FAMILY TI

Kaye & Ward have also reprinted the following novels by Marguerite Steen

THE SPANISH TRILOGY

The One-Eyed Moon
Matador
The Tavern

Anna Fitzalan
Stallion
The Tower
Woman in the Back Seat
Bulls of Parral

FAMILY TIES

MARGUERITE STEEN

KAYE & WARD · LONDON

First published by Collins 1939

Reprinted by Kaye & Ward Ltd
194-200 Bishopsgate, London E.C.2
1971

Copyright 1939

ISBN 0 7182 0873 0

Printed in Great Britain by
Lowe & Brydone (Printers) Ltd, London

CHAPTER ONE

Too late, it occurred to Simon that he should, perhaps, have taken the visitor downstairs himself: should have steered him through the chaos of the outer office and, while a clerk—dispatched by a flicker of his employer's eyebrow—went to make sure the chauffeur was on the alert, have glossed the formalities of leave-taking with some suave little phrase that should leave the departing guest not unaware of the compliment implied by his host, in personally escorting him to the door.

It was the kind of thing Daniel would have done perfectly. On second thoughts, he felt the ordinary procedure better became both the occasion and his own personality. He was not a courtier, and compliments, when he was constrained to pay them, sounded—at least in his own ears—a little fulsome. Still, there were times when they were, if not indispensable, useful; and Daniel paid them with great grace. It was annoying he had not been there; a faint superciliousness in the lift of the visitor's eyebrow betrayed the fact that he was accustomed to small flattering attentions, and had the contrary effect of rousing in Simon the antagonism which any suggestion of arrogance evoked. It was foolish, of course—foolish and humourless—to be affected by such trifles; one should stick one's tongue in the cheek and give people what they wanted. A little harmless bootlicking was a cheap price to pay for advantages—if only the attitude of the licker were not so confoundedly undignified. Daniel could lick boots and look charming over it; or perhaps that was an unfair way of putting it. Daniel had been reared in an environment of suavity, of pleasing insincerities, of graceful social antics which Simon might have imitated, if he could have brought himself to do so without feeling a fool. He recognized their value.

As it was, his lack of ceremony had probably cost the firm a couple of thousand. If Daniel made an appointment, why couldn't he be there to keep it in person ? He knew Lord Mynte; he knew what the Mynte memoirs would be worth to Crome and Lygon, and knew exactly how to handle the combination of touchy self-assertion, pretentiousness and underlying sagacity which had earned its owner a peerage, and splashed his name across the news sheets of Great Britain and the States. Where Simon saw only an infuriating self-sufficiency, Daniel saw humour; the arrogance of the newly-created baron, which enraged Simon, was, to Daniel, the more exquisite sort of joke, to which he delighted in pandering.

Daniel *ought* to have been there. Simon felt guiltily that little was likely to come of the interview; in fact, Mynte had as good as given him to understand that his memoirs were too valuable to be entrusted to a firm like Crome and Lygon, lacking, as yet, the prestige due to so momentous a publication.

Simon could see exactly how Daniel would have handled the situation: how warmly he would have agreed with the other's objections—even going so (unnecessarily, in Simon's opinion) far as to praise rival firms, to weigh the advantages of one over another; gravely pretending to defer to the author's opinion, delicately adulating his "literary" (save the mark!) gifts—all to an accompaniment of the firm's sherry and cigars which, since Daniel had chosen them, were beyond the criticism at least of a Mynte! Daniel, playing the exoletus to an elderly voluptuary, artfully seducing him, amid fumes of Habana and Jerez, from the fastness of his native shrewdness, to ultimate capitulation. "Well, take it, my boy, and see what you can do with it. After all, youth must make a start!" And Daniel's sudden, nauseating coyness: "I don't want you to commit yourself to anything you might regret later; hadn't you better think it over? After all, we are only a young firm——" "Youth at the helm, eh? Well, well, perhaps even youth won't despise a helping hand——" A contract produced, signed. More compliments; Daniel smirking now—the firm's

white-headed boy! As likely as not, an invitation to dine—
with, as a patent afterthought: "You'll join us, of course,
Crome?" Daniel, as "the Head of the Firm," winking behind
the victim's back and, as the door closed: "Oh, my God, do
I really look as if I've just left Eton?"

That was the way it ought to have gone. Actually, there
had been ten minutes of stiff conversation, five of them taken
up with apologies for Daniel's absence. A few publishing
generalizations—and a half-promise to look in "some other
time," which meant exactly nothing. Meanwhile, Gosschalk,
Bartholomew Rice or Jackford would get the memoirs.

Simon Crome ran his hands through the hair which, at
thirty-seven, was no longer as plentiful as it should have been.
It was no use getting mad with Daniel, because his approach
to the business was that of the amateur. Simon was even
willing it should be so: that he should bear in the background
the burden of the firm's responsibilities, while Daniel did his
playboy stuff for the benefit of the clients. He did it brilliantly
—and had the sense to leave more serious matters to Simon;
but lately—Simon had been obliged reluctantly to recognize
it—the quality of his performances had gone off; worse, he
could not even be relied upon—as witness to-day—to put in
an appearance. Sooner or later there would have to be some
sharp speaking: a detestable necessity between partners, and
particularly detestable in the present case, when one's nerves
were already on edge with a thousand and one other things.
In his over-tired condition, Simon found himself teased by a
thought which, though constantly recurring, he managed in
less anxious moments to thrust into the background. Had he
made a blunder in taking Daniel into partnership? If so, it
was too late to consider it now; he would simply have to
redouble his efforts to build up the business in which were
involved, not only his small amount of capital, but the whole
future of himself and his family.

Simon's secretary was in the room, smiling at him. She

was a tall slim woman, very calm, with dark hair and eyes, and a silk scarf the colour of the lipstick that lent accent to her pale, accurately drawn features. Simon knew she was a widow, with one boy whom she kept at boarding school. He did not know much else about her, except that he liked her and was glad of her efficiency.

"Well, I'm here," she was saying; her lips twitched into an amused smile. "I mean," she explained, with a nod towards the desk, "you'd better take your elbow off the bell, or someone will think the office is on fire."

"What's the time?" He knew she would not expect him to apologize. Not for the first time, he compared her, to her own advantage, with Daniel's scornful blonde.

"It's just eleven minutes to four. Isn't Mr. Lygon here?" She added, on a note of surprise: "I thought it was his appointment."

"It was. Look here, what have I got to-morrow?"

"Rather a lot of things, I'm afraid. By the way, Mrs. Crome rang through a few minutes ago to remind you about dinner to-night. A quarter to eight, and she hoped you'd manage to be in time to change."

". . . Well. Anything else?"

"I've just been through the Bratislav proofs; Jeffreys brought them to show me. They're awful: about fifteen pounds' worth of overrunning. Could you have her in and speak about them?"

"Find out when I'm free and send her a note. Anything from Combridge?" asked Simon wearily. Combridge was the firm's solicitor; Simon reflected ironically that there, at least, was someone who was doing very well out of Crome and Lygon.

"Yes. Rather a discouraging message, I'm afraid. He thinks the book's definitely dangerous, but he'd like to see you about it."

"We can't afford dangerous books. Did he say what's the matter?"

"Libel, I suppose. He didn't say much, except that he advises you strongly against accepting it in its present form, and he'd like to come in and discuss it with you to-morrow morning."

"With a view, I suppose, to asking the author to remove the libellous passages? You know what'll happen: first of all she'll deny the libel; then she'll accuse us of 'mutilating' her work—do it up and send it back. I've got enough on my plate without dealing with disgruntled female novelists." A look on her face silenced him. "I suppose you think it's good?" he accused her.

"I did think it showed more promise than a lot of the stuff we've had in lately. What about letting Combridge see Mr. Lygon, and leaving him to deal with it?"

"I'll think it over." He ran his finger down the engagement pad she offered him. "Look here, this is awful. I can't possibly get through it all to-morrow. It's Henry's birthday, and I practically promised to take the kid out for the afternoon."

She nodded seriously.

"You mustn't scratch that. It's quite time you had a holiday, anyhow. You've not even had a Saturday since we started."

"What about yourself? And, look here: I can't have any more of this nonsense about overtime."

The girl's face coloured, her brows twitched together.

"It isn't nonsense. Why should I take money for something I do of my own free will? You forget I've got a stake in this outfit too, Mr. Crome; and I'd much rather work on Saturdays, at my leisure, than cram a lot of extra stuff into ordinary working hours. I mean, the things have got to be done, and it's just a matter of choice between scamping them or doing them thoroughly. You know yourself, scamped work's nothing but a nuisance in the long run."

"We really need another clerk, don't we? But I don't see how it's to be managed for the present."

"It's not necessary, either; at least, it won't be, if we can get a better organization into the office. I don't think that new girl's much good; we ought to have an older woman, someone with a bit of authority with the juniors—she'd be worth her salary if she kept them in order."

"All right. I'll see what can be done. Now, about to-morrow: can't some of these be staggered? What's Daniel doing? Why the devil can't he come in? I haven't seen him since lunch."

"Wasn't he lunching with the editor of *Column*? Perhaps he's in his room now. Shall I find out?"

"Send up for Miss Thomas. Wait a minute," he added, as her hand went to the receiver. Turning in his chair, Simon directed a long, considering, upward glance at the calm, intelligent face. Definitely a woman to be trusted; the last few months had shown him that. "What do you make of Daniel?"

The question took her by surprise; startled, she raised her brows, and Simon smiled.

"It's all right; I'm not asking you for a criticism of my brother. I mean, do you think he's well?"

"I don't know," she said slowly, having paused to consider. "One has to know a person for rather a long time before one can tell things like that about them; I don't see as much of Mr. Lygon as I do of you—and one has to allow for differences in temperament. It's been a trying time, hasn't it —for everybody?"

"And it looks as if it'll be worse before it's better," said Simon grimly. "We're used to trying times; but it's different for Daniel. I've been wondering if he's cracking up a bit."

"I think he's very nervy, and of course that makes him irritable. He's one of the people who have no sort of capacity for relaxation." As she said it, Simon realized how much their relationship of employer and employee owed to the apparently illimitable capacity for relaxation that made Nancy Rowland-son so soothing a companion. "And—I hate talking personalities, as you know; but he isn't a happy person, is he?"

"Daniel's a bitter devil; it's odd how few people realize it. All that easy charm and amiability—a brilliant fake. *Au fond*, Daniel's about as amiable as a scorpion."

"At any rate"—she was smiling—"you're an admirable combination. He dazzles, and you inspire people with confidence."

"Dull, but necessary. So, incidentally, is the dazzling. I only thought Daniel's light seemed a little paler lately; I suppose the fool's overdoing it. Even allowing for the difference in years, I couldn't, at Daniel's age, have pulled my weight in the business and given myself up to the social racket every night—as he seems to be doing."

"It's very difficult to know where to make the cut; especially nowadays, when so much seems to hang on this social stuff. It's not a bad idea to have somebody who takes all that off your hands—especially when you haven't much taste for it yourself."

"The question is, how much of Daniel's energies can be spared to this somewhat dubious business of ' making contacts,' and how much ought I to insist upon his reserving for the straightforward work of the firm?"

"Is it wise to insist——? Oh, excuse me; I wasn't criticizing——"

"Don't be silly. Go on."

"I was only thinking—it takes more than six months to make a publisher; and, for the present, Mr. Lygon's probably more valuable to us out of the office than he would be in trying to pick up the threads of a business which no one's got much time to show him. Our organization's still at sixes and sevens, and even routine jobs have to be shuffled and shifted from day to day, to meet emergencies. It's all right for people like us—I mean you and me, who've served our apprenticeship; but it must be very confusing for someone who's never had anything to do with publishing before. Confusing and, in some ways, disheartening——"

"Between ourselves, a good many things are disheartening," admitted Simon. "Since the Cratchitt biography, we practically haven't had the smell of a decent manuscript. Nothing but floods of first novels from the agents; the Bratislav thing—we'll be lucky if we sell five hundred—and a perfectly good thriller nobody's noticed."

"I thought Gascoigne had promised you something in *The Kingsway*."

"They wouldn't use it. I suppose we'll have to buy some space in that as well. Let's face it; there's a hell of a lot more money pouring out of this business than we're likely to see back, given reasonable conditions, in the next five years."

"We've got our Aldebaran edition," she reminded him. "And we've done quite well with Cratchitt. What about Lord Mynte?"

"Down the drain, I'm afraid. That was Daniel's job, and he wasn't here to handle it."

"What a pity." Her tone showed that she recognized the seriousness of the default. "You look awfully tired. I'll make some tea; and perhaps, before you go home, you wouldn't mind looking through these estimates with me——?"

Yes, he was tired. His brain felt like a piece of used-up blotting-paper, incapable of assimilating another idea, and he had the comfortless, unkempt sensation of a person who has not had time to pay attention to his appearance since morning. On the mantelpiece, between the photographs of Henry and Jemima, Christian had put a little square mirror: "Just to remind you to see if your tie's straight, darling, before important people are shown in!" He rose stiffly and picked it up.

God, what a graceless, unwashen-looking object for the head of a publishing firm! What an old, anxious face! Simon found himself instinctively rearranging his features, slipping back the mask that preserves the decent privacy of the human mind. Had he looked like that when Mynte came in? He was fairly sure he had not; yet even now, with the mask in position, there was no evading the truth—that the last eight or nine months had aged him more than the whole of his previous

Fleet Street experience. He looked a great deal more than his thirty-seven years of age; the rather agreeable, dusty-brown hair was not only thinning, there was a grizzled patch over each of his temples. His skin had the old, leathery look of the person who lives a sedentary life, and made two heavy folds between the flange of the nostrils and the corners of the tightened lips. As a man who had always taken pride in his physical fitness, Simon winced. At this rate, he would be an old man by the time Henry was through his public school! Sickening—after looking forward so long to the time when they would enjoy together all the things which were now postponed "until Henry's grown up." Riding in Richmond Park, shooting, tennis—the real thing—down at Hampton Court: all the things which Simon loved, and had voluntarily forsworn, while he built up Henry's inheritance to these and other pleasant joys. Even music—the dear passion of his heart: what time had he for attending concerts? The Glyndebourne season had opened and would close without his hearing an opera.

He went to the lavatory and, after washing and brushing his hair, felt a little better. Nancy Rowlandson had brought in the tea, and stood by the desk, pouring it out—an unconsciously domestic figure. It flashed across him that that was what she should be doing at this hour: pouring out tea in a home of her own for a man of her own, instead of doing office-boy work for a pittance. He was ashamed of the salary he had had to offer Nancy; he had not expected her to accept it. Agreeing with him that it was very little, she considered the question calmly before making her decision. "I have a little money of my own, and it's always worth while getting in at the birth of a new venture." Simon accounted himself the gainer by her longsighted view of the situation.

"Mr. Lygon's come in," she was saying. "He's dictating some letters, but he'll be down in a few minutes."

"Then we'll run through the estimates." The hot tea bit his tongue and cleared his brain; he settled down to a close discussion in which she showed herself no less acute than he. Her experience on a woman's paper was invaluable to Simon; it was a relief not to have to explain each step, as one was obliged to do, with Daniel.

When Daniel came in, she gathered up her notes and went quickly out, as though delicacy forbade her being present at the meeting of the partners. Simon said, "Hallo," in a non-committal kind of way; he felt that, for once, it was up to Daniel to make the running.

Daniel said, "Hallo," and sat down on the fenderstool, with his hands in his pockets. At thirty he had not quite grown out of the 'Varsity manner; the somewhat drooping elegance of his long limbs was lent substance by "classic" tailoring; his fairness and pallor lent, at first sight, a spurious youthfulness to features which, to a closer observer, yielded up their secret of age-old cynicism. One could see Daniel doing his playboy stuff with the cold, moonlit heartlessness of Pierrot, and, in the next breath, freezing those whom he had lately charmed. His lower lip could be cruelly stubborn. So, remembered Simon, could their mother's: the lovely blonde creature who had run away from Simon's father to Daniel's. Simon had never blamed her; so ardent, gay and life-loving a being was out of place in the humdrum household of an elderly, conventional Civil Servant. He was glad his father had been generous enough to divorce her, although, as he grew older, he could guess what it had cost that hide-bound conventionalist to publicize his domestic failure. There was generosity, too, in an arrangement that kept Rose Lygon in contact with both her sons; ten-year-old Simon was often asked to play with three-year-old Daniel, who came to his public school at the beginning of Simon's last term, and had the advantage of his half-brother's protection and advice during those initial and difficult months of adaptation from prep. school leniency to the harsher standards of public school discipline. It was only when Daniel went up to the 'Varsity that the half-brothers lost contact. To Simon, labouring in Fleet Street, there seemed to be little in common between himself and a brilliant young member of the Union and the Bullingdon. Or perhaps it was just that Daniel was rich and he poor; there is nothing like the strong tide of financial inequality for drifting people apart. . . .

At the end of ten minutes Daniel had neither spoken nor moved. Simon stared at him curiously. Yes, the chap looked ill. His pallor had the greyness of shell, and a patch of light that the lamp on the corner of the mantelshelf threw on his upper cheek brought up a seaming of fine lines. He wasn't being theatrical, either; it was more than obvious that he did not care whether or not any one was looking at him—and this, in Daniel, was itself disquieting.

"Anything up?" Simon was constrained to ask. As Daniel made no immediate reply, he continued acidly: "I suppose you know Mynte turned up while you were out?"

"Anything doing?" asked Daniel, as though it were no affair of his, but politeness obliged him to feign an interest he did not feel.

"I shouldn't think so. Why on earth didn't you come back?"

"I shouldn't think his stuff's much good," said the incalculable Daniel.

"You didn't take that point of view when you rang me up last night to say you thought the Mynte biography would be a pretty good gamble. And it was you who fixed the appointment."

"I don't suppose we'd have got much out of it. He'd be sure to want a packet, and, as a millionaire, he's got about the least publicity value on the market. Nobody'd want his memoirs."

"It's a change of tune on your part—that's all I can say. Why on earth were you so het up about it yesterday?"

"Call it a touch of boyish enthusiasm." A grin seared Daniel's face like a flash of lightning. "I happened to sit next to him after dinner, and the talk got on memoirs. The success of Otterbrook's book seemed to be under his skin—you know they're bitter rivals. I suppose I said the obvious things——"

"Such as what?" asked Simon, with heavy sarcasm.

"Oh, you know—that a Mynte memoir would wipe Otterbrook's eye." A faintly diabolical glint appeared in the corner of Daniel's own.

"But you've just said——"

"Hooey, darling, hooey. The uncontrollable Lygon charm making itself felt. He got frightfully serious about it, and I naturally followed up, until, I suppose, I very nearly convinced myself that we'd got a best-seller under our thumbs. Mynte was positively fawning on me by the time I let out that I was a real, live publisher——"

"I'm glad you call it live. I kept him waiting twenty minutes, because I felt it wasn't my line of country; then, when I saw him, I suppose I bungled it."

"What's it matter?"

"It matters this much, Daniel: that if we can't find another Cratchitt pretty soon, you're likely to drop your five thousand and I'll be up against a very unpleasant conversation with my father-in-law."

Incredible as it seemed, Daniel was not listening. His eyes were narrowed as he got up to help himself to a cigarette from Simon's box. As he lit it in silence, a person unaccustomed to Daniel's mental processes might have thought he was pondering upon Simon's words. His first remark showed that they had not penetrated his consciousness.

"Have you ever heard of a chap called Caffard?"

"I don't think so," frowned Simon, after a pause for consideration.

"You must have come across him, out and about," said Daniel, who could never be brought to realize that the Cromes did not go, in his sense, "out and about." "A dislikeable-looking person, with fuzzy hair and toffee-apple eyes; sings as if he was gargling cream, and does things with a piano that make you go hot all over."

"Do you mean some sort of a performer?"

"He's at the Caille d'Or. He's got a string of women the length of Piccadilly after him." Daniel paused. "Eliza's among them," he concluded. The cigarette shook for a moment, then straightened itself defiantly between his lips.

"Oh—hell!"

No wonder Daniel looked chawed to pieces. Simon sought for words of consolation, knew there were none, and started drawing squares on his blotting pad. This was a nice new complication! If this went on, Daniel would be about as useful to the firm as a sick headache. It was the most unfortunate thing in the world that he still minded about Eliza.

"So I'm through," said Daniel quietly.

"How do you mean, ' through '?"

"I've stood in my time," said Daniel, "for five gentlemen, an all-in wrestler and a trick cyclist; I've got ideas about a certain revue star, and I'll take even fivers on a week-end Eliza *says* she spent with her sister down at Newmarket. It may have been coincidence Orris was riding, but my view of Eliza is, she's too clever to risk coincidence. Anyhow, I draw the line at a half-breed emotion merchant with blue nails."

"What are you going to do? Take her away?" It could be managed somehow; he and Nancy Rowlandson could carry the firm for a few weeks.

"Take her away? Lord, no. After Caffard, any one can have Eliza." For all his cold, light voice, Simon knew Daniel was going through hell. The inevitable formula of sympathy prescribed itself.

"Have a drink."

"I'll divorce her," said Daniel, taking no notice.

Simon sat very still. The self-protective instinct which rises uppermost in every man when his own interests are involved, stung him with the realization of what Daniel's divorce might mean to a firm like Crome and Lygon, with its Nonconformist backing and—so far—jealously guarded reputation for propriety.

"Well, Daniel. It's your affair, of course."

"It is, isn't it?" asked Daniel flippantly.

"I suppose it's hardly a thing that can be fixed by—talking over."

Daniel laughed.

"Eliza and I have come to the end of our talking. I'm sorry I let you down this afternoon, Simon, but we lunched at Boulestin's, and it struck me, as I was down that way, it would be a good idea to have a word with my solicitors. So I went down to Clement's Inn and fixed it all up. Dear Eliza will receive what I believe are called her papers some time before the end of the month."

"Citing the emotion merchant?"

"Well, no. Even taking into consideration the limitations imposed on the Press, Lygon v. Lygon and Caffard would raise too much of a stink. Mrs. Daniel Lygon and a cabaret turn! It can't be done. Fortunately, Eliza's volatility has provided me with a wide range of co-respondents from whom to take my choice. Privett—that's my solicitor—and I have agreed to pick out the most presentable. I wanted to go and call on the chap and ask him if he minded, but Privett practically had epilepsy at the suggestion. It appears there's a thing called collusion. . . . Of course, if I wanted to be nasty, I could turn in a whole list; but so long as Eliza behaves herself, I'm quite prepared to be the little gentleman."

"It's a rotten set-out for you," muttered Simon, feeling thankful for small mercies.

"Inconvenient, as much as anything," said Daniel lightly. "I suppose I've got to shift all my stuff over to the club now; I'm told I can't divorce Eliza while we're both living under the same roof."

"I never thought of that. What a perishing nuisance."

"I believe in the good old days it was quite the thing for the deceived husband to turn his wife into the street. The arguments against that are—a, I've never been deceived; Eliza has always been painfully candid about her affairs; and b, I don't suppose for one minute she'd go. She's just had her bedroom and the drawing-room re-decorated, and there's no hope of her getting tired of them for another three or four months. When boredom sets in, she might make a move——"

"Look here. Why don't you clear right out for a few weeks? Take a holiday, I mean. I knew something was getting you down. I wish you'd told me before. Mrs. Rowlandson and I can carry on—and you'll have a chance to pull yourself together."

"Thanks, I'm all right. I mean, I'm better off for work. This was part of the reason, you know, that I suggested the partnership. I didn't flatter myself I'd be any good to you, in an operative sense; I just wanted something to fill up my time. And now I've got things moving I don't give a damn. What are you doing to-night?"

"Family dinner-party—unfortunately. Christian's people are in town for a few days; I suppose I'll be required to render an account of my stewardship to father-in-law after dinner!"

"I don't think Old Harry cares much for me."

"He'll care for you a darn sight less when he gets wind of the divorce. Damn you, Daniel!" said Simon good humouredly. "Why do you have to involve me in fighting your battles with my Nonconformist in-laws?"

"It's none of their business, is it?"

"I agree; but the man who pays the piper is apt to call the tune. Having given us our backing—apart from your five thousand—the old boy thinks he's got a right to a finger in our moral, as well as our financial, pie."

"Well, damn his eyes," said Daniel easily. "Pity you're fixed up. I was going to suggest dinner together. Look here, I can fix that Mynte thing, if you like; but I honestly don't think there's much in it."

"Better leave it alone. But, for God's sake, Daniel, keep your eye skinned for anything that may be of use to us. We've had about a ton of tripe this week from the agents; I don't believe any of them are any good, but of course we daren't refuse to look at the stuff they send us. It's only a heart-breaking waste of time."

"You forget we turned down *Black Brother*; Gosschalk sold twenty thousand copies, and I'm told Rice is doing pretty well with *Aspasia*; I wanted you to have both of those."

"My dear Daniel, what's the use of my telling you that neither would have been a farthing's worth of good to Crome and Lygon? If we'd published *Aspasia* we'd have lost our backing at one fell swoop—old Harry would never have stood for it. We can't afford to follow our own taste yet—and, I'll admit, it looks as if we shan't be able to do so for some time to come. You know as well as I do that we're practically pledged to moral uplift——"

"Well." Daniel shrugged his shoulders. "It'll be interesting to hear Old Harry's comments when he sees the dividends."

"There won't be any—not this year, at any rate."

"Exactly. Moral uplift into dividends won't go—at least, not in the publishing business."

"That's rot. Look what Hyne makes out of his Sermon on the Hearth series!"

"Of course; because Hyne's gone baldheaded for religion. There's a lot to be cleaned up on sheer Tractarianism, if it comes to that ; but there's nothing in this facing-both-ways stuff."

As usual, when Daniel talked what he knew to be horse sense, Simon felt irritated. He said shortly that he was going home, and offered Daniel a lift, which the latter refused.

Instead of ringing up the garage, Simon decided to walk round and pick up the car; he wanted "a breath of air," and a little respite from the mental tension of the office. He was annoyed, on arriving, to find that some minor adjustments he had ordered had not been attended to. The mechanic was apologetic.

"Very sorry, sir, but we've had a perfect deluge of rush jobs."

"Oh, well, see to it to-morrow. I want to get away now."

"Well, sir, we've got your car on the tracks at this very moment. The steering's not true, and the brake's pretty bad, as you said. We can have her ready in half an hour. You did say half-past six, didn't you?"

"Hal-*lo*, Mr. Crome! You don't mean to say you're still running the old Morris." It was the manager, a cheerful, loud-mouthed individual whom Simon usually avoided. He was there grinning, radiating prosperity from every fold of a rubicund countenance. Why don't you chuck a fool job like publishing and come into the car business? he seemed to be asking. "Come now, when are you going to turn her in? You know a car of that age is going to be a liability, instead of an asset, in a few months' time. Just let me show you the new Hillman—a beautiful piece of work! You ought to bring Mrs. Crome here and let her try it; a real lady's car——"

By the time Simon made his escape the shops were closing, and a stream of suburban shoppers poured towards the Tubes. He felt that they were tired, irritated people like himself; his aimless figure was jostled by women impatient of courtesies at this hour of the day. He scowled, wondering where to take refuge from the violence of tired, untidy women, and remembered a popular restaurant on the corner of the next block. He was too tired to risk alcohol, but a cup of tea would furnish a pretext for sitting down until his car was ready. He bought an evening paper and passed through the gilded portals.

The ground floor, beyond the banks of *petit fours*, of cocktail oddments, pastries, flowers and fruit, seethed with customers. Simon looked with distaste across the crowded tables. Harassed waitresses threaded the aisles with loaded trays—mixed fruit sundaes, ice cream sodas, bloated pastries, the rubbish women put into their stomachs when they are tired! A supervisor moved with the air of a field marshal, overlooking the tables: a hard-faced, gritty female, with a sash of office worn across her iron-clad, black satin bosom. "Plenty of room upstairs," she informed Simon, who had meant to escape, but now found himself the victim of a relentless compulsion which drove him towards the lifts.

The lift was packed with women in fur coats, with stale make-up caked on their faces and arms loaded with handbags and parcels. Several looked resentfully at Simon, as though they disliked his intrusion upon their disorder. His nostrils contracted against the smell of women—closely-packed, over-heated women; he loathed that woman-smell, compound of powder and stale scent and the exudations of female bodies; he loathed it partly because it offended his senses and partly because it destroyed the illusion dear to his sex of the im-maculacy of women. He hated to be forced so close to a woman that he could see the little greasy patch at the corner of an unpowdered nostril, the smut on a forehead, the graceless sprouting of a curl from its pin, the pale line of lip inside the dark line of partly eliminated lipstick. He thought quickly of Christian, of her flower-sweet freshness that remained, after twelve years of marital intimacy, one of the loveliest and most changeless of her charms.

The lift stopped, and Simon, pressed into the background by mink and musquash and synthetic fox, waited to be liberated; to his horror, no one got out, the lift gates opened only to gulp another fur-muffled figure. With lips only a couple of inches away from the brownish nape of a Jewish neck, Simon managed to gasp:

"Is this the tearoom?" But he was too late; the lift was again ascending, and the attendant chanted, "Second floor—restaurant, restroom, ladies' toilette," without troubling to turn her head. Glaring at the green-flaxen roll above the pseudo-military collar, and the thick matt surface of an over-rouged cheek, he found himself thinking, "A lift attendant's job is hell; it's a wonder more women don't go mad at it."

The landing was crowded with women coming from the toilette: uniform powdered faces, sleeked hair, waited with patronizing impatience the lift's delivery of its dishevelled burden. Musquash and fox and mink retreated on ludicrous pegs of patent leather and near-silk.

In the restaurant, the tables were less closely placed than downstairs, but none was unoccupied. A few men had an air of helpless, even shrinking, surrender to the female horde; at tables for two were more fur coats, little black hats, patterned veils. . . . Women have no originality. Whether in clothes or in literature they seek a well-established pattern.

"Do you mind if I sit here?" Despair halted him by one of the small tables. A girl of eighteen or nineteen looked up from her novel, muttered something and hurriedly snatched a pair of gloves and a parcel out of the way. She had small, plump, very clean hands, with a ring on one of the unimportant fingers.

CHAPTER TWO

A young woman in spectacles, with a curtain of lank, black hair, repeated for the fourth time a phrase of one semibreve and two minims on a historic Steinway, and, in answer to a gesture from the instructress, fifteen little boys and girls in apple-green tunics doubled their fists, thrashed the air with skinny arms and patted the parquet tentatively with bare toes. "One, two, three, four—Jemima Crome! One, two, three, four——"

"She's quite off the beat," murmured Christian resignedly.

"Never mind," her sister comforted her. "Look how beautifully Henry's doing it. I suppose he'll be going up into the next class soon."

"I hope he won't. Poor Jemima's got enough to bear already. Henry beats her in everything—clever little beast!"

"Does she mind? I thought she adored him."

"It's not much fun being beaten every time by someone two years younger than yourself."

"Jemima's got an angelic nature; rather like yours, Chris, at the same age."

"She'll grow out of it. Oh dear, look at the poor sweet; you'd never believe I spent nearly an hour yesterday, trying to make her do those stupid semibreves. And she does so hate it. I wonder if I'm being a brute in making her go on."

"Well, it helps her music, doesn't it?"

"I'm afraid Jem's music is a myth—though I daren't tell Simon. I wish the young woman at the piano didn't play quite such *cerebral* chords. I can't help thinking the children would so much rather have a tune they could sing to; and I'd enjoy it more myself, if I hadn't got the feeling we're all expected to be so frightfully spiritual and highbrow."

"They're rather a Garden City lot," admitted Lydia, as she glanced round the chairs occupied by mothers or nurses, most of whom had an air of painful concentration upon the efforts of their offspring. "I feel that for two pins the woman in the brown hat—which, however you choose to look at it, darling, and we all know your charity is boundless as the ocean, is *quite* a calamity—would burst into 'Summer is i'cumen in,' and I'm sure they all belong to Groups."

"The mother of that fat child with a band round her teeth asked Jemima and Henry to a party, and Jem rather put her foot in it by saying we were going to the circus that afternoon."

"I didn't know circuses were improper. Or is that some sort of new Leftist notion?"

"It seems it's wicked to encourage performing animals."

"Whatever made you join this cranks' party?"

"It's so difficult to give the children a proper amount of exercise through the winter months, and they both loathed the ordinary dancing class. Even Henry got bored with the waltz."

Henry had just been chosen to demonstrate the exercise to the still struggling class, which he did with an expression of uplift that made his mother grit her teeth.

"He looks positively pansy! I can't have him going on with this," she muttered. "Thank God, they're doing triplets now; even Jemima can do triplets."

"It doesn't sound decent, at her age. Christian, are the parents dining with you to-night?"

"Yes, they are, and I hope Simon gets back in decent time, for once. Poor darling, he's having such a rotten time; he really might as well not have a home at all."

"Well, how's business?"

"I don't know. I never ask about office things, you know; it's such a bore, when we see each other so little—and, of course, he tells me if there's anything special."

"It's rather a bad time for publishing, isn't it?" asked Lydia, after a little pause.

"Isn't it always?" Christian was focusing on her daughter; yes, Jemima was actually managing to keep up the beat with her arms.

"Printers' strikes, I suppose, and increased costs of production," said Lydia intelligently. Christian turned to look at her in surprise.

"I'd no idea you knew so much about publishing."

"I get it all from father. He's rather seeing himself these days as a sort of vicarious publisher, and impressing us all with his inside information on the trade! I told him I was surprised he hadn't insisted upon calling the firm Crome, Lygon and Matlock; it would be rather resonant—don't you think? Or *don't* you?"

"Oh, I think Crome and Lygon's quite long enough," said Christian hurriedly. "Besides, father isn't a partner——"

"Well, when are you going to give us some really thrilling novels? I'm sure they're the things that make money nowadays—with all these book societies, and books of the month, and literary lunches that every one goes to. I went to one last week; I wanted to see what Margaret Greer looked like —after *Bleak Harvest*, you know; and Pratt Somervell was in the chair——"

"Well, did you enjoy it?"

"Not at all. Margaret Greer is a tall woman with grey hair—quite too devastatingly Girton; she's got a thin, whispering voice with a lisp, and she had a lot to say about the modern novel and politics. Not a bit interesting to the lay mind. I don't think writers ought to let themselves be seen; too, too shattering for their admirers!"

"I haven't read *Bleak Harvest*. Is it good?"

"It's marvellous how little you know about books—for a publisher's wife. Yes, it's *good*——" Lydia wrinkled up her charming nose. "But like all her work, it leaves a sort of sour taste in your mouth. Frightfully humorous, you know, but every laugh seems to have a nasty little twist in it which spoils one's enjoyment. I should imagine she's rather bitchy —lots of brilliant women are, aren't they? Particularly if they happen to be virgins."

Jemima, Henry and their friends were now pretending to

be "fountains"; the impersonation involved a strange, crouching position and occasional spasmodic upward dartings of curiously agitated hands and arms.

"Who's that rather theatrical-looking red-haired chi' next but one from Jemima?" inquired Lydia, after a brie. interval of contemplation.

"That——? Oh, that's Rachel Hawke's little girl."

"Oh—one of the primroses?" As Christian did not seem to grasp the allusion, Lydia expanded. "You don't mean to say you haven't seen *My Primrose Path*? If one can believe the advertisements, they've sold twenty-five thousand copies already——"

"I haven't seen it. What is it?" asked Christian.

"My darling mugwump, it's Rachel's autobiography; and it's fluttered more dovecotes in Mayfair than anything since the Cardigan memoirs, that Edward the Seventh was asked to indict!"

Christian made a little restless movement.

"I do so hate these books by Society exhibitionists! I enjoy a nice, *risqué* novel, but I dislike personal revelations and anything coarse and—well, unnecessary."

"Darling, you *are* so like mother at times! But I must say, I think Rachel's gone too near the bone. There's one story she tells—missing out the names, of course: I suppose even Rachel's scared of libel, or perhaps her publisher got nervous —and everybody says it's about Eliza Lygon."

"How beastly for Daniel."

"I should think Daniel's getting fed up. Really, Eliza's past a joke. It's that dago at the Caille d'Or now."

"Oh, no—don't be silly."

"Well, darling, that's what people are saying. As you know, I don't run with Daniel and Eliza."

"Goodness, I do hope father doesn't hear anything. He'll make it so beastly for Simon if he does."

"Has he met Eliza?"

"Only once—for a minute. I managed to get rid of her."

"Well?"

"Oh, it was all right. She started to vamp him."

"He doesn't care for Daniel, does he?"

"I don't think he does; but it doesn't really matter. Daniel never butts in on Simon's affairs."

"Daniel's frightfully fascinating, isn't he? I wouldn't mind making a pass at him myself—if it wasn't for Eliza."

"I shouldn't think Eliza would make much fuss; but I do hope they'll settle down," said Christian. Infinitely "settled" herself, she had that desire common to most people who are happy and contented with their lot—that contentment should be universal. She was always afflicted when she heard of disturbances among her friends, and, although she knew Eliza very little, considering that Eliza's husband was Simon's half-brother and partner, she always worried a little about her and about Daniel.

"I don't think Daniel's a very ' settling ' sort of person; if you ask me, I think they're heading for a bust-up," said Lydia.

Some tone in her sister's voice recaptured Christian's attention from the "fountains."

"You haven't got a crush on Daniel, have you?"

"I'm not sure."

"Oh, Lydia."

"You needn't be shocked. I'm not thinking of seducing him as an experiment, to find out what my feelings about him really are. I was only thinking that some time—oh, millions of years off yet!—I might fall enough in love with Daniel to marry him, if he had finished with Eliza."

"I don't think Father would be very pleased."

"I shouldn't think he'd be here by then. I'll probably, after an interval with the dye-pots, have allowed my hair to go white, and be known as the handsome Miss Matlock! Why is ' handsome ' such a stuffy adjective? I'll look like a marquise and Daniel like an ex-Viceroy, and we'll make a most romantic couple. No. I don't think Daniel will ever be romantic; he'll be sheathed from head to foot in glittering cynicism, and terrify every one—except me—with his mordant wit."

The flights of Lydia's fancy did not reassure Christian. She realized, with a shock, that Lydia was very much in love with Daniel, and, being the kind of person who sees nothing but tragedy in an attachment between people who have no possibility of getting married, she made a mental note to avoid, as far as possible, bringing Lydia and Daniel together. They had met a good many times at her house, and no one had ever noticed anything. Christian did not think that Daniel could possibly be in love with Lydia, for all the latter's charms. How could a person love Eliza and love Lydia? Daniel's taste, she had often thought, was for the exotic, the decadent, the slightly vicious and exciting: there were none of those qualities in Lydia.

Henry came capering up, with a minute beading of sweat all over his earnest face. He looked exactly like Simon, thought Christian, resisting the desire to hug him; she wished profoundly that Lydia had got married as well—someone like Simon, who would adore her and give her lovely children like Jemima and Henry. She had a sudden twinge of love for Simon, so sharp it made her start; she wondered if they would be able to afford another baby some day, and thought what fun it was, bearing Simon's children.

"Miss Martindale says I can start counterpoint," said Henry, importantly. Jemima, quite unquenched by her recent ignominy, was chattering to the child with a band round her teeth; leaning against Christian's knee, Henry scowled at his sister. "It's absurd Jemima shouldn't know her notes by now; I don't think she concentrates," he pronounced. Then he remembered something, and smiled angelically at his aunt. "It's my birthday to-morrow."

"I know, Henry. I've brought you a present."

"Thank you very much," said Henry politely. "I hope I'll like it. I'll be nine."

"He's going to school next term," said Christian, wishing

he was not; he seemed so very small and tender to take chances among older, rougher boys.

"I'd have gone last term," Henry was saying, "if it hadn't been for my squint!" He had disconcertingly developed a rather bad cast in one eye, and Christian had wisely decided to keep him under her own care, to make sure he wore his glasses all the time. "Next year I'll have my birthday at school, shan't I? Can Father take me out, even if I'm at school?"

"Simon's taking us to a theatre," explained Christian. "I do hope nothing crops up, but we've been so unlucky lately, each time we plan to do something together."

She wondered, when Simon came home, if they were going to be unlucky again. He had that air of tense abstraction which had become almost habitual to him, and kissed her as if he was thinking of something else.

"Have a drink, darling? It'll help to pull you together—for to-night." She brought him a full glass. "I put dinner as late as possible, to give you time for a rest before the others come."

"Any one beside your father and mother?"

Christian shook her head.

"No. I thought you'd want to talk business, later on. What are you smiling at?"

"Can't a man smile at his wife? As a matter of fact, I was wondering how you manage to be so different from the rest of your sex, Chris. Don't you ever get sick of the way I neglect you?"

"Often!" She smiled back at him. "Never mind; we'll pull through—shan't we? And then we'll have a glorious holiday and get to know each other all over again. I've got all sorts of vague recollections of you, darling, and I'd like to check up on them, when you've got time."

"It's like you to make a joke of it, but it's no laughing matter, to me. Apart from ourselves, it's not good enough that Henry and Jemima barely know me by sight these days. What have the kids been doing to-day?" Simon stretched himself in his chair and closed his eyes; he remembered Nancy Rowlandson's remark about relaxation. It was blessedly easy to relax in Christian's company.

"Lydia and I took them to their dancing class—and Henry's got his usual Tuesday afternoon swelled head. I sometimes wish things didn't come so terribly easy to him, Simon! I'm afraid of his being rather unsympathetic and superior when he grows up!"

"We'll soon see to that. I've got the seats for to-morrow," said Simon, easily.

"Oh, have you? I'm so glad. I was so afraid you wouldn't manage it."

"I'm not sure, yet, if I shall. Chris, there's hell's delight between Daniel and Eliza."

Her heart sank.

"What's happened?"

"Daniel says he's going to divorce her. For God's sake, keep it to yourself for the present; there'll be an awful row when your father hears about it."

"I'm afraid there will. How sickening, Simon! But perhaps Daniel will change his mind."

Simon shook his head.

"I'm afraid not—this time. He's gone into a flat spin over some chap Eliza's running about with, and I'm afraid he's going to be quite useless until it's over. That means, of course, that I shall be much more tied. . . . I suppose it's a good thing, in a way; I mean, his going through with it. Eliza's been a disturbing element ever since we started; Daniel's only given about a third of his mind to the work—the rest's been taken up with fretting about Eliza."

"Poor Daniel. It must be beastly to have to fret about someone you care for."

"Foul," agreed Simon, thinking that, if anything so unimaginable could happen, it would break him up completely, to fret about Christian. As though the thought communicated itself to her, she was looking at him deeply; the blue penetration of her eyes went right into the depths of him, disturbed all the deep essence of his love for her.

"Nothing can be worth while, can it, if you lose confidence?"

"Nothing."

"I've often wondered——" They were in their bedroom, and Christian had slipped out of her dress; in a satin slip, the colour of rosy moonshine, she looked absurdly young—young enough to be the elder sister of Jemima; she stood by the dressing-table, combing out the thick, soft curtain of her hair. "I've often wondered just how far confidence goes. Do you see what I mean? There must come a point when believing in a person is sheer folly; yet, if one's fond, it must be very hard to decide when that point's reached. After all—it's a confession of personal failure. I mean, if you love a person, your instinct is to trust them completely, and even when you find out they aren't to be trusted, you have to go on, for the sake of your own self-respect."

"I know what you mean. You're really defending your own foundations, aren't you?"

"And it really comes down to a question of how much it's worth while to defend a rotten thing. People talk so lightly about divorce—it's really so complicated; such a muddle of pride and pain. Simon, would you divorce me, if I behaved like Eliza?"

"Yes, I suppose so. Father divorced mother," muttered Simon clumsily.

"But for my sake, or your own?" she persisted.

"For both, I suppose. It's a pretty low trick to act dog-in-the-manger, and there can't be much pleasure in keeping someone tied to one against their will."

"I wonder. You know, I'd find it awfully difficult to divorce you if you were unfaithful to me. To begin with, I simply shouldn't be able to believe it; and then I'd feel so sure the thing that had come between us would pass like blight.

Nothing evil could ever persist, could it, between you and me?"

She was standing before him, looking up with eyes so radiant with candour, so deeply calm with her confidence in him, that Simon's heart turned over.

"Darling, what's all this heavy thinking on divorce about?" he asked presently. "If you're wanting to experiment, I warn you, you haven't a dog's chance—on me!"

"Haven't you ever seen anybody you got excited about, since we were married?"

"Have you?" countered Simon.

"Only Herbert Marshall," said Christian seriously. "I do think he's rather a sweet—and I'd get a frightful thrill if I ever had a chance of meeting him."

"My precious, you shall! Remind me, next time we're in Hollywood."

"I'm only fooling. And you haven't answered my question; I asked you first."

Simon appeared to think.

"Let's see. There was a girl called Sheila; I was rather keen about her, until I noticed she got lipstick on her front teeth. And that reminds me——!" He broke off to laugh. "I got picked up this afternoon."

"You didn't."

"I did. By a sweet young thing in a teashop."

"What on earth were you doing in a teashop?"

"The true wifely note. The car didn't happen to be ready, and I had a blazing thirst, and nothing to do for half an hour; so I went into one of those god-awful tea palaces close to the garage and got picked up."

"Serve you right. Sure you didn't do the picking up?"

"That's not worthy of you, Mrs. Crome."

"No, it was pretty cheap, wasn't it? Sorry." Her lips brushed the back of his hand that tugged at the collar stud. "Was she lovely?"

"Let me see. Oh, I suppose so. Aren't all young women lovely, in this year of Max Factor?"

"Young?"

"*Ça va sans dire.* Haven't you noticed? My hair's getting thin on top; it's the time an old man's fancy lightly turns to thoughts of the *détournement des mineurs.*"

"Idiot!" She laughed; her warm, contented laughter that suggested that Christian got a lot of quiet enjoyment out of the mere fact of being alive. "What a humbug you are, darling! Do you know, you're all pink and bright eyed. I believe you got an enormous kick out of your adventure."

For some reason, this grated slightly. The word "adventure" suggested, to begin with, that one had so settled into the groove of middle age and matrimony that the flirtatious flicker of a typist's eyelashes constituted excitement. Simon found himself resenting the implication—wholly innocent as he knew it to be—that he was senile. An "adventure"—to speak to a chit in a teashop!

"What did you talk about?" pursued Christian.

"Oh, God—I don't know," mumbled Simon, hunting for a tie.

"I hope you paid for her tea."

"Ought I to have done so?" Taken unprepared, Simon paused, aghast at what Christian appeared to regard as a solecism.

"It depends. Lydia says it's quite usual, nowadays, for the girl to do the paying," said Christian, solemnly.

Sensing her amusement, he went through into his dressing-room. Her voice followed him, still a little tremulous with laughter.

"Of course, if she was a lady, she wouldn't let you pay for her!"

It was ridiculous to be ruffled by her teasing; Simon forced himself to laugh, as he replied:

"I don't suppose she'd pass your standards of ' ladyhood.' As a matter of fact, I thought she was just a school kid, until I was sitting opposite to her. She'd got on a sort of little round hat and a collar like Jemima wears"—he paused to recall further details—"oh, and the usual make-up, and rather pretty nails."

"What did you talk about?" asked Christian again; she had come to the door, and was smiling in at him, fastening the belt of her evening gown. "Or were the nails so pretty the conversation didn't matter?"

"Oh, hell. I'm sorry I told you about her."

"Simon!" Her arms were round his neck, her soft body pressed to his. "I'm a fool. I didn't mean a thing—I was only ragging you, because—because you look so enchanting when you're ragged! So little, and young, so like Henry——!"

He returned her kisses.

"I'm dead tired, old girl—that's the long and short of it. Is there time for a bath?"

"Of course. I'll keep the others in play until you're ready." She ran to turn on the taps. "I've put in some of the salts Lydia gave me—they're heaven."

When he had bathed, and while Christian was finishing her dressing, Simon went along to the nursery, where Jemima and Henry, pyjamaed and in their dressing-gowns, were eating bread and milk and arguing over the current instalment of Henry's novel.

The nursery was very warm and full of fire and shaded lamp-light, and smelt of bath soap and Jemima's Ovaltine. It was very modern, with its shiny, apricot-coloured walls and cellophane curtains patterned with heraldic-looking lions and unicorns. Simon wondered if the children liked it, or if they ever thought about it at all. It did not seem as though it would be possible to feel, about a nursery like that, as one had felt about the pleasant, untidy old nursery of one's youth, with scrap screen and big rag hearthrug in front of the high brass-topped fireguard; with the shabby furniture with stubbed framework and upholstery that Christian condemned as "too germ-carrying," and the Christmas Supplement pictures miscellaneously framed on the cretonne-patterned walls.

This nursery was, and looked, expensive; most of it had

come out of Christian's pocket—which meant, out of the pockets of Christian's parents. It was difficult to make a stand about a thing like that, which involved the advantage of one's children. Christian understood how he felt about it, and the nursery was the only "show" room in the house. He made it plain from the beginning that, though Matlock money might provide hygiene for his offspring, it should not lay down his carpets and drape his windows.

As Simon sank into Nana's chair, which she vacated at his entrance, he was glad that the intellectualism of his second-born spared him the formula of the "romp." Left to herself, Jemima would certainly have expected to be romped with; but her natural instincts were controlled by Henry, who, seated at his table with his chin on his clenched fist and the scowl of an infant Balzac, had the air of one who had definitely said farewell to childish things. Jemima, blinking and verbose, as she always seized the opportunity to be when Henry was laconic, claimed her father's attention.

"You see, Daddy, I think Buzzwheel's a *silly* name—even for a dentist. I do think made-up names are silly, don't you, Daddy? I mean, nobody's ever going to believe in a dentist called Mr. Buzzwheel."

"Jabez Buzzwheel," enunciated Henry, as though she had not uttered. "He had it on a brass plate on the door of his house, which was in Pont Street——"

"You see, Daddy. Why *Pont* Street?" chimed in Jemima, obstructively.

"Why not?" Simon felt bound to rejoin.

"Because there *aren't* any dentists in Pont Street," cried the triumphant Jemima.

"There might be some day," sulked Henry. "And anyhow, it avoids libel. Hence Buzzwheel," he ended, on a lofty note that consigned Jemima and her objections to limbo.

"What's this—a new book?" inquired Simon, not recognizing the preliminaries.

"I scrapped the other," said Henry, dismissing past efforts

with a wave of the hand. "For one thing, it had been done
before. Now, nobody's ever written a novel round a dentist—"

"How d'you know they haven't?" interrupted Jemima.
"Do you mean that among all the millions and billions of
books in the libraries there isn't one single one about a dentist?"

"Well, is there?" Henry appealed to his father, still, for
him, the supreme arbiter on such matters.

"I haven't come across one," admitted Simon. Henry raised
an eyebrow at his sister. It was one of Jemima's grievances
that Henry never said "Sucks!" or "I told you so!" like other
little boys of his age. He took up a few sheets of paper which
were under his right elbow and read, very distinctly, with a
slightly precious pronunciation which he reserved for the
public reading of his own works, and which Christian called
his B.B.C. voice:

"'It was a beautiful spring morning, and as there were
no customers, Mr. Buzzwheel called White his dog and locked
up the door of the surgery and told Miss Jenkins his secretary
to say he had gone to the Riviera for the week-end.'"

"Had he?" pounced Jemima.

"No," admitted Henry. "Only to Bognor."

"Then why did he tell a lie?"

"To make a good impression," said Henry rapidly. "'Slipping a few odd teeth in his pocket——'"

"No, no," said Simon. "You can't do that."

"It's necessary to the plot," explained Henry. "You see he
got lost and he had a hole in his pocket and the teeth dropped
out and the police found him because of them." He scowled
a challenge at his father. "Don't you like it?" he asked, as
Simon continued to be silent, with a strained expression on
his face.

"Not much, old boy. I don't much like the teeth touch.
It's not aesthetic."

"Oh, well." Henry shrugged his shoulders. "You can't
please everybody. I suppose if it isn't a Crome and Lygon
book there are plenty of other publishers."

Simon winced; he seemed to have heard that a good many times lately. Without any idea of being tactful—a quality foreign to her nature—Jemima saved the situation.

"Are we going to the matinee to-morrow, Daddy?"

"Yes, you are. I've got the tickets—at least, I've given them to Mummy, in case I can't get away in time."

The expression of the disgruntled author gave way to a brief gleam of satisfaction. Henry said politely:

"Thank you very much," and was cut short by Jemima's whoop of delight.

"Oh, Daddy. Oh, *good*. But you must come—it's only half as much fun if you don't come."

"I shall if I can; it'll be all right, because it's a box." Christian had asked for a box, in case Lydia could come. "I don't see nearly enough of Lydia, considering she's my only sister; and matinees are just the sort of time she's likely to be free."

"Daddy, suppose you can't come—couldn't Daniel?" pleaded Jemima. "Henry likes Daniel—don't you, Henry?" She appealed to her brother. "Of course, it's Henry's treat; but you *do* like Daniel, don't you?" urged Jemima piteously. No one knew about the deep and hopeless passion she cherished for Daniel.

"Oh, yes, I don't mind Daniel," said Henry, off-handedly.

"Well, we'll see what can be arranged," said Simon, getting up.

"Can't we have just one game of Lexicon?" pleaded Jemima. Henry always beat her at Lexicon, but she bore it cheerfully, having a vicarious share in all Henry's triumphs.

"No, I've got to dress; your grandparents are dining with us to-night."

Simon bent down to lift up his daughter; Jemima's arms and legs wrapped themselves round him tightly, her soft, sweet-smelling hair, newly washed, made a web that enclosed their two faces, as she kissed Simon good-night in her usual thorough fashion: each eye separately, ears, nose, and finally mouth. As usual, at the conclusion, she gave a deep sigh of satisfaction for a task adequately performed. Simon put her down and turned to Henry, who had got out of his chair and stood waiting, with his hands in the pockets of his brown dressing-gown, looking very small and childish, with the cast in his eye—corrected during the day-time by the glasses which Nana put carefully away before he had his bath—lending a wistfulness to his upward glance which was hardly in accordance with Henry's firm and self-reliant character.

"Good-night, old man."

"I wanted to ask you," said Henry gravely. "Do you think it's time I stopped kissing?"

"It depends what you feel about it. Do you?"

"I shall be nine to-morrow," said Henry, "and the next term I'm going to school. One has to stop some time, hasn't one?"

"Do you want to stop to-night?" asked Simon.

Henry looked taken aback.

"That's different, isn't it? I mean—you and me?"

"Yes, I think perhaps it is," said Simon carefully.

"And mother, and—perhaps—Jemima. But I think I would rather like to start to-night."

"How do you mean?" asked Simon, not for a moment grasping his meaning.

"Well, there's grandfather and grannie, isn't there? They always come up and say good-night to us, when they come to dinner."

"Oh, I see. Well, Henry, it's up to you. But I'll mention it downstairs, if you like."

"I think it would help if you did. I can manage Nana," said Henry, more firmly.

"Good-night, old boy." Simon held out his hand. Henry laid his own small fist in it very gravely, looking up into his father's face. Then, suddenly smiling, he lifted his mouth for the accustomed kiss.

"Good-night, father."

Growing up, growing up. Something gripped Simon's

heart, as he went downstairs from the nursery floor. Paternity
—the man fulfilling himself in creating mankind; handing
on to posterity no mere physical imprint, a matter of bones
and hair and skin and a certain blueness or brownness of eye,
but something of the intangible that makes up the living
whole—emotions, desires, the tendency to react in a special
way to special stimuli. From primordial instinct, he was
thinking, as he used the military brushes sharply on either
side a widening parting, derives all the constructive effort of
the human race—all of the urge to personal betterment, which
means, in the long run, betterment of the family, of the group,
of the race. From his children a man draws, not merely the
will, but the inspiration to build himself a position in the
community: the equilibrium which helps him to maintain
his stability among conflicting influences: the courage to
embark upon the enterprise which, lacking that inspiration,
seems too much for a person to tackle alone. The man working
for himself may gamble with the future, but the head of a
family must leave gambling to the irresponsible, must concentrate the whole of his forces upon a future which means
safety and prosperity for those whom he loves. "Perhaps I'm
a prig for looking at it in this way," he apologized to himself.
"Perhaps I'm excusing my own jog-trot temperament, that
finds salvation in security. Marriage, of course, has accen-
tuated that; I gambled enough—after my own fashion—before
I met Christian."

He looked comfortably, possessively, round the big square
room; it was a comfortable although old-fashioned Victorian
house which they had taken soon after Jemima's birth—in a
Bayswater square that had resisted, so far, the "reconstruction"
mania which has turned so many of its kind into flat colonies.
He and Christian had chosen it because it had a solid, family
air of mid-Victorian prosperity. "Such a nice house for
children, Simon! And I do want Jemima to have as many
brothers and sisters as we can afford." The rent and rates were
something of a drain on Simon's resources, but optimism had

governed their decision, and optimism inclined them always to the view that things would be better "very soon." Old Harry had approved the choice. "A very dignified and suitable place, my boy; you couldn't have done better for yourself—as well as Christian. She's like me—can't stand these flats, and moving on every year or so. Give a woman a place she can really call home, and you can take my word she'll make a home of it for her husband and children. You'll be here until you move into Belgrave Square!"

Such doubts as Simon may have had when he signed the long lease soon vanished in Christian's happiness; any sacrifice, he felt, was worth while that secured her her air of quiet content, as she moved about her big, airy rooms, taking housewifely pride in their immaculacy. Used as she was to the enormous spaces of her own home, she could never have settled into the cramped environment of a flat. She never seemed to suffer, as other women in houses did, from that which is euphemistically termed "servant trouble"; at least, he never heard her complain of it. They had few changes, and these were accomplished with decent calm and dispatch. Simon sometimes felt they were living beyond their means, and there were many improvements that Christian would have liked to have made if there had been more money—or if Simon had allowed her to spend her own. But he was adamant on the subject of providing for his own household. "Spend on the kids, if you like," he told her, "but please, dear, if you care about my feelings, wait until I can give you all the rest. The time's bound to come——"

"Of course it is. Don't I know that, without your telling me?"

If Daniel and Eliza had had kids, he was thinking, as he slipped the oddments from the pockets of his day suit into his evening clothes, it mightn't have held them together, but it would have given Daniel some sort of ballast to face the mess he'd got into now.

Daniel had got to be helped. It was the last promise that

Simon had made to their mother, when he visited her in the
nursing home which she left, only to die in the South of France.

"I know you two can't have much in common these days;
but Daniel has always looked up to you, darling! You'll always
do what you can for him, won't you? I'm afraid this marriage
of his is going badly, and he has so little in himself to make
up for it." Simon could still see the nervous hands plucking at
the sheets, smell the over-sweet perfume of the flowers with
which the room was filled. To spare her feelings, he avoided
looking too closely at his mother; Rose Lygon was trying
so desperately to die elegantly, as she had lived, and death,
it would seem, was jealous of elegance. Her second husband,
Daniel's father, had died some years before, leaving "not nearly
enough money, darling, for people like Daniel and Eliza,
though I spare them all I can, and of course they'll get everything eventually. Don't blame Daniel, because I've brought
him up to have expensive tastes; I'd have done the same for
you, if there'd been any money to do it on. But I don't suppose
you've been any less happy because of it. I never could understand your father—he seemed to *like* working, and being
poor!" She flickered her lashes. "Anyhow, you've married
a rich wife, haven't you? So sensible of you, darling."

He wondered whether, in the depths of her misunderstanding, she imagined he had married Christian for her
money. It was the kind of thing a woman like Rose Lygon
would think; but it did not seem to matter now. For the rest
of the time he was with her, her talk was all of Daniel, her
love and anxiety for him so transparently greater than her
regard for her elder son that a less generous person than Simon
might have been wounded. It was the memory of this conversation which, against his better judgment, had made
Simon agree to Daniel's rather surprising suggestion that they
should pool their resources and go into partnership in publishing—an ambition which Simon had cherished for many
years before he made up his mind to turn his back on Fleet
Street and fly after higher game.

CHAPTER THREE

It was one of the minor blessings of life, Simon reflected, that taking it all in all, he liked his parents-in-law. Sir Harry Matlock—the title was still new enough to titillate pleasantly the vanity of its owner—was a fine, picturesque old fellow, proud of the thick white thatch that covered his big, squarely modelled head and of the Vandyke that added importance to a chin less prominent than might have been expected from Sir Harry's character. It had been, in fact, before its owner had the inspiration of masking it with a beard, rather an ignominious little chin: soft, round and dimpled, sensuously good natured and very misleading to those who trusted its mild contours and declared, on the strength of it, that "there was a soft side to Old Harry." Sir Harry himself had become aware of it at an early stage in his career, and, from that moment, had, in a sense, declared war upon it. It was as though he were always conscious of that soft little chin, lying in wait to betray him: for to counterbalance its effect upon other people he had cultivated a tight, thin-lipped expression which went with the deep furrow concentration had drawn between his brows. It was not until some years after his marriage that he had had the inspiration of the Vandyke; and with that to lend confidence to his lower features, the upper part of his face had insensibly relaxed, so that, in middle life, the general effect was urbane, if not positively genial.

Only those who had dealings with Old Harry knew that he was as hard as rock: as hard as the commodity out of which he had built his fortune. While yet under age, he inherited from his father a shaky little business, a small, doubtfully-run factory turning out hardware and farming implements. When Harry—young Harry then—looked over the ledgers he remembered how they had lived, ever since his childhood, in a state

43

amounting to genteel poverty, while his father, amiable, well meaning, honest, muddled along with the little factory, running always a losing race against more able competitors, perpetually agonized about his relationship with the bank, with the one or two fairly reliable customers, with his work-people. It was not a scheme of living that appealed to young Harry—thrustful, ambitious, with a commercial college training behind him.

It was a mystery to most people what means of persuasion Harry used, to obtain a large grant from the bank which his father regarded with such timorous respect. Certainly the soft little chin had nothing to do with it!—nor with the ruthless system of reorganization that swept through the works, scaring the slowcoaches and galvanizing departments which, for a month or two, were plunged into hopeless confusion by Harry's methods. "There is one thing about young Harry: we'll either be broke or made by the time he's through," was the general comment.

Now, from the windows of the train which brought him to St. Pancras, Old Harry could enjoy the prospect of his "Ironmongery Town," as the popular press had dubbed it—the long, pale glass palaces that were the factories; the tree-speckled avenues of workmen's model dwellings; the Institute, with its swimming baths for men and women (mixed bathing strictly prohibited), its lecture and recreation halls and free cinema, where news and instructional films were given three times a week, with lighter fare on half-holidays and at the week-ends, its gymnasium, billiard saloon and broad, adjacent playing fields. Three model public houses provided for the thirst of the inhabitants. "Ironmongery Town" had its own technical college and its own hospital, of which an important feature was the maternity clinic; but the architectural feature which dominated the whole of the lay-out, as seen from the railway, was the Congregational chapel, which rose with the grandeur of a miniature cathedral from the only elevation the landscape afforded. "Old Harry's way of squaring the

Almighty," the cynics called it. Old Harry's religious fanaticism was no less famous than his commercial hard-headedness: the combination of the two had put the seal upon his credit in circles peculiarly susceptible to the nice adjustment of religion to business.

"I'm sure father comes up to town by train just for the sake of that view of the works," commented Lydia astutely. It was undeniable that, although the Rolls was invariably sent up for Old Harry's use in town, he never made the journey otherwise than by train.

He had married, as soon as his prospects permitted, the daughter of an insignificant county family, thus assuring to his children that strain of breeding for which Old Harry, like the majority of his class, had a genuine respect. Lady—at first Mrs.—Matlock had settled comfortably into the setting of luxury it was Old Harry's pride to provide for her, sharing with him an interest in the expensive education of their two daughters, one of whom, it was tacitly understood, would provide Sir Harry with a son-in-law to carry on the works, since a slight but vital operation after Lydia's birth had disposed of their hopes of a son. When Christian had chosen to marry a "literary" man, the responsibility had narrowed down to Lydia, who distressed her parents by a seeming disinclination towards matrimony, and had celebrated her majority, when she "came into" the money put aside by Sir Harry for his daughters' coming of age, by taking a flat in London and living a life which seemed very irregular and inexplicable to her parents.

So Christian, having got herself respectably, if not brilliantly, married, was the favourite, and it was partly on Christian's account, and partly because of some vague yearnings towards the intellectual life which he had had so far no opportunities to cultivate, that Old Harry had surprised Simon by offering to finance the publishing firm which he had once, in a moment of expansion, admitted to his father-in-law was an ambition of his to establish.

Old Harry's approach to the idea was characteristically cautious. He did not allow himself to be carried away by Simon's enthusiasm. He spent a month in making inquiries here and there, before he was satisfied that publishing held wider prospects than Simon's present editorial position, and that a son-in-law in the publishing business carried more kudos than one in journalism. Old Harry could afford to be, and was, a snob. He was also, although he did not admit it, tickled at the prospect of having a finger in the publishing pie. From ironmongery to books!—a piquant transition. It is not too much to say that he saw himself, during the time it took to draw out the contract, as the future apostle of literary uplift: for of course he had made it clear that his money was not to be used to graft more of what he described as "scribblers' filth" on to the market.

He was a little doubtful of the Lygon end of the partnership. Before Old Harry's money came into the picture, Simon and Daniel had practically decided to take the plunge. Daniel had five thousand pounds: admittedly a drop in the bucket, but enough, they thought, to get started in a small way. Simon coached Daniel carefully in his approach to Old Harry. "For God's sake none of your quips and sallies; the old boy won't understand them, but he'll resent you for puzzling him." Accordingly, Daniel behaved as though butter would not melt in his mouth, and, as usual, got away with it; but not to the extent of making Old Harry like him.

Christian was wearing a new brooch. Her glance as she showed it to him held a touch of guilt. He knew she would rather not have worn it just then, but that she was doing as they expected of her. He admired it dutifully.

"Pretty thing, isn't it?" purred Lady Matlock. "I saw it in the Burlington Arcade; I had to get it—it seemed just the thing for Chris."

The "pretty thing" had cost, even to Simon's inexperienced eye, not a penny less than fifty pounds. He had grown past the bitterness of jealousy, that it should be her parents, and not he, who provided Christian with her jewels; yet he could not help wishing they would wait a while, and give him a chance.

The drawing-room had always, to Simon, a slightly foreign and unaccustomed air when his parents-in-law were in it. It was a pleasant, lofty room, with a few plain but (Simon flattered himself) well-chosen pieces of furniture scattered about its beautiful parquet; with tall windows draped in a heavy satin for which Christian had wanted to pay, and he had refused to allow her, and pale walls with Breughel reproductions and a pair of old Empire mirrors with candle-sconces which both he and Christian refused to have fitted with electric lights. A simple and quiet room, it appeared, on the occasions of the Matlocks' visits, to become faintly demoralized, as though it caught the infection of luxury from Lady Matlock's furs, her jewels, the layers of softly scented material in which she folded her plump, matronly figure.

Simon's reverence for his Bechstein was outraged by the appearance upon the polished lid of a plethoric vase from which sprouted a lush selection from the Matlock hothouses. Christian cast him a comical look of apology; Simon went very quietly, and, using of necessity both hands and an absurd amount of muscular energy, removed the offending object to the top of a bookcase.

"Oh, Simon dear, don't you like them there? I thought the reflections were so charming."

Simon passed some vaguely mollifying comment, and wondered why the room looked as if it had gone mad. "You know what Mother is," Lydia, who sympathized, had once said to him. "She's never happy unless she's got her rooms *lousy* with flowers." Looking at the flaring bouquets she had brought with her, Simon reflected that Lady Matlock must be very happy. Oddments of silk and lace, showered from her hands in passing, strewed chairs and the settee upon which she conveyed throne-like attributes, by the mere act of sitting there with her small, regal smile. A Pekinese lolled against her waist; Sir Harry stood behind her, as though posing for one of his many press photographs, beaming satisfaction. "There you are, my boy," he seemed to be saying. "That's the way to provide for a wife!" Simon wondered with a pang whether Christian missed the diamonds and orchids and Pekinese he had never been able to give her; she must, after all, have grown up thinking that these were natural concomitants of the married state. Yet could anything be more blissful than their lives together?

"Darling, I've brought you a marvellous recipe for trout," Lady Matlock was saying, as they drifted into the dining-room. The fire had not been lighted early enough, and Lady Matlock's plump shoulder blades contracted. "Rather chilly, isn't it? Harry, dear, will you bring me my wrap?"

The parlourmaid, who had learned to be prepared for such contingencies, laid the garment over her shoulders.

"You must try my trout!" she purred, cosily content beneath her tent of sable.

"Do you think my cook could do it? We haven't got a chef, you know, Mummy," said Christian cheerfully.

"That'll come, that'll come," chimed in Sir Harry. "When Simon's found that best-seller he's always threatening us with!"

"They take a bit of finding," admitted Simon, as the soup went round. He saw Christian taste hers anxiously, relief dawn faintly as it came, evidently, up to standard. Dear Christian—always so anxious that their *ménage* should pass muster with her people: not for her own sake, but for his. She flung her head up with a little laugh.

"Have you brought any manuscripts for me to read?"

"Just a couple—I'm afraid they're not much good."

"Do you know I'm reading for Crome and Lygon?" she challenged her father. "I think I ought to get paid for it, but Simon says the business won't carry an extra salary just yet."

"I thought it was Lydia who was the authority on literature, not you." Old Harry's smile rested upon his favourite daughter, as he scrupulously touched up the ends of his moustache with the napkin.

"For a publisher's wife," admitted Christian, "I'm scandalously ignorant. I can't see what use I can possibly be to Simon."

"My dear stupid," said Simon, "your illiteracy is much more valuable to me at present than other people's erudition. I can get twenty readers to tell me if a book's a good 'un—I'm even capable of judging that for myself; but you're the only one who can tell me if it's likely to be a seller; and from that point of view I'd back your judgment against mine any day."

"That sounds flattering," grunted Old Harry.

"She's got one supreme quality: she judges everything she reads on its personal appeal to herself. She doesn't give a hoot for construction, or realism, or literary values. She either likes or doesn't like it—which, when you come to think of it, is exactly the point of view of the average subscriber to the fiction libraries."

"And a very good point of view, surely?" reproved Lady Matlock, scenting criticism.

"For us as publishers—excellent."

"Though really, one can hardly trust the libraries nowadays," complained Lady Matlock. "Even my girl at Harrod's —such a nice young woman! I always ask her advice before choosing my books—even she's quite nonplussed, sometimes, to find me something I'll *really* like. Of course, as she says, it's almost impossible to find something nowadays that one can recommend to all the subscribers."

"Of course it is. But I'll guarantee Christian's choice to go for eighty per cent of the library public." He was anxious to avoid the denunciation of modern fiction which he saw gathering like a thundercloud about his father-in-law's brow.

"There are advantages in having only a very ordinary brain," said Christian, smiling very sweetly. "I like stories about comfortable people; people with enough money to have fun—and a spot of glamour. I do most of my reading in bed in the morning, and it seems to start the day off pleasantly if one enjoys the people one reads about."

"I always say," said Lady Matlock, feeling for her lorgnette to inspect the dish which had just been presented at her elbow ("*Rouget*, Mummy dear," put in Christian hastily). "I always say, if you want to read about the working classes, or unemployment, or the slums, there's plenty of that sort of thing in the newspapers. I don't think it's proper matter for fiction." Swallowing a sigh, Simon resigned himself to the usual argument. "Don't misunderstand me, dear; my objection isn't frivolous. Harry and I"—she straightened her plump little figure—"have always taken the greatest interest in the working classes; in fact, I'm sure you might say we have devoted our lives to the improvement of their conditions. I myself know a great deal more about poverty and sickness among the poor than half the writers of these slum novels—which of course I never read!—whose accounts are always grossly exaggerated and give quite a false impression to the general public of what is really being done for the lower orders. I always say, why *should* I read about them in my spare time—especially as the authors seem to take a positive pleasure in dwelling on all the coarse and vulgar episodes which any decent-minded person prefers to ignore."

"I'm afraid I agree with Mummy. I don't get a kick out of descriptions of navvies spitting on the floors of pubs, and servant girls taking medicine to get rid of their illegitimate babies. I hate being disgusted, and I hate having my feelings harrowed by imaginary events," said Christian. "And I simply loathe 'land' novels, about farm hands reeking of sweat and cowbyres, and I don't much care for long descriptions of scenery, unless it's some place I know; I usually skip them."

"My darling," said Simon, smiling at her, "go on. You are worth a million a word to the publisher in search of a best-seller. You are the Average Reader in a nutshell."

"But surely you agree with her, Simon? I do think so much of the fiction published nowadays shows not merely a complete lack of morals, but of good taste."

"After all," said Sir Harry, "there's nothing to beat a good, clean thriller as a selling proposition. Look at Septimus Thatch; look at Hilda Munnings—though," he added, "she might leave out some of that unnecessary stuff about the private lives of her characters that doesn't contribute an ounce to the plot. What you want to look out for is a Septimus Thatch——"

Simon, who was quite hardened now to being told by his father-in-law what to look out for, agreed that there was room for another writer of first-class detective fiction.

"I had a very promising book in yesterday," he mused. "It was about Roumania——"

"Roumanians in Roumania, or English people in Roumania?" pertinently questioned Christian.

"Roumanians in Roumania."

She shook her head. "I'm afraid it wouldn't go. People don't like reading about foreigners—especially if the book is written *well*. Don't you remember that Book Society choice a few years ago—all about Maoris, by one of the women novelists——?"

"I bet she never saw a Maori," chuckled Old Harry. "What can a decent Englishwoman know about blacks? Stupid subject for a woman to write about—only makes folks laugh who know their subject——"

"As a matter of fact," said Simon quietly, "I happen to know she was brought up among Maoris, and her grandfather was one of the first pioneers to go out to New Zealand."

"Stupid subject for a woman," muttered Old Harry, resenting, as Simon knew, the idea of a woman's knowing about a matter on which he was wholly ignorant.

"Well, anyhow," went on Christian, "the first book sold, because of the Book Society; and then she did a string of Maori novels—two or three, anyway—and nobody read them at all. Because they were too Maori, do you see? I mean, they were about Maoris and written from the Maori point of view. That never goes in England; it disturbs our imperialism, or something."

"I'm afraid she's right," said Simon. "Nothing but sheer pigheaded insularity can excuse the indifference of the general public to such a book as *Mawai*. The truth is, that for all the education in this country, its cultural influence only reaches a very limited circle. The majority of readers still seek relaxation, rather than intellectual stimulation, in their fiction——"

"Well, well, after all, we are English, and, I hope, proud of our own country," boomed Old Harry. "They say it's the fashion nowadays to run down patriotism. Ha! That's what the intellectuals are doing, aren't they? Well, thank God, the nation isn't run by intellectuals. Never mind them, my boy: concentrate your attention on the big-hearted, simple man in the street—the backbone of the nation! If he wants relaxation, give it to him—full measure. I don't mean, serve him slop. That isn't what he wants—it isn't what the British lion cut his teeth on! But give him subjects and characters that appeal to him; that rouse his emotions and touch his sentimental spot. Books—the greatest force for good that the world possesses! But they must appeal to the heart, my boy, not only to the head. Don't forget that."

Simon, who always went hot under the collar when Old Harry paraded the British lion, caught a saving gleam from Christian's eye, and mumbled something placatory.

"What's the most successful book you've published up to date, Simon? The Cratchitt biography, isn't it? And let me tell you why: because it's the straightforward record of an honest Englishman rising by his own efforts. No intellectualism in old Joe Cratchitt—God bless him! Industry and ideals

—ideals and industry, that's what brought him to the top. Where will you find anything more typically English than that? King and country—hard work and hitch your wagon to a star—do you wonder that book strikes home to every decent Englishman—ay, and Englishwoman too—who gets hold of it?"

Biting his tongue, Simon managed to hold back the comment that the Cratchitt biography was one of the most unpleasant examples of hypocritical horn-blowing he had ever handled; but there was no doubt the public had eaten it.

"That book," went on Old Harry, warming to his subject, "that book was like a clean wind across a sewage bed. The ladies will excuse me—sewage bed was my expression, and I mean it. Fifty per cent of the so-called literature of to-day is plain sewage—and the publishers know it. They deliberately make capital out of the prurience in human nature——"

"Father, dear," said Christian, "would you like to finish your wine with Simon, or will you join us in the drawing-room for coffee?"

"There's a book on the counters," went on Old Harry dangerously, "that, if we'd got anything of a censorship, would be burnt in the marketplace. Some dirty revelations of a so-called Society woman—a nice sort of Society we've got, if we take her at her word!"

"Darling," Christian tried again, "when you begin to talk about Society it always makes me a bit nervous; we're all in 'Society' of a sort, and you know it's just as mixed as life down at Granedge—good and bad in equal spots. Do you mind if Mummy and I have our coffee now?"

"Coming," said Sir Harry, gulping the remainder of his wine. Although a connoisseur of vintages, his puritanism led him to believe that by remaining in the dining-room to drink with Simon he would be showing a bad example to the younger man. At Simon's age a glass of port represented his acquaintance with wines; he secretly deplored, while enjoying, his son-in-law's cellar.

"It will be nice to get into the warm room," smiled Lady Matlock, rising as though relieved to have done with her martyrdom. "Simon dear, you really should instal central heating, now you and Chris have settled down! It's so inexpensive, in comparison with a few years ago, and such an economy, after you've paid for the installation."

"Well, I dare say we'll manage it presently. The diningroom ought to have been warmer, but I suppose the servants didn't allow for its being a particularly cold evening." Simon had learnt to take with unfailing good humour his mother-in-law's hints that he was not looking properly after Christian's comfort. "Have one of your own cigars, sir?" He opened the cabinet which Old Harry had given him at Christmas.

Old Harry accepted one and lit up. His blue eyes twinkled at Simon down the cylinder of tobacco.

"Nasty expensive habit, my boy! Mustn't give way to it. Do you know how old I was when I bought my first box of cigars? I mean, of course, apart from business: you've got to have a good cigar to offer people when they come to talk big business. But I never smoked 'em myself—no, sir! I was fifty, before I treated myself to a hundred Ramon Allones, and, by George, I felt like a criminal every time I looked at the box."

"He's always been mean with himself and wildly extravagant with me," put in Lady Matlock, with smiling satisfaction.

"That's as it should be," grunted Old Harry.

"Well, considering your views, you've done your best to lead me astray, haven't you?" pointed out Simon. "It's all very well to give a man a taste for the best and tell him to smoke gaspers!"

"Have patience, have patience. You can console yourself with the thought that when I've smoked my last Ramon you'll be buying cabinets like that for Henry."

"I don't find any consolation in *that* thought," said Simon. It always surprised him to find how fond he was of Old Harry. It might occasionally be galling to be treated as an ignorant and struggling beginner in the book trade, to be used as an audience for the old boy's lay sermons and chidden—albeit obliquely—for his slowness in providing for Christian upon the scale Old Harry had provided for her mother; but it was impossible to ignore the fact that Old Harry was truly and deeply fond of him, finding in him, probably, some consolation for the son he had never had.

"It's Henry's birthday to-morrow, isn't it? I want to give him a pony."

"Good God!" Simon was moved to ejaculate. "You can't do that! I mean, sir, it's extraordinarily generous of you; but a pony's a bit difficult in town, isn't it? He gets plenty of riding when we're in the country, but now he's just off to his prep. school——"

"He can take the pony with him, can't he? I don't hold with children learning on riding school nags; Henry'll get much more confidence and sense of responsibility out of a pony of his own."

Simon stood silent, biting his lips, trying to think how it would be possible, without mortally offending Old Harry and hurting Christian's feelings, to refuse the gift. It was necessary some time to call a halt to the Matlocks' generosity, which bound shackles upon him of which even Christian was not aware. He would have liked to cry out, "To hell with your presents! They're robbing me of my independence, of the right that belongs to every man of providing for his own family according to his means." Forbidden such truthfulness, he thought how lightly and easily Daniel would have dealt with such a situation, as he mumbled:

"It's awfully kind of you, sir; I hope you won't misunderstand me when I say that we—Henry and I—can't accept it."

He saw Christian's eyelashes flicker and felt a pang. Old Harry had flushed crimson.

"What on earth do you mean?"

"I think I know what Simon means, Daddy," cut in

Christian—and Simon drew a breath of relief, for if any one could manage Old Harry it would be Christian; but he felt unhappily she was going to support him at the sacrifice of her own feelings in the matter. "I think he means that you've already given us so much—both us and the children—that we can't, for the present, accept any more."

"Nonsense. What I choose to give is nobody's business but my own."

"And ours. I'm with Simon: it would be lovely for Henry to have a pony of his own. But wouldn't it be a little silly, for a boy in his position? It's not one of the grand prep schools, where most of the children have their own mounts; it's a very simple school, and most of the parents are very nice, not very well-off people, who are making a great effort to give their boys a good education. Simon and I do so want to economize while Henry is there, so as to have plenty in hand by the time he is ready for Charterhouse."

"You're talking like a pauper!" said Old Harry, contemptuously. "You know perfectly well the boy'll be seen through his public school——"

"Yes, Daddy: by us—not by Mother or you. Does that sound ungrateful? Please try to understand. Simon and I have talked it over a lot lately, and we agree that the children are our responsibility. We didn't have them carelessly, or without calculating exactly what we should be able to do for them. You're already making me a generous allowance; we took that into our calculations. Mummy, you ought to be able to understand: wasn't part of the fun of having Lydia and me all the planning and contriving you had to do, to give us the things you wanted us to have? Oh, I know your planning was on a bigger scale, even then," she added hurriedly, as Old Harry's lip curled, and Lady Matlock smiled in a patient and humouring fashion. "But it was *your* planning and *your* fun —and how you'd have hated any one who tried to take your fun away from you, as you, with the dearest and kindest intentions, are trying to take it away from us!"

Later, when they were going to bed, Simon asked her, "Did you really mean that about fun?"

"What about fun?"

"The fun of having children, and planning and economizing for them? Is it really fun, Chris—for you?"

"Of course it is, silly! It's the most exciting thing in my life—apart, of course, from you."

"You're really marvellous, Chris," he murmured, as he held her tightly. "Why should you feel like that? Why should you ever have to think about money at all? I don't suppose you knew the difference between a penny and a pound when you were a child."

"You're wrong there; Father saw to it that we'd got a very clear idea of the difference between pounds and pence, and we were certainly brought up not to waste pence. But, don't you see, my sweet, it's having had everything without the slightest effort that puts such a kick into the way we're living now? I really do get a genuine thrill out of doing littls sums to see if I can afford a new party frock for Jemima and/or the gloves at Fortnum's that go with my tweeds. And it's positively delirious to balance the price of Henry's underwear against ovenware for cook!"

"All the same, you were disappointed Henry didn't get his pony."

"I was—rather. He'd have loved it so much——"

"Then why didn't you say so?"

She withdrew a little from his embrace to look at him.

"Don't you know?"

"Tell me."

"Because in a thing like that—that we'd talked over so often—I couldn't have gone over on to Father's side; it would have been letting you down."

"If I choose to give my grandson a pony," Old Harry was muttering, "it's my own look-out."

"Not entirely," said Simon. "I wouldn't for the world say a word to hurt or offend you, sir; but I wish you'd try to see our point of view. Even if Crome and Lygon becomes one of the big firms like Gosschalk or Rice, my scale of living will never approach yours."

"Do you mean to say you'll never be able to afford to give your son a pony?" taunted Old Harry.

"A dozen ponies, I hope, and a jolly good hunter, when he's old enough; but owning a horse doesn't give one the millionaire outlook. I don't want young Henry to start off too big for his boots. I don't want him—it may sound selfish, but I've got a good reason—to enjoy advantages his Father can't give him; in short—forgive me for putting it bluntly —I don't want him to grow up with the idea at the back of his mind that he's got a grandfather who will give him whatever he likes to ask for. I do desperately want him to be independent and work for his living: you ought to sympathize with that," ended Simon, scowling.

"It sounds to me as if it's all what *you* want and nothing about Henry. Learning to ride is part of a gentleman's education——"

"I fully agree with you. Henry shall learn to ride, with the other fellows at his prep, but he's not going to swank about on his pony and think himself the king of the castle because he's the only chap with a mount of his own."

"I think you're rather hard on the poor child," put in Henry's grandmother.

"Henry's not a child any longer: he's a little boy of nine, with rather too much intelligence for his age. He's on the verge now of the worst swelled head of any child I ever met, and I'm not going to help to swell it."

The crease on Old Harry's brow had smoothed itself out; his anger was as brief, usually, as it was sudden; had he not had a trying little habit of harking back to old arguments, reviving old grievances, he would have been a good-tempered man. As it was, he was moody, and one could never quite rely upon him, after a quarrel was made up, to forget it or the cause of it.

"You're a good lad, Simon; you're sensible. I bet the women would make a mess of young Henry, if they had their way." He characteristically ignored Christian's espousal of her husband's cause—partly because he did not believe in it, partly because he disliked to acknowledge the possibility of her opposition to him. "I'll have the pony sent down to Granedge; he can ride it when he stays with us."

"You've actually bought it?"

"Of course I have; a nice little sorrel—a bit spirited, perhaps, but it will do him good to master it."

"And now what are we to give Henry to-morrow?" demanded Lady Matlock, to whom birthdays were as serious a matter as the major festivals of the Church.

"Get him some bricks," Simon was beginning—when the door opened, and the parlourmaid entered.

"Mrs. Lygon, madam."

Their eyes met in a flash of apprehension. Eliza, who had not been near them for twelve months, would of course choose this disastrous moment for re-introducing herself into the family circle.

Simon was out of his chair and half-way across the room before Christian had spoken.

"I'll see her in the study——."

But before the door closed behind him, Eliza's strident accents—indifferent to servants, to strangers, to the bourgeois convention of keeping one's personal affairs private—rang through the hall:

"Look here, Simon, you must make Daniel give up this dam'-fool notion of a divorce!"

CHAPTER FOUR

Lydia shared a flat somewhere near Marble Arch with a girl called Anna Pryde who had something not very serious to do with a film agency. Between them they had enough money to "do" themselves very well; the flat was spacious, and lent itself to their frequent hospitalities, as well as to the privacy which each regarded as an essential of a *ménage à deux*. Beside the dining- and drawing-rooms, which were flung into one when the girls gave a party, each had her private sitting-room, which, in Anna's case, was also her bedroom; Anna insisted upon Lydia's taking the only other available room because she paid the larger share of the rent.

Christian had taken Henry to the oculist, and, having sent him home with Nana, it was natural to drop in and see Lydia on her way back. Unexpectedly alone, Lydia was delighted to see her sister, whom she had not met since the afternoon of Henry's birthday, when they had all gone to *Julius Cæsar*. Over their sherry, Christian found herself telling her about Eliza's visit, which she had had no opportunity of mentioning when they met at the theatre, Daniel having taken Simon's place at the last minute and Lydia departing before the fall of the curtain for another engagement.

"You mean she just walked in——?" said Lydia, her eyes on the "twig" she was eating with her sherry.

"Not into the drawing-room, fortunately—although she might just as well have done, bawling at Simon about the divorce before he could shut the door."

"Divorce——?" said Lydia.

"Oh, I forgot you didn't know." Christian bit her lip; she had not meant to mention the divorce to Lydia, although it was inevitable she would hear of it in the course of the next

few days. "Yes, I'm afraid they're going to do it. Isn't it
sickening, for everybody?"

"Who's doing which?"

"Daniel, of course, is divorcing Eliza. At least, that's as
it stands at present. Eliza doesn't seem to want it, for some
reason of her own. That's why she came to Simon; she thinks
he has influence over Daniel, which I'm afraid isn't true, the
way she means. According to what Simon says, there doesn't
seem much sense in stopping it—they'll never get on together,
and Eliza's behaviour is pretty bitchy."

"That Caffard thing, I suppose."

"No, it's somebody else. Oh, the whole thing's frightfully
disagreeable, and I'm so sorry for Simon."

"I should have thought you might keep your sorrow for
Daniel," said Lydia, getting up casually and strolling to the
window.

"I was thinking of Father; of course, he'll be livid, and
he'll take it out on Simon, as he's barely on speaking terms
with Daniel."

"He knows about it, does he?"

"Well, of course he couldn't help hearing what Eliza said.
They both started to pump me, and I tried to laugh it off
as one of Daniel's and Eliza's little disagreements—but you
know how impossible it is to get past Father with a thing like
that; and, anyhow, what's the good? Everybody'll know in a
day or two. Oh, I do wish it hadn't had to happen just now,
with Simon up to his eyes in worry about the business. Poor
sweet, he always seems to come in for the tough end of other
people's affairs   "

"Of course, they never could bear Daniel," said Lydia,
speaking of her parents. "He's just all wrong from Father's
point of view. The mere fact of his being the son of Rose
Lygon——"

"Isn't Simon?"

"She was Mrs. Crome then, darling, and when Daniel was
born, her first husband was very much alive. You must see

that, as a divorcee, she was, from Father's point of view, a Scarlet Woman, and the colour ran—unfortunately—into poor Daniel!"

"Well, I suppose he can't help his way of looking at it. After all, Daddy and Mummy are Victorians, and I suppose we've got to put up with it."

"What did they say to Simon?"

"They'd gone before he had finished with Eliza. I tried to keep them, because I thought it would be so much better to have it out there and then; but they wouldn't play cards or listen to the wireless, and it was so absurd—the three of us sitting there—me trying to make light conversation, and being headed back every time with scathing remarks on Simon's partner!"

"I thought you looked a bit wan at the matinee, and it struck me once or twice you were unnecessarily short with Daniel."

"He's nothing but a nuisance, involving us in trouble with Daddy!" said Christian, with, for her, unwonted sharpness. "And the worst part is that I sympathize with him—I mean Daddy—really; it's such an unpleasant thing to happen in connection with the firm—when we're only just beginning—"

"I think you're being rather Victorian yourself, darling," said Lydia coolly. "Nobody makes heavy weather nowadays about divorce, and you surely don't expect Daniel's to affect the sales! And, talking of sales—I know a chap who has written a book."

"Oh, darling, don't we all?" cried Christian, on a note of relief at having shelved the subject. "It'll soon be much more distinguished to say, 'I don't know a soul who writes.' Only nobody'll believe it."

"I know what you mean," said Lydia, "but this is different. No, I'm not in love with him. As a matter of fact, I don't like him, much. He's one of Gwen Audley's chaps, and it was Gwen who wished his book on me. I've had it for weeks— you know, lying round——"

"Oh, it's been published?"

"No, just a nasty lump of typing; I'd never have read it, probably, if Anna hadn't forgotten to bring in the *Saturday Review* and I'd got nothing to read in bed. So I happened to remember Gwen's chap's book, and I got so interested I couldn't put it down. I mean, in spite of the beastly typing and those brass things that catch in everything. I simply read straight on, and this morning the light was still burning, and the bed was covered with bits of chapters and I finished it in my bath."

"Did you drop it in your bath?" inquired Christian, knowing her sister's habits.

"No—not all of it," said Lydia truthfully. "The last few pages are a bit fuzzy and curly, but it's quite readable."

"Well, you'd better tell Simon about it."

"As a matter of fact," said Lydia, on a note too elaborately casual to deceive Christian, "I wondered if I'd be too unpopular if I dropped into the office some time this afternoon."

Their eyes met.

"I don't think Daniel's there to-day," said Christian bluntly.

"I suppose," said Lydia slowly, "you think I don't think of anything much—except Daniel."

"I'm afraid not. After *Julius Cæsar*."

"Well, why did you ask him, if you don't approve of our being friends?"

"You know I didn't. He was a stop-gap for Simon, who couldn't get off at the last minute."

Lydia shook her head.

"You needn't worry. I don't cut any ice on Daniel."

"I thought you seemed to be cutting a lot."

"Because we've got the same line in talk? Have some more sherry. To hell with Daniel," said Lydia, raising her glass. "Funnily enough," she went on, "I hadn't meant to chase Daniel this afternoon. Funnily enough, that book's got me. I don't know if it's a seller or not; probably it isn't—I can't tell about those things like you can, but, if you'll excuse my putting it that way, I've got a darn sight more appreciation of literature than you have, and I've got a shrewd idea that Gwen's not very likeable young man has written something rather first class. Anyhow, I think I'll ask Simon."

"Yes, do. Poor darling, he's rather lowered at the moment. Paper's gone up again, or something, and he's afraid it may affect the price of Aldebarans. You know, our one-and-sixpenny classics. They're our sort of backbone at present—Simon's been counting on them to get us over the flop on the fiction side."

"I'd better ring him up and make a date." Lydia moved to the telephone. "What's the name of that secretary of his?"

"Nancy Rowlandson. But why not speak to Simon himself?"

Simon, it appeared, was not in, but the appointment was made. Lydia dropped the receiver back on its stand, and went restlessly to jerk the curtains back from her windows. A flood of sunshine poured across the flowering window boxes; the sky above the geometrical design of roof and chimney stack was exquisitely clear and fragile; Lydia's flat was on the top floor.

"What a day to be in town!" she exclaimed petulantly. "What idiots people are—I mean, people who can do as they like—clinging by their stupid engagement books and taxicabs and Berkeleys——! I've got to lunch with a man at half-past one."

"Why don't you cut it?"

"Too much trouble. Do you remember a day at Arundel, a few years ago? It was just about this time of year. Gathering willow catkins—and there were hundreds of little flies round the trees—they couldn't have been mayflies, could they, in February? And the trees were red—they'd got a sort of glowing, inflamed look, as though they were just waiting to burst into bud——"

Christian looked lovingly at her sister.

"Darling, I'm afraid——"

Lydia looked dangerously back.

"Can't I even like trees?"

"Can't you find someone who would like them with you? I wish you'd get married," said Christian very gently. "You're too pretty and sweet a girl, not to be married."

Lydia seemed suddenly to become flaccid.

"I don't think I'm the sort of girl men marry," she said quietly.   "Anyhow, I've never been asked.

"I don't believe it!" It was indeed not credible that Lydia, with all her delicate grace, her exquisite taste in personal adornment and her gift for charming and amusing people, should not have had many proposals.

"I get on the average," said Lydia, with simplicity, "one proposal a week—strictly dishonourable. I am the married man's idea of heaven. So far, though few people believe it, I'm a virgin, because I've never happened to come across a powerful enough inducement to part with that which, to a woman, is supposed to be more precious than rubies. Personally, I've never thought much of rubies." She gave a hard little laugh. "Are you thinking about Father and Mother? What a shock they'd have if they ever got a glimpse of my mentality —the real me! Mother wanted me to go down to Granedge with them."

"I suppose you got out of it—somehow?"

"I can't cope with the life down there. It's not so much the place and the people; it's the atmosphere of nonconformity —family prayers and chapel on Sunday——"

"Well, we were brought up to it. It's a bore, but——" Christian shrugged her shoulders, then laughed suddenly. "Jemima and Henry get a terrific kick out of it! Henry's one ambition at present—apart from writing—is to be a lay preacher."

"What about Simon?"

"Rather a strain for him, poor sweet; but he at least gives Father and Mother credit for their sincerity."

"Are they sincere?" asked Lydia, disturbingly. "Personally, I can't line up all this high living with Christianity. What it seems to boil down to is, that Father's made capital out of religion. I bet he gets fifty per cent of his publicity out of his religious stunts. I wouldn't blame him if he was honest about it."

"Well, how can he be? I mean, if he *isn't* sincere, as you say, which, personally, I don't believe. I mean, if his religion is a 'stunt,' you can't expect him to give it away."

"I don't mean, to the general public. But he might give a wink to his family, now and then."

"Well, he doesn't, and that proves his sincerity, so far as I'm concerned," said Christian stoutly. "Granted that the poor dear's a trial some ways, my goodness, we've got plenty to thank him for! I don't know how you feel about it: but I've always enjoyed being rich. I mean, *consciously* enjoyed it. I've perhaps never enjoyed it so much as since I was married to Simon."

"You mean, you miss——?"

"Heavens, no. It's rather difficult to explain. You see, to begin with, it looked as if my money was going to be a barrier between us. Well, somehow—I can't even remember how—we got over that. I suppose we cared for each other so much that we couldn't allow a thing like money to separate us. Well, now, the way things have turned out, I've got the consolation of knowing I'm not a deadweight on Simon. I even think that my having money and Simon's not having so much has brought out decencies in both of us that we didn't know were there. It made Simon generous about accepting, and I suppose it made me tactful about giving. I was awfully inclined, at first, to take advantage of the fact I was the rich one by just getting whatever we both happened to fancy; I was too stupid, or perhaps I hadn't enough imagination, to see that I was cheating Simon out of pleasure he'd got a right to expect in his marriage."

"What sort of pleasure?" asked Lydia curiously.

"You probably won't understand. I wouldn't have done, a few years ago. Giving presents was a thing we always took for granted; it meant nothing more to us than spending a little time in the shops and writing a cheque or two. For Simon, every present he gave meant calculation, saving up—perhaps going without something for himself. When I began to realize that, I hated, for a while, taking things from him; then I began to see that that, for him, was part of the pleasure of giving. In some way, it made the gift more valuable, not only to the receiver, but to the giver."

"You're awfully in love with Simon still, aren't you?"

"Crazily," admitted Christian. "It's mutual, thank goodness."

"Don't you ever have rows?"

"Not serious ones. Naturally we have differences of opinion, but we've grown awfully civilized about those."

"You're the born wife," sighed Lydia. "And I suppose I'm the born mistress. At least, that's what people seem to think."

"I hope you won't become Daniel's mistress."

"Why?"

"I don't believe you'd be happy. Honestly, Lydia, I like Daniel very much; but he's nobody's business—I mean, he's no good to a woman. Least of all to you. He's the most inhuman thing I ever knew. I dare say there's quite a lot to be said for Eliza."

"Sure; I'm not criticizing Eliza. I haven't even got any illusions about Daniel. I don't suppose I could cope with him, if I had him. To hell with Daniel," said Lydia, for the second time. "I ought to be getting ready for my lunch; I wish I could have had you lunch with me instead."

"I'll go and catch a bus," said Christian, beginning to collect her belongings.

"Well, for crying out loud! I suppose Simon's got the car."

"It's time we had a new one; the old Morris is always in for repairs—no wonder; it's the one Simon bought for our honeymoon, but he refuses to get another until business looks up. We hire a Daimler for state occasions."

"Why don't you get one of your own?"

Christian shook her head.

"It isn't necessary, and I don't think Simon would like it."

"I don't think he should object to your providing yourself with a bit of common comfort, at your own expense."

"He wouldn't. But I don't think this is quite the moment for splashing money on cars, when we're in for an economy drive. I'd rather put the cash into the business, if Simon would let me."

"You look as if you could do with a bit of cherishing, Chris. Aren't you very fit, these days?"

"Do you mean I'm looking plain?" Christian sounded surprised. "I thought I looked pretty good in this blue thing; I've not had it on for weeks, but it was such a lovely morning, I thought I'd go gay and chance it."

"Makes you look the least bit yellowish," said Lydia, with the candour of a sister. "Why don't you put on some make-up? I've got a heavenly new pink I keep for my hang-over mornings."

"I look frightful in a make-up; it's the worst of my sort of skin. I'll go on the top of a bus and try to get to an open window—it's only lack of fresh air."

"You're not, by any chance," said Lydia, "in for another baby?"

"Gosh, no! At least, not to my knowledge. After nine years? Of course I'm not," cried Christian. Her hands twitched on the clasp of her bag. Inside her bag was her diary, but she simply could not take it out under Lydia's nose and verify her denial. Besides, she was so sure! Simon and she had agreed, for financial reasons, to be most conscientious over their precautions since Henry's birth.

All the same, when she found her seat on the top of the bus, her knees were trembling, and it was several minutes before she had the courage to draw the diary out of her bag.

Contrary to Simon's expectations, Daniel was in the office: leaning back with his feet on the fenderstool, reading type-

script. He looked, as he did most of the time nowadays, as
though he had a bad hang-over: the scrupulousness of his
grooming seemed rather to increase than to diminish the
signs of unholy nights that wrote themselves in semi-circles
of discoloration under his heavy eyes.

"Come, come, sir; late again! This won't do at all," was
his facetious reception of his partner, as Simon walked in.

"Where's Nancy?"

"Dealing, I'm told, with a crisis in the packing-room."

"Damn, I want to dictate some letters." Simon irritably
pressed the button on his desk. Daniel laid the typescript on
his knee and looked critical.

"Not quite our usual bright self this morning?" he
murmured. "Perhaps the junior partner can supply a little
stimulant. Cautious as we must ever be in raising hopes too
seldom fulfilled, we believe ourselves to have here"—he tapped
the typewritten sheets with an immaculate fingernail—"a
work of quality all too rare in these days of agents' sweepings.
If Crome and Lygon don't take it they're ruddy fools. Thus
spake Zarathustra."

Simon snorted sceptically.

"A second *Aspasia*, I suppose?"

"A second nothing." Simon turned impatiently aside,
while Daniel continued imperturbably: "Written by a *soi-
disant* girl friend of Madame Lupescu, what it does not reveal
of the goings-on in Roumanian high life is, as the current
phrase goes, nobody's business."

"Don't be such a damned fool, Daniel! If the scrapings of
Mayfair garbage pails are no good to us, do you imagine we
care two hoots for Roumanian scandal?"

Daniel shook his head and looked wise.

"Roumania's in the air," he propounded, in the voice of
a seer. "If you spent ten minutes outside your disgusting
workshop——"

"Yours as well," put in Simon, adding acidly, "though
nobody'd think it."

"—You'd know," continued Daniel, as though he had not spoken, "that everybody's galloping off to Roumania; that there's a sort of feverish *entente* working up between this country and Carol's; that Roumanian diplomatists are actually subsidizing British writers to work up pro-Roumanian enthusiasm. If you hadn't got your nose inside this beastly office every hour of the day and night you wouldn't need to be told this. Have you ever heard of a thing called getting in on the crest of the wave?"

"With a book of Court scandal by some renegade Jewess!" snorted Simon. Before Daniel had time to refute this statement, Nancy Rowlandson was with them.

"I'm sorry; I didn't know you were in," she said to Simon.

"Anything the matter?"

"Only a misunderstanding; it's cleared up now." She produced her notebook. "I'm afraid I've had to book you some appointments—I've made them all provisional, as I didn't know what you might have fixed up before you got here."

Simon groaned as she enumerated them.

"And Miss Matlock rang through, a little after twelve, to ask if you could see her about three o'clock."

"Did she say what about?"

"No. She just left her love, and said it was all right if you were busy."

"Well, we must see." Lydia could see him at any hour of the evening she chose; he wondered if there was something she wanted to tell him without Christian's knowledge. "Are you going to be in this afternoon?" he shot at Daniel.

"I don't see why not. As a matter of fact, Mynte more or less said he might drop in and talk over that matter of the plates. You might give me a few notes on what you're allowing the old boy."

Remembering that, for all his shortcomings, Daniel had saved the Mynte situation, Simon controlled himself to mumble that they'd better see if the book was worth it before they started making offers for plates. "And as for that

Roumanian tripe, you can stop wasting time on it and have a look through the stuff we've just had in from Nettlefold."

Daniel raised his brows.

"I think I'll finish it in my own room. When Crome and Lygon have gone into liquidation, perhaps you'll have the kindness to remember I recommended you to accept this book. It'll probably have made a fortune, by then, for one of our rivals."

He stalked out, and for a moment there was silence. Simon was watching Nancy Rowlandson's face.

"Well?" he snapped presently.

"Well what?" Her serious eyes were raised from her notebook.

"Well, what are you thinking?"

"Since you ask me, that it's rather a pity to hear you two quarrelling. You're each so good, in your different ways."

"You see what it is—Daniel simply refuses to recognize the policy of this firm. It isn't as if he hadn't had it fully explained to him; he knew exactly what it would mean when we accepted my father-in-law's backing; he knows what it'll mean if we don't keep our word to our backer. He's just been urging me to accept some Roumanian garbage——"

"Well, Roumania's very much in the air at the moment."

"*Et tu, Brute!*" He looked at her in half-humorous despair. "I know it is; but if we want to increase our reputation, and likewise keep topsides with Old Harry, we've got to get hold of something by an accredited author who won't let down our prestige."

"Why don't you commission something? Get Cowper Merrill—he's worth the money—or somebody like that, to do a serious book on Roumanian ideology; send him out there to get the stuff——"

"Isn't Hesketh Crowne out there already?"

"You know the sort of thing *he'll* turn in!" Nancy's lip curled. "He'll fawn on princes and have platonic flirtations with half the nobility; his book will creak with discretion.

Did you ever know any one so consciously, painfully discreet as old Hecky? A breath of simple truth would blast him for ever. Merrill will bring you something worth while; even if it costs the earth, I believe it's worth the gamble."

"I think you're right. Supposing he won't?" Since the conversation with Daniel, Simon was in a defeatist mood. "He may have too much on hand; he may be in America——"

"Then," said Nancy, "why don't you send Mr. Lygon?"

"You're mad," said Simon briefly.

"Please listen to what I've got to say. I'm not at all sure it's not a better idea than Merrill; it's a lot cheaper, anyway."

"It might be—if Daniel was capable of carrying it out."

"I think he could, if he was given a free hand. He's got the right sort of personality—and he can arrange all the right kind of contacts. Look here, Mr. Crome: it's obvious he's miserable here at present. Why not give him the chance? Let him send back his stuff in letters, and someone—I myself, if you like—can lick it into shape. Won't it solve a problem which I can see is getting both of you down?"

"You know Daniel's in a mess over his wife."

"I guessed that was it."

"You knew about Eliza?"

"Only common gossip. I'm so sorry. It seems rotten luck, when you've just started, and need to put all you've got into the work."

"I think your suggestion is worth thinking over. It's yet to be seen if Daniel can be talked into treating the matter seriously. He's pretty impossible these days."

"Business or pleasure?" inquired Daniel, as he pushed the cigarettes across the desk. Lydia helped herself to one and lit it with what she felt was, in the circumstances, creditable calm.

For one moment, when they told her that Simon had been obliged to go out, but Mr. Lygon would see her, if she liked, she had been tempted to turn tail and bolt. It was the kind of thing that happened in one's more schoolgirlish dreams: coincidence doing its damnedest to further the cause of romance. She said coolly that she would be much obliged if Mr. Lygon would give her a few minutes, and was promptly conducted up the narrow flight of stairs to Daniel's room, which was on the floor above Simon's, and which she had not visited before. It was about the same size as Simon's, and similarly decorated, but there were details that Simon would not have chosen.

"Business, mainly," said Lydia. "Christian and I were brought up not to crash people in office hours without a proper excuse." She stared at a race fixture card without recognizing its purpose. "It wasn't so nice of Simon to go out without letting me know; I made an appointment——"

"'Once more the hand of Fate brings them together.' We seem to be seeing quite a lot of each other these days."

"Well, if you call a matinee last week a lot——!"

"The speed of modern living hastens the pace of making acquaintanceships," said Daniel idly. "In the good old days of the barouche you had to meet a person a dozen times before you got through the necessary social preliminaries. Nowadays, you meet them at a cocktail party, and either separate at the end of an hour, enemies for life, or become soulmates in the course of a White Lady!"

Lydia sought in vain for a reply to this, then, suddenly recollecting the parcel on her lap, transferred it to Daniel's desk.

"I brought that in for Simon to read; perhaps you'll have a look at it as well, and tell me what you think."

"The story of your life?" Daniel arched his brows.

"Don't you know that no nice girls have life stories?" she mocked him. "It's got nothing to do with me; it's a novel, by Marius Lear."

"What a god-awful name!"

"It is, rather," admitted Lydia, brightening. "I'm not sure, either, that he's not rather a god-awful young man. He goes to parties in tweeds and boots with hobnails in them——"

"Ah, Bloomsbury."

"I doubt it. I met him at Gwen Audley's, and then at some people who have a flat in Bennett Street. They're awfully Right and pro-Franco and that sort of thing, and I noticed him gritting his teeth at a piece of wall where someone had chalked up ' *Viva el ejercíto!* '"

"Novel political?" inquired Daniel, still with cocked eyebrow.

"Well, to do him justice, it isn't."

"Thank heaven for that. About the only subject on which my partner and I are in agreement at present is our mutual dislike for this dirty liaison between politics and literature. Fond of books?" he shot at her.

Lydia nodded.

"So am I—although, to judge by our lists, you mightn't think it."

"You're pretty indiscreet, aren't you?—considering that I'm the senior partner's sister-in-law."

Daniel laughed.

"I'm his brother. It doesn't seem to weigh on us."

The conversation creaked on; Lydia, in refuge behind a smoke-screen—she was normally a moderate smoker—took in most of the things about Daniel that betrayed his state of mind. There was a muscle which jerked up and down in his cheek, making a rictus of an ordinarily pleasant smile; and his fingers were restless with a horribly smooth kind of restlessness, as though their owner were quite aware of it and was curbing them, just enough, but not too much. It reminded her of a morning in the shires: of a meet to which Daniel had taken a very fidgety young bay, and they had all admired the way he handled her.

But as for getting near him, as for striking any personal note upon that smooth, metallic shield with which Daniel was covering himself—the idea was preposterous. As for Christian's hope she would not become Daniel's mistress——!

"Well," said Lydia, "I'd better go; I've got a date at four."

"Well," said Daniel, rising, "I suppose I'll be seeing you —out and about?"

"Give Simon my love. If you could manage a fairly quick opinion about that book, I think it might make a difference to Marius Lear. I mean, I think he's not one of these young men who write for their own amusement."

"Has he done anything else?"

"Only a few poems, I think. I haven't seen them. Well, good-bye."

"Good-bye," said Daniel. "If we don't meet before, I suppose you'll be turning up for my divorce. It promises to be quite a circus."

Lydia felt the blood burning up her cheekbones; certainly no one could equal Daniel for putting you off your step. She heard herself saying sharply:

"Well, that's one name for it."

Daniel looked surprised.

"Don't you think it's a good one? I'm sure it will occur to a lot of people, after watching Eliza and me going through our hoops. By the way, the court's sure to be crowded; I'll see you have a card if you're in town."

She felt her eyes filling with angry tears, that she jerked her head away to conceal.

"Do you think I enjoy seeing my friends having a filthy time in public?"

"Don't you?" said Daniel quizzically. "If you don't, you're the only girl I ever met who didn't."

"You must know a rotten lot of girls!"

"Bless them, do you think I grudge them their bit of fun?"

When Lydia got home she found Anna in the midst of the dregs of a sherry party; most of the people had gone, but the room stank of smoke, and was littered with empty glasses, chipolata sticks and cigarette ends. Anna hailed her with relief, and a few minutes later managed to bundle the remaining guests through the front door. When she came back, Lydia was lying on the sofa, frowning with disgust upon the debris.

"Aren't people pigs? I forgot you had a party."

"A funeral party, darling. The office is closing down, and we've all got our notices to finish on Saturday." Anna shrugged her shoulders. She was a tall girl who looked as though she had been forced through an icing tube into the black gowns she habitually wore. The one she had put on for her party was as severe, to use her own expression, as a slap in the face, and had no adornment except wide bracelets of dull gold. "*Hic jacet* the British Film Industry!" said Anna, draining her glass.

"So what?" asked Lydia.

Anna shrugged her shoulders again.

"A holiday, so far as I'm concerned. I think I'll go to Austria for a bit. They say it's going to be impossible soon, but I've got plenty of friends scattered round and I'll pay some visits."

"You don't want to give up the flat?"

"Heavens, no; though I may have to owe you the quarter's rent for a month or two." Anna lit a cigarette. "I wondered if you'd let me off my share of the servants' wages, as I shan't be using them while I'm away. It seems mean to ask, but I'm going to be rather short until I find a new job."

"That's all right," said Lydia. "It'll be queer—here—by myself."

"Why don't you shut it up for a while and take a holiday as well? Why don't you come out with me? You've never been to Vienna; you could have a lot of fun, and when you've had enough of it, the von Schnabels would love to put you up. They've got a divinely comic castle near Starnberg."

"I don't think I want to leave London at present."

"Budding romance, darling?"

"No such luck," said Lydia, trailing to her room.

CHAPTER FIVE

Christian and Simon were dining at the Hanover, a favourite resort of theirs for dinners *à deux*. They liked the slightly clandestine suggestion of the small room with the open fire, the outmoded décor and the exiguously draped ladies who soared upwards through billows of chiffon upon a rococo panelling of tarnished gilt and café-au-lait. It was a pleasant place in which to be quiet, and Simon was not obliged to change when he left the office late. They had the corner table behind the screen, and had reached the coffee stage before Christian told Simon she was going to have another baby.

Simon was lighting a cigarette; the match burnt itself down to his fingertips before he spoke:

"Are you sure?"

"Quite. I wouldn't tell you until I'd been to find out."

"My poor sweet!"

"Poor nothing. It'll be heavenly to have another baby around. Nana will go crazy when she hears." Christian hesitated a moment. "Do you mind?"

"Good God, why should I? You've got the minding to do. Of course I'll have a fit when the time comes. When does it, by the way?"

"About the middle of September." Christian cheerfully added sugar to her cup. "Darling, I've got some things to say about it. That's why I brought you here; because of course you'll want to argue, but you won't be able to bawl me down in public. At least, not so much as if we were at home."

"Go ahead." Simon managed a smile, but his brain felt like the overwound spring of a watch. With Jemima and Henry, he was just managing to keep his head above water.

Another child—perhaps a boy—meant another prep school, another public school, for which fees would have to be found. It was the sort of unforeseeable thing that shakes the foundations of security, at a time when one has already begun a little to doubt one's ability to pull through.

"Do you remember," Christian was saying, "what it cost us to have Henry?"

"Do I remember! But you can't have children for nothing. Anyhow—your Father paid most of it." Simon's brows creased involuntarily. Another obligation to Old Harry.

"Well, listen. I absolutely refuse to have another show-down like we had over the other children. That frightful nursing home—sixteen guineas a week, without the extras! And every mortal thing, from a box of matches to a telegraph form, was an extra, so far as I remember. You were rooked for the stair carpets and the lifts and the flowers in the waiting-rooms and the commissionaire who addressed everybody as 'my lady' and 'my lord'; for the visitors you had and the visitors you didn't have—do you remember being charged six teas every day for a fortnight, and Mother and Lydia were the only people who ever had a cup of tea with me? It was just one colossal racket, and nothing will induce me to go through it again."

"Of course, you must do as you like about that. So long as you can square your Mother."

"It's not her baby, it's mine," said Christian, and he noticed, with a touch of speculative amusement, how much the lines of her mouth and chin had gained of firmness since the day when he married her. "She had all the fun she wanted over Jemima and Henry. She had so much fun, I sometimes felt as though I was having them to oblige her, instead of on my own account! She simply revelled in that nursing home, and I shouldn't think they ever came across any one so willing to be rooked as Mummy!"

"You're right there," admitted Simon.

"But this baby's got to be absolutely ours, Simon! There's

going to be no nonsense over his birth, any more than there'll be, I hope, over his upbringing." He noticed how confidently she spoke of the coming child as a boy.

"I'd like it to be that way, Chris. I'll go and see Palliser myself, and get some tips about nursing homes——"

"Nursing homes my foot. Don't you see what I'm getting at? I refuse to go into a nursing home. If I can't have my baby at home—which I suppose would mean rather an upheaval, and anyhow, it'd be impossible to keep Mummy out of the way and she'd demoralize everybody—I'll find a nice hospital and book a private ward——"

"You'll do nothing of the sort."

Christian sighed.

"I knew you'd start to bawl me down. *Will* you listen? I know what I'm talking about, this time. It was different when I had Jemima, and felt scared, and liked the idea of being fussed over and treated like something rather precious and extraordinary—as if no woman had ever had a baby before! But I know all my stuff now, and so long as I'm in a nice clean place, with a cheerful nurse who knows her job, and a doctor who has no antiquated notions about the moment for a spot of anæsthetic, I don't give two hoots for the rest. In fact, I like the nice, business-like, jump-to-it feeling of a hospital. I do *not* want to wallow about in carnations and quilted satin bedspreads, like I did with poor darling Henry: I want a bright, clear room with white walls and a shiny floor, and hard and fast rules about visitors and when to get washed in the morning!"

"If you suppose Old Harry will stand for the hospital notion——!"

"If he'd got sense he'd let me go into the works clinic. It's got the best-equipped maternity wards in the country—I mean, from a medical point of view. But I don't think it would be very satisfactory; it's too much on the doorstep, and Mummy would never be out of the place. They wouldn't dare to order her about, because she's on the board of governors!"

"Well, I hate the hospital idea. It doesn't seem suitable."

"Darling, you're not being snobbish!"

"Chris, if you were as strong as a horse, you could go and have your baby in a by-lane, so far as snobbery goes. But you know what a rotten time you had over Henry. I'm only afraid that in a hospital you won't get the extra attentions you're used to——"

"And I never wanted! Did I ever have a moment's peace in that damned home? Was I plagued to death with 'extra attentions' I'd have been thankful to do without? I *have* heard of girls going into nursing homes and having to ring for a quarter of an hour before any one took any notice; but Berrill House certainly wasn't like that. I suppose Mother put the fear of God into them."

"Well, we must see what Palliser says," temporized Simon.

"*Not* Palliser, please, darling."

"Why ever not? He saw you through the other two——"

"And he's a famous gynæcologist and attends the accouchements of minor royalty—I know, I know! And he's hand and glove with Mummy, and it was he who suggested Berrill House and made all the arrangements. Do you suppose he'd help us over a thing like this? Not on your life. What about his rake-off?"

"I'd no idea you were so canny about these matters! But Palliser's a hell of a big noise in obstetrics, and I don't much fancy the idea of trusting you to someone with less experience."

"Not having a plate in Harley Street doesn't mean lack of experience, darling. It may mean bad luck, or lack of means, or just plain integrity! Nancy Rowlandson's put me wise to a lot of things like that."

"Did you tell her—?"

"Before I told you——? We were talking about the children; she was telling me about her boy. What a nice woman she is, Simon."

"Nancy's the salt of the earth. I don't know what I'd do without her."

"I give her ten for courage. Apart from the question of ability, I don't believe I'd have the gumption to go out and earn my living, if it were necessary, even to keep the children."

"Of course you would—if you had Nancy's training."

"Well, we got on the subject of babies, and I started to tell her about that awful nursing home—really as a joke; it's funny enough when you get it in perspective; but Nancy didn't even smile. She said, ' It must have been hell,' and told me all about having her Dennis in hospital."

"I shall have to have Nancy on the mat, for putting ideas into your head."

"You'll do nothing of the sort. She told me how charming every one was, and what a marvellous rest it seemed—she'd been through rather a rough time at home, poor dear, with her husband sick and one thing or another. She said the calm, matter-of-fact atmosphere was so confidence-inspiring. She went in rather jittery, because it was her first baby, and they made her feel it was as simple as falling off a log."

"That depends on the patient. Nancy's got a marvellous constitution."

"So have I," insisted Christian. "I suppose you're thinking of that stupid old miscarriage. If a girl can't be allowed one miscarriage, without having it thrown up at her for the rest of her life——!"

"Sorry. Well, what else does Nancy say?"

"Of course, she says it's not easy to get into the maternity hospital, unless you're genuinely hard up. In fact, she rather quenched me by saying that she didn't think people who could afford nursing homes should monopolize hospital beds, even if they pay. I didn't like to say that we *are* genuinely hard up, for the moment—because it wouldn't be strictly true. Father would jump at paying the bill. . . . Anyhow, I got the name of her doctor out of her, and I went to him this morning, to make sure about the baby."

"Was he all right?"

"Charming. Rather a serious old boy, with beautiful hands.

He gave me a most flattering account of myself, and I said I'd be glad if he'd see me through."

"Did he agree to it?"

"I thought he jibbed a bit. I'd told him, of course, about Jemima and Henry, and I think he wondered why I'd come to him, as I must have a doctor already."

"Well, you seem to have got it all fixed up——"

"All except the hospital. I wanted to tell you about that, before I got him to make the arrangements."

"I'd better go and see him," frowned Simon.

"Have you got time? It would be nice if you could. Don't do the prosperous publisher too heavily, will you, sweet? Or he might feel like Nancy, and refuse to help us over the hospital."

"Prosperous publisher! Do I look like it?"

"You look very distinguished: though I wish you hadn't started such a lot of little tiny lines round your eyes. Do you think we could manage a bit of a holiday soon?"

Simon shook his head.

"It doesn't seem likely. Especially if Daniel goes to Roumania." So far, Daniel was toying with the Roumanian idea, and had said neither yes nor no.

"How are things between him and Eliza?"

"Finished—so far as Daniel's concerned. The divorce is going forward—it's too late, of course, for the Hilary sittings; but Daniel's lawyer hopes to get it well forward in the Easter lists."

Christian wondered whether to say anything about Lydia; decided against it, and suggested going home.

"Sure you wouldn't like to go on anywhere?"

"No, bless your heart."

"I don't seem ever to give you any fun nowadays, Chris."

"Do you think I'm dull?"

"It's hardly ten. I've not had a night out for weeks. Come on; let's have an hour at that place of Lydia's. You know —where she took us on her birthday."

"Don't you have to be a member?"

"I can fix that."

"We aren't changed."

"Lots of people weren't, the other night." For some reason he felt impelled towards frivolity: an impulse rare enough to command surrender. He nodded to the page who was waiting to get them a taxi. Within its darkness, he flung his arms about Christian and kissed her deeply. "My darling, to think of you going through all that again, for me!"

"You are glad, aren't you, Simon?"

"I'm too stunned to be glad or sorry just yet," he told her truthfully. "I never thought of its happening, after all this time."

"Nor did I. But I'm terribly thrilled."

"Lydia's place"—which was one of those dance clubs that flourish for a season or two under the patronage of Mayfair, and then, losing their *cachet*, peter out, usually by way of the Bankruptcy Court—was not overcrowded, as the theatres had not closed and the supper mob had not yet started to drift in. Simon and Christian found a table, waved to two or three people, and presently danced to a band which made up in quality for what it lacked in numbers.

The floor was very silky, the lights flickered between gloaming and near-dark, picking up the spangled ornament on a girl's dress or a jewelled bracelet. Held close in his arms, Christian moved as though she were part of himself; their perfect physical adjustment seemed the logical complement of their perfect spiritual affinity. If ever two human beings "sang in tune," he thought gratefully, it was Christian and himself. Neither had known, to begin with, that it was going to be like that; deeply in love, it had taken years to develop their singularly happy partnership, and now it was as though each had overflowed a little into the other, so that there were little hollows and cellules in Simon which were filled with pure Christian, just as in Christian there were vesicles whose analysed content was so completely Simon that only a blood test could fully have resolved their separate entities. And now, between their closely-pressed bodies, lay something that was both Simon and Christian, a growing seed of the love which was the most dynamic element in Simon's life. He felt almost insupportably tender towards her as they circled slowly round the pleasantly empty floor, pursued by the neurotic croon of the microphone, the Paphian bleat of the tenor sax and an undercurrent of nerve-teasing rhythm contributed by the drums. Christian—his wife, his mistress. How many people found as complete fulfilment as he had done in their married lives?

"What are you smiling about?"

"I was thinking about the time when we were engaged, We haven't had so many dances together since we were married, have we?"

"We must try to have some more." Daniel is right, he was thinking: we ought to do more of this kind of thing. But how? Such evenings as were not filled with work were given over to the rather pompous functions a publisher is supposed to attend, to sober dinners or to an occasional night at the club.

"There's Lydia," said Christian suddenly.

"Who's she with?"

"Gwen Audley, I think—and a young man I don't know at all. He doesn't look exactly Lydia's cup o' tea!" Christian laughed and waved; the two girls waved back, and the young man stared dully through horn-rimmed glasses. He had considerably too much hair, bunched darkly about his brow and sprouting angrily from the crown of his head; a pale, lantern-jawed face and a dinner-jacket that seemed, from the way he tugged at the back of the collar and on the fronts, to be at the root of his apparent hatred of humanity.

"What fun meeting you!" Lydia looked rather distraught and naked, but beautiful, in a gown with no shoulder-straps, and her hair pulled up from the nape of her neck into a topknot of heavy curls.

"Who's your boy friend?"

"Not mine—Gwen's. It's Marius Lear. Gwen won't forgive me if I don't bring him over and introduce him to Simon."

"What a bore. I did hope there wouldn't be any business nonsense to-night," murmured Christian, as Lydia went to collect her companions. Simon pulled a face; he was half-way through Lear's book, and was curious to meet the writer.

Marius Lear shook hands with obvious reluctance, and stood, looking sulky. He evidently had no ideas about making himself agreeable to strangers. Simon wondered what accounted for his presence in "Lydia's place"; it was inconceivable that he was a dancer, and only a fool would have assumed he took pleasure in his surroundings.

"Won't you share our table?" asked Christian, after being introduced to Gwen Audley, a stout young woman with anxiously proprietorial airs over Marius Lear. When the women were talking, Simon said to Lear, who had not so far given utterance to a syllable,

"We've got one of your books in now." He rightly judged that his companion would have no small talk.

"Not 'one of' my books; it's the only one I've written." He seemed to resent the implication of productivity.

"I've not finished it yet," said Simon, controlling a smile.

"I shouldn't bother," said the other rudely. "I don't know who sent it to you, but it's not a Crome and Lygon book, anyway."

Simon stiffened.

"I'd like to hear your views on what constitutes a Crome and Lygon book."

Marius Lear looked surprised.

"You know yourself, don't you?"

"Hardly. We're a new firm, you know. We've naturally got a certain policy, but our character, as a firm, is still rather embryonic. In fact, we're waiting for someone to give us the big lead."

Marius Lear pouted; it would be more accurate to say

that he rolled out a further section of a lower lip already unduly prominent.

"Then you're not interested in first novels."

"Why not? It's not unheard-of, for a first novel to be a best-seller," said Simon, trying not to be annoyed by the other's ungraciousness.

"I'm afraid I'm not interested in best-sellers. My sort of work doesn't run that way. You needn't think I regard myself as a genius—or my book as the herald of a new epoch in fiction. I don't even expect to get it published; it was written for my own satisfaction, and, up to a point, it's succeeded. It's shown me my present limitations, but that isn't to say I shan't do a better one later on."

"Do you spend all your time in writing?"

"No. I earn my living," said Marius Lear tersely.

"How?" persisted Simon. His curiosity was stung by this odd, uningratiating person, who possessed the rare quality, from a publisher's point of view, of detachment towards his own work.

"I teach, in a so-called college in South London. I write in my spare time." He shot a curiously sly glance at Simon. "I suppose you're wondering how I come to be here?" he mocked him. "I don't fit in, do I? My clothes are wrong, my behaviour's wrong and I'm not sleek enough!"

"You're extraordinarily aggressive, Mr. Lear," said Simon coldly. "I don't quite know why. And now I'm going to have another dance with my wife. It may surprise you to know that we haven't had a night like this for about ten months. A publisher's life—like a schoolmaster's—doesn't leave many opportunities for amusement."

"It depends on what you call amusement." Lear curled his lip.

"What the devil do you come for, if you aren't enjoying yourself?" snapped Simon, losing his temper.

"Is the bear supposed to enjoy itself? I'm surprised you haven't grasped my position." He jerked his head ironically towards the back of Gwen Audley's fat, sallow neck. "Having danced for two hours for the entertainment of her visitors, I got dragged on here. I'm just not sure enough of myself to walk out. Silly, isn't it?"

"Sounds crazy to me," admitted Simon; but he had recovered his temper, and his interest was quickened by the other's confession. "Look here: we can't talk in this place; but I'm genuinely interested in your book. You might drop in some time, for a chat with me and my partner. You'll find the address in the directory."

"I'm only free on Thursday afternoons," said Lear, looking surprised.

"All right; make it Thursday. That's a week to-day. And give me a ring to say what time you'll be along."

"You might," said Lear, rising, "let me have that manuscript back; there are two or three things I'd like to alter."

"Very well, when we've done with it. Won't Thursday be soon enough?"

"I should think you'd be glad to get it out of your way. Aren't publishers' offices cluttered up with dud manuscripts?"

Simon also had risen; below the two men, Christian and Lydia and Gwen Audley carried on their feminine chatter of first nights and dress shows; in that upper air there was freer breathing, their masculine encounter simplified itself.

"What's the idea of calling your work 'dud'? You don't believe it."

"I don't; and it isn't. But so far as you're concerned, it might as well be," was the blunt rejoinder.

"Would you mind telling me exactly what you mean by that?"

"You're backed by Old Harry Matlock, aren't you?"

"By my wife's father—certainly."

Marius Lear seemed taken aback by this revelation of publishing politics of which, evidently, he had been ignorant. He hunched his shoulders, and made a clumsy little movement of apology.

"I didn't know he was a relative. Sorry."

"There's no need to apologize. My father-in-law, although
he is our chief backer, doesn't happen to be a partner, and
Lygon and I agree upon the value of your work."

"I suppose I ought to be gratified."

"Well—aren't you? Or have you got such a conceit of
yourself that other people's opinions don't count?"

"No, it's not that. I—I——" Suddenly the barriers went
down; his hands were thrust into his pockets, he looked Simon
straight in the face. "It matters like hell to me whether that
book gets published or not. But it's been to seven publishers
already, and they've all ' agreed on its value ' and sent it back
to me within three weeks!"

"I think I know why that is. There aren't many firms
nowadays that care to gamble on a first novel, unless they see
a reasonable chance of its making its advance." Simon paused.
"There's real quality in your work, Lear, and you've got a
fine, disciplined vocabulary that might serve as model to some
of our major authors, but——"

"That's writing verse!" said Marius eagerly. "Whatever
poetry does for you, it does make you respect words! There's
too much god-damned fake about modern writing; half the
novels you open might as well be plays—strips of dialogue
with a few stage directions thrown in——"

"That, unfortunately, is what the greater part of the
reading public seems to like. You, Lear—you're too classic
ever to be popular! But there may be something better waiting
for you."

"At least there can't be anything worse!" He shot a glance
at the gossiping women and drew nearer to Simon, with an
odd movement of confidence. "What d'you think I've been
doing this evening? It isn't the first time either—a chap like
myself isn't in a position to chuck away a couple of guineas
when they come his way. I've been giving a poetry reading
at that Audley woman's flat! A fellow I know put me up to
it, and introduced me to her. I thought it sounded easy, and

would pay a week's rent. My God! Have you ever read poetry
to a roomful of Society women——?"

"Heaven forbid," said Simon. "Well, look here, Lear——"

"Simon." Christian had risen, and her hand was laid on
his arm. "This tune! Don't you remember? It's one of our
old favourites. Do let's dance this one."

As they manœuvred their way into the now crowded space
left for the dancers, she asked him:

"Were you having a very bad time, darling? I shall scold
Lydia next time I see her, for bringing shop into our play-
time. I do think Gwen Audley's chap is a dreary young man."

"Not so dreary as you think," said Simon, steering her clear
of a couple who showed signs of rehearsing Big Apple in the
middle of the floor. "I'm glad Lydia introduced him, and I've
practically made up my mind to take his book."

"The one Lydia's so keen about? Won't she be pleased!
Gwen Audley says he's clever, but I didn't pay much attention
to her. Did you know he'd been doing a poetry reading in
her drawing-room? I don't seem to fancy poetry in drawing-
rooms; I once got let in for some, and it made me feel terribly
hot and undressed! I somehow can't imagine Marius Lear
. . . Is his book really good? Is it going to make a nice lot
of money?"

"Not a penny; and it will let me in for an awful row
with Old Harry."

"Oh dear—*that* sort of book." She delicately wrinkled
her nose.

"God dammit, Chris, I can't let your Father dictate the
whole policy of the firm to me! I may be a tradesman, but
I've got a certain amount of self-respect to keep up, as a critic
of literature, and some of our recent fiction makes my gorge
rise. It hasn't even the virtue of having made money. Neither
will Lear's book; but if it's handled properly it will surely
contribute something to our prestige with the reviewers; it'll
show the general public that the name of Crome and Lygon
isn't synonymous with tripe——"

"What about Gerald Wells's garden book, and the Cratchitt? They surely aren't tripe."

"It's fiction that counts, Chris—unless you mean to stick to belles lettres. I believe—how easy it is to prophesy!—but I honestly believe Lear's going to do great things some day."

"Why?" she inquired, rather flatly.

"It's difficult to explain; it's not fair to draw conclusions on ten minutes' conversation. But he's given me an impression of integrity one doesn't often meet with in these days. I don't believe he cares for anything except writing as a pure creative art, and he doesn't care if the public fawns on or curses him, so long as it leaves him in peace to write what he believes to be the truth."

"You must have got on very well together, if he told you all that." In spite of herself, Christian was unable to prevent a faint note of jealousy from creeping into her voice. It was not usual for Simon to contact so quickly with a stranger—particularly a stranger of the writing confraternity.

"He didn't tell me a word. I just got it, from the way he looked and spoke. I assure you he's far from being an oncoming kind of person! If he ever becomes famous—which I don't think unlikely—Miss Audley and her friends will have their work cut out to make a pet of him."

Christian looked curiously at him.

"I've never heard you speak so warmly of any one you've only just met," she said, in a troubled voice. "I wish I liked him more. I mean, I do like to be nice to your favourites, Simon, but I don't seem to be able to get up a warmth for Marius Lear."

"Don't worry. He won't be affected, either by your chill or your warmth," said Simon dryly.

"Well, tell me about the book."

"Didn't Lydia tell you?" he temporized.

"No. She only said she'd sat up reading it all night, and dropped the last chapter in the bath in the morning."

"Well, it's an odd piece of work. By the way, he told me

he teaches in some college or other. I wonder what his subject is?"

"Gwen mentioned it—it's languages. Spanish, French and German."

"That explains it."

"Explains what?"

"The queer sort of cosmopolitan flavour he gets into his work; it's not what you'd expect from an English writer. I suppose he's visited the countries——" Simon became speculatively silent; yes, there were a number of things that required explanation in Marius Lear. "The book?" he added, as Christian gave his arm a little pinch. "Well, Chris, I don't expect you'll like it. It's about prostitutes—mainly."

"Father certainly won't like it," said Christian with decision.

"I'm afraid he won't; because, unfortunately, he's incapable of realizing the philosophy which runs at the back of the characters."

"Will anybody? Prostitution's not a very popular subject in England, is it?"

"Great heavens, doesn't one consider anything but popularity?"

"Isn't that what we're obliged to consider, for a while? And anyhow, I may be old-fashioned, but I agree with Mummy that some subjects are right out of place in fiction. There must be plenty of text-books and things on white slave traffic, and I honestly can't see what people gain by making heroines out of those poor girls in Sackville Street."

"In answer to your perfectly just comment—a, most people won't be bothered to read text-books, and b, the name White Slave Traffic—which was coined by the popular press to spare the susceptibilities of the public when words like brothel and prostitute weren't allowed to appear in print, doesn't happen to cover the form of sexuality with which Lear's book is concerned."

"Why do people make such a fuss about sex, Simon? Why

don't they just get on with it and be happy—like you and me?"

"My dear, sweet darling! What a question to raise at a moment like this. And, by the way, it's getting late. What about going home?"

"I was just going to suggest it. I suppose it's no use to offer Lydia a lift?"

"I don't suppose so. Let's just dance this out, shall we?"

"I'm rather surprised Lydia liked a book of that sort," said Christian, after a short pause.

"I'm not. I can't imagine any person with pity and imagination and human sympathy in their make-up *not* liking it. The trouble is that such qualities aren't more generally distributed."

"I suppose you mean Lydia's got a nobler mind than I have," said Christian, in a small voice.

"Not nobler; perhaps a bit broader," substituted Simon.

"Do you find me very narrow-minded?"

"I think you've had a very narrow experience of life; you've been very sheltered; you've known hardly any people who weren't what your Mother would call ' nice,' and you've never had an opportunity of developing your sympathies in other directions."

"Lydia's had exactly the same upbringing," pointed out Christian.

"Lydia hasn't married, and she has been living her own life for a good many years. It's given her a wider outlook; besides, Chris——" Simon paused, a little afraid of hurting her feelings.

"Yes—what?"

"Even in your own small circle, you've come across people —and incidents—that wouldn't exactly fit into that idyllic pattern you seem to expect in your reading. You know about Eliza Lygon; you've known and received in your own house people who weren't sleeping with their own husbands or wives, and were having affairs ' on the side ' which sometimes came out in the divorce courts and sometimes didn't, according to the degree of discretion or complaisancy in the persons involved. And you've always taken these things very much for granted—at least, you gave that impression——"

"Because I didn't talk about them, or make a fuss at the time? I loathe gossip, and being mixed up in other people's affairs. And it isn't the same thing; the other's so squalid——"

"Because it's not in your world—is that it? Prostitution in Mayfair, between people whose names are in Burke or *Who's Who*, is quite a different matter from the same thing in Long Acre, when one of the parties has her name in the police records! What a little humbug you are."

"Don't be an ass. You're mixing up adultery and prostitution; they're completely different, though each is nasty enough——"

"Excuse me; the act of offering your body, if you're a woman, to a stranger—which you may mark any time you care to cast your eye round a place like this—is, by whatever pretty name you like to call it, prostitution; and allow me to tell you there are as many prostitutes to the square acre in Mayfair as you'll find in Soho, and Eliza Lygon's one of them."

"Well, darling, I don't agree; and, anyhow, I shan't read Marius Lear's horrid book."

"It's not a horrid book," said Simon evenly. "It's a tender and pitiful account of a homeless boy, who has affairs successively with three cyprians; and of how each of them according to her kind contributes something to his wisdom and knowledge of humanity, so that he ends up a darn sight finer person than he was when he started out." He added angrily, as Christian's eyebrows rose: "For God's sake, can't you realize that such women have virtues of their own—the strong, fierce virtues of their environment?"

"I can't see what possible interest such women can have for any one like ourselves," she answered, her eyes dangerously bright. "You may think I'm bitchy, but I hate everything to do with them. I hate what they stand for; I hate this modern fashion of sentimentalizing them and their lives, of making heroines out of them, like the French novelists——"

"There's nothing like that in Lear's book!"

"You've just said the boy was a finer person for knowing them. It isn't *possible*, Simon. And I hate to think of the people who'll buy the book—for the sake of all the beastly details——"

"Any one who buys it with that idea will be disappointed," said Simon, trying to speak patiently. "Practically the whole book consists of three long, philosophical conversations——"

"It doesn't sound very realistic," she sneered.

"Dammit, it isn't meant to be realistic. It's no more realistic than some of the Old Masters. If it was, I suppose it would be a best-seller; it would raise Cain among the bishops and galvanize Bloomsbury and be sniggered over in Tooting. But as it is practically a philosophical treatise about two hundred people will read it, and about ten will recognize it as the work of a rare mind, and about three will profit by it, and feel that it's added something to their own philosophic stature. It will mean a dead loss to Crome and Lygon of about five hundred pounds——"

"Simon, have you gone crazy? Why are you publishing it?"

"For the sake," he said quietly, "of my self-respect. It could do with a little bolstering, these days."

They went to find Lydia and her companions, to say good-night, and, to their surprise, found her sitting alone, smoking a little cigar and scribbling in her engagement book.

"Marius Lear had to go, so Gwen made him take her home first. Did you like him?" she asked Simon.

"Very much."

"And what about his book?"

"He's coming to talk about it on Thursday. Would you like a lift? Chris and I are going home."

Lydia looked restlessly about the room.

"I don't think so—thanks. It's rather early, isn't it?"

"Don't you mind being by yourself?"

"Someone's sure to turn up. Every one comes here now," she answered vaguely.

At the foot of the stairs a man was paying off his taxi-cab; when he turned, it was Daniel—elegant, dissolute, with stone-cold, insolent eyes; he had evidently been drinking, although he was not in the least drunk. He began to laugh softly as he came face to face with Simon and Christian, and, as an attendant came forward to take his coat, he removed from the sleeve, with elaborate delicacy, a small piece of fluff, which he proceeded to puff into the air.

"What book was that?" he inquired, as he allowed his hat to be taken.

"Too easy." Christian, knowing the game, shook her head at him.

Daniel regarded her gravely, flattening his hair.

"You're too clever. That's the trouble with women nowadays; you're all too, too clever. Where are you going?"

"Home, to bed. You look as if you'd better do the same," said Simon.

"Old Slug-a-bed Simon! Old Jog-trot Simon Crome!" Simon jerked his shoulder away from Daniel's too-affectionate hand. "It's no use telling him the things he misses by going early to bed. It's only people like me"—he addressed himself to Christian, with his charming, indifferent smile—"who realize that all the most exquisite things happen between midnight and dawn."

"You'll find Lydia upstairs. I hope you'll see her home before dawn, at any rate," said Simon shortly, as their taxi came up.

In the taxi Christian said to him, "I wish you hadn't said that about Lydia."

"Why?"

"He'll probably tell her, and she'll think we—sympathize."

"Sympathize—with what?" As Christian was silent, he found her hand; it clung to his. "Lydia—and Daniel? You don't mean——? Oh, damn!" said Simon softly.

CHAPTER SIX

"You see, my dear Lydia," said Daniel, his eyes half-closed and hardly moving his lips, so that, lying back in the corner of the sofa upon which, at four in the morning, they still found themselves sitting, the effect was uncannily ventriloquial, and Lydia, shuddering slightly, found herself instinctively seeking some demoniacal dummy upon the speaker's knee, "attractive as I find your proposal, and tempted as I am to accept it, there is a thing called the King's Proctor. . . ."

"I thought he'd been abolished—by A. P. Herbert, or something," Lydia heard herself saying vaguely.

"No. At least, I don't think so. I'm still extraordinarily indistinct upon the functioning of our new divorce laws, but I'm prepared to lay generous odds that the K.P. still functions, though whether before or after the balloon goes up, I would not like to say. I mean, whether one is at liberty to indulge one's propensity for loose living up to the moment one makes one's appearance in court, or whether the green eye of the little yellow Prog is focused upon one's in-comings and out-goings from the moment one ' enters an appearance,' I simply do not know. It's a point I must take up with my solicitor."

His voice came to her distantly, through the darkness of her own fatigue; there was not a corpuscle of her blood in which weariness had not taken up its apparently permanent abode, weighing down in her like drops of lead, so that all the lovely lines of her limbs sagged and she could feel the loosening of the muscular armature of her face and the lines dragging downwards from the corners of her lips. On the other side of the room she could see in a glass dimly the reflection of a Lydia so unlike her normal, daytime self that, had she not been exhausted to the point of indifference, she must have shuddered. The room was almost empty; the band played a last, lagging fox-trot for the benefit of three elderly, epicene couples, and a moribund group of waiters stood, with sullen patience, against the curtains that shut out the deserted street.

"Well, what's the use of waiting? We can't spend the night here," she roused herself to say.

"Why not? You're a member. I'm a member. Can't turn out members. It's against the regulations," he said portentously.

"Are you drunk?" she asked, indifferent to his reply.

"Oh, God, I wish I were."

"You'd better," said Lydia, in a dying voice, "you'd better go back to your hotel, and have some more to drink, and sleep—and sleep—right through to-morrow."

"Oh, balmy counsellor!" he jeered at her. "I've never been drunk in my life. I haven't slept for a week, and hell fire won't drive me to my hotel to-night. My bedroom's got a red satin chair in it, that's so exactly like a woman I used to know that if I drop off for a minute I wake up screaming and think I'm in Vienna. Or was it Carlsbad? One gets so confoundedly mixed up with these middle-Europe places."

"You'll have to go somewhere. Look, every one's gone, and they've started to put out the lights." She began to fumble with her fur cape; she felt drenched with hopelessness.

"Perhaps I'll go along to Jermyn Street and see Rosa and hear some more about the days of wine and roses, when the gay young blades used to finish up a thick night by knocking out the bobby."

"Don't be silly; Rosa's been in bed hours."

"Don't delude yourself. Rosa's a wise woman; she never goes to bed. No wise woman ever goes to bed, unless——"

"Daniel!" cried Lydia in desperation. "Daniel, are you listening to me? You can't stay here—I won't let you; and there's nobody else for you to talk to at this time of night."

"Morning," he corrected her gently. "'The grey-ey'd morn

D

smiles on the frowning night, Chequering the eastern clouds with streaks of light, And fleckéd darkness like a drunkard reels From forth day's path and Titan's fiery wheels.' Sixpence if you can give me the context of that."

"Listen," she said again, laying her hand over his. "If you're bothering about the King's Proctor, it's madness for us to stop here, with all these waiters staring at us and wondering what we're up to."

"Even the King's Proctor," said Daniel, "might baulk at imputing impropriety to us, in the presence of four witnesses."

"Here's the key of my flat; I happen to have Anna's as well—she's away. Take it, and if you've got any sense, use it!"

"What's the idea? It's very sweet of you. But why should I use—this?"

"Do you think I'm blind, Daniel? You can't pretend to me, you know. You're all set for a smash, but you shan't do it—if I can help. Oh, for God's sake, Daniel, why can't you relax, and talk sensibly, instead of fooling about, as if it was all one big joke——?"

Something to her surprise, he made no reply. She rose, swaying a little with weariness. A waiter came over to them quickly.

"A taxi, madame?"

"Yes. Wait a minute. You'll want one as well, won't you?" She pushed her knee against Daniel's. He looked up stupidly.

"What? Oh, yes, I may as well have one too." As the man went away he got up stiffly, stretching his body upwards from the waist; a lock of hair that had separated itself from the smooth swathe across the crown of his head hung over his brow; his face was ashen. "All right. I'll be along presently."

"Honest? No cheating?"

"I'll just pop along to the club and see if there's any message. I suppose we'd better not follow each other in too obviously."

"The key opens the street door, as well as the flat; and you have to work the lift yourself. You can manage that, can't you?" she told him anxiously.

It was heaven's blessing that, with Anna's departure, she had given the cook a week's holiday. The parlourmaid did not sleep in; she arrived, from her distant suburban fastnesses, at an elastic nine o'clock; when Anna was away—the only member of the household who was bound by a time-table— it was tacitly assumed that half-past nine would do; Lydia knew she could be trusted not to come earlier.

She bathed quickly, brushed her hair, re-made her face, and waited, with strangulation in her throat, for the faint scratch of the latchkey which would announce Daniel's arrival. Would he keep his word? In the excitement of apprehension her tiredness vanished; a thin, young, eager reflection met her from the mirrors, as she moved quickly about the sitting-room—seeing it through Daniel's eyes (it was his first visit to the flat), collecting hastily a few faded flowers and carrying them to the garbage pail. There must be nothing drooping, nothing that suggested staleness or disorder in the personal setting in which Daniel would see her for the first time. She cleared away newspapers, emptied an ash-tray, shook up cushions. The peach-coloured wrapper she had taken from her cupboard had just returned from the cleaner's; she sniffed it fastidiously, to make sure no trace of the benzine odour lingered, and, to make doubly sure, sprayed herself carefully with her favourite hyacinth perfume.

Suppose he did not come? The hands of the clock were creeping towards five: so little of the night left!

. . . Daniel was standing in the doorway, with his hand on the doorpost, smiling at her. For the rest of her life, she knew, she would see him as he stood there, drooping a little sideways, like a puppet on a slack wire. Whenever she was alone, she would only have to look up, to see him standing there. . . .

"I've got some hot consommé ready," she said quickly.

"Why?" asked Daniel.

"Well, you said you've had no dinner, and you've eaten nothing all the evening. Sit down by the fire, and I'll bring it in here for you."

She watched him cross the room unsteadily; his hat was still on his head, the crown flattened on one side to a ridiculous, a clownish angle, and as he walked the white silk scarf he was wearing slid round the back of his collar and fell on the floor. Daniel looked at it as though he would have liked to pick it up, but, with all the goodwill, could not muster the energy.

Lydia brought the tray, upon which she had already arranged the silver; the soup was in a little brown casserole, steaming hot; while he looked on, she tipped a glass of her best sherry into it.

"You remind me," said Daniel, "of Calypso ministering to Odysseus."

"If you're suggesting I'll presently turn you into a pig—!"

To her surprise, he reached up and took her hand; his own was very limp and burning.

"Not you, Lydia. Not you," he said gently "It's not women like you who turn men into pigs Besides, you've got it wrong; that's Circe, not Calypso. I was thinking of fountains four set orderly, and a gadding garden vine."

"Drink up your soup."

After three or four spoonsful, he laid down the spoon and his head dropped forward on his chest.

"Daniel, finish your food."

"I'm so tired . . . so tired. . . ."

"All right, my dear. Then come." Passing behind him, she slid her hands under his armpits to help him rise; he made no resistance, and did not seem to question her actions. It was only a few steps to the bedroom, but she felt as though she would never get him there; it was like carrying a corpse, save that the eyes of the corpse were open, and it made comments upon its surroundings.

"Nice flat. All women's flats nice nowadays. Gone crazy

about decoration. No sooner through with one idea than
they're off on the next. Woman I know's just had all her books
bound in magenta to go with Chinese yellow drawing-room.
Crazy notion. Never know if you're picking up the Bible or
Ruff's Guide." She managed by some means to tip him on
to the end of the broad, low bed. Suddenly, without a word,
Daniel rolled over and was asleep.

His position looked so wretchedly uncomfortable, his
clothing so disordered, that she tried to remedy both. It was
obvious a bombshell would not rouse Daniel.

She had never undressed a man, and swore softly under her
breath as a nail-tip broke under the stress of the encounter
with stiff masculine buttonholes. Long, limp and thin, a
shattered Harlequin, he lay at last, in his silk underwear; a
shiver shook Lydia from head to foot, and quickly, not knowing why she did it, she snatched the corner of the sheet and
drew it across the limbs so helplessly displayed.

The hands of the clock had moved relentlessly on; three
hours were the most she dared allow him of sleep. Supposing
she slept herself? Terror of being surprised by their discreet
and conventional Agnes drove Lydia to the cook's bedroom,
in search of the little alarum that ensured the punctuality of
Anna's morning tea. She set it for ten minutes to nine, placed
it at a sufficient distance from the bed to mitigate the shock
of so unaccustomed an awakening, then, quickly, so as not
to have time to think, stretched herself at his side and drew
his head on to her bosom.

Dawn had already slipped through the division of the
curtains when his stirring awoke her. With a leaping heart she
looked down upon Daniel, still fast asleep, pale as ash, with
rings of darkness under his eyes. Her cramped arm tightened
involuntarily about him, and, as though grateful for the
sweet assurance of protection, he turned towards her, flinging
his arm across her neck and bosom; she felt his lips against
her naked shoulder.

"Eliza—my dear—my dear sweetheart!"

It was one of those gay March mornings which the climate inconsequently wishes upon the astonished Londoner: a morning when optimism crackles in the bright blue and gold air, blazes from the windows of florists and the barrows of street merchants and falls glittering from the bright drops of the fountains which the breeze carries in a sideways rainbow across the pavements of Trafalgar Square.

Stepping briskly westwards along the Strand, Simon, infected by the sunlight, felt a recrudescence of physical and mental energy, which he put down in part to the mild dissipation of the previous night. It was no use thinking he could go on, as he had been going on, day after day, with his nose to the grindstone; the result was flatness, staleness, enervation. One lost edge, lost one's sense of proportion, became too easily affected by trifles, slipped into the attitude of defence, rather than attack. Of course things were going along all right! He had just been allowing himself, as a result of overwork, anxiety and lack of recreation, to get into a mood of nervous defeatism. Last night's dance with Christian had acted like a purgative, had cleared his outlook of its jaundiced tinge; the world upon which he looked this morning was a world of opportunity, of which, for the first time for several weeks, Simon's felt fully equipped to avail himself.

For once, details of office routine did not present to him a tangle of irritating incompetency. He dealt sharply with some contretemps that had arisen in the publicity department, drawing from Nancy Rowlandson the half-exasperated, wholly admiring comment: "What a fool I am not to have thought of that for myself!"

"Why should you? The publicity's not your business."

"It's my business to keep a check on all the departments," she retorted. "I don't know what's the matter with me to-day: a rush of Spring to the head, I should imagine."

"What about taking a day off?" suggested Simon. She looked at him as though he had gone mad. Presently her lips curled into an appreciative smile.

"I believe you've got it worse than I. What about the whole staff prancing off hand in hand to pick primroses by the river's rim?"

"Don't be an ass. You've not had a day for months. Go on—go down to the country and take Dennis out for the day."

She shook her head firmly.

"The children aren't allowed out with their parents, except at week-ends and half-terms," she explained. "I'm saving up to take Dennis to Dieppe for his half-term week-end—if it happens to fit in with our work here."

"I'll see that it does. Well, what about the letters?"

"Nothing very important—— Oh, Mr. Lygon rang through about half-past nine, to say he was sorry to be late, but he'd be down by ten."

"*What?*" Simon gaped. "See here: Spring's Spring and a joke's a joke, but I'm not buying that one. Since when have you felt it necessary to protect Daniel by inventing messages for him?"

"It's not invention; I took the call myself."

"He's pulling our legs," muttered Simon, drawing the letters towards him.

"I don't think so. I suppose he's been rather inconsiderate lately, but he's obviously having a bad time——"

"Yes, yes." Daniel put it across Nancy as he did across every one else! "Hallo, this is better!" He read through the Book Society's notification of their recommendation of a Crome and Lygon novel. "A move in the right direction; now perhaps we'll get the ' choice ' with her second book; it's definitely better than *Wine and Song*. Bertha Bradlaw has been asked to speak at one of the Foyle luncheons, and wants to come and have a word with us about it. It's a pity it's her," reflected Simon ungrammatically. "Old Bertha's dam' bad propaganda for her own work when it comes to public appearances. You'd better deal with her: find out her ideas—if she's got any—and coach her up a bit."

"If I'm to take on the job of lecture coach," smiled Nancy, "I'll certainly apply for a rise in salary."

"You'll have earned it," he said shortly. "Lady Whipple will be delighted if I'll lunch with her on the twenty-first. Who's Lady Whipple? I've never heard of her. Try it on Daniel, and if he can't, or won't, send a pretty refusal; I can't waste my time these days, lunching in Belgravia."

"Do you think perhaps you should? You do know Lady Whipple—she's Lord Mynte's sister-in-law——"

"Definitely not my cup of tea. Send it up to Daniel's room."

"And her daughter married Reggie Targett."

"Targett of the *London and New York*?"

Nancy nodded.

"It might be a useful contact. They always give us stinking notices."

"It certainly might." Simon bit his thumbnail. "All the same, it's more Daniel's affair than mine. I'm no use at the social racket."

"You know, I think you'd go down better with these Whipples than Mr. Lygon. They're rich, narrow-minded Nonconformists——"

"Hey!"

"Well, you've had plenty of practice," grinned Nancy. "They're very much in with the Matlocks—I should think that explains the invitation. And it's worth while getting in on the ground floor with Targett——"

"I know it is; but it doesn't say he'll be at the luncheon."

"He won't, because he's just gone to the States; but his wife's in town, staying with her people——"

"How on earth do you know these things?"

"I happened to see it this morning in the Court Circular: ' Mrs. Reginald Targett has arrived from California, and is staying with her parents, Sir Albert and Lady Whipple——' "

Simon gazed at her.

"You don't mean to tell me you read the Court Circular?"

Nancy laughed outright.

"I read anything: from the Circular to *The Daily Worker*," she told him. "A catholic taste in reading's the best way of picking up useful bits of information; and I assure you, it would pay us if you managed to talk pretty to Reggie Targett's wife. She's the managing director in that firm!"

"All right—make a note of acceptance. I'd like to get hold of Targett; he could do a lot for us, if he chose."

"While I remember," said Nancy, "Mr. Blandon's frothing at the mouth about Agatha Mott's notice in *The Athenian*. As you know, I don't usually pay attention to disgruntled authors, but honestly, I think she's gone a bit too far. Why on earth do people bring personalities into reviewing? It's obvious that any one like Mott's going to loathe Blandon's work, but the lamming she's given it is positively spiteful, and only defeats its own object."

"Did you say so to Blandon?"

"Of course; but he's quite unconvinced, and went off rumbling about lawyers and libels and what-have-you——"

"He won't catch Agatha out on libel! She's got the tongue of a serpent, but she's as sharp as a weasel when it comes to crossing the line of what may and what may not be said with impunity. As for her virulence defeating its own object—I wonder if you're right. She carries a lot of weight, you know; she can raise a laugh against any one with that spiteful humour of hers."

"Are you talking about Agatha Mott?"

Daniel had lounged into the room; he looked pale, but healthier than of recent weeks, and the hand in which he held a lighted match was almost insolently steady.

"Poor dear Mott—she's not as black as she's painted. I once had the most frightful row with her; we happened to be alone, so I said, ' Agatha darling, if you'll allow me to express my own opinion, you're nothing but a damned dyspeptic old 'Varsity virgin.'"

"No wonder we get rotten notices from *The Athenian*," said Simon.

"On the contrary," said Daniel, "she adored it. She spends the whole of her life calling other people the dog's dinner, and it was divine to get a nice straight slice of her own poison handed to her slap out of the oven on a hot plate! I've been a favourite of hers ever since."

"You'd better tell Blandon that."

"Has she been biting our Blanny? No, no, that's too naughty. We can't have our woolly little Blanny mauled by Agatha, even in fun. I suppose she hadn't got anything handy to sink her claws into. When is his next book out? I must remember to ask her to lunch; it'll make all the difference. A woman appreciates these little attentions—especially when people are inclined to forget she's a woman, and regard her purely as five feet eleven and a half of drainpipe filled with neat sulphuric acid."

Daniel was evidently in form. When Nancy left them, he proceeded to make himself comfortable in the arm-chair.

"Well, here we are again—partners in conference. What can I do for you to-day, partner?" he inquired genially.

"I've got to go down to Camden's about the Book Fair," said Simon. "And afterwards I'm seeing a man about some sort of a special show for Bertha Bradlaw; this Istanbul book of hers has made quite a bit of a fuss, and Christina Foyle has asked her to speak at one of the luncheons——"

"*Sacré nom d'un chien!*" said Daniel piously. "Has C. F. *seen* her?"

"That's C. F.'s affair—not ours. By the way, there are last week's sales." Simon tossed him a sheet of paper, which Daniel glanced over vaguely.

"Up a bit, aren't we?"

"Cratchitt steady, Bradlaw well up, the rest we might describe as pullulating. The market's started to move, Daniel, and we've got to move with it."

"Quite," said Daniel, registering alertness. Simon frowned.

"Look here: I may have to lunch with Camden. But I

made a half-promise to meet Alec Ray at the Ivy. Can you carry on, if I'm not back?"

"The Ivy being one of my favourite spots for imbibing nourishment—with pleasure. You've no idea what a zip it puts on a *truite de rivière Monagasque* to watch our leading West End actresses greeting each other with Borgian embraces."

"Well, if you'll kindly cut out the embraces and concentrate on Alec, we might get something better than four lines in next Sunday's columns for young Dunfy's *Guns over Lyonesse*."

"I wish I were a critic," mourned Daniel. "It seems one has very little to do except contract cirrhosis of the liver by lunching luxuriously at the expense of people who yearn for a little easy publicity. It's just the job for me; like the orchid, I flourish in corruption."

"And look here: you might try and work in a word about Marius Lear."

Dropping his attitude of frivolity, Daniel looked up quickly.

"Are we taking his book?"

"Yes."

"I'm glad. If we could get a few more Marius Lears on our lists I should begin to take this business quite seriously."

"If you took it more seriously," Simon was tempted to reply, "we might have had several Lears by now." But he restrained himself; when Daniel was obviously in a good mood, there was no point in aggravating him.

"Tell Alec about him; try to get him interested. The interest of a person like Alec's worth columns to a beginner. Like the elephant, he never forgets, and he talks—in the right places, to the right people. It's a pity the days of patronage are over—that's really what a writer like Lear needs: a patron, to launch him on intellectual society."

"What about Bertie Manders?"

"I must try and fix up a meeting between them; but

Bertie's got too many protégés—they're crusted on to him until the poor chap can hardly move for them."

"A pretty simile," conceded Daniel. "I see Bertie, like some rich Ragusan argosy, sunk to the plimsoll in Mayfair tides, with limpets round his hull."

"I don't think Lear would have much use for him either; he's too ignorant of Bertie's world to appreciate the rich Ragusan idiom!" smiled Simon.

"Lydia said you met him last night," said Daniel easily.

"That's what decided me to take his book."

"And they say personal contacts don't count!"

"Who say? I thought they were the only things that did."

"Of course they are; but it's the cry of the art-for-art's sake crowd: of the woolly-backs like Blandon: of all the not quite successful people who blame everything but their own want of social competence for their lack of success."

"I shouldn't credit Lear with much social competence! He did his best to insult the firm—represented by me—for ten minutes——"

"And you bought it, of course. Really, Simon, there's nothing to choose between you and poor dear Agatha! Fawn on you and you snarl; abuse either of you, and you fall supine with pleasure. You're like a couple of cats, asking people to scratch your stomachs——"

"Don't be an idiot. You raved about the book yourself."

"Naturally. It's a first-class book—and I suppose you're having a special presentation copy done in half-calf for Old Harry."

"Really, Daniel, you're the least soothing person——!" Simon made a movement of irritation.

"But stimulating—*hein?*" Daniel joined his long, well-kept fingers, tip to tip. "Admitted that the query comes somewhat late in the day—what *did* induce you to take Old Harry's money? We could have managed quite well on our own; I could, at a pinch, have raised another couple of thousand."

Simon waited for a moment before answering. Daniel was within his rights to ask the question; it was typical of his lack of financial acumen that he had never seen fit to raise the point before. Old Harry's backing was a matter entirely between him and his son-in-law, which Daniel, at the time, had accepted in child-like good faith.

"I may have made a bloomer, Daniel," he said slowly. "The next few months—and, incidentally, Lear's book—will tell their own tale. But I acted in what I thought were the best interests of Christian and the children. I know we could have got along somehow on our own capital, but it would have been a pinch, and darned slow going. It didn't seem fair to Chris not to accept her Father's help over a matter which involved the whole of our future, when I've taken it—God knows unwillingly enough—in smaller ways. You must realize, Daniel, that this business, which amounts to a hobby from your point of view, is a serious thing for Chris and me." He paused lamely. Of course Daniel knew that; it sounded foolish, put into words, but a sudden, irrational and even childish longing for understanding from his half-brother and partner drove him to express, in this inadequate fashion, the anxiety which the gay day and his sense of renewed well-being had banished temporarily from his mind.

"Well," said Daniel, "I'll feed Alec oysters and Clicquot; I'll coo in his ear gently as any sucking dove; I'll make the babbling gossip of the air cry out, ' Dunfy!', and if he doesn't come back suitably on Sunday, I'll give myself the pleasure of ringing him up and telling him my opinion of his filthy ingratitude."

"Don't make it too glaring; even reviewers have their *amour propre*," said Simon dryly.

"I thought they earned a thousand a year by selling it to their papers. Well, on with the dance," said Daniel. "The junior partner of Crome and Lygon proceeds to earn his pittance by the exercise of the charm for which his side of the family is famous." He looked quizzically at Simon. "What on earth you will do without me when I go to Roumania I can't imagine."

"Are you going?"

"I think I might as well. It'll take some time to arrange and I've got to find out the date of our party at the courts."

"How long do you think you'll be away?"

"Won't that depend upon exactly what I'm expected to do?" Simon looked at his watch.

"There isn't time to discuss it now. What are you doing to-night? Could you dine with us?"

"Yes, if you like. I should think you got enough of the shop without carrying it home with you in the evenings."

"I'll give Christian a ring; I'm practically sure we're both free. Eight o'clock—unless I hear to the contrary—and don't bother to dress."

When Daniel had gone to his room, Simon put the call through, and was puzzled by a note of hesitation in Christian's voice.

"Is anything wrong? Are you all right?" A sudden pang of fear, that went back to the time when Christian was carrying Henry, sharpened his inquiry, but he was at once reassured by her laugh.

"Of course I am. It's only—as the devil has it!—that I've asked Lydia to dine." There was a little pause. "It's beginning to look pre-arranged."

"Couldn't you put her off? Daniel and I want to talk shop. We shan't have much time to be social."

"I'll see if I can get her, but she was going out somewhere, and I don't suppose she'll be back at the flat before changing time."

"Oh, hell, I suppose that means dressing. All right, I'll tell Daniel."

"And I'll try and get Lydia upstairs after dinner, and give her a good talking to. I can't bear to think of her making herself miserable about Daniel."

"Well, she'll have plenty of time to get over her misery, if we send Daniel to Belgrade."

"You've not forgotten we promised to go and have cocktails with the Hattons, have you?"

"Oh, no, we haven't, have we?"

"I'll make excuses, if you like, but it was you who said we had better accept, because of meeting Cowper Merrill."

"It doesn't matter now that Daniel's doing his job. I wish you'd get me out of it. Will you, dear? We've been to such a heap of cocktails lately, and they're such a waste of time—most of them."

"I wondered if it would be a good idea if we gave one ourselves. It's an easy way of seeing a lot of people, and I think authors and agents like it. I'll tell you why I mention it now: we're bound to have one before the end of the season, and the sooner the better for me—see? When does Daniel go? We might make it a sort of *bon voyage* party for him—but I ought to be getting the cards out now."

"We'll talk about it to-night. I think you've got enough on your hands without taking on office propaganda."

"Oh, Nancy Rowlandson will help; you must lend her to me for a morning, to help me make the lists. I do want to throw one good-sized party, before I go into prudent retirement!"

"Well, why don't you—a party of your own friends? You won't get much fun out of a literary rout."

"Yes, I will. I want to make myself useful. I can't do much, but I'd like to feel I was pulling my weight."

"You do that all right," he assured her, as he hung up the receiver. Bless her heart! There really was not—would never be—any one like Christian. It was like her to choose this practical form of "making up" for her lack of sympathy over Marius's book. No apology was complete, to Christian, unless she had found some way of expressing, actively, her genuine regret. It touched him the more, in that he knew that her opinion was unaltered, probably unalterable. Her stubbornness, inherited from Old Harry, was a thing beyond her own control, although her love could often conceal its more inconvenient evidences: and on the few occasions when they both suffered from its results, his own pain was increased, rather than mitigated, by his tenderness for her and his appreciation of the fact that she did not want to be stubborn, but was wholly the victim of her own inherited temperament.

He rang for Nancy, ran off half a dozen notes, and picked up his hat.

"Do you want a taxi?" asked Nancy, with her finger on the bell which summoned the office boy.

"Christian's talking about throwing a party: shop window stuff," he said, as he reached the door. "I suppose it's a good idea?"

"It's the sort of thing people seem to expect nowadays," she frowned. "I loathe literary parties, but we've had a lot of invitations, and I'm afraid you're bound to do it. It's nice of Mrs. Crome to take it on."

"I'm not sure if she ought. She's going to have another baby."

She gave him a quick, sympathetic look.

"I'll give her all the help I possibly can."

"I suppose we'll have to ask the whole Zoo. Try and find a date that will suit us—it will have to be before Daniel goes, of course."

Simon ran down the stairs; the taxi was waiting; he stepped into a flood of sunlight on the pavement. "God, what a day!" he said aloud, as they swung into the traffic stream of the main road.

CHAPTER SEVEN

"I'm afraid we can only offer a twenty-five pound advance," said Simon.

A smile—the first he had given—curled the corners of Marius Lear's big mouth; when he smiled there was something attractive in his ugliness. His small eyes, with the upper lids completely hidden by the fold of skin which descended from his viciously sprouting eyebrows, twinkled at Simon.

"That'll do. It's more than I expected."

"You're a bit of a phenomenon in authors, Lear!" Simon could not refrain from remarking.

Marius shrugged his shoulders.

"Books are trade, aren't they, as much as potatoes? My father kept a greengrocer's shop; I know something about overhead expenses and profits. I don't suppose you'll do much more than cover the advance."

"We may not; but, as a business man, you'll know it sometimes pays to drop money." Simon pushed the cigarettes across his desk. "You'd better have a talk about the contract with my secretary, Mrs. Rowlandson; she'll explain to you about royalties and things."

Again the slow, humorous smile lit the other's face.

"I shouldn't think there's much need to discuss those, is there?"

"Well, there's the usual three-book option, and the royalty question may arise—I hope it will on your next."

"Oh, well, I'll leave that to you."

"I'd rather you didn't—even if money's no object, as appears to be the case, with you."

The smile vanished and the upper lip lengthened.

"It's a fool impression to give. I certainly want the money."

"I wish we could make it more. Don't you smoke?"

"I haven't been doing for some time. I don't think I'll start again, thanks. As a matter of fact, I cut it out because smoking's too costly unless you keep it down to a minimum, which, unfortunately, I don't seem able to do."

"I smoke far too much," said Simon absently. Through the smoke he took stock of his companion, wondering what it was about Lear that so appealed to him, in spite of the man's uncomfortable abruptness, his uncouth mannerisms and clothing. Lear was, in fact, very much what he might himself have been, had it not been for the civilizing influences of a career which calls for the cultivation of some social graces. It was, perhaps, because these were often so uncongenial to Simon, so unwillingly exercised, that he felt a marked sympathy with Marius Lear. It was an effort, often, to remember to go to the barber, to have one's hands manicured; it would be pleasant, sometimes, not to fuss about such things as clean linen—he found himself envying Marius his evident indifference to such artificialities.

"You said you teach, didn't you? It must be pretty hard to find time for writing with a job like that."

"I've chucked it" said Lear, surprisingly. "As a matter of fact, I gave in my notice for the end of the term, as soon as I got your note about taking the book."

"Was that not a bit premature?"

He shrugged his shoulders.

"Premature or not, it's done; I should have done it before."

"Have you got anything to live on?"

"Twenty-five pounds."

"You're crazy!"

"It doesn't cost much to live my way, and the money'll last me quite a while. I'll have my salary, of course—half of it; I had to sub the other half, because I'd spent up last term's during the holidays. I always meant to save; I thought I might save enough to have a cottage somewhere out of London, and give up my time to writing, but it never seemed to come off. The pay was rotten, and there was going abroad; I had to do that, to sluice off the term's muck."

"You won't get far on twenty-five pounds."

"Oh, that won't matter," he said easily. "I don't care, so long as I'm not doing something I loathe for twelve hours out of the twenty-four. I always hated teaching, and you've got no business to take money for doing something you don't believe in. Teaching's strictly vocational, anyhow, and—well, I suppose I haven't got the vocation."

"Well, but how do you propose to keep yourself, when your capital's gone?" insisted Simon. "Are you going to try journalism?"

Marius shook his head.

"I haven't the least gift for it. Now and again I get a poem into print—of course that only means a few shillings. But I suppose it's not wholly unlikely I might make a living out of my books, later on?"

"A good deal later, I'm afraid." Simon shook his head. "It's no use beating about the bush; your work's not the type that has a big, general appeal. We'll do our best, of course, to place your novel in America, and we might do a bit with foreign rights; as a matter of fact, if we found a good translator, it might go quite well in Germany. That sort of thing only brings in a few pounds——"

"I could do the translation myself, if it came to that."

"I'd forgotten you specialized in languages."

"Who told you I did?"

"I forget—oh, I think Miss Audley told my wife."

Marius grunted.

"One thing I'll have done with: poetry readings in parlours to women with faces like Pekinese!"

Simon laughed.

"You needn't grudge that part of your apprenticeship. It's not a bad way of laying the foundations of your future public. Not, I fear, that your book's likely to cut much ice with Miss Audley's friends. I've got a suggestion. It doesn't amount to

much, but it might be worth your consideration. Have you
got another appointment?"—as Marius looked at the cheap
watch strapped on his wrist.

"No—that's to say, there's a concert; someone gave me a
ticket for it. I thought I might get in for the second half."

"What is it?" Simon marked this fresh proof of his affinity
with Marius Lear.

"Delius, mainly——"

"I wish I'd known. What's the use of saying it? There's
never time nowadays. . . . Look here, this is my suggestion:
It doesn't happen very often, because we haven't got any sort
of reputation yet with foreign agents—but now and again we
get the offer of a French or German book. When it's French,
either Christian or I manage to read it; but we have to send
the German stuff out, and pay for a special report. You could
do that sort of thing for us, couldn't you?"

"I suppose so; if you'd be satisfied to take my opinion."

"I'd risk it—though we've yet to prove if you've got any
idea of what's likely to go down with the public."

"I could do you an abstract, and leave you to judge that
for yourself."

"And if we took it, would you be able to do the translation
for us?" pursued Simon.

"I should think so—provided it wasn't technical, or some
sort of a scientific text-book. You'd have to get a specialist
on that."

"I suppose you know translation's rottenly paid?"
Marius nodded.

"I did a book once for Gosschalk; someone mentioned my
name and I was rather tickled by the idea. It took me the
best part of three months and paid for a week-end in Paris.
I thought it was worth while."

"Well, I'll bear you in mind. I don't think we've got
anything in now, but I'll notify them to let you know if
something turns up." Simon held out his hand. "I'm glad
to have your name in our lists, Lear, and I'll do my best to

make you glad as well. You must come in one day soon and meet my partner; he's a great admirer of yours. Don't forget to see Mrs. Rowlandson, as you go out, about the contract."

He turned to work on his desk; it was a complicated collection of accounts, calling for the closest attention, and he was anxious to master its contents before the expected visit of the firm's auditors. He was also expecting a call from Old Harry, whose secretary had telephoned to say that Sir Harry was in town, and would try to get in to see Mr. Crome before the office closed. Yet, despite his efforts at concentration, he found himself thinking about Marius Lear. It was almost as though the man were still there, slumped in the arm-chair, filling the room with a personality that, in some way, took possession of it, driving out the fainter emanations from other people whose right to be there was, on the surface of it, better defined than his. Suddenly Simon knew what it was: it was Lear's singleness of purpose, his blind concentration upon his own objective and his indifference to any difficulties which fortune might place in his way that lent him such a formidable strength of personality: and with these a sweeping quality of freedom which roused Simon's envy, without his even recognizing it for what it was. And he knew, with sudden clearness, what he wanted: which was to find some way in which their association should be strengthened and his know-ledge of Marius increased, because he felt that in such an association he would find augmentation of his own forces, and attain to a higher independence of thought and action than he had hitherto allowed himself to indulge.

He had faced, deliberately and in moral solitude, exactly how far the publication of Marius's book would involve him in trouble with Old Harry, and, instead of being enervated, was stimulated by the prospect of a tussle. After all, in accept-ing his father-in-law's backing, he had not sold his soul; what he had offered, in exchange, was the benefits of his own experience, for the increase of their mutual fortune. In putting money into the venture, Old Harry had accepted Simon's ability to make good on the managerial side, and, while the latter had expressed his willingness to respect the prejudices and principles of his backer, the final decision, when it came to the rejection or acceptance of a manuscript, must lie with him. Telling himself this, Simon had a momentary pang for occasions when he had timorously allowed himself to be overborne by the weight of his father-in-law's opinion—followed immediately by a recrudescence of self-respect over his present self-assertion. If it came to a show-down, he could at least produce strong evidence of support: from Daniel, for whose opinion Old Harry had no regard, and from Nancy Rowlandson, for whose discretion and common sense he had a very strong one.

He attempted again to concentrate upon the accounts, but this time it was the thought of Daniel that teased him. Daniel, and Lydia. Christian must have been wrong about that. Neither had shown any signs of secret understanding on the evening they dined with the Cromes. Daniel, quite serious for once, entered into full discussion of the Roumanian project —a discussion from which the women were tacitly excluded: Christian listening with her usual quiet attentiveness, and Lydia, strangling yawns, hardly troubling to conceal her boredom. She left early, pretexting her need of a "long night" after the previous short one.

"What time did you go home?" Simon had casually inquired.

"Oh—morning-ish," said Lydia, vaguely. "You know how it is—one never knows the time, after midnight, at those places."

"She wouldn't allow me to take her," drawled Daniel. "I said no nice girl went gadding home alone at such an hour, but it didn't seem to make an impression."

No. If anything, the two seemed bored by each other. They kept to the fine edge of courtesies when it was necessary to address each other directly, but only an inflamed imagination could have detected in Daniel's attitude to Lydia, or in hers to him, a more than conventional interest. He remarked on it afterwards to Christian, who pursed her lips and shook her head.

"I tell you, she's admitted she's in love with Daniel."

"Well, if that's so, it's a pity; because it's as plain as daylight he doesn't care two raps for her—thank goodness," said Simon tersely.

Why should the evening return to his mind, to plague him now? He was very fond of Lydia; but her affairs were none of his—so long as they did not concern Daniel. That, of course, would be a father-and-mother of a tragedy! Anything between Daniel and Lydia, on top of the former's divorce, would blow the firm sky-high, if it came to Old Harry's ears. Surely Daniel must realize that? The possibility of giving him a word of warning crossed Simon's mind, to be instantly dismissed. Apart from the fact that it would be a give-away for Lydia, Daniel would quite rightly resent interference with his private affairs. It was a good thing he was going away for a while. Lydia was a darling, but a fool. It was time she got herself a husband, and stopped taking interest in charming detrimentals like Daniel.

The door opened, and Nancy Rowlandson came in.

"Oh, there you are. For God's sake come and give me a hand with these figures."

"Lady Matlock's here, Mr. Crome; she wants to see you."

"What?"

It was the first time his mother-in-law had visited the office, and, much as he would have liked to assume that her call had no more than a friendly motive, common sense made Simon reject the easy assumption.

"Do you know what she wants? I'm expecting Old Harry."

"She didn't say; but she's in my room. I thought I'd better not leave her downstairs."

"I suppose I'll have to see her; but you must play the watch-dog. If I don't ring in a quarter of an hour, come in with something. And—I say! If Old Harry turns up, you'd

better ring through to me. Goodness knows what the old
lady's up to, but she may not want to run into him as she's
leaving."

Nothing was less clandestine, however, than Lady Matlock's bearing, as she overflowed with her sables, her violets
and floating chiffons, from Nancy's room into Simon's. When
the discreet double doors which preserved managerial privacy
were closed, she pushed up her veil and bestowed a kiss on
her son-in-law. Her plump cheek had the soft coolness of a
petal, and smelt, like a baby's, of orris-perfumed fuller's
earth.

"Simon, dear, I thought I'd give you a surprise! What
charming quarters you have—and *such* an attentive staff.
While I think of it, I left a little parcel with your secretary:
just something for the children. I thought you wouldn't mind
taking it home."

Catch-phrases came into Simon's mind: "The smile on
the face of the tiger," and "When the Greeks bring gifts . . ."
Anything less like a lean habitant of the jungle, more like a
pampered domestic cat than his mother-in-law it was impossible to imagine, yet Simon had the impression that those
softly curled paws were prepared, on this occasion, to unsheath
more than the gift of which she spoke.

"It's my day for massage, so Harry and I came up together.
I've got such a clever woman; my dear, you ought to persuade
Christian to go to her. How is Chris? I thought she was
looking the least bit peaked when we dined with you the other
night. I do wish you'd take her away for a little change; it's
been such a long winter, and she's much more delicate than
she looks."

Simon glanced sharply at her, wondering whether Christian
had yet said anything about the baby; he did not think it
was likely.

"I think she's all right; but I'll see if I can send her to
the country for a long week-end. She won't go without the
children, and she doesn't like interrupting their lessons, you

know. I'm expecting Old Harry," he told her, hoping it might hurry her to the point of whatever she had come to say.

Lady Matlock shook her head and pursed her lips.

"I doubt if he'll manage it. He's had a very trying morning, and there's a shareholders' meeting this afternoon. We lunched together, and he was quite worn out. He said he'd telephone if he was kept later than four. We're floating a new company," she said vaguely. "I'm sure I can't imagine why: Harry's terribly overworked as it is, and I'm so worried about him."

"I don't suppose you need be; he's got endless staying power," said Simon. She answered him sharply:

"We are not growing younger, Simon, and the doctor says he should be taking much more rest. It's not only the works, it's the enormous number of outside responsibilities he takes on, apart from business. And now they're bothering him again to stand for Parliament! I tell him he can't possibly do it, but I know he's tempted."

"Where do they want him to stand for?"

"Granedge, of course," said Lady Matlock proudly. "Naturally, I understand what he feels about being the first to represent in Parliament the town which owes its existence to him. What a record, when one remembers that little handful of squalid cottages; and now——! Ah, Simon, there aren't many who live to see their life's work so splendidly realized as my dear man. It brings tears to my eyes, each time I look from our windows over our beautiful town. 'A triumph of righteousness,' I tell Harry. I know what his answer will be."

"No doubt," said Simon absently. "Well——"

"He never speaks, but he points silently to the church, and I know what he means. Our witness; our acknowledgment of Divine guidance——"

"A very handsome acknowledgment, I'm sure. Would you care for a cup of tea? I generally have one about this time."

"That would be delightful." She dimpled at him, drawing off her gloves; her small plump hands, the nails manicured to pink shells, the fingers loaded with diamonds, folded themselves on her lap. "So you see, don't you, why I'm so anxious not to add anything—not to have anything added—to Harry's load just now. When this Parliament thing's settled, and before he starts the election work, I want to take him away for a nice holiday. The Whipples have asked us to join them on their yacht—the very best thing for Harry, if his mind's at rest, and he can really give himself up to a few weeks' laziness, as he calls it! But of course, if he's going to worry about things at home, we might just as well not go at all."

"Has he any particular cause for worry?"

Lady Matlock bit her lip, appeared to hesitate, made up her mind to continue.

"You must know he's very much upset about this divorce."

Some unholy levity prompted Simon to raise his eyebrows and grin at his mother-in-law.

"I'd no idea Old Harry had got himself involved in a divorce!"

It was a foolish jest to make to an utterly humourless woman. Lady Matlock stiffened, her plump, indulgent face hardened into lines of indignation.

"You know perfectly well what I mean. Mr. Lygon's divorce."

"Well, Mother," said Simon, on a conciliatory note; he repented of his folly. "I agree with both of you that it's a very unfortunate thing, and very inconvenient from the point of view of Daniel's work; but I can't see how it affects any one beside ourselves."

"You surely see how unpleasant it is to have the name of the firm mixed up in a divorce case?"

"That, again, seems entirely Daniel's affair and mine; they're our names."

"Every one knows of Harry's connection with you!"

"Do you mean with me, *quâ* son-in-law, or with me as Daniel's partner? Certainly every one knows I married

Christian Matlock, but so far as his share in the business is concerned, I don't suppose a dozen people outside ourselves are aware of it, and the rest don't give two hoots—so long as we meet our liabilities!"

"You are quite wrong," said Lady Matlock icily. "Harry's connection with the firm of Crome and Lygon is a matter of public knowledge."

"Oh, well, if he chooses to publicize it——" said Simon, rather testily.

"There is no need for you to lose your temper, Simon— any more than there is for Harry to publicize his affairs. His interest in book production has been shown for years in connection with the public libraries. When our Granedge branch was opened, it was Harry who insisted upon a much stricter censorship than the librarian at first exercised; he was determined to stamp out this miserable tendency among young people to fill their minds up with smutty reading. In fact, he gave two addresses: one, I think, on ' Our Glorious Heritage of Literature,' and the other on ' Reading for Profit.' He made a great impression, I remember, by saying that if he were a publisher, he would devote all his power to the purification of English fiction. The applause was quite overwhelming; as Harry said afterwards, it only went to show that people *do* want the highest——"

"It depends on what you mean by the highest," said Simon. "The publisher, like the shopkeeper, exists to supply the public demand. Refusal to publish tripe won't prevent a certain class of reader from getting what he wants elsewhere."

"Surely one does not cater for that class?" queried Lady Matlock superbly.

"Well, well," said Simon, hanging on to his patience. "I still don't see what this has to do with Daniel's divorce."

"It means," declared Lady Matlock, "that Harry is financing an immoral concern."

Simon gave an irresistible yelp of laughter.

"Oh, come, come, Mother! That's altogether too much of

a good thing. What on earth has Daniel's private morality to do with the business? And, in any case, Daniel's doing the divorcing; the immorality is Eliza's affair."

"It is, perhaps, natural for you, Simon, to treat these matters lightly." Their eyes met, and Simon's narrowed. She had got to take care, this bigoted old woman. Christian had hinted at trouble, before they were engaged, on the score that Simon's mother had been divorced, but, to do them justice, neither of the old Matlocks had ever referred to this regrettable incident to Simon himself. "From our point of view—I mean from the point of view of people who know the circumstances —it may be that Mr. Lygon is not to blame. Though I really do not care for that young man. There's too much levity in his general attitude towards life, and we both feel, personally, that this divorce is a symptom of his lack of moral seriousness. Look at it as you may, Simon, it is a most unpleasant thing for the firm to be associated with, and Harry feels it very keenly—especially as his own strict views are generally known, and it will really appear, to a great many people, as if his money is being used to free your half-brother from his responsibilities."

"That's ridiculous," said Simon, stung at last to indignation. "Daniel has money in the firm, besides a considerable private income of his own——"

"You know the kind of thing that people say." She shrugged her shoulders. "You can't make a public statement about a thing of that kind, and when you think of the opposition Harry brought to bear, through influential friends in the Lords, to A. P. Herbert's Bill, I don't wonder he feels hurt by the assumption that he is false to his own principles."

"His opposition didn't effect much, did it? No one's going to bother about Old Harry's principles, though a few may respect him for holding them; and if you saw this year's lists, you wouldn't bother about the very small amount of attention Daniel's case will command from the general public."

"There's bound to be publicity, because of the Lygons' position."

"Well, what about it? Old Harry's name doesn't come into it."

She pressed her lips together.

"I think you must move in a very narrow circle, my dear Simon," she told him acidly, "if you can't realize how quick people are to connect a name like Harry's with any scandalous event that finds its way into the papers. It seems"—her large, blue eyes filled with tears—"it seems as if our very integrity exposes us to the malice of people who are jealous, I suppose, of Harry's good name, and take pleasure in throwing mud at a thing they can't imitate."

"Well, I don't suppose much of it sticks," Simon felt bound to comfort her by saying. "Look here, Mother. I could understand your being upset if this divorce concerned Christian and me——"

"Which God forbid," said Lady Matlock, earnestly.

"Certainly. But as Daniel and Eliza haven't an earthly thing to do with either of you, I hope you'll forgive me for saying that I think you're making a mountain out of a mole-hill, and the sooner you put the whole thing out of your mind the better. It will all blow over in a month or two, and really, if you knew as much as I do of the circumstances, you'd say it was a jolly good thing."

"Perhaps I know more of the circumstances than you think," she retorted. "I overheard a conversation this morning that would have made me sink through the floor, if I hadn't remembered that they couldn't possibly recognize me, and that gossip among that set is usually as unfounded as it is devoid of decency."

"What set?" muttered Simon, tired of the discussion.

"Evidently friends—or I had better say acquaintances—of Eliza Lygon." She spoke the name as if it were sickening. "Two women of the fast set, who didn't seem to care who was listening. I don't understand how such people don't get sued for libel. You can imagine my feelings when I heard them making jokes about the divorce, and laying bets upon which of her lovers the husband was naming!"

"Oh, there's always a certain crowd who'll do that; they don't count, anyhow. And if things are like that, Mother, don't you think it's much better that Daniel should make a clean break, and get away from Eliza?"

Her little, obstinate chin stiffened.

"If he takes on obligations, it is his duty to look after them. ' Those whom God has joined together——'"

"If you knew Eliza, I don't think you'd quote the Bible in this connection."

"Simon"—her tone altered, became beseeching—"can't you do anything to stop this horrid thing?"

"I certainly cannot; and I would not, if I could."

"You must have so much influence with your brother: you're so much older—you've had so much experience——"

"Not, happily, in the kind of situation into which Daniel has got himself. Leave it alone, Mother—and try to forget it."

"How can I forget it, when Harry thinks and talks of nothing else? We've never," said Lady Matlock tearfully, "had anything of this kind in the family before."

"Do try and think clearly, Mother. You haven't got it ' in the family ' now. I'm touched—genuinely—by the way in which you both choose to identify yourselves with my personal interests, and I don't want you to feel that I'm ungracious in assuring you that you're overdoing it. I'll have a talk to Old Harry——"

"You won't alter his opinion. And I hope you won't make him feel that you're taking the Lygons' side; you certainly seem to sympathize with them a great deal more than I expected."

"Don't you expect me to be sorry for Daniel? He's my half-brother, as well as my partner. I always deplored Eliza, but she wasn't my business. She isn't now, whatever Old Harry likes to make out."

"I don't believe in this modern tolerance," said Lady Matlock, viciously. "I hold with the old saying: ' Touch not pitch, lest ye be defiled.' I hope, by the way, that you aren't allowing Christian to receive that woman, now this has happened."

"Chris and Eliza were never very ' thick.' There's no question of ' receiving her,' for the very good reason that Eliza's never been near us since the night when you, unfortunately, were dining with us. We hadn't seen her for months before that. I can't think of any possible reason why she should come again."

She rose, dropping her gloves and handbag, which Simon stooped to collect for her.

"You haven't drunk your tea; I'm afraid it's cold by now. Let me ring for another cup."

"No, no. I must get back to the hotel. Harry and I are going down on the five-thirty—at least, I hope he catches it; it doesn't look as if he is coming here."

"Well, I'll make a point of seeing the old boy, and talking him out of his fussation over Daniel's affairs. When does he come up again?"

"I think you are taking this too lightly, Simon," she told him, giving him her hand coldly in farewell. "However easy your own attitude may be, don't forget that honour is everything to Harry. He is not only a great financial power, but a great moral force in the world of business, and no amount of verbal quibbling will make him depart from his determination never to be associated with anything that is not absolutely beyond reproach in the eyes of the Christian community."

"Phew!" said Simon, when Nancy returned, having seen Lady Matlock to her car. "I've just been through the hoops on Daniel's account. For sheer blind interference in other people's affairs, commend me every time to Nonconformists."

"They're no worse than other sorts of Christians. Religion has that effect on people, I find. It makes one awfully anxious about one's own children."

"How?" asked Simon, startled.

"Well, I don't want Dennis to grow up religious, but I don't exactly want him to be a little pagan. I've known several children from atheistic homes, and they seem somehow to lack background. I do think that 'Gentle Jesus, meek and mild' and saying Grace before meals does something for one when one is small—helps, as it were, to steady one in one's universe. But it's very hard to know where to draw the line, and it's terrifying to think of them growing up into self-righteous humbugs like so many people who have been brought up on religion."

"I sometimes get scared about Henry," admitted Simon. "He is very suggestible, and his visits to Granedge are always followed by nauseating outbursts of holiness. I found him holding a prayer meeting in the kitchen one night, with all the servants down on their knees, spellbound by the little beast."

Nancy burst out laughing.

"What did you do about it?"

"Slapped his bottom and sent him to bed. It worried Christian rather."

Daniel came in and took more gravely than Simon had expected the account of his conversation with Lady Matlock.

"Blast Old Harry. I always felt he was a dangerous old devil, under those white whiskers and mellifluous boomings. God, wouldn't I like to catch him out in some bit of nonsense of his own!"

"You'd be lucky. People have spent their lives in trying to catch him out, and have died defeated. It's preposterous, of course; nobody builds an 'Ironmongery Town' out of strict evangelical principles. He must have done some large-scale racketeering in his time."

"I didn't mean in his business; give the devil his due, I'll bet Old Harry has got that armour-plated, as far as the investigations of amateurs like myself are concerned. But I'd like to know about some of the little, purple moments with which he's enlivened the drear, domestic round."

"Don't be an ass. I shouldn't think he's ever looked at a woman since he got married."

"Think not? Then, by God, he's for it! He's just reached the time of life when fellows of his sort go off the rails."

"Not Old Harry," said Simon, with conviction.

"You wait and see. I shouldn't be surprised if he's paying blackmail already to a couple of his factory hands."

"Rot," said Simon. "You don't catch Old Harry being such a fool as to foul his own works."

"Well, the irresistible impulse will come over him one day to tickle a typist, and then the fat will be in the fire. Don't you agree with me?" He appealed to Nancy, who sat patiently, the pencil poised over her pad, on the farther side of the desk. She shook her head.

"I like Sir Harry. I don't usually like old men; most of them are creepers——"

"Mark that, Simon, and be careful what you start in your old age!" threw in Daniel.

"I mean, they give you an uneasy feeling, even when they're being perfectly respectful and pleasant to you. But I've never felt like that with Sir Harry."

"That's a good mark to him, at any rate. Are you going to clear out, Daniel, or do you want me for something? Nancy and I have to go over these accounts before I go home."

"I've just got to sign my letters, and then I think I'll push off. I want to drop in at the Roumanian legation on my way to the club."

A tap on the door heralded the appearance of the girl Simon had christened Daniel's Scornful Blonde, a tall, languorous creature who looked more like a mannequin than a secretary. Daniel called her his "Hollywood touch," and said she made him feel more like the film producer's ideal of the business man.

"Miss Matlock's on the phone," she drawled, with erubescent fingertips laid to the short, platinum crest of her hair. "I wasn't sure if you and Mr. Crome were in conference, so I came to ask before putting her through."

There was a little pause before Daniel answered.

"All right, I'll take the call upstairs. Isn't she a bit of crackling?" he inquired, as the door closed behind the blonde. "I live in one long cold sweat for fear somebody's talent scout spirits her away from me; I know I'll find a note on my pad one morning, and recognize her a night or two later in three spangles and a feather in the cabaret. Well, good-bye, my sweets. See you in the morning."

"Shall we begin with Finch's account?" asked Nancy, as Simon was silent. Lydia and Daniel. Daniel and Lydia. Daniel was better these days: more like his normal self. Did it mean——?

"Is anything the matter?" asked Nancy quietly.

Simon threw down his fountain pen and thrust back his chair.

"I'm going to leave these damned things until to-morrow. I've had as much as I can stand for to-day."

CHAPTER EIGHT

Simon had lent Nancy to Christian for the day, and Christian had asked her to lunch with her.

"I suppose you wouldn't believe I'm scared stiff of the party?" said Christian, when they were having coffee in the drawing-room.

"What are you scared of?" asked Nancy, thinking that Christian did not look as well as she should, but putting this down to nervousness about the coming ordeal.

"I've always been scared of meeting strangers. It's ridiculous, isn't it? I'm so thankful neither of the children has inherited it; they're both as bold as brass with every one they meet."

"I think it was very decent of you to throw this party; you needn't have done it," said Nancy. The more she saw of Christian, the better she liked her.

"I suppose I needn't—in a way. But the Gosschalks and Rices have both thrown big parties, and we've been asked to them; and you know, although I hate cocktail parties almost as much as Simon does, I'm beginning to see the point of them. They're a sort of compliment to the people who work with you, and they keep you in touch with hundreds of people you couldn't see in the ordinary course of a busy life like Simon's. I quite see it's bad business, in his position just now, to let go of strings that may bring up a big fish one of these days!"

"Of course, it isn't the first big party you've given."

"It's the first of this sort. My teeth simply chatter when I think of all these people that I mostly know only by name, surging all over the house and talking about subjects on which I'm wholly ignorant. Literary people are such toughs, aren't they?"

"They're toughs all right," said Nancy grimly. "But you needn't worry. No one as attractive as you need worry."

"Do you think I'm attractive? I often think I'm an awfully bad advertisement for Simon. It was all right while he was just an editor, and I never had to meet any of his business friends; but I do think a publisher's wife ought to be better read than I am, more capable of taking the lead—at least in her own house. You'd do so much better than I, Nancy—you don't mind if I call you Nancy, do you? I wish we could change places to-night."

"Nonsense. I'm a commonplace in that crowd; you're so different, you'll have an enormous success. I hope you're going to have a good rest this afternoon; you ought to undress and go to bed properly—I never think lying down on a sofa is much use."

"I'd rather have some fresh air, and I'm going to take Jemima and Henry in the park for an hour. It's Nana's afternoon, and I always look after them when she's out."

"Why don't you let me take them? I've got nothing to do, and I'll take them up to the Zoo, if you like; they'll settle down all the sooner to-night for a little extra excitement."

For some reason, however, Christian was obstinate about her walk. Jemima and Henry, hatted and booted, rushed into the drawing-room, and announced their desire to be taken to Kensington Gardens.

"Why the Gardens?"

Henry and his sister exchanged glances. Henry scowled through his glasses, while Jemima burst forth:

"Because there's a woman there—and Nana says she's mad —but Nana says madness is really being possessed of the devil —and Henry and me want to see if we can cast out the devil by walking behind her and saying the Lord's Prayer—and we have to say it a special way—and take one step for each word —and Henry wants to see the devil come out—because he thinks the devil looks like a bat with fire coming out of its ears and perhaps a long swishy tail with an arrow-shaped bit on the end like in Grandma's Bible——"

Christian and Nancy suppressed smiles, as Jemima panted for breath.

"Well, you can't go in the Gardens to-day," said Christian firmly.

"I'll wait a bit and see if there are any more telephone calls," volunteered Nancy, "then I'll run down to the office in case Mr. Crome wants anything. I'll be back before the caterers arrive, and see that they've got all they want."

With the two children at her side, Christian went into the damp, slightly foggy park: Jemima, straight and sturdy in her coat of rose-pink tweed, Henry, slight and a little under-sized for his age, barely touched her elbow with the crown of his little head. They were both very excited about the party, and demanded to be told all the details.

"What are you wearing, Mummy?"

"The brown velvet thing, I think—it won't matter if things get spilt on it."

Henry nodded critical approval of his mother's choice.

"I think you ought to wear brown velvet always; it suits you."

"Stupid!" jeered Jemima. "How could she wear brown velvet *always*? Brown velvet in the summer—brown velvet for tennis—brown velvet for bathing! Wouldn't a brown velvet swimming suit look *silly*, Mummy?"

"Not at all," said Henry calmly. "Seaweed's brown, and some sorts look exactly like velvet."

"But *Mummy* isn't *sea*weed!" cried Jemima triumphantly. "I do think Henry's too silly sometimes, isn't he, Mummy? I do think for his age Henry's *awfully* silly!"

Were there to be games? they demanded. Music? Dancing? When Christian admitted there were going to be none of these amusements, they allowed it to be seen that they did not think it was going to be much of a party.

"But what are people going to *do*, Mummy? They can't just stand about and talk all the time."

"Grown-up people," pontificated Henry, "never want to do anything but talk and drink. I think it is rather stupid. I'll do you a charade, if you like." A passion for charades had succeeded the passion for literature, and one of the characters in the charade had always to be a minister, to give scope to Henry's gift for the extempore sermon.

"I'm going to sit down for a little while," said Christian suddenly. "You two can play until I call you."

She felt so heavy, and all the morning energy had expired, leaving her limp and listless. She put it down to the weather; she had felt so well since the new baby started—had not even had the morning sickness that was so tiresome before the other two were born. Of course, she had worked herself up about the party; now that the time had come, she felt she must have been mad to think that she could handle a thing like that, without any previous experience. Of the two hundred invitations they had sent out, there had been a hundred and thirty acceptances, many of which bore names which, to Christian, meant no more than a line of advertisement, or gilt letters on a binding. Simon, from his editorial days, and Daniel, through his wanderings "out and about," seemed to know everybody; it was very difficult to limit the invitations to two hundred, but their rooms would not conveniently hold even so many, and she had drawn a breath of relief for each refusal that came along. "Never mind, it will be all over by to-morrow," she comforted herself. If only she felt more like herself—more energetic—less at the mercy of all those formidable intellects which would make hay of her poor attempts at intelligent conversation!

"I'd no idea," murmured Daniel in Lydia's ear, "that women novelists still draped themselves in window curtains. It takes me back to the days when my mother took me to call on Ellen Terry."

"Did she collect novelists?"

"No, I don't think so; but the place was a-wash with

strange pre-Raphaelite relics: you know, djibbehs and amber
beads and lumps of that blue stuff with black streaks in it—
what's its name?—turquoise matrix. Several of these women
only want a string of mothballs round their necks to make
the resemblance perfect."

"Aren't you quarrelling with your bread-and-butter?" said
Lydia, while appreciating the suggestion.

"I loathe bread-and-butter. The nearest I get to it is a
slice of thin toast with Gentlemen's Relish."

"Well, there's Agatha Mott," pointed out Lydia. "I should
think she's got enough flavour for your vitiated palate."

More and more people were shown into the room, which
resounded with voices; there were a few honest, hard-working
writers, slightly stunned by their surroundings, and any
number of sleek young men with divine manners, who danced
attendance upon the more elderly and famous of the writing
set. Most of the young men had written a little book on
interior decoration or some aspects of the ballet, which entitled
them to be coyly secure of their inclusion in such gatherings.
A few tough, elderly women, with square-cut grey fringes,
drove purposefully into corners the more yielding of the
editors and reviewers, to hold them pinned there until they
had accomplished their object. One or two aged, hard-bitten
critics resembled rock pinnacles in their rugged disregard of
attempts made to capture their attention, while agents watched
modestly and anxiously the gambols of their clients, jealously
observant of successes scored by the protégés of rival firms.
Aggressively earnest members of the Left Book Club washed
down their chipolatas with quantities of Franco sherry,
babbling of Nazi enormities. Authors lied seriously and (in
their own opinions) with conviction, about the amount of
their advances and American sales, and publishers, overhearing,
stuck their tongues in their cheeks, and got a very useful idea
of what it would be politic to offer So-and-so on his next novel.
The reputed Queen of the West End stage was consciously
featherheaded on a sofa for the benefit of her admirers, whose

laughter concealed their wincing appreciation of the fact that most of the feathers were dipped in vitriol.

Lydia found her sister temporarily withdrawn from the crowd. Christian's lips were parted, and she was gasping a little, from heat and over-excitement.

"You do look adorable in that brown velvet thing—so fashionable and reassuring!"

"I'm not the only fashionable person here." Christian's eyes strayed over the assembly, with which was mingled a spattering of that section of Mayfair which enjoys coquetting with literature. "Is that Mrs. Reggie Targett? She's got a divine frock."

"New York, darling. She's a paralysing woman: that awful combination of erudition and smartness that leaves a poor, well-intentioned fish like myself grounded and gasping. You know—old Bertie Whipple's girl. You wouldn't think she came from a good home, like us!"

"Do you think they're enjoying themselves?"

"Good God, no. These people don't enjoy themselves. How can they? They're on the stretch all the time, for fear someone says something a little cleverer, makes a ruder remark, attracts more attention than they do themselves."

"Poor Simon. He looks as if he's having a hard time. Who's the girl he's talking to?"

"I can't remember—friend of Daniel's. One of the debs. I expect she's trying to get him to publish her first novel. By the way, I haven't seen your Great White Hope yet!"

"Who do you mean?"

"Who but Mr. Marius Lear? I hope Simon remembers he has me to thank for finding that for him."

"I sent him a card." Christian frowned. "I don't think he looks the sort of person to care much for parties."

"You never can tell," said Lydia wisely. "It's amazing, the effect it has on some people—I mean, getting into the literary swim. Take a look around you: fifty per cent of your guests started out in life as nice, simple creatures, rather despising our frivolous kind—even holding themselves consciously aloof from us. But after discovering that we bought their books, and that our sherry was good, and our houses comfortable—well, it speaks for itself, doesn't it?"

Marius Lear was met, as the door opened, with that roar of conversation that marks the successful party. Sensitive to his ignorance of the conventions, he was conscious of the parlourmaid's quickly averted glance at the shabby tweed overcoat he wore over his ill-fitting dinner-suit. He watched it disappearing into the cloakroom, gave a tug at his cuffs and a hopeless scrape with the fingers to his ungovernable hair, and prepared to keep his word to Simon. Simon had made him promise to come.

"It's the least you can do. We're doing all we can for you, but it's no good if you don't pull your weight. This book of yours isn't to be put over with advertisement; you've got to meet people and make them remember you. It's the only way nowadays for writers of your class."

Only his personal liking for Simon had made Marius agree to a measure so foreign to his tastes and sense of personal dignity. He had, by now, met and, on the whole, disliked Daniel, and it was unfortunate that it was Daniel who happened to be nearest the door when Marius's name was called into the room.

Daniel turned quickly, his expression of somewhat synthetic charm—for he was being pleasant to a man he disliked intensely—changed to a sincerity which was lost upon Marius, who was aware only of the easy grace of Daniel's manner, his distinctive good looks, and the contrast between these qualities and his own appearance.

"Oh, there you are, Lear. We've been waiting for you."

"Who have?" asked Marius abruptly.

Daniel gave his easy laugh and waved a hand vaguely.

"*Le beau monde des arts et de la littèrature*," he said lightly. "Come along; you must meet a lot of people. Let me see." His considering eye swept the nearer groups, wondering which would be the most valuable, from Marius's point of view. "Oh, there's Margaret Greer—you know her work, of course. Margaret!"

Miss Greer turned a pale, powdered face, drooping eyelids and the slightly peevish expression of a female don, in Daniel's direction. She was drinking something straw-coloured out of a glass; Marius thought it looked like cold tea. He muttered some acknowledgment of the introduction, Daniel smiled brilliantly and left them. Miss Greer and her companions, a West End playwright and his novelist wife, stared coldly at Marius, and proceeded to turn their backs upon him.

It did not seem to him unnatural. Why should they be any more interested to meet him than he was to meet them? The name of Margaret Greer conveyed nothing in particular to Marius; he had the smallest possible opinion of contemporary literature and never read reviews; he was therefore untroubled by the knowledge that he had just been snubbed by one who was, not only in her own opinion, but in the opinion, probably, of every person in the room, excepting Marius Lear, the *doyenne* of intellectual fiction.

It was Simon who rescued him from his isolation, thrusting through the crowd to clap him warmly on the shoulder.

"Well, there you are! I want you to meet Alec Ray and Roger Burke. We've been talking about you."

Ray he knew from Simon's accounts to be the most powerful and important of the critics; Burke was a novelist whose superiority over Margaret Greer was a subject of acrimonious argument among their mutual supporters. Feeling like a bear on a chain, he suffered himself to be led by Simon towards the two men, and found them reassuring. Ray was a tall, grave person with longish grey hair which gave him rather a prophetical appearance, and Burke, a big, rubicund, cheerful individual, whose faint air of patronage was so agreeably mitigated by his evident desire to put a nervous new-comer at his ease that Marius was not irritated by it. Simon had evidently paved the way well; they knew about and were interested in his ideas, and plunged almost immediately into a lively discussion upon the revival of classicism in English prose, a topic upon which Marius held strong views.

As Daniel was crossing the room to speak to Lydia, who sat on the fenderstool, looking rather forlorn and surfeited with society, a small foot in a high-heeled brown satin slipper reached out and tripped him. He looked down, to meet the bright, spiteful upward gaze of Agatha Mott, who was sitting on the floor with Cowper Merrill, her chosen *copain* at such gatherings as these.

"Who's your young man with the baggy trousers and the boots?"

Daniel shook at her an admonishing finger. It amused him, at times, to take advantage of the fact that he was probably the only person in the society which she frequented who was not secretly terrified of Agatha Mott.

"Now, Agatha! You're to let our new find alone."

"He looks rather exciting," drawled Agatha. She had a wide, brilliantly red mouth and small, prominent, but pretty teeth.

"He's not at all exciting, and he's far too underdone a morsel for an old, jaded palate like yours."

"I want to know him," she pouted, trying, through the forest of legs, to focus Marius, who was still talking to Simon, Ray and Burke. "Get him away from those three fools and bring him over to me."

"I shall do nothing of the kind; he's not ready for rough games yet. But if you're panting for a change from Merrill, you'd better go and purr your apologies to Aubrey Blandon. He's not forgiven what you wrote about him in *The Athenian.*"

Her expressive lip curled.

"He's dam' lucky I didn't say more. You should be ashamed of yourselves for publishing such muck."

"Nice little sales, Agatha—very nice little sales. Now get up and let me pass, there's a good soul; you can't sprawl about the floor, pretending to be a great schoolgirl, when

everybody knows you're a vicious trollop whose place is in the
bridewell. There's Celia Glynne—go and romp with her; she's
used to your goings-on."

"Imbecile!" said Agatha Mott; but it seemed to be the way
to handle her. She scrambled up and joined Celia Glynne on
the stairs, where the latter was posed, as for her portrait, in
a velvet tippet and muff. She was not very pleased at Agatha's
joining her, because she hoped that Bragg, the cartoonist, was
making notes for a sketch of her, and she did not want Agatha
to be included in the drawing; but it suited her at the moment
to feign a welcome, as she had a new book coming out, and
relied upon Agatha for a suitable notice in *The Athenian*. As
the third volume of Agatha's Victorian trilogy was also due,
and Celia had influence with one of the many societies that
had recently sprung into being for the furtherance of the
literary trade, the two settled down to an amicable
conversation.

In turning away from his own group, Simon came face to
face with Nancy Rowlandson, slim and tailored-looking in a
dark red gown. She gave him a shining smile.

"Your party's a terrific ' go!' After midnight, and nobody
seems to think of leaving."

"Keep an eye on Lear, will you, Nancy? I expect Ray and
Burke will be moving on presently, and I don't want him to
fall into that tigresses' den on the stairs." Simon jerked his
head humorously towards Agatha and Celia, settled in the
silken folds of their petticoats, with bright, predatory eyes
upon the company that seethed below them.

"Don't you think he can look after himself?"

"Not yet. We don't want Agatha to start one of her
poisonous little jokes at his expense—he's so naïve, the first
thing he'd do would give her an opening."

"All right; I'll be the shepherdess of your pet ram,"
promised Nancy. She hung about unobtrusively, until, as
Simon had expected, Ray and Burke bade good-night to Marius,
and left him to say farewell to their hostess.

"Mr. Lear, will you take me to have something to eat? I'm getting ravenous."

"Is there some food?" Marius seemed surprised. "I thought there was only drink."

"There's quite a lot of food in the dining-room, and there's room to sit down. These crowds are awfully overwhelming, aren't they? Let's rest our feet and eat some sandwiches, and I'll tell you who some of the people are, if you like."

"I don't suppose I'll remember if you tell me," mumbled Marius, as he followed her into the dining-room.

"You must cultivate a memory. It's one of the really important things in this racket."

"So you admit it's a racket?"

"Of course it's a racket; but it's quite harmless, so long as one preserves one's detachment. The pity of it is," she added, "that so many people don't. They attach quite a ridiculous importance to affairs like this evening, so that it becomes an obsession, and they end by living for it. Of course, it ruins their work in the end."

"So I should imagine. I think it's poisonous; I shan't go to another."

"I think you're wise." She looked at him consideringly. "After all, there are plenty of ways of meeting the people one wants to—if one can make the time."

"I don't want to meet people. I want to get on with my work."

"You stick to that." She laid a hand impulsively on his arm. "Do you notice what a lot of young men and girls there are here to-night? Poor little fools—they all think they're made if they get a word from Alec Ray or a smile from Margaret Greer."

"That must take a bit of doing," grunted Marius, and told her of his own experience. Nancy grimaced.

"It's like Margaret. I'm afraid she's spoiled. She's easily our best novelist, but every one knows she's a bitch. I suppose it's hard not to be, in an overcrowded profession like ours;

and every one makes an enormous fuss of her, because she's easily the most influential of the reviewers."

"I thought she was a novelist?"

"So is Celia Glynne, so is Agatha Mott; but they all do reviews, and," added Nancy, "I suppose naturally, give their friends the places of honour in their lists. It's only human, isn't it? But it's one of the reasons that unknown writers find it so hard to get a showing nowadays; it's why Mr. Crome was so anxious for you to show up here to-night."

"What a lousy system!"

"I know. I've listened to hundreds of arguments for and against novelists being reviewers as well. It's not a bad thing that a writer's work should be judged by a company of his peers—if one can rely on the judgment being impartial. To be fair, I think it usually is; but there are some glaring examples of back-scratching, of course. You see, for one thing," went on Nancy, "it's much harder to make a living out of writing nowadays than it was ten or fifteen years ago, and a reviewer's salary makes a very welcome little addition to the income of a writer whose sales aren't big enough to keep him, or her, in sufficient comfort by themselves. But you'll find all these things out for yourself as time goes on." She broke off. "I saw you talking to Burke just now. Did you like him?"

"A very sensible fellow, I thought," said Marius, non-committally. She stifled a smile at his refusal to be drawn, pointing out to him a well-known Jewish author and the poet Glover, at whom, knowing his work, Marius looked with interest.

"I'd like to know him—not now: some day. When I can meet him as an equal, on his own ground."

"You're not humble, are you?" asked Nancy, doubtfully.

"Not really. Actually, I suppose it's a sort of inverted vanity that makes me not like meeting people who I feel are my superiors."

"Here's Prudence Thrale!"

A massive lady entered, escorted by three young men. Her

progress was reminiscent of an enormous liner coming into dock; as she anchored beside the table there was a perceptible displacement of currents. The young men hovering about her like cast-off tugs, she turned a beamingly benignant smile upon the rest of the company.

"Shall I introduce you?" whispered Nancy.

"God forbid. Who is she?"

"I told you—Prudence Thrale. Don't you know *anything* about your contemporaries? She's a grand historian, and she's just published a huge novel of the Georgian period——"

"People who write historical novels should be indicted," said Marius firmly. "The historical novel panders to the half-baked public that won't read history unless it's served up with fictional trimmings."

He had spoken loudly; Nancy hastily interposed herself between him and a baleful glitter which had come into Prudence Thrale's eye. Simon's pet ram was going to be hard to look after!

"Well, what do you think of your first literary party?" she asked him, a little later.

The answer was slow in coming; she repeated her question.

"Do you really want to know?"

"Of course I do."

"Well, it's been interesting in a way, but I'm bitterly disappointed."

"In what?" She was startled.

"I suppose I had the naïve ideas of how celebrated people behaved and talked when they got together. After all, I don't see why they should be naïve," he defended himself, although she had not spoken. "After all, if people have achieved certain things, you expect more of them than you do of the ordinary individual. Do you suppose that a party with Byron, or Tom Moore, or Thackeray in it was as stinkingly dull as we've been to-night?"

She was silent for a moment, frowning at his childishness.

"How do you know it wasn't? It's easy to endow the past

with glamour but I thought only children or hopelessly simple people did it. As a race, we aren't noted for our conversational powers; I'll admit that by comparison with a nineteenth century *salon*, to-night's been pretty deadly. But I don't suppose the standard's any worse than you will find in any similar gathering in any part of the country to-day. You haven't," she could not refrain from throwing at him, "made any very notable contribution yourself, so far as I'm aware!"

"I know I haven't." To her relief, he took the accusation in good part. "It stifles me! Except for the few minutes with Ray and Burke, I haven't heard one remark of value, of interest, of simplicity or un-selfconsciousness since I came in. There's surely something wrong there?"

"You expect too much," said Nancy, lowering her voice. "You forget that, on occasions like these, it's very difficult for people to be natural. They have a feeling of being on show, they're anxious for their own reputations——"

"That's exactly what I mean! Do you know the feeling I get from listening to and watching all this? That if these people were more sure of themselves they would not be so artificial. Half of them, at least, are conscious all the time of being humbugs——"

"Is a humbug ever conscious?" she questioned lightly. "If so, I don't quite see how the humbug comes in. The real humbug starts by fooling himself. . . . I dare say a few of them manage to do that, but not more, surely, than in other classes of society."

"People who set out, as these do, to lead the public with their writings, have no business to be humbugs; they're betraying their own art."

Nancy looked at him for a moment.

"I can't quite make out if you're a prig or a crusader," she said. "Do you see what the time is? Simon and Christian look as though they're longing to get rid of us. Where have you to get to?"

"South of the river," he told her carelessly.

"But, my dear man, how are you going to do it—at this hour of the morning?"

"The trams will still be running. What about you?"

"Oh, my flat's down in the city; it won't take me long to get home."

"I suppose I ought to offer to take you," muttered Marius, "but I haven't got the money for a taxi."

"Share mine, and I'll drop you on the Embankment," said Nancy on the spur of the moment.

"Nonsense; it's out of your way."

"Can't I take a bit of a drive if I feel like it?"

"No. You don't feel like it."

"Look here: I'd rather have company than go home by myself. There's something about a lonely taxi that gives me the creeps. If you won't let me take you to the Embankment you can at least drive back with me as far as the Charing Cross Road; it will save you part of the walk."

Daniel and Lydia had found temporary refuge in Simon's study, now deserted.

"Shall I come round to-night?"

"It's our last chance. Anna will be back to-morrow."

"Then I'll be along in about half an hour. Sure it's all right?"

"As all right as it ever was," said Lydia, with a touch of bitterness. "Heaven knows what cook will think of my packing her off night after night to sleep at her sister's; she obviously guesses something, but I suppose she'll be appeased when Anna's back and we return to our usual blameless routine!"

"It's not going to be so much fun for us, is it?"

"Do you mind?" She turned up her thin face, pale with fatigue. He bent lightly, to kiss her lips.

"Of course I mind. You've been an angel—it's been marvellous all along."

"Marvellous enough to make it worth while going on?"

"What do you mean?"

"You're going away in a fortnight, aren't you?"

Their eyes met. He muttered something, and put his hand quickly on her arm. She drew it away, glancing through the open door to where Simon and Christian stood in the hall, still speeding their lingering guests.

"We'll talk about it later. Good-night, Simon. Good-night, Chris darling. It's been a wonderful party, though I feel definitely subnormal, and I don't quite like having so very many lions growling all round me!"

"Well, thank God that's over!"

Simon was undressing, and Christian had gone into the bathroom, leaving the door ajar. He spoke loudly to make her hear.

"The way to get things out of people is certainly to feed 'em! What do you think of this? Margaret Greer's promised me something for our spring list. Not fiction, of course; she's tied up for that. But her *belles-lettres* stuff is nearly as popular as her fiction. Won't it give Old Harry a kick to see her name in our list?"

He paused for Christian's reply.

"Chris! Are you listening?"

He heard her call out: "Simon!" on a note that chilled his blood. He was leaping towards the door when she pushed it towards him from the inside; he heard the latch click.

"Don't come in——" Her voice was muffled by the closed door. "Don't come in, Simon—go—quickly—and fetch Nana."

CHAPTER NINE

When Daniel arrived at the flat, he found to his surprise Lydia standing, fully dressed, as he had left her, in front of the stove. She looked up with a smile as he entered, but made no demonstration of welcome, beyond holding out her hand in a friendly fashion and then dropping it to her side.

"Are you hungry? Do you want anything?"

"Only devilish thirsty. Have you got anything?"

"There's some beer in the refrigerator, and a big bottle of cider—if you prefer it."

"Lady, don't you know you should never ice beer?" asked Daniel, as he returned with the bottle.

"Anna and I like it that way sometimes, when we've come back from a hot party with our eyes full of smoke."

"So Anna comes back to-morrow."

"There was a wire to-night, when I came in to dress."

"So that's the end of our fun."

She made a restless movement.

"I wish you wouldn't call it fun."

"I agree; it's a silly word. A blasphemous word, for all you've done for me. Dear Lydia. Kind Lydia." He pulled her to him with sudden roughness and set his mouth hard on hers. When they separated for want of breath, he added: "I'm going to miss it like hell. That's the worst of all the lovely, stolen things; you can't go on stealing for ever, and when they come to an end it's worse than if you had never known about them. I'll think about them a lot—in Roumania."

"I hate your going off to Roumania," she told him. "I've got an idea you'll do fool things, and drink more than is good for you, and probably meet someone who'll play you up like —like——" The name faded on her lips. How bitterly she had come to hate Eliza Lygon she could not have described;

147

she had been astonished to discover such wells of hatred within her.

"Do you think I'm a complete wrong 'un, then—all through?" asked Daniel. She shrugged her shoulders.

"What is a wrong 'un? If you're one, then I suppose I'm one as well. Why shouldn't you do as you like? It's your business if you ruin your health and—get your heart broken again."

"No, no. That doesn't happen twice. Shall we go to bed? There's not much time for sleep before that god-awful alarum goes off in my left ear." Setting down the empty glass, Daniel delivered himself of a long, exaggerated yawn, and came out of it to find her looking at him in a tender, almost a motherly fashion that pricked his none-too-sensitive conscience a little. "Lydia, how divine you look to-night. You've got something about you that simply tears the heart out of one's body. I can't believe I'm your first lover——!"

"You should know," she answered simply.

He suddenly flung his arms about her, burying his head in the soft curve of her waist.

"Why can't we be happy together, without consulting any one but ourselves?" he muttered. Presently he lifted his head to ask: "What did you mean by what you said about its being marvellous enough to make it worth while going on?"

"It was only an idea that came into my head. About me going to Paris, when you go to Roumania."

"You going to Paris? You didn't tell me that before."

"I only thought of it to-night. I often run over to Paris about now—to look at clothes and things, and make whoopee with some Americans I know who live in the Quarter and call themselves painters. It's going to be awfully deadly in town, now that we shan't be able to see each other, Daniel; so I thought I might go over——"

"And then——?"

"And then I'd be there, when you go through on your way to Belgrade. We could have a day or two, if you like the idea—"

"If I like the idea! There's nothing I'd like better than a time with you that wasn't limited by that blasted clock. Of course we'll do that. I'll try to get off a day or two earlier, because things are pretty well fixed up, the Belgrade end, and it will mean a frightful to-do if I alter the date of my arrival——"

"You think it's not too risky? We mustn't mess things up, must we, because of El—Eliza."

"I'll take dam' good care we don't. Besides, I'd loathe to get you into any sort of a mess."

"I'd loathe it too, darling! But honestly, there's not the least fear, so far as I'm concerned. I wouldn't have suggested it, if there had been."

She stood there droopingly, looking into the scarlet bars of the stove as though she were regretting the lack of danger; her lips had curved into a wistful line, and the wide satin folds of her full skirt seemed to drag downwards from the tight bodice with an inexpressible effect of mourning. Rising quickly—he had flung himself on the couch—Daniel slipped the narrow bands of material from her shoulders, and laid his lips to the soft hollow in front of the armpit on either side; then he proceeded, with gentle deftness, to unhook the bodice. The dress slid, in flakes of reflected light, below the waist, the knees, to crumple about her ankles. Then he finished undressing Lydia.

At some wakeful hour of the night, with Daniel's breathing soft, even and peaceful at her side, the foolish tears of utter loneliness flooded her eyes.

Some people would call it insanity, after staying a virgin all these years, to part with their virginity under circumstances like these! I suppose I should have waited until I knew Daniel really was in love with me, before giving myself to him the way I have. Oh, to hell with waiting. I gave him what he wanted, when he wanted it, because I love him, and there's no other way, if you love the way I love Daniel. Christian and Simon. Christian adores Simon; she talks sometimes as if she'd got the monopoly of love. But she'd never have done for Simon what I've done for Daniel. She isn't made that way. There's a kind of shutter that closes down between her and all the things that aren't supposed to be "correct," according to the law and the Church and the way we were both brought up. Perhaps that's why she's so happy. That, and being able to trust Simon; knowing that he loves her as well, that he'd sacrifice anything and anybody to make her happy.

Moving cautiously, so as not to disturb her companion, she slid down again under the sheets, and pressed her burning face into the pillows. Love, trust, companionship—Christian had them all; while she had nothing—nothing but her foolish love!

Christian's miscarriage swept the earth from under Simon's feet for the succeeding twenty-four hours. Although the doctor assured him it was not unduly serious, and only meant lying up for a fortnight or so, and some care, until her system recovered from the shock, he was demoralized by the sudden and sweeping realization of how vital a part of his life she stood for, so that her suffering became his, and he looked, as Christian told him, laughing weakly, as if it had been he, and not she, who had gone through the unhappy experience.

"Look here," said the doctor, who called later in the day, to see how the patient was getting on, "I suppose you realize you're in a worse state than your wife? Why don't you both take a holiday? You're obviously burning the candle at both ends."

Simon explained that it was impossible for him to leave town; that, by the time Christian was fit to travel, Daniel would have gone abroad, and all the business of the firm would rest upon his shoulders.

Daniel, when he heard about it, was most considerate, and instantly offered to cancel the Roumanian trip. This, however, Simon would not hear of. Apart from the fact that all the arrangements were made, it was as well to separate Daniel and Lydia for the present; he felt that, although he might manage to handle Old Harry over the divorce, it would take a superman to deal with him if any chit-chat about Lydia and Daniel came to his ears.

It was arranged that, as soon as Christian was well enough to move about, she should go down to the coast with the nurse who at present was looking after her, and the children, with Nana and the governess, were to go down to Granedge—a prospect which filled them with glee. They both adored the pomp and circumstance of their grandparents' home, the freedom of the park, the expeditions to the works, to which their grandfather always insisted upon taking them, proudly showing off Henry as the future master; and they were now old enough to appreciate the advantages of living in an environment which, by its very existence, paid tribute to the name of Matlock. They loved having hats touched to them, and notice taken of them whenever they went out, and invariably returned somewhat the worse for wear—with ideas about their own importance which were quickly taken out of them by Nana, in the wholesome, corrective atmosphere of the Crome nursery. Christian hoped that the attendance of Nana on the present occasion—she was usually sent on holiday when the children went to Granedge—would do something to counteract the spoiling of the grandparents.

It was two or three days before the departure of Daniel that Nancy Rowlandson came down to Simon and laid down an ultimatum.

"If you don't take a rest, Mr. Crome, while you've got the chance, I shall throw in my hand."

He seldom lost his temper with Nancy, but her suggestion, coming at such a time, seemed wholly irrational.

"Don't be a fool!" he snapped at her. "The work has to be done, hasn't it? And there'll be more when Daniel has gone."

It was surprising, indeed, how much he was going to miss Daniel, who, since he pulled himself together, had shown more intelligent interest in the business than he had done since the beginning of their partnership. He had the great gift of getting through an immense amount of work, while pretending to do nothing, and for several weeks had practically dealt single handed with the publicity department, whose former organizer had fallen to bribery from another firm, and left them stranded, just at the moment when the Aldebarans were being launched on the market. With no previous training in publicity, but a very astute sense of what catches the public eye, Daniel, with Nancy's help, had concocted a series of slogans which, reproduced in the three-colour process, were willingly accepted by the booksellers for their window displays. He had also relieved Simon of much of the firm's correspondence—no small consideration; and it had to be admitted that Daniel's epistolary style, although far from orthodox, brought forth a response that was lacking to Simon's short, dry notes.

"Exactly," said Nancy, to Simon's comment on the future. "And it will be grand for everybody, won't it, when you crack up, and I have to carry on by myself?"

"You know as much about the work as I do," muttered Simon.

"Thanks; but I don't seem to fancy the prospect. What I really came to suggest was, that we should get someone in as a stop-gap while Mr. Lygon's away."

Simon stared at her as if she had gone mad.

"Do you mean in Daniel's place? It's not usual to fill in with a vice-partner when one goes away on business."

She shook her head patiently.

"Haven't we fixed that Miss Thomas and I are to split Mr. Lygon's work between us? That's to say, the routine stuff, that actually goes on here, in the office. But we seem to have overlooked the fact that my ordinary work remains to be done, and, with the best will in the world, I don't think I shall be able to keep up with that and the extra stuff as well. I suppose you realize that we've got nearly three times as much business in hand as we were doing before Christmas?" she added, with a note of pride in her voice which showed Simon how completely Nancy Rowlandson identified herself with the interests of the firm.

"We'll have to increase the staff, at this rate," he smiled at her.

"Yes, but we don't want to get new people in haphazard," she said hastily. "It pays to be particular, in our job. The suggestion I was about to make"—she paused; Simon, looking up quickly, saw, to his astonishment, a faint glow of colour in her usually colourless cheeks.

"What the devil are you blushing at, Nancy? Get on."

"I'm not blushing! I only wondered whether you'd care to take Mr. Lear, on trial? I believe he'd be very good indeed. He's genuinely interested in book production."

"By George," said Simon. "That's a whale of an idea. But do you know if he's free? Doesn't he teach, or something?"

"The term finishes next week," said Nancy. "I think he'd be very glad of the chance; he's very short of money."

"I must let him have his advance," muttered Simon. "Well, you seem to know a lot about Marius Lear! What do you suppose he could do?"

"I should try him on the secretarial," was the prompt reply. "He says he knows shorthand, though he hasn't got much of a speed; I should think he could manage your letters —you aren't a quick dictator. Of course he can type, and he's got an extraordinary memory for detail and a fairly good mind for organization. I should think he'd train up quite well."

"So you're proposing to resign your post in favour of Marius Lear! How on earth do you come to know so much about him?"

"We've met a good many times in the office—he turned in the report on that German book on decoration in record time, by the way; it's waiting for you when you have time to look at it, but I don't think it's anything special: no better, at any rate, than our own writers can do. And I asked him to have

tea with me last Sunday," concluded Nancy, on a note of
defiance which so amused Simon that he laughed outright.

"Well, you needn't get so annoyed about it. I should
think he was awfully pleased; I don't suppose he meets many
of his own kind in the course of his profession. Do you like
him?"

"Very much."

"So do I. You might drop him a line, to come in and talk
it over. I suppose you didn't tell him you were going to
make this suggestion to me?"

"What do you take me for?"

"All right, all right. How touchy you are this afternoon!
By the way, did you say his term ends next week?"

"Yes; on Friday."

"I suppose that means they're all breaking up—for Easter.
What about Dennis?"

Nancy's colour faded.

"I've arranged for him to stay at school for the holidays;
he won't be alone—several of the children whose parents are
abroad stay there as well. They'll have quite a good time."

"That's bad, Nancy! For you, I mean."

"Well, it's not so bad for Dennis as hanging about the flat
all day, while I'm at work."

"I wish I could give you your holidays now."

"That's all right." She gave him her bright smile. "It's
all in the day's work. It's good for Dennis to learn that, while
he's little."

"Look here: why shouldn't he go down to Granedge with
Henry and Jemima?"

"Well—why should he? I don't know the Matlocks—at
least, not in that way——"

"Leave it to me; I'll fix it."

"You are thoughtful. Dennis will nearly blow up with
gratitude. I—I'm nearly blowing up myself," stammered
Nancy.

Lydia went to see Christian in the afternoon; she felt ashamed and guilty, because she knew she should have offered to go with her sister to Littlehampton, and also had a shrewd idea that Christian had guessed why the offer was not forth-coming. But she had put off her visit to Paris for nearly ten days, and did not want to leave England at the same time as Daniel, for fear of its being too obvious.

Christian looked very well and pretty, lying flat in bed, with the new library books, a box of chocolates and one of Simon's typescripts scattered about the eiderdown. The contrast of her sister's life with her own filled Lydia for a moment with bitter envy, and she turned quickly away, to hide an irrational gush of tears. What had Christian done, always to be beloved and sheltered: married to the only man she had ever cared about, and mother of two children who idolized and were idolized by her?

"That suit looks good, Lydia!"

"I expect it'll look punk in Paris." Lydia had hastily, under pretext of powdering herself, dashed away her tears. "It is time I got some new things; I wish you were coming to help me choose them." She did not, as she said it, quite manage to meet Christian's eyes, feeling lest she should read there recognition of her own hypocrisy. "Gosh, who brought you the lavish chocolates? They don't look like Simon, somehow."

"Father came in, just before lunch. Have one; I daren't touch them—lying here and taking no exercise! I don't even let myself wonder what I'll look like when I put my clothes on again."

"You're getting better, aren't you, Chris?"

"Of course I am. I feed like a fighting cock, and sleep like a log; it's sheer affectation, keeping me flat like this, day after day."

"I'm glad; I should have hated to go away, leaving you ill."

"I've not been ill; only my silly inside, that got slack, or something. When do you go?"

"To-morrow morning. It's awfully boring in town just now. I hope it's better in Paris."

"Don't take any notice of Father if he's a bit short with you."

"Why, what about?" asked Lydia.

"He and Mummy have some silly idea you might have come away with me. I said it wouldn't have been much fun for either of us—you'd have wanted to do things, and wouldn't have done them because of me, and I'd have been peevish, wanting to do them, and feeling I was keeping you from having a good time."

"I shouldn't think there's much good time to be had now at Littlehampton; it's too cold for bathing."

"And think how bored we'd have been, crawling along the sea front and resting every few yards! I don't care with nurse —she's paid to crawl; but we both hate walking slowly, and we'd have got so low-spirited!" Christian broke off to laugh. Lydia thought: "Is it possible she doesn't know I'm going to Paris to meet Daniel?"

"I might run down for a day or two when I come back, if you are still there; you'll be better by then, and we shan't need to crawl so much."

"I wish you would! Father said he'd come down, but he's not such good company just now—poor darling; he can't talk about anything but Daniel's divorce."

Lydia walked about restlessly.

"Why on earth there's so much fuss about Daniel's divorce I can't imagine! It's nobody's business, except his—and Eliza's."

"Well, you know what Daddy is. Things like divorce, and birth-control, and sex novels—they're red rags to a bull. I think myself Daniel might have kept his affairs to himself, until it was over. It's so hard on Simon."

"You can't keep a divorce to yourself," snapped Lydia.

The telephone purred while Nancy and Simon were

together, and she leaned forward and lifted the receiver. With her hand over the mouthpiece:

"It's Mrs. Lygon," she said.

"Hell fire! She can't want me. The call's for Daniel."

"It's not a call; she's downstairs in the office. They've just rung up from the desk."

"Where's Daniel?"

"I think he's gone down to the passport office about his visa. I can find out from Miss Thomas."

Daniel was not in his room, and Miss Thomas was not sure if he meant to come in again that afternoon.

A few minutes later, Eliza Lygon stood in the doorway. She was tall and as thin as it was possible for any living creature to be, her thinness exaggerated by the black tailor-made she wore. She carried her hat and a pair of gloves in her hand, and a great, belligerent crest of hair, burnished to the redness of copper, was flung back from a brow as broad and noble as the lower part of her face was mean. The short black lashes that fringed her eyes of sea-green lent her face a strange, painted look, like the funerary portraits on Egyptian coffins. People who disliked her said that Eliza looked cheaply theatrical; the others raved about her "distinction."

"Good-afternoon, Eliza," said Simon coolly.

She ignored the greeting.

"Look here. You've got to get Daniel to call this divorce off."

"I've told you once, Eliza, that I've got no influence whatever with Daniel, and you must arrange your own affairs between yourselves."

"It's no use saying that, if he won't see me."

"Well, write, or telephone him."

"He sends back my letters unopened, and when he hears my voice he hangs up," said Eliza sullenly. "That's a nice way to treat your wife. I say, that's a hell of a nice way to treat your——"

"It's no business of mine how Daniel treats you. I suppose

you knew what his behaviour was like when you married him."

She sat down on Daniel's favourite corner of the fenderstool, swinging one leg across the other; round her left ankle, under the stocking as thin as a cobweb, she wore a narrow anklet of gold. Simon saw that the only other jewellery she was wearing was her wedding ring.

"Well, he's got to call it off, or name another co-respondent. I won't have Gavin dragged into this."

"It's a pity you didn't think of that, both of you, before."

"Yes, you would be self-righteous," she sneered at him.

"Well, have you come to offer an understudy to Daniel's co-respondent?" There was one thing about Eliza: she absolved one, by her conduct, from most of the decencies.

"I've come to tell him that if he doesn't stop the whole thing, I'll make him—in a way he doesn't like," she said quietly.

"Well, Eliza, it's no affair of mine, and I'd be very much obliged if you'd save this up for Daniel. I'll try to persuade him to see you, if you like—but I must warn you, he won't have much time; he's going abroad the day after to-morrow."

"I know about that; I've got a pretty good tab on Master Daniel!" said Eliza. "And as for it's not being your affair, you may find out it is. Anyhow, it will pay you to hear what I've got to say. You can pass it on to Daniel or not—just as you choose; but I fancy he won't be very pleased if he hears, afterwards, that you knew, and didn't warn him."

"Oh, cut the drama and come down to it, Eliza. What have you got up your sleeve?" asked Simon impatiently.

"If Daniel goes on with this divorce," she said slowly, "I'll cross-suit him."

"Don't be silly. That won't stop the divorce, and you won't gain anything by a lot of muck-raking on both sides."

"Shan't I? Shan't I—if I cite Lydia Matlock?"

"You're crazy," whispered Simon.

She laughed scornfully.

"I've had Daniel watched. He's been seen, going into Lydia Matlock's flat after midnight; and if that's not evidence enough for divorce, the cook's been questioned. She says she's been sent to sleep out, five out of seven nights, since she got back from her holiday."

"What a filthy trick!" said Simon, wondering how Lydia, or Daniel—either of them—could have been so mad . . .

"Any worse than spying on me? I know Daniel; he thinks he's been very clever, finding out about all the people I'm supposed to have had affairs with. But he wasn't quite clever enough to keep his own actions dark until the divorce was through."

"I won't have you say these disgusting things."

"My dear Simon, don't you know that Daniel's any woman's business, providing she's pretty enough? Lydia Matlock's been after him for ages——"

"That's a lie. Will you kindly remember Lydia's my sister-in-law——?"

"That's why I came to you about it." She narrowed her cats' eyes at him and smiled. "You aren't having any too good a time with Old Harry, are you, over our divorce? Well, it's nothing to what you'll have, if I bring Lydia Matlock into it."

"Well, if you've finished what you've come to say, Eliza, you may as well get out. I'll tell Daniel, of course, and I hope he'll find his own way of taking it out of you."

"Thanks very much," she mocked him as she rose. "You might tell him also that if he doesn't put a stop to this before he goes abroad, I'll instruct my own solicitors to get on with it."

"Stop a minute," said Simon. She stood where she was, turning her head on its long neck insolently across her shoulder; she was wearing a white scarf that looked like a stock, and the red of her hair, which came nearly to her shoulders, the black of her coat and the high white bandage under her chin made her into a magazine cover. He had the ludicrous sensation of playing a part in a cheap short-story. "What's it all about, Eliza? You may as well come clean—you've got no credit to lose—with me!"

"You always loathed me, didn't you?" Her lips curled, as if she drew some obscure gratification, even from Simon's dislike. Recognizing the fact, he thought, Yes: there are women like that—women who don't care what emotion they rouse, so long as it's an emotion. He did his best to cheat her of her satisfaction.

"I never particularly thought about you."

Her smile broadened. As though any one could help thinking about Eliza Lygon! Practically in her perambulator she had aroused either adoration or hatred, just by lowering the lashes over her odd, green eyes.

"You aren't doing this on account of Gavin Trufitt!" stabbed Simon.

"Why not? He's my lover, and he's in the diplomatic; and it will ruin him if Daniel drags his name into the court."

"And a lot you care. You aren't doing this to save Trufitt, but to spite Daniel, and to get back on Lydia, for succeeding where you've failed."

"What do you mean by failing?" She gazed at him with genuine astonishment. "If you mean Daniel's fallen out of love with me, and in love with the Matlock girl, you must be insane. He's crazy about me."

"Then you ought to be ashamed to treat him the way you do."

"Supposing you mind your own business? I could have Daniel back to-morrow, if I liked," she boasted.

"I'd like to see you try."

"I might, if he gives up this idiotic divorce, and gives up the Matlock."

"Do you come in anywhere on this 'giving up' programme? Do you give up Trufitt—and the rest?"

She looked at him coldly.

"I didn't come in here to discuss Daniel's or my future with you. Will you please give him my message, and say I'll wait until dinner-time for his answer?"

When Daniel was told about it, he first applied an unprintable epithet to Eliza, and then swore there wasn't a word of truth in it.

"You needn't trouble to play the fine old English gentleman," said Simon wearily. "She's had the pair of you watched."

"The hell she has!"

"How on earth," Simon bitterly commented, "you came to be such a blithering fool—or Lydia either—passes my comprehension. You knew Eliza didn't want the divorce, and you might have guessed she'd do all in her power to scotch it."

"I've got a good mind," said Daniel, chewing his thumb, "to let her carry on, and ask for the discretion of the court."

"Oh, yes? That'll go with a swing on the President. It'll be marvellous for Lydia, and, of course, Old Harry will be delighted. I shouldn't wonder if he put an extra couple of thousand into the firm, on the strength of his daughter's seduction by the junior partner."

"Sarcastic, are we?" Daniel arched his eyebrows. "There are moments, Simon, when it would give me the greatest possible pleasure to slap your face. Just because your own affairs are all what they call ' open and aboveboard ', and you don't happen to have put a foot wrong since you left your stinking little public school, you think you're entitled to your smug superiority——!"

"That's a lousy thing to say, when you know I've taken your side all along about Eliza——"

"It didn't cost you anything, did it?"

Disgusted, Simon began to pile his papers together. Daniel found and lit a cigarette.

"I think you're right, all the same, about her motive," he went on, as though he had not previously insulted his partner. "The Trufitt stuff is a blind. Eliza doesn't want a divorce, because it suits her to be a married woman; it gives her a background and a kick each time she goes over the rails with some poor fish who imagines, for the moment, that she's as

F

mad about him as he is about her; and it provides her with a graceful means of escape when she's got tired of the game. Can you see any good reason why I should continue to be a bolt-hole for Eliza?"

"None whatever. In fact, I'm not interested in Eliza. I'm not even," said Simon coolly, "deeply interested in you. It's Lydia I mind about; Lydia—and the god-awful situation there is going to be with the Matlocks if this gets about." He leaned back in his chair and closed his eyes. "You've certainly got us beat, when it comes to pure egoism, and indifference to other people's welfare."

"I wish it hadn't been Lydia," said Daniel, in a low voice. "Lydia's a nice girl, and it's a damned shame."

"I'm glad you own it."

"Eliza'll give her hell. She's always given girls hell."

"Any girls, or just the ones you've had to do with?" inquired Simon pointedly.

Daniel gave a sharp sigh.

"I suppose Old Harry'll smash us."

"I don't quite see how, without dropping a lot of money; but I don't doubt he'll have a jolly good try."

"And I'll drop my five thousand and you—I suppose you'll be in the cart as well?"

"Well in. Charming for Chris and the children, isn't it?" He leaned forward, bringing his fist down heavily on the desk. "You god-damned fool, Daniel! What did you want to go and do this for? I hope you pay with all you've got for your infernal selfishness—just as I'll have to pay for my own folly in taking a chap like you into partnership."

"Hold on," said Daniel. "There's no need to start cursing and swearing over something that hasn't happened. I'll chuck the divorce, of course."

"And blame me for the rest of your life, for doing you out of your freedom, I suppose."

"One never knows; Eliza herself may get sick of me one day."

"It seems to me more important you should get sick of Eliza."

"That's all right. I'm sick of Eliza." He got up, went to the cabinet in which the drinks were kept, and mixed himself a formidable dose. "If it wasn't for one thing," he said, as he set down an empty glass, "I'd go right ahead. Yes, I'd sacrifice myself, and you, and let Old Harry stew in his own juice. I can imagine myself being perfectly ruthless—if I was in love with Lydia Matlock."

"You positively enjoy making yourself out a cad, don't you?" said Simon bitterly.

"It depends on what you call a cad. Maybe it's caddish to take all that I've had from Lydia, and not stand up to it. Maybe it would be more caddish to involve us in a divorce which might or might not end in freedom for myself and Eliza: and then marry a girl I'm not in love with, by way of straightening things out. But I happen to be too fond of Lydia to choose that line of country. Lydia's a nice girl. She's a dear girl. She's worth something better than to be married —out of politeness."

"Even if she'd rather have it that way, than not at all?"
Daniel nodded.

"Yes. It wouldn't be so bad if she didn't happen to be in love with me," he said simply.

"Poor kid. What the hell did you want to play about with Lydia for, if you didn't care for her?"

"Oh, be your age," drawled Daniel

"It would be a rotten thing to do with a stranger; but with Lydia—so close to all of us—such a nice person——"

"You needn't rub it in. The devil of it is, I do care about her—tremendously—in a way. But it isn't her way. She knows that herself."

"Doesn't she want you to marry her?"

"Blast you, of course she does."

"Then I should have thought your course was plain enough."

"You're an odd bird, Simon," said Daniel reflectively. "Full of all the virtues, and just about as imaginative as a cock sparrow. One has to put things into words of one syllable for you."

"I don't see who you are, to decide what is best for Lydia's happiness," scowled Simon.

"Perhaps not. But perhaps I know Lydia too well—perhaps I've got too much regard for that queer, childish idealism of hers, to bring her Eliza's leavings," said Daniel quietly.

"That sounds very good, Daniel. You might have thought of it, all the same, before you started playing about with her."

"I agree. But you might do me the justice to admit that young women of Lydia's age are supposed to know the rules of the game."

That was true enough, Simon thought. No doubt, Daniel and Lydia were equally to blame, when one talked about "blame" in an affair of this sort.

"It's a rum thing. But I've never been ' that way ' about a woman since I married Christian. I suppose that's luck."

"I'll say it's luck," was the grim rejoinder.

"Well—I suppose you'll ring up Eliza?"

"I'll send her a note; I don't seem to have a taste for Eliza's conversation, just now."

Simon allowed himself a breath of relief after Daniel had gone. So that cleared out the divorce—which meant peace with Old Harry. Daniel had "withdrawn for private reasons": that would do for the Matlocks. But would it satisfy Christian? They were so used to being wholly in each other's confidence that she would inevitably sense that he was withholding something from her, and then it would all come out—about Lydia. Christian would be heartbroken. Poor, silly Lydia! She was in for the very devil of a time. With Eliza on their heels, the lovers could risk no further meetings; her malicious tongue would set up a scandal that would burn up London, and would, in time, almost inevitably penetrate even to the Matlocks' circles. Lydia could not possibly be such a fool to risk her allowance from Old Harry, and the conclusion of her independent life.

After leaving Christian, Lydia took herself to a cinema, largely for the sake of sitting in the dark and surrendering to emotions which discretion and self-respect obliged her to conceal in public. She had already seen *Carnet de Bal*, but as she bought her seat, she felt that the effect of following once more this poignant record of withered romance might be an astringent one: that the rustling of lovers' vows, like dead leaves, through the air of the valse would serve to remind her how transitory such loves must be, and that the time might come when she had outlived her love for Daniel, and would be able to look back upon it with the calm sentimentality that one feels in reading an old love-story.

For she was desperately in love with Daniel, and, true child of her age, had not the faintest glimmer of optimism about its outcome. All that mattered was to take all that one could get of the bitter-sweetness of the present, and let the future take care of itself. It would be marvellous in Paris . . .

"Goodness," said Anne, when Lydia walked in. "You do look a wreck! Where have you been?"

"Studio One—gorging myself with tragedy."

"So it appears. I don't want to be cattish, darling, but tragedy's rather attractive in small doses. An overdose is damned unbecoming."

"I'll have got over it by morning," said Lydia, flinging her gloves on the bed.

"Meaning, that you're not going out to-night?"

"I've got my packing to do; I'll have something on a tray."

"That reminds me. I think we'll have to get rid of cook."

"What's she done?"

"I don't know what you've been up to while I was away," said Anna, "but her manner's grown distinctly fresh. I had to speak to her about singing in the kitchen when I had visitors, and she shrugged her shoulders and more or less insinuated that as we were all girls together, what the hell——? Perhaps you can bring her to her right mind about it."

"Oh, I'll say something if she does it again," muttered Lydia. She also had marked a growing familiarity in the cook's manner, and knew she was to blame for it. For, of course, the woman had known something was going on, when she was sent home to sleep each night. You might say servants are not paid to think, but it does not stop their thinking; and her attitude to Lydia during the last fortnight had plainly shown that she was aware her mistress had gone in for the gay life. Lydia was afraid to dismiss her for fear of something coming out; that was what almost always happened, when you sacked a servant—things came out, and Lydia knew she dared not face the risk. "Any messages?" she asked, to change the subject.

"Some man rang up, about five minutes ago. He wouldn't leave a message; he said he'd ring later."

Daniel!

"Didn't you know who it was?"

"No—none of my crowd," said Anna carelessly. Once more Lydia had cause to bless her divine incuriosity about other people's affairs. "I'll give you a hand with your packing if you like; I'm not going out until later."

"There's hardly anything to do," said Lydia. "I think I'll have a little lie-down, and you might tell cook to do me a boiled egg." She felt ashamed as she said it, of not wanting to face the cook, and went to her room, while Anna, secure in her innocence, pulled a face and rang the bell. Through open doors she heard Anna's coldly given order, and the woman's jaunty "O.K.!" Lydia's ears burned; the creature would have to go. She had been so punctilious, with her "Yes, madam," and "No, madam." Now, if they were to be treated as if they were a couple of chorus girls——! It was not, thought Miss Matlock, as she softly clicked the latch of her bedroom door, what she was accustomed to.

What had Daniel wanted? Perhaps it was to suggest one of their "accidental" meetings; perhaps he had found some place where they could safely have supper. She must do her face carefully and have a very hot bath. . . .

She had hardly slipped into her dressing-gown and lain down across the bed when the telephone bell rang.

"Hallo."

"Hallo. I rang up before, but you were out."

"Yes, I'd been to a flick." She held the wrist which supported the receiver in her other hand, to steady it.

"Listen. Some rather bad news."

"You aren't coming to Paris." The bottom fell out of one's world, but one's voice remained cool and steady. Weren't women wonderful!

"No—that's all right. Eliza's bitched up the divorce."

"What on earth for?"

"She's found out about us."

"Daniel! You can't mean that—we've been so cautious!"

"Not cautious enough. She's had me watched. She knows I've been with you in the evenings."

"Well—it won't make any difference, will it?"

"I'll tell you about it at the week-end. I'll be over on Friday. You've got the hotel address?"

"Yes, in my purse."

"I'll be there for lunch. Till then—*au revoir*, my sweet!"

She heard him hang up. Her heart was thudding, and all her limbs were trembling. Eliza knew! That meant, if she knew Eliza, that about a hundred other people knew as well. And every day, more and more. . . . All London gossiping about them. . . . To hell with all London. There were three clear days ahead, with Daniel, in Paris.

CHAPTER TEN

After Easter, there was a great fuss about getting Henry off to his preparatory school, in which Jemima—always a liver in the moment—took ardent part. She insisted upon accompanying her mother when Christian went to buy Henry's outfit, and her feverish interest embraced every detail—from the pattern and quality of Henry's new pyjamas to the marking ink chosen to initial his belongings. Henry remained rather superbly aloof from these activities, engaged partly in finishing off his dentistry novel—to which, with a pertinacity that resembled his grandfather's, he had returned, after a short excursus into dramatic interests—and partly in the compilation of a biography of Wynken, the Crome tortoise, sole survivor of a family of three which had been presented to the children while Henry was yet unbreeched. Henry wished to take Wynken to school with him, but had considerately given up the idea for the sake of Jemima, who wept at the thought of parting from him. "After all," said Henry reasonably, "I shall have plenty of other interests, and a girl needs something to keep her busy about the house."

"Henry'll have an awful time at school," said Christian ruefully, "if he comes out with some of what Nana calls his 'old-fashioned sayings '!"

"It'll do him good. You mayn't have noticed it, my dear, but our Henry's got the makings of a first-class prig. I only pray he won't be head of his form this first term; that test they sent seemed to me absurdly easy," said Simon.

"Don't you like your children to be clever?" reproached Christian.

"Not too clever. And Henry's been intolerable since he came back from Granedge. I don't think he'd better go down there in his next holidays."

"Simon! They'll be desperately hurt."

"I know, and I'm sorry; but Henry's my son. His granny makes him into a drawing-room performer, and he comes back patronizing everybody, from us to the window cleaner. Do you know what I found him doing the other day, when the nursery windows were being washed? There was young Henry, sitting at his table, like the lord of creation, waving his pen and ordering the window-cleaner to get out of his light! 'Now, then, my good fellow,' the little brute was saying, 'you've been quite long enough on that job, and I want to get on with my work.' Old Harry's voice to a semi-tone! I fetched him a good-sized clip on the ear——"

"Oh, Simon, I've told you so often not to box the children's ears; it's so dangerous."

"My own have survived plenty of it. I bet that cuff will seem nothing to Henry, by the time he's been shown his place by some of the elder lads at the Manor."

Yet how he adored Henry was brought forcibly home to Simon, when he and Christian and a snivelling Jemima gathered at Victoria to cheer Henry's departure into the new world that would absorb not quite but nearly all of the little boy they had known for nine years. He felt as poignantly as Christian that it would be another Henry who would return to them at the end of his three-month term, and, mentally execrating himself for sentimentality, he joined with her in mourning the end of Henry's childhood.

He was pleased, however, and surprised, to see how well the child showed up, in spite of his seeming fragility, among the mob of little boys in bright blue caps and light grey freize overcoats red cheeked, shrill-voiced and totally indistinguishable, except, presumably, to their parents, who stood, a constrained group, looking on. The new boys were easily recognizable, nervous, with sidelong-glancing eyes; stiff with anxiety not to make themselves in any way conspicuous, avoiding the staring curiosity of the old hands.

Henry bore himself, both Simon and Christian were relieved

to see, without a shade of embarrassment, yet without the
the bumptiousness of which his father had been apprehensive.
Mortified by Jemima's heaving sobs, her scarlet cheeks, which
she kept mopping with a soaked handkerchief, he stood a little
apart from her, his spectacles twinkling intelligently over the
unfamiliar scene. Presently a newsboy came along, wheeling
a barrow.

"Would you like anything to read?" asked Simon.

Henry stepped confidently up to the barrow and reflected.

"I'd like *The Daily Sketch*, please, and you might get me
two copies," he added, as Simon tossed the copper on to the
folded papers.

"Why two?"

"There might be another boy in my carriage who would
like one," said Henry.

Simon winked at Christian.

"He'll be all right. I think the diplomatic service will be
the measure of our Henry," he told her. She laughed, blinking
rapidly her eyes, which were a little too bright.

"What about the works? Father's not likely to spare his
successor to diplomacy." It was a question they often fought
shy of discussing, but Simon felt sure that she was with him,
in his determination that Henry's future should not be sacri-
ficed to Old Harry's sentiments, save with Henry's own
approval. What about Crome and Lygon? It seemed on the
face of it much more likely that his son's tastes would turn
to publishing than to the output of ironmongery.

"It's queer how quickly they find their level—if they've got
any sense of their own," he commented, when they were in
the taxi.

"Henry isn't short of sense!"

"He shouldn't be. I'll let him put me down here." He
rapped on the glass for the driver to stop. "Cheer up, Jemima!
Henry's not gone for ever—and he'll soon be back for half-
term."

"I ought to have let him have Wynken!" the little girl was

sobbing, in an access of compunction for her selfishness. Jemima's tenderheartedness, her bouts of contrition for real or imagined naughtiness, were often a source of embarrassment to her family.

She was being rather an anxiety to them, at that time; she had suddenly taken it into her head to grow enormously, and was a great deal too big and heavy for a child of her age. Her governess gave unsatisfactory reports about her lessons, but agreed that these must be excused, on the score that Jemima was outgrowing her strength. It seemed a strange description, for Jemima was as strong as a young bull, and twice as clumsy. She could push Henry over with the least possible exertion of her muscular young forearm. Christian had stopped the Eurhythmic classes, which were just so many hours of hell for Jemima—who had now added self-consciousness to her other shortcomings—and sent her instead to a gymnastic class, where she did not make quite so bad a showing: although if a line was crooked or failed to "number off" correctly, it was almost always the fault of Jemima Crome. She still, however, when not shadowed by consciousness of her social unwieldiness, had an enchanting nature, and Christian found herself taking more and more pleasure in the child's company.

It was, in fact, only over Jemima that she ever had any differences of opinion with Simon. Simon was a little inclined to be sharp with his daughter, whose clumsiness, gift for dropping and breaking, for slamming doors and generally drawing criticism upon herself, was rather irritating to a man who came home, drained of energy, wanting only peace and quiet in his family. Jemima's very anxiety to oblige made her more nervously prone to create disturbances, and Christian found herself constantly on edge in the defence of her daughter.

She knew that the very best thing for Jemima would be to send her to boarding school, but, knowing how hard pressed Simon was for money, did not care to force the point, although

she and her mother frequently discussed it, and Lady Matlock
had on many occasions urged Christian's acceptance of
Jemima's boarding school fees, which, out of loyalty to Simon,
Christian always refused. She resented, nevertheless, this
sacrifice of Jemima to Simon's pride, and took, guiltily, as
much as she dare, in clothes for Jemima, who outgrew her
frocks with horrifying speed, and, at eleven, cost nearly as
much to dress as Christian herself.

Henry had been at school about a fortnight, when Jemima
went to have tea with a friend; and it was just two or three
days afterwards that Christian was rung up by the mother of
the little girl who had been Jemima's hostess.

"Oh, Mrs. Crome, I'm so sorry to tell you Naomi's got
measles! I thought I'd better let you know, so as to keep your
eye on Jemima."

When told about it, Nana took the robust and old-fashioned
view that all children had to have measles, and it was a pity
that, Henry being at school, they couldn't both have got it over
together. Christian did not take it quite so easily. In nine
cases out of ten, she knew, childish measles could be as trivial
a thing as a cold in the head; but it might turn out a very
nasty, tricky business, leaving horrid effects behind. She
watched Jemima like a lynx, and, sure as fate, on the eve of
the very day when she should have been clear of infection,
the fiery little rash made its appearance on Jemima's plump
white chest.

It was one of those gay April days when even a dull London
square is vibrant with the intimations of spring. Jemima had
not yet been out, for her vitality was still so low that she only
managed to sit up for a couple of hours round about tea-time.
She looked very plain and unattractive, poor child; a great
deal of her hair had come out, and the rest made a stubbly
halo round her pale, puffy little face. She had grown out of
all her clothes while she was in bed, and her big, bony wrists
stuck out of the sleeves of the old dressing-gown which was

to be thrown away as soon as Jemima was well enough to dispense with its use.

She was terribly bored; not interested in reading, and easily tired by the table games that Nana played; tired, even by conversation, when it went on too long, she pined for the change of scene which, as yet, she was not considered strong enough to seek.

Her illness had gone its rather unusually stormy course. She suffered pitifully from ear-ache, and her aching eyes had been bandaged to keep out the light which, if it were totally excluded, meant exclusion of air as well. She was as bad a patient as most energetic little girls are, and needed constant watching to keep her from doing herself harm—either by flinging off her bedclothes or by tearing at the spots which, poor child, tormented her night and day, and, when she was prevented from scratching, made her whimper with irritation. Her temperature chart had resembled a silhouette of the Andes, and she had lost far more of the "too, too solid flesh" than her weakened constitution could stand.

"When's Daniel coming back?" she asked repeatedly. "I want Daniel to come and see me. Why does Daniel have to be away such a long time?"

Christian thought it better not to say that Daniel had returned, and that he had gone down into the country, where he was writing up his Roumanian notes for Simon—the latter not too pleased at this continued furlough, which Daniel had requested since, as he said, "it's pretty hopeless to get anything done in the day-time, and you know what nights are like in London. If I can take a fortnight or three weeks in the country I could practically knock the stuff off at a sitting."

"Well, it's up to you," Simon had said reluctantly. "But don't forget you're pretty badly needed up here."

"By the way," said Daniel. "I've gone back to Green Street."

"You have, have you," said Simon, wondering if Lydia knew of this.

"I saw no point in paying the father-and-mother of a hotel bill, with a perfectly good house for which, whether I use it or not, I've got to pay the rent for another ten years, sitting more or less vacant. As a matter of fact, Eliza and I have agreed to cut it up into a couple of apartments; she'll have the first and I'll have the ground floor, and the servants can fight it out as they like overhead. She's having a front door with a lock fixed at the head of the stairs, and to all intents and purposes we'll lead separate lives."

"I should have thought it would have been more satisfactory if you'd had separate establishments."

"Why? It's not so easy to find the kind of accommodation we want for ourselves, and we both like Green Street. I can't turn her out, and I don't see why I should be turned out myself —so that's the end of it," said Daniel curtly.

"Well, if you want it, I suppose you'd better take another fortnight away from the office. I hope you'll manage to get it done in that time, Daniel, because you're more valuable to us in town than down in the country. I've got awfully out of touch with people while you've been away; there simply hasn't been time for all the gadding round that seems to be expected of one, and I must admit," he added dryly, "that your point that it pays in the long run has proved itself pretty effectually. I'm practically sure we'd have got the Fordyce manuscript if I'd managed to keep that luncheon appointment with old Fordyce that I had to scrap because of rushing off to the courts on the Leverson libel. By the way, I want you to think up something for Marius Lear's book when you come back; that stunt you pulled over the Aldebarans was a great success, and I'm looking to you to help us to put over *Cypriana* with a bang."

"I expect I'll get a brainwave when the time comes," said Daniel negligently.

"When *is* Daniel coming to see me, Mummy?"

"He's got lots of work to do," evaded Christian. "You know he'll come the very first moment he can." She did not feel much like welcoming Daniel, since Simon had told her, as in the end he was obliged to do, about Lydia.

"Then Lydia," whined Jemima, as though the name had echoed from her mother's mind to hers. "Why doesn't Lydia come? I know she's back from that old Paris—and I'm so tired of this old room—and Nana's old silly games—and old everything!"

Lydia might have come, Christian was thinking. She always professed to be so fond of the children, but she had hardly been to the house since her return from Paris. When she came her manner was nervous and evasive; she talked and laughed a great deal, but said little about her Paris trip. And not a word about Daniel. It made their conversation so difficult. They had never had secrets from one another; Christian hated to think that Lydia now had a secret over which she was suffering alone.

"Mummy, why can't you ring up Lydia and *tell* her to come?"

Christian had, as a matter of fact, rung up that morning, and had been told by the servant that Miss Matlock was away. She tried with all her power not to connect Lydia's absence from town with Daniel's. Lydia could not possibly be such a fool, since the ultimatum from Eliza, as to risk herself, and all of them, in that way!

They had just finished tea, and Nana had gone for a short walk. One of the maids came up to say that Lady Matlock was on the telephone.

"You're sure it's her ladyship—not Miss Matlock?"

"No, madam; it's her ladyship—speaking from the country."

She would have to answer it; it was Lady Matlock's usual hour for ringing up for the bulletin about Jemima. She rose, looking anxiously at the child, slumped in her chair.

"I must go and speak to Granny. You'll be quite quiet, won't you, until I come back? Have you got a book?"

"I've got this old magazine," grunted Jemima.

"Be a good girl, darling; I'll only be a few minutes."

Alone in the nursery, Jemima let the magazine drop to the floor. Goodness, how sick she was of that old nursery—of the lions and unicorns on the curtains, of the stupid faces of the furniture, of the picture over the mantelpiece of a large red and white cow in a yellow field, with Robert Louis Stevenson's verse printed underneath it: "She gives me cream with all her might To eat with apple tart." Stupid cow, stupid field, stupid verses. Henry's were more exciting than that.

Shining sun, and a bright, light blue sky—Cambridge colour. How lovely it must be in the Gardens! If only they let her go out she knew she would be better at once. Old Fusspot of a Nana—and everybody paid as much attention to her as if she were God! Even Daddy and Mummy listened to her, and did as she told them, just as if they were children and Nana was told to look after them. Nana said who could come, and sent away visitors if they stayed too long—generally just as one was enjoying oneself very much indeed; and it was Nana who had said, "As soon as we have a nice, mild day, we'll see what a little toddle will do." What was to-day but nice and mild?

Jemima stood up impatiently, the blanket Nana had insisted upon packing round her knees sliding to the ground; her knees —that felt so funny. No wonder they felt funny; what could you expect, when they never got used? She suddenly remembered the gym lesson—the jumping stands and the lovely springboard on which one stamped very hard and went bouncing over the rope. Naomi was there now—she had had measles very lightly, and was back at school as soon as she was out of quarantine. Naomi, who always wobbled when she walked along the bar, and Miss Trimmer had to hold her hand—Jemima never had her hand held, not even when she nearly fell off. Perhaps, for the first time or two, after going back, it might be wise to hold Miss Trimmer's hand. The floor waved about oddly—not quite so badly as a week ago, when she got up for the first time, but enough to make one feel as though one was at sea, in a very small boat that bumped over every wave.

Jemima went to the window and peered wistfully into the square. Nothing very exciting ever happened in the square; there was a notice forbidding street music, and all the odd things which might have enlivened the outlook, but it gave one a kind of thrill, after all that time in bed, to see people walking about, the world going on just the same as though Jemima Crome had never had measles and nearly died! She was convinced that she had nearly died; no one could feel as bad as that and not be near death. She had felt so bad that she had not even made her will, a business to which she and Henry were addicted every time they had a little cold and a temperature and spent a day in bed. She remembered worrying about the last will, which was somewhere about, in which she had left things to Nana, and to all the servants, and to several of the girls at the gym class—because, of course, if she died now, she wanted to leave everything to Henry. But perhaps the last will had been destroyed; Nana had a way of picking up odd bits of paper and tearing them into slips for book-markers in the *Tatlers* and *Sketches* she was unendingly reading.

Jemima watched two dogs sniffling along the railings; one was a Pekinese—it must have escaped out of one of the houses, perhaps number eleven. They kept on the opposite side of the square, which was bright and sunny; the near side, Jemima's side, was in shadow, and the shadow extended nearly half-way across the square in a solid block of purplish grey. The Pekinese's hair was all ruffled forward, which made it look like a feather duster.

Suddenly, in the inconsequent fashion of dogs, the pair made a dash across the square. They were now on Jemima's side, right beneath her, and she could not see them. The only living, moving things in the square, and they had moved out of sight; the loss was intolerable. She craned her neck, but from the closed, third-floor windows it was quite impossible to see the near pavement. A sudden burst of weak resentment filled her eyes with tears and flushed her cheeks. Stupid old Nana, with her continual: "Keep out of the draught," and "Don't you go near that open window!" As though an open window could do one any harm, on a day when the sun was shining and dogs were playing along the railings.

Exerting the whole of her strength, Jemima flung up the sash and leaned out. The sudden rush of air made her gasp and cling tightly to the sill; she closed her eyes, opened her mouth and felt the sweet taste of the air on her tongue. Lovely, lovely; so cool, after stuffing up against the fire all the afternoon.

She leaned ecstatically on the sill, no longer thinking about the dogs, but of how lovely it was at last to feel the fresh air blowing softly in her face and down the open neck of her jersey. Fresh—and the least bit cold. Not really cold, of course, only cold because one had been in a stupid, stuffy room for so long. "Why, I was simply sweatin'!" said Jemima aloud, as she hugged her breast with her arms. She lifted them up presently to cool her armpits, and to her own surprise, gave a tiny shiver. It was almost a voluptuous shiver; she told herself it was lovely to shiver, after being hot for all those weeks. Presently she coughed: just one, short, husky bark.

Hearing the approach of footsteps, Jemima hastily shut the window, less from deceitfulness than from the desire to avoid the wearisome argument which experience had taught her invariably succeeded any attempt on her part to evade the "fussiness" of Nana. When Christian returned, she was again sitting by the fire, with her nose buried in the rejected magazine. As she opened her mouth to answer her mother's first question, the cough took her again, this time more purposefully, more painfully. Jemima avoided her mother's anxious look with a feeling of guilt.

At night it was pleurisy, and, by morning, pneumonia. Simon and Christian held hands, and watched darkness thin into dawn, and the electric light grow pale, across Jemima's little bed.

Marius answered the telephone when Simon rang up the office.

"You'll have to carry on as best you can . . ."

"That's all right," came Marius's steadying voice. "I don't think there's anything special in this morning; if anything turns up, I'll run round with it at lunch time."

"Is Mrs. Rowlandson there?"

"Yes; do you want to speak to her?"

"No—let her know the way things are."

"I will. Could either of us be of use, if we came along now?"

"I don't think so, thank you, old man."

Simon thought, as he rang off, how quickly Marius had slipped into his place in the office. A fortnight after he came shambling in, very sullen and dubious about his capacity for fulfilling his new duties, it seemed to Simon as if he had always been there, like a shaggy, half-bred retriever whose place is always at his master's heel: often in the way, occasionally kicked and sworn at, but painfully missed when absent.

Carefully coached by Nancy, he soon mastered the essentials of his post—which was practically that of a glorified office-boy, but he did not appear to find any indignity in it. When Simon rang off he turned to Nancy, who had come through the open door of her room on hearing Simon was on the line.

"Someone ought to let Mr. Lygon know," she commented, when Marius had given her the bad news. "It's not fair to leave everything to Mr. Crome, and though we can manage, so far as routine goes, I think we ought to be in touch with one of the heads. Put a call through; I'll speak, if you like, when they answer."

Marius glanced at the clock, picked up the receiver and told the girl on the switchboard to get the number of the country hotel at which Daniel was staying. After some delay the bell rang; Nancy left her typewriter and came to Marius's desk.

"Can I speak to Mr. Lygon? Half a minute: say it's urgent—an office call."

There was another wait; Daniel did not seem to be available. The three small, irritating hoots went off at the end of the first three minutes, before a click heralded a crisp, feminine voice:

"I'm afraid Mr. Lygon's gone out. Can I take a message?"

Blessed with a keen ear and a retentive memory, Nancy at once recognized the voice. She had only once spoken to Lydia, on the first occasion when the latter rang up to make an appointment with Simon about Marius's book, but she knew as certainly as though they were standing face to face that it was to Lydia she was speaking, and her trained discretion warned her at the same time to conceal her recognition.

"Please say that Mrs. Rowlandson rang up, and that it's a matter of importance. Will you ask Mr. Lygon to ring the office as soon as he comes in?"

There was a brief hesitation before the reply came.

"I—I don't really know what time he's expected back; it might be possible to get a message to him. Could you tell me exactly what it is?"

"Well," said Nancy, speaking with careful clearness, "as a matter of fact, I'm Mr. Crome's secretary, and I'm ringing up entirely on my own responsibility, because I think Mr. Lygon ought to know that his partner isn't in the office. He may not be in for two or three days. I only wanted to make sure that we could get into touch with Mr. Lygon, if anything turns up that we can't deal with ourselves."

"I see." Lydia sounded doubtful. "Is anything the matter? I mean—is Si—is Mr. Lygon's partner ill?"

"No; it's his little girl; she's got pneumonia. I'm afraid they're anxious."

"Good God. All right; I'll see Mr. Lygon gets the message within the next hour."

"I suppose that means you'd better go up to town," Lydia

was saying to Daniel, who had been in the bath when Nancy's call came through. Daniel was most reluctant to be disturbed when taking his bath, and had pooh-poohed Lydia's misgivings about taking the call.

"How should they know it's you? Pretend you're someone to do with the hotel, and say I'm out," he instructed her.

"Suppose it's Simon? He's sure to recognize my voice."

"Well, if he does——? It's no damned business of his," grunted Daniel, prone among soapsuds.

"Daniel!"

"Well, if you must know, he knows all about us already. Eliza blew the gaff. I didn't tell you, because I didn't see the sense of upsetting you more than I'd done already."

"Then Christian knows too——!"

"Darling, *would* you mind answering that call? It's probably something quite drivelling, but there's always the chance that the office has gone up in flames——"

When Lydia returned from her conversation with Nancy, her hands were to her head. After giving him Nancy's message, she said:

"But I can't *think* why you didn't tell me Simon knew about us. I understood—you made me understand that you'd had all that out with Eliza—you never said a word about Simon!"

"What was the point of it?" asked Daniel rather sullenly. He had acted out of what he considered genuine consideration for Lydia, in suppressing the account of the scene in Simon's office. "Eliza chose to drag Simon into a matter that was no business of his, and I only thought it would make you uncomfortable if you felt he was ' in ' on it."

"Then of course he's told Christian, and I've been behaving and talking all these last weeks as if there wasn't a cloud in the sky! She must have thought I'm completely mad—or bad —or something!"

"What on earth does it matter? Hell, yes; I suppose it

means I'll have to go. It'll look odd if I don't. You'll stay here, won't you? I'm sure to be back in a day or two."

"I don't think I'll stay; I think I'd rather be in town. Besides—Christian might like to have me with her, until Jemima's better."

"Well, that's for you to decide, of course. I'll just give the office a ring, and say I'm on my way up."

"Blows our holiday to blazes, doesn't it?" said Lydia brightly.

"We can pick it up again—later on."

"It's never quite the same, is it—'later on'?" she murmured, turning away, to open drawers and take out the things —Daniel's and hers—which had to be packed for their departure.

It had just been one of the things which are too good to last: this business of coming away together and signing "Mr. and Mrs. Lygon." Actually, it was the first time they had had so to label themselves; in Paris and in Berlin (where, unknown to her family, she had also accompanied him) it was simply a matter of handing over passports, and the rest concerned no one but themselves. There was just a wild and lovely sense of romantic adventure in sharing a room—a thing which each solemnly declared nothing would induce them to do, if they were married. There was complete abandonment to the pleasure of the moment—an abandonment which heightened the tempo of their loving, and imparted, at least to Lydia, the illusion of an eternal bliss. She knew, after the trip to Berlin, that Daniel was, at last, in love with her, and, like most women in her position, she persuaded herself that he felt as deeply as she did herself the importance of doing something to mark the permanence of their relationship. She attempted to discuss it with him, on their last night in Berlin, only to find him doubtful and evasive, keenly aware of the difficulties of continuing such a relationship as theirs, after the return to England.

"But we must do something!" She was aghast; it had

never occurred to her that Daniel would, by crying "Halt!"
put their romance on the level of the kind of affair in which,
she knew, a good many women of her own acquaintance were
in the habit of indulging. This must be different—different!
This was not a vulgar, week-end arrangement—it was *love*,
love as deep and strong, though not as blessed, as Christian's
and Simon's.

"Why not leave it to arrange itself, my sweet?" he answered her lazily. "It's so easy to spoil a thing like ours by
driving it too hard, and it's been so marvellous, up to now!"

"But we might, surely, help it along a little? It's going
to be so foul—not being able to have you at the flat."

"Of course it is. You must realize, darling, that any sort
of meetings in town, after this, are going to be a confounded
risk. I don't mean for myself, but for you."

"I suppose Father'd cut me off," said Lydia. "Well, I expect
I could get a job? Anna's just got a frightfully good new job
—I had a letter from her this morning: she's a sort of social
adviser to a company that helps people to give parties! I
think I'd do a job like that frightfully well——"

"Don't be a sweet ass. And, for God's sake, don't let's fetch
Old Harry down on us; the firm won't stand it. Why not
be patient, darling? It's no use blinking the fact that, for the
present, Eliza's got us in a vice, and she won't hesitate to
tighten it if you do any public poaching on what she considers
—erroneously, I'll admit—to be her preserves."

"I won't—I promise; I suppose I daren't. But we must
have something for ourselves, Daniel: some place where we
can see each other without being terrified of Eliza. Suppose
I was to find a cottage somewhere——?"

"I don't think bucolics will suit either of us particularly,"
said Daniel coolly. "You overlook the fact, my love, that we
are children of luxury. . . . I hate like hell the idea of not
having you when I like and for as long as I like: particularly
after our wonderful time out here—but I've just got enough
sense left to realize that we'd be the worst sort of fools if we

brought the roof down on our heads for the sake of continuing to enjoy ourselves as we've done for the last ten days. I've taken more than a chance in sneaking this extra time when I ought to be in Belgrade, and I haven't yet decided what I'm going to tell the people I'm supposed to be staying with——"

With this she had to be content, and reaped what she considered to be her reward when Daniel telephoned her a few days after his return to England, to suggest they should go down to the country together.

"We'll find some unheard-of pub and go rustic for a fortnight. Can you manage it?"

The first cloud upon the shimmering blue-and-goldness of her mood was when Daniel joined her after scribbling something at the reception desk.

"What did you put?" she asked him, out of curiosity. Daniel's brows gave the odd little twitch they performed when he was uneasy or irritable.

"I had to put Mr. and Mrs. Lygon; I've got to use my own name, in case any one rings up from the office."

"Of course," said Lydia lightly, "we could have had separate rooms."

"It didn't occur to me," said Daniel simply, and she did not know whether to be glad at its never occurring, or to be hurt by the implication that, if he had thought of it, he would have arranged things otherwise.

During the days they spent together, Lydia had ample means of proving that such an affair as theirs, which seemed so natural and graceful when its setting was a foreign country, was beset by English prejudice with many small but galling disadvantages. Unused to such expeditions, she had carelessly brought away with her a handbag stamped with her own initials, which she had to remember to conceal: an inconvenient state of affairs, because it meant that she had, often, no place to carry her comb and powderpuff, and had to use Daniel's pockets as a repository for all the oddments a modern young woman carries about with her. It would hardly have mattered if Daniel had not had an almost feminine regard for the shapeliness of his garments; his reluctance to bulge pockets and spoil the shape of his jackets with a collection of feminine junk was not invariably concealed, and Lydia was often obliged to feel apologetic, and would even go un-powdered, rather than disturb him in the middle of some temporarily absorbing occupation.

Even more thoughtlessly, she left in the lounge one evening a letter addressed to her in London, which was brought to her later by one of the waiters. The immediate result of this was that it became apparent that every one in the hotel, from the management to the boots, knew she was not Mrs. Lygon.

"Blast it," said Daniel, when she confessed her carelessness to him. "If we'd been at one of those down-the-river places it wouldn't matter; they take it for granted that no man goes away for the week-end with his wife. But I believe this manager's a pillar of the local chapel. I was wondering why he and his wife were giving you such dirty looks when we were in the bar. The old swine! Shall we leave?"

"No, of course not. It would probably be the same any-where else—and anyhow, I'm proud of being with you, whether we're married or not."

Then there was the trying circumstance of Daniel's encounter with some friends of his and Eliza's, who insisted upon his joining them for a round of golf. He went leaping up the stairs to warn Lydia to keep out of the way.

"They've got the loosest-hung jaws in the county, and she and Eliza are bosom friends. I'll have to play their beastly golf. Thank God they aren't staying here; they want me to lunch with them at the clubhouse."

"Have I got to lunch alone?"

"I'll break my neck to get back as soon as we've finished, and I'll loathe every minute I'm away from you."

She wept a little, after he had gone. It wasn't so good, after all, being Daniel's mistress: at least, not in a country like England, where every one pretended to a morality they did not possess. "The wages of sin is nervous breakdown, loss of income and being starred as Number One Fool in the categories of Daniel's crowd," she thought miserably. "Let's face it. Apart from the time he's making love to me, Daniel isn't really enjoying this party; his book isn't going well; it isn't the right *milieu* for him."

Daniel, who needed all the stimulation of cosmopolitan gaiety to get the best out of himself, was stubbornly trying for two hours every morning to lick his Roumanian notes into shape. They had a small, private sitting-room, with a table covered with a plush cloth with ball fringe, a host of fluted glass vases, in each of which nodded three daffodils, which had the air of being sadly discomposed by their genteel receptacles, an old-fashioned and uneasy "saddlebag" suite and a piano in a bird's eye maple case. It was impossible not to compare these sordid surroundings with their balconied room in Paris, with the chromium-fitted efficiency of their apartment in Berlin: as impossible as it was not to feel a little ludicrous in such surroundings. It was Lydia who first noticed that her conduct was slightly infected by the setting in which, for the first time, she found herself; and who observed that Daniel, without realizing it, was also under its baleful influence.

The mere fact of their bedroom and bathroom not communicating, and the latter having to be approached along a public passage, accounted, on the face of it, for the abandonment of their light-hearted custom of strolling about naked; but it was Lydia who discovered, on a warm, sunny morning when, on returning from the bath, she flung off her peignoir and bent to do her exercises before the mirror, that it was impossible to be naked without self-consciousness in surroundings of such bourgeois propriety. And it was Lydia who rightly ascribed the sour looks of their elderly chambermaid to the fact that the pair of them had been overheard, laughing and talking in the bathroom. She suddenly remembered that the sharing by two people of opposite sexes of a bathroom was regarded as an offence against decency, not only by people of the chambermaid's class, but of her parents'. Never, she was sure, had her father seen her mother, save draped in the teguments of civilized virtue.

These and other incidents helped to reconcile her to Daniel's abrupt termination of their holiday, and determined her never again to risk an experiment of the kind, unless it were to be made abroad, or in an environment of her own devising, where she could, as it were, control the repercussions of their actions.

When they arrived in town, she got Daniel to drop her at Simon's door. The servant who let her in told her that Jemima was thought to be dying.

CHAPTER ELEVEN

The little enamel clock on the shelf punctually indicated half-past seven. Three switches: milk, coffee and water for her egg—Nancy pressed them down, one after another. She could imagine doing it in her sleep. With her usual neat, economical movements, she sliced bread, and pressed down a fourth switch for the toast. In striving towards efficiency, housekeeping had practically de-humanized itself. In another generation or two, words like "fireside" and "toasting fork" would have passed from the popular vocabulary, to survive only in antique shops, with anachronisms like "warming pan."

For all that, Nancy passionately loved her home. One of the happiest moments of her life had been when, upon her appointment as Simon Crome's secretary, she had given up her Pimlico rooms, and taken the little three-roomed flat for herself and Dennis. It was the first time, since the early years of her married life, that she had a place to which, without affectation, she could apply the word "home," and the fact of exchanging the uncertainties of Fleet Street for an assured and regular salary (small though it was) had given her courage to assume responsibilities from which she had shrunk, while at the mercy of editorial fluctuations and changing policies.

While eating her breakfast, she opened and re-read parts of the advance copy of *Cypriana* which Marius had given her. The book affected her profoundly—as it had affected Lydia Matlock. Marius had the great and indispensable quality of the novelist, of creating character; taking as his leading figure the flat, pale, neutral personality of an inexperienced youth, he proceeded, through three hundred and eighty pages, so to amplify it that it leapt from the concluding chapter a complete, three-dimensional force. The sum of his argument was that no man can fulfil his place in the cosmos until he has attained sexual equilibrium, and the three women whose conversations provided the three sections of the book were presented as three mayas, helping the hero to work out his destiny.

It was an exotic subject for an English writer, and Marius had handled it in a fashion to give the least possible satisfaction to the seeker after pornography. As realism it hardly began to exist; the very form of semi-metrical prose, in which he had couched his dialogue, carried the characters and the situations on to a plane whither it was doubtful that the reader of mediocre intellectuality would have patience to follow them. It was a book at once limpid and profound, deriving from the French models to which Marius had given his literary allegiance: such a book as rarely finds appreciation during the lifetime of its author, but seems destined inevitably to find a place upon the shelves of *cognoscenti*. Full of the faults of his literary inexperience, it nevertheless contained, as Nancy recognized, qualities not to be found in the works of the majority of his superiors.

The thud of the morning papers falling on the mat disturbed her in the middle of a paragraph. Nancy rose, putting the book down reluctantly; the arrival of the papers signalized the beginning of her day's work. From her Fleet Street days, she had acquired the habit, invaluable to the journalist and useful in her present employment, of making a quick survey of the day's news, from as many different angles of Press politics as possible. She therefore took in four papers, remarkable for their catholicity of opinion. Of these, " The Daily Moron," as Daniel called it, *The Cable*, as it was more politely known to its contributors, was usually reserved for her journey to the office—the subject matter calling for the minimum of concentration, and the entertainment value at least equal to that offered by the advertisers in the Tubes and buses.

As she bent down to pick up the papers, the thought of Simon flashed through her mind: whether Jemima would be better, whether he would be back in the office. It was not too peaceful with Daniel in command; he and Marius did not hit it off—a state of affairs which called for the continual exercise of Nancy's tact. It was unfortunate that there should be friction between the two men at a time when Daniel was engaged in chaperoning Marius's novel on to the market.

It was, therefore, not until she was half-way to the office that she reached the middle page of "The Moron," and the diagonal line of block lettering with which "The Moron" was wont to drive its more violent pronouncements into the quivering jelly of its readers' minds. "FATHERS! WHAT OF YOUR DAUGHTERS?" howled the heading. The print at the left-hand top corner of the page burst into capitals to announce, "Eric Neil's Appeal to Englishmen to Defend the Purity of their Homes."

Always fascinated, from a clinical angle, by "The Moron's" rhetoric, Nancy turned, with twitching lips, to the beginning of the article.

"I have had through my hands to-day a production of which any decent-minded person might well be ashamed. I say 'have had,' because this noxious object is now a heap of ashes in my grate: in spite of which I feel that my soul is stained with an unforgettable evil."

"Give it 'em, Eric!" grinned Nancy, settling down to enjoy herself.

It was not until she had finished the paragraph that Nancy discovered—at first incredulously, then with an overwhelming passion of anger—that the article was an attack on *Cypriana.*

She felt the flesh tighten on her cheeks, and found that her hands and knees were trembling. The print blurred before her eyes; it was several moments before she could continue reading. "The Moron" had always been noted for its catch-penny morality, but this time it surpassed itself in calculated hysteria—the one irresistible form of appeal to its public, not one of whom, as Nancy knew, would have the wit to read a paragraph of *Cypriana*.

"How many of your wives and your daughters," jibbered "The Moron," "have access to the public libraries? How many of you have paused to think that a library subscription may be the passport to hell? Let every voice in the country be raised in One Clear Call to the powers which alone can save our women from widespread corruption!"

There followed a scabrous description of the contents of the book—the type of description that makes pornography-hunters lick their lips—and a personal attack upon Marius, carefully framed so as to evade the possibilities of libel. The death-blow was reserved for the final passage.

"It is hardly to be believed that this vile book is issued by the firm of Crome and Lygon. This firm, a new-comer to the publishing world, is financed by Sir Harry Matlock, whose name, for so many years, has stood to the public for the highest ideals in the world of Big Business, as well as for a great public example of probity and religious conviction. It is inconceivable that Sir Harry is aware of this cynical abuse of his support. We call upon him with confidence to protect the purity of our womanhood, the innocence of our youth and the high tradition of English literature."

Shaken with nausea, Nancy arrived at the office; as she went through the outer room, she caught sight of a copy of "The Moron" being hastily smuggled out of sight. Daniel's blonde was in the cloakroom, shaken out of her waxen poise by the event of the morning.

"What on earth are we going to *do*?"

"How the devil do I know?" snapped Nancy. She knew there was nothing to do except withdraw the book, but she was not in a frame of mind to discuss the matter with Miss Thomas. She went into her own room and shut the door.

Marius had not yet arrived. Nor had Daniel. She wondered what to say, if, or when, Simon rang up before the arrival of his partner; she wished, desperately, that it was Simon, and not Daniel, in whose hands, for the moment, the management of the firm's affairs reposed. She knew Simon did not take "The Moron"; unless someone rang him up at his own house, it was unlikely that he would hear of it, until news went through from the office.

Marius walked in calmly. Marius, also, did not take "The Moron." She allowed him to settle down at his desk before handing him, silently, Neil's article. He read it through without comment, dropped it on the floor, and slid a sheet of paper into his typewriter.

"Well?" said Nancy.

"Well what?"

"You know what it means?"

"Why should it ' mean ' anything? It's obvious enough—I don't know this Neil, or whatever he calls himself, but he—or somebody that employs him—has got a down on the firm."

"Don't be so childish. It's finished your book."

He looked at her with honest amazement.

"You don't mean that any one's going to pay attention to a rag like that?"

"Don't you know anything about the laws of censorship?" Nancy sighed. "Don't you know that an office boy can get a book indicted, if he lodges a complaint about its morality? No firm can proceed an inch against an attack like that."

"I don't believe it. The article's obviously written by some sort of a sexual frustrate, and they've chosen to run it as a selling stunt."

"I know all that; it makes no difference to the response of the class of people who are now reading it over their eggs and bacon. I suppose ninety per cent. of them are sexual frustrates as well; anyhow, this is exactly the sort of thing that will set them howling for our blood."

"Bosh!" said Marius rudely. "You needn't tell me that the English masses are moral reformers. One of the best things about our working classes is that they don't give a dam' for religion or morals or what-have-you, so long as they've got their wages and their pint of beer." He laughed. "Let 'em read it, if they want; it won't do them a ha'porth of harm."

"Of course it wouldn't; but do you suppose 'The Moron' cares about that? Marius, can't you understand? There's no question of genuine attack, either on you or on the firm. There's not even any question of public morality. If it paid them to boost smut, they'd do it; but smut doesn't pay, in a big way, in England. It always pays to appeal to the high standard of English morals, to persuade people they're better than their neighbours, to set them cackling about national purity! Half the people who read Eric Neil's article betrayed their wives last night, sniggered over some dirty picture or story they're ashamed of this morning; that's why they're grateful to 'The Moron' for reminding them that they're part of the great, upright, pure-minded British Empire, that defends womanhood with the last drop of its blood!"

Marius raised his eyebrows.

"You're a bit overwrought, aren't you?"

"God, I haven't worked for papers like 'The Moron' without learning their methods!" said Nancy bitterly. "The editor wants a new 'uplift' stunt; they've run out of material; the public's fed-up with the usual stuff—white-slaving, convent scandals, under-payment of nurses. Clear out and find something new; have a go at literature—get hold of somebody's body and roast it——!"

"It's my book, you know, not yours," said Marius calmly.

"It's the firm's as well, isn't it? And the firm's got as much as it can carry, at present, without a public slap in the face like this."

Daniel came in; at a glance it was obvious he had seen "The Moron." For once his dilettante air had deserted him;

G

ignoring the formality of the morning greeting, he snapped at Nancy:

"Who sent Neil a copy of *Cypriana*?"

"I can't imagine, Mr. Lygon. Only a dozen copies have gone out—we haven't even sent out the review copies yet. Mr. Crome told me to hold them up until we'd heard from the special people."

"Have you a list of the people to whom they were sent?"

"I think I can tell you from memory." Nancy proceeded to recite the list, which included Roger Burke, Bertie Manders and Prudence Thrale, all three of whom, by general consent, were above suspicion. Both Burke and Prudence had written about the book in terms of enthusiasm, and Bertie Manders, meeting Daniel at a first night, had sung its praises in a breathless treble, which, according to Daniel, was worth five inches of double column in *The Sunday Times*. "I don't think Neil's friendly with any of those," she concluded.

"He's the sort of sycophantic little beast that oils in anywhere," pronounced Daniel. "He's either picked up the book by accident, and seen a chance of stunting it, or it's been supplied to him deliberately by someone who's got a grudge against us." He leaned against the mantelpiece, biting his thumbnail. "Simon must be kept out of this for the present."

Nancy made no reply. She had her own strict standards, by which personal affairs must always be subordinated to public ones, and she could not repress a feeling of doubt regarding Daniel's capacity for handling the situation.

"Have you heard anything about the child?" she asked.

"There seems to be no change. I said I'd let him know if anything out of the ordinary turned up. You'd better get Combridge," he threw across his shoulder at Marius, who, although the author, seemed so far to have been excluded from the discussion. "If there's the least loophole," said Daniel, while Marius was looking up the solicitor's number, "we'll fight it. God Almighty!" he exploded. "The book hasn't

even got to the reviewers! If literary censorship is to be left
in the hands of some thieving hack——!"

He was taking exactly the attitude that Nancy had foreseen and feared. So far as publishing was concerned, Daniel
actually knew very little more than Marius. Simon, she felt
sure, would agree with her: that whatever might be the loss
to the firm and to Marius, either was better than the expense
of taking the case to court—to be judged, in all probability,
by illiterates, or by some person with an *idée fixe* upon the
subject on which Marius had chosen to write.

She found herself in an impossible position: torn between
her loyalty to Simon, and what she felt sure must be his point
of view, and the difficulty of representing this to Daniel, who,
after all, was Simon's partner, and authorized to act in his
absence, and who was not prone to take kindly to advice. She
hoped that Combridge would be able to talk him out of his
present decision; she heard Daniel asking him to come round,
and saw him replace the receiver and turn to her.

"We've got to justify ourselves, for the sake of Old Harry.
It's infamous, the way his name has been dragged into it."

"How can we justify ourselves?" she thought, adding aloud,
"It's terribly unfortunate Mr. Crome is away. Do you think
he should be asked——?"

"Simon's got quite enough on his plate for the present.
He's in no state to give judgments in an affair like this. Take
this down, will you? Who's the editor of *The Cable*?" he
broke off to ask.

"I think it's Ricketts—he took over from Lafarge, when
they amalgamated; but I'll check up on that later."

"We are very much surprised," dictated Daniel rapidly,
"by your article in this morning's *Cable*: the more so that
we are unable to trace any reference among our records to
the despatch of a review copy, either to your paper or to your
contributor personally. It is therefore to be assumed that he
obtained it by methods for which the term unauthorized may
be accepted as a euphemism, and to which we beg to call your

attention, as editor. Meanwhile, the firm of Crome and Lygon wishes to state that it has no comment to make, and no intention of acting upon your contributor's suggestion."

"That'll show the bastards we're prepared to fight, anyhow," concluded Daniel, upon a note of satisfaction.

Not trusting herself to speak, Nancy pressed her lips together. She knew that Combridge would dispose of Daniel's "hot air." Her heart ached for Marius, but a fight at this stage could only be disastrous for all parties.

For the next hour the telephone rang almost continuously; people who "wanted statements," people with messages of sympathy, people advising them to fight, people advising them not to fight, people clamouring for copies of the book, people clamouring for the destruction of the book. An elderly, effeminate-voiced inquirer wanted to know if the author could be persuaded to autograph a special copy for the speaker's library. A Church of England clergyman asked for an appointment—he was sure he could convince them of the urgency of the suppression of a book of this description. An officer of the Salvation Army called in person, and seemed bitterly annoyed because he could not obtain a copy of the book "for his private use." ("What do you think he *means*?" asked Miss Thomas naïvely. "Search me," said Nancy.)

"Sir Harry Matlock's secretary on the line; Sir Harry is in town, and would like an appointment at twelve."

"All right; bring on your lions," muttered Daniel.

"Am I to say Mr. Crome's away?" inquired the blonde, fingering freshly plastered curls.

"Better not; he'd probably go crashing down to Simon's. Say the appointment's booked. You'd better stay and see him," said Daniel, to his companion.

"Not on your life! I'm afraid I can't manage it," said Combridge, a small, grey man with a crisp manner. "In any case, I've got nothing to add to what I've already said: that I can't advise you to fight it."

"But, hang it, can't you see—it's not an ordinary case of

censorship," fumed Daniel. "The book has not been circulated, except to a few privileged people. The reviewers
haven't got it, the booksellers haven't got it, our advance
people haven't got it, the publication date is nearly a month
away, and the writer of this article has almost certainly
obtained his copy by theft. Do you mean we've got no redress
against a thing like that?"

"I dare say you might have. All I can say is, it won't do
you or the firm a ha'porth of good. The cat's among the
pigeons and you'll do more damage in trying to get it out
than by letting it kill its bird. The fact is, you won't
get a jury in England, now, that isn't prejudiced by the *Daily
Cable* article; even people who sympathize with you won't
dare to take your side openly, for fear of prejudicing their
own standing with the moralists."

"I can bring fifty witnesses to prove that the book's not
merely perfectly moral, but a literary masterpiece!"

Combridge wagged his head.

"You might get away with it if these things were in the
hands of a literary commission. You know as well as I do,
Lygon, that the people through whom the censorship operates
have, most of them, not opened a literary work since they
read Scott for School Certificate. It will cost you a lot less
to scrap the book and let the *Cable* have its own way. After
all, grim as the thought may be, it represents the bulk of
public opinion."

"'Tscha!" said Daniel impatiently. "It's been done too
often, Combridge. Whatever sort of fatuous numskulls take
their opinions from *The Cable*, I don't believe the general
public is willing to have its literature dictated to it by a penny
newsrag."

"Don't be naïve," said Combridge, who had been legal
adviser to literary firms too long to retain any illusions. "We
aren't dealing with the general public, but with *The Cable's*
public. It doesn't give two hoots for literature; it doesn't
give two hoots for morals either. All it wants is an artificial

stimulus, which is supplied to it by its own Press organ, to give it the illusion of being both moral and literary—a very different thing, my dear Lygon, a very different thing."

"Of course I know that. But doesn't it strike you as a criminal state of affairs, that a paper like *The Cable* can control, not only its own public, but the entire reading population—through an article like that? Of course, you haven't read the book," muttered Daniel. "You can't be expected to feel as strongly about it as we do."

"You'd better be out of the way," Nancy was saying to Marius. "It won't make things easier, when Sir Harry arrives, if you're around."

Marius lifted his head from the typewriter. The untidy lock of hair was sprouting over his brow, and sweat glistened in the deep, leathery lines of his face. She saw with a pang that he looked both tired and discouraged. He had not said a word about his book since Daniel's arrival. Nor, so far as she knew, had Daniel, steeped in his own point of view, spoken a word of sympathy to its author! How selfish they had all of them been—thinking only of the firm, while Marius was there, taking his blow in philosophical silence. For herself, Nancy had hardly dared to think of the book; it was like thinking of something lovely and still-born, and it filled her throat with bitter and scalding tears. She wondered whether Marius also wept inwardly for the miscarriage of his labours. She had not felt able to say a word, so far, of sympathy to him—too much afraid, by betraying her own sorrow, of adding to his.

"I'd like to see him," he said unexpectedly.

"To see Sir Harry?"

"You've all gone on," said Marius, getting up, and hitching his slacks about his narrow hips, "as though this business had nothing whatever to do with me."

"Marius—we didn't——"

"I wrote the book, and I can write another. All the fuss can't take away what I've done, and it can't kill my ability to do it again—better, perhaps, than before. Of course the thing will have to be withdrawn. It's no use Lygon thrashing about and starting a case. Besides"—Marius shrugged his shoulders—"he's not fighting for the book, or for me, but for his own prestige as the publisher. I don't feel bitterly—in his place, I'd probably do the same myself. It's mortifying to have your output controlled by the penny Press, but that's how it seems to be in England. I can get this book done in French, or in German. They might even publish an English version in Paris, if I could get at the right people. I dare say Crome could help me. He'll have to do that"—he laughed— "if he wants to get back the advance I've spent already!"

"You don't suppose he'll worry about that? Mr. Crome is as generous a person as I know," said Nancy indignantly.

"To hell with generosity. I don't want charity," snapped Marius. "All I want is a reasonable chance of getting on with my work; then some day, may be, I'll be generous, and I'll be charitable, and I'll grin like blazes when people throw it back in my face!"

"You've got a lot to learn yet, Marius Lear," said Nancy, after a pause. "You've got to learn not to resent kindness when it is offered to you; you've got—oh, leave it alone! I don't see what good you'll do by meeting Sir Harry. He's very bigoted and very touchy about public opinion; he must be raging over *The Cable's* use of his name in connection with this affair."

"Exactly. And I want to explain to him that I'm perfectly prepared to withdraw the book, and that if Lygon wants to fight it's against my personal wishes," said Marius. He had a kind of untidy dignity about him that, involuntarily, impressed Nancy. It was not easy to imagine Marius being brow-beaten by Old Harry; would it, however, conduce to peaceful settlement of a very awkward business, to allow them to come together?

The office palpitated when Sir Harry Matlock's name

travelled through the departments. A general feeling of thankfulness, that none of them stood in Daniel's shoes, circulated among the staff, as Sir Harry pushed through the swing-door and started, unannounced, to mount the stairs to the partners' rooms. The girl on the switchboard had just time to gasp his name through to Nancy, and she had not yet made connection with Miss Thomas, in Daniel's apartment, when Old Harry thrust open the door of Simon's room, to find himself face to face with Marius.

The two faced each other: Old Harry sullen and empurpled behind his glossy beard, Marius cool, with the pipe to which he had recently taken in the corner of his mouth. He removed it, to point with it to the chair Daniel had recently vacated.

"Won't you sit down?"

"Where's Crome? I've got a noon appointment with him," blustered Old Harry.

"Crome's not in; Lygon's expecting you. He'll be down in a minute."

"I don't want to see Lygon! My appointment's with Crome."

"He's not been in this morning. His daughter's ill."

"His daughter——?" The wind was patently taken out of Old Harry's sails. "Do you mean Jemima—my grand-daughter?"

Marius nodded.

"Very ill," he thought fit to elaborate.

"But—but—— What's this nonsense about? The child's had measles—we know all about that; but she's getting better. The last news we had——"

Daniel came in; he looked surprised to see Marius, but could think of no pretext for dismissing him. After all, he was the author, and might as well be present at what promised to be a very disagreeable interview. Old Harry wheeled upon Daniel as he came in.

"What's the matter with Jemima?"

"Pneumonia," said Daniel laconically. It seemed inhuman,

yet inevitable, to be glad of a circumstance that had evidently
checked Old Harry's onrush. "Well, sir, I'm afraid you've
not come on pleasant business to-day," he said, Daniel-like,
following up his advantage. "I'm sorry Simon isn't here to
talk it over with us—by the way, have you two been introduced? This is the author, Marius Lear."

Ignoring the hand which Marius pushed out towards him,
Old Harry dropped into a chair. He was obviously at a loss,
between his desire to know more about Jemima's illness, and
the business on which he had come. His dislike for Daniel
embittered the situation; he resented receiving news of his
grandchild from one whose society he had always avoided as
much as he deplored his association with his son-in-law, and
he was angry that Christian and Simon had neglected to
inform him about Jemima.

"I thought she'd got over measles," he muttered. He was
pitiably confused, between his wrath and his grandfatherly
sentiments.

"She caught a chill. I'm afraid she's pretty bad."

"Why weren't we told?"

Daniel raised his brows.

"I shouldn't think they've had time to think of telling
anybody. It was very sudden, and Simon hasn't been down
to the office since."

"What does he say to this *Cable* business?"

"Nothing. You see," said Daniel, opening a box. "Have
a cigarette, sir? No? I thought it better not to tell him for
the present. He's having quite a bad enough time"—Daniel
shrugged his shoulders—"but I'm afraid he's bound to hear
of it, before the day is out. Of course, sir, I can only offer you
the firm's sincerest apologies for the way in which your name
has been brought into this very nasty business. You realize,
without my telling you, that we aren't responsible for *that*."

"Responsible! I suppose you'll say next you aren't responsible for the publication of the book?"

"We're prepared," said Daniel quickly, "to justify to the

hilt our choice of this particular novel. It's perhaps a little difficult to eulogize a book in the author's presence"—he flashed his bright, beguiling smile at Marius, who pushed his lower lip out and turned his head away—"but our own high opinion of Mr. Lear's work has been endorsed in quarters which you yourself, sir, are bound to respect. Roger Burke, for instance, regards it as a valuable contribution to literature."

"A catch-phrase, that's been used to cover all sorts of indecency, from Boccaccio to Lawrence!" exploded Old Harry. Marius's mouth tightened. "I've said again and again that I'll have nothing to do with this modern trick of calling dirt 'literature' and foisting it on the public! What do you suppose I felt like this morning—what do you suppose my friends felt like—when they saw me pilloried as the backer of a firm that specializes in filth——?"

"Excuse me," said Marius. "Have you read the book?"

Old Harry turned his lowered head, like a bull elephant preparing to run amok.

"You have nothing to gain by insulting me," he said dangerously.

"It's my work that *you* have insulted. If you have not read the book, what business have you to apply the disgusting epithet you have just used to my work?"

Old Harry's eyes narrowed. He opened his lips, as though to speak, closed them again, and looked at Daniel, as though, of the two, he preferred to deal with him. Marius Lear was a type anathema to him and his kind; after one look at the fellow, there was no sort of indecency with which it was not possible to credit him. Writers, for Old Harry, fell sharply into two classes: the collared and the collarless. Of the former, Hugh Walpole, John Galsworthy and Horace Annesley Vachell were excellent examples; Old Harry was pleased to acknowledge them as gentlemen and to claim acquaintance with them. In dismissing the latter, he ascribed to them all the literary outrages against which he set his face. Marius, in his open-necked, dark-grey flannel shirt, was easily the worst specimen he had encountered. It was inconceivable that Daniel—who, for all his undesirable qualities, was incontrovertibly a gentleman—could stomach him.

"You will appreciate, sir," Daniel was saying, "that *The Daily Cable's* version of Lear's novel was well in accordance with the usual class of its news. Every one knows the sort of rag *The Cable* is, and the public it caters for——"

"What everybody knows is no concern of mine; its circulation is——" Old Harry mentioned a startling number. "I suppose it doesn't mean anything to you and the author" —he infused the word with vitriol—"that my name's a byword by now in half a million homes of Great Britain."

It flashed across Daniel and Marius simultaneously that Old Harry was less concerned with "the preservation of female innocence" than with his own reputation, and Daniel, at least, recognized how much more dangerous to the firm was the attack on Old Harry's self-esteem than the offence to his propriety.

"On the contrary," pointed out Marius, "the articles absolve you in the most explicit fashion from any responsibility at all. Its writer even goes so far as to name you as champion of his cause against our evil intentions!"

Daniel shot him a warning glance; it was no moment for trifling with Old Harry. The warning came, however, too late. The old man rose, with a vicious glance at Marius.

"We'll conclude this discussion, Lygon, when my son-in-law is here. I'll wish you—and your author—good-day."

Daniel rose as well.

"Just a moment, please. You see, Simon's return is uncertain, and we can't leave this in the air until he comes back."

"I'll go down and see him myself."

Daniel looked politely doubtful.

"That, of course, sir, is as you choose. But may I remind you it isn't the best of moments to get his full attention to a matter like this?"

"Perhaps you'll leave me to judge that for myself."

"Well, naturally. I hoped, however, that you would lend us your co-operation in fighting the case."

"I don't see what that's got to do with me."

"We took it for granted you would wish, as I do, to vindicate the firm's position," said Daniel suavely.

"Who took it for granted?" said Marius, unexpectedly. "I didn't. I'd like to make my position clear now, as Sir Harry is here to listen to what, so far, I haven't been asked to give my opinion upon! After all, the book's mine, and if I choose to withdraw it, and cancel my contract, that ends the matter, doesn't it? I don't see that the firm can do much if the author refuses to publish."

Daniel, taken aback and angry, began to argue the point.

"What about breach of contract?" he fumed. "The firm has taken on the onus of the book's production; the costs of printing, binding and advertisement—a good deal of which is already in hand—have got to come out of the firm's pocket."

"The firm," said Old Harry slowly, "and everybody in connection with it can go to hell, so far as I'm concerned. I've finished with it. Good-day."

"And that," said Daniel, as the door closed behind his visitor, "is that." He turned furiously upon Marius. "Why the devil did you have to butt in? You've done nothing but put the whole lot of us on the rocks."

"Not more than you're proposing to do, with your talk about fighting the case," said Marius calmly. "Even if we win—which I don't suppose we should—the book's done for. It'll come out in a cloud of scandal; all the dirty bookshops round the West End 'll buy it up, and decent people 'll fight shy of it. I'd rather it were burned!"

"I dare say," sneered Daniel. "I don't suppose it troubles you that we're faced with a dead loss of—however many hundreds of pounds it may be; I don't know the financial end of the business—Mrs. Rowlandson will tell you. I don't suppose that it occurs to you that a thing which is less than a flea-bite to Gosschalk is a serious matter to a young firm, that's still struggling to find its feet. If Old Harry gets out, we're probably smashed; and you haven't even the common decency to back us up, when we try to save something out of the wreck——"

"Oh, shut up," drawled Marius, replacing his pipe between his pouting lips. "If it's the financial loss that's worrying you —do you suppose that *Cypriana's* the end of my work? I'll see you have it back—every penny of it—out of my future stuff. Maybe you don't believe in that? Well, to hell with your unbelief. You can just wait—and see."

Daniel picked up the telephone receiver.

"Get me Mayfair 0098."

". . . Is that you, Daniel? I thought you'd forgotten I was alive."

"Did you? I say, we're in a frightful mess."

"What about?"

"You haven't seen this morning's 'Moron'? I mean, *The Cable*?"

It appeared Lydia had not; Daniel gave her a brief outline of the situation, which she interrupted with exclamations of concern.

"What a ghastly to-do. Does Simon know?"

"Not so far as we're aware. He hasn't rung up this morning. I suppose that means the kid's desperately ill."

"I spoke to the nurse for a minute, about an hour ago. I'm afraid they're expecting the worst. It'll kill Christian."

"Damn. Look here: Old Harry must be stopped from going down there and plaguing them."

"Oh, surely he won't? He adores Jemima."

"He didn't seem to know about it, until we told him; that didn't go with a swing. I didn't know they were keeping it from the old people."

"It's natural they should. Mummy's got a heart of gold, but she's intolerable when there's illness about. She takes charge of everything and countermands the doctor's orders and tells the nurses they don't know their job. It wouldn't be so trying if she weren't right every time!"

"You couldn't get hold of Old Harry, could you, and calm him down a bit? It can't do any real good—I mean, so far as the firm's concerned—but it might ease him off for a day or two, and give us a chance to find our feet."

"I'll try"—but Lydia sounded doubtful. "I'm not exactly in good odour, you know, darling. I think they both feel I've been neglecting them—but I'll ring through to the Savoy, if you like, and find out if he's lunching with any one."

"Do it quick, for heaven's sake, before he gets at Simon," implored Daniel.

Sir Harry had a suite permanently reserved, which he occupied on his frequent visits to town. When Lydia rang up she was told that he was expected in at any moment; so far as the speaker knew, he was lunching alone.

"Tell him that, unless she hears to the contrary, his daughter will be lunching with him. No, not Mrs. Crome— Miss Matlock." She left her number, and went hurriedly to dress.

CHAPTER TWELVE

At home, Simon sat in his study, striving to concentrate upon work which had to be done, in spite of one's private pre-occupations. No one had time to pay attention to him, and he could not, apparently, be of use to anybody: but he felt that, simply by being there, he was being of some comfort and support to Christian, whose present calm was more disturbing than her original agitation.

In defiance of advice, she had insisted upon doing most of the nursing herself: even Simon could not persuade her to leave the sick-room for more than a few moments at a time. Cold, concentrated, remote from the people who wished to help her, she seemed to have reached some supernatural state of physical endurance, in which she had no need of support save that of her own indomitable will. "If any one can save Jemima, it will be me," she said simply, when they reproached her with over-taxing her only recently recovered strength. It was, Simon supposed, the natural, maternal thing to say: but seeing her at long distant intervals, each time a little darker under the eyes, more drawn, tighter about the lips, it was difficult not to make a purely selfish appeal. What on earth would happen to him if he lost Christian? He gripped his temples and tried to be sane. He detested the angular, North of Ireland nurse— they had unfortunately not been able to get the one who had helped to nurse Jemima through measles—who was supposed to do the day nursing, and, rather than sit down *tête à tête* with her, had trays sent to his study. Christian never came downstairs for her meals.

In spite of the fact that things were going well on the whole, Simon sometimes thought that, had he known to begin with as much as he now knew about publishing, he would have kept out of the risky venture. During the last few months he had had some startling demonstrations of the impossibility of getting a fair deal in the Press, unless he spent more money in advertising than the present fortunes of the firm warranted. Again and again his books got passed over, or dismissed with a perfunctory line or two among the unsigned reviews. He had, of course, known all about the close relationship between advertising and reviews, but he had depended upon the goodwill of editors (for many of whom he had worked) to give him at least a reasonable show, until events proved that proprietorial blood was a great deal thicker than comradely water. The reviewers were not to blame; they had their livings to make, and worked under the tacit, if not openly expressed orders of their editors, who, in their turn, were answerable to the proprietors if advertising dropped. Simon knew of at least a couple of instances of an irate publisher, incensed by not receiving from the reviewers sufficient adulation of his authors, cancelling his advertising with a particular paper: an action which resulted, indirectly, in the dismissal of the reviewer, since, in a country where reviewers are two a penny, and the literary page exists only by virtue of its advertisements (who in England cares about literary news?) the loss involved was too serious to risk a repetition. Simon did not flatter himself that any accounts department would be affected by the withdrawal of his inch or so of space in the Sunday papers: he realized that his only form of self-defence was to purchase more.

So while Jemima rocked between two worlds, he sat, puzzling over how a little more money could be squeezed out of another department, to put into the advertising: seeking some evidence of extravagance that could worthily be diverted into another channel: wondering whether he ought to be lunching at the Ivy, on the chance of getting a word or two with people who might bring their influence to bear on critics, and worrying over the absolute necessity of making a success of this business, upon which the whole of Christian's and his future depended.

It was terribly difficult to concentrate, for, besides Jemima, he was troubled about Daniel and Lydia, about Old Harry's reaction to *Cypriana* and about Christian's lack of sympathy with his publishing ideals. His mind felt red-hot with thought and he was so tired it was almost impossible to keep awake.

Christian came in, to say with a dreadful self-control that tore at Simon's heart:

"Do you think Henry ought to be told? He's so intelligent, and it would come as a terrible shock to him, if he only heard —afterwards."

"Honestly, Chris," said Simon, getting up to give her a chair, "I think better not; it isn't as if he were at home, where we could keep an eye on him. He's too young to cope with it by himself."

"Well, you know best." She spoke almost as though he were a stranger. "I think we'll have to let them know at Granedge, now."

"Do you mean——?"

"She's losing strength all the time, and she hasn't known any of us for the last two hours. Nurse thinks it really *is* sleep, just now, but it was simply a stupor up to a little while ago. It doesn't seem believable—that a few weeks ago——" The hard, controlled voice stopped; Christian sat motionless, with the palms of her hands upturned on her knees, staring across the room. "Do you suppose there really is a God? I've done nothing but pray—and nothing happens."

"Would you like Lydia to be with you?" He touched her hair gently, almost shyly. This cold being was not the Christian he knew; he tried not to be hurt, that sorrow should take her so far away from him, instead of drawing them together.

She shook her head decisively.

"If we tell them at Granedge, will you promise not to let Mummy come here? I—just—couldn't—stand—it," said Christian slowly, "if Mummy was here."

"I'll promise you shan't be disturbed, my dear. It may——"

He checked the words of difficult optimism that came to his lips. "Has the doctor been yet? We'd better wait to hear what he says."

"It won't make any difference. . . . He said he'd be here about ten. What time is it?"

"Only a little after nine. Couldn't you take a rest, Chris? The child's asleep, you say. I'll sit with her, if you like."

She took no notice of the suggestion.

"The days seem so short and the nights so endlessly long. If only it wouldn't be night! It's in the night I lose courage: even with Nana there. I can feel her drifting away from me. She used to be afraid of the dark when she was little: do you remember? I believe it was the fault of that Shropshire woman we had before Nana came to us. I'm going back now; if you come up, mind that loose board in the passage, just in front of her door. She sleeps so lightly, and sleep's the best chance she's got."

"I'll just look over my letters, darling; then I'll come up."

"Look over mine as well," said Christian wearily. "If anything wants answering, put it on one side; I can see to it this afternoon, when nurse goes off duty."

The morning dragged itself away. He knew he should telephone the office, but his working morale seemed to have collapsed: a fact easily enough accounted for by the cumulative effect of months of overwork, to which the present anxiety contributed the last straw. In his present state of mind it did not seem to matter much what happened at the office; in fact, unless he could find a way through this advertising problem, there would soon be no office. In view of the forth-coming appearance of *Cypriana*, he had got to do something desperate: even to the extent, if necessary, of interviewing the bank for an extension of his overdraft, but he could not think where to find more security, the bank having already every scrip he possessed. The ardour with which he had previously applied himself to every detail, no matter how trivial, of office management—even to the extent of neglecting his home and Christian—now seemed to him fantastical, and his fear for Christian was no less than his fear for Jemima. Her reserve of strength must be nearly exhausted; such as it was, she had been drawing on it extravagantly ever since the beginning of Jemima's measles, and the doctor, when he came, spoke gravely about her, and warned Simon that his wife would presently need as much care as his daughter, unless she were forced to husband her resources.

"What about the child?" Simon forced himself to ask. "Why can't you say straight out——?" He heard the flutter of febrile anger in his own voice. The doctor looked at him steadily; Simon, ashamed, turned aside, and started to stuff his pipe, with fingers that trembled slightly.

"There isn't anything to be said. She's weaker this morning —what can you expect, with a temperature like that? The most one can say is that she's got a first-class stamina, that may help her to pull through, if we can arrest the present tendency. She's too sick to help herself much, now—poor Jem!"

They had just brought lunch to him in his study, when the clap of a car door outside the open window drew his attention to the square. He recognized the Matlock Rolls, and caught a glimpse of Old Harry, mounting the steps to the front door. Having made sure his mother-in-law was not there, Simon, without waiting for him to ring, sprang into the hall and opened the door himself. He had never in his life been so glad to see his father-in-law. The assurance of a rocklike stability which emanated from the old man's personality was exactly the quality most grateful to Simon, in his present condition. He felt like a scared small boy, grateful for a grown-up person's company.

"Come in, father! I'm terribly glad to see you."

It creates a difficult situation, when the person you have come to overwhelm with your just wrath greets you with the most unconcealed and innocent pleasure. Old Harry stood for a moment, stiffly, in a favourite position—his weight on one leg, the other slightly advanced and his fine white head

flung back, a forensic attitude which he frequently adopted
when, as lay preacher at Pleasant Sunday Afternoons, he
exhorted young men to "play up and play the game," to
"march breast-forward," to "run the straight race," and
generally to perform the muscular antics which are regarded
as inseparable from sporting Christianity. At such moments
his blue eyes would flash with an angry integrity: as though
the mere notion of a Christian lounging about, say, with a
novel, or staring at a picture show offended his highest ideals.
The blue eyes were flashing now: or rather, they smouldered
in an ugly fashion over the purplish pouches towards which
mounted the clipped white hairs of Old Harry's immaculate
beard. Simon saw that he was angry, and assumed at once
that he had heard—through Lydia or someone—of Jemima's
illness, and resented being left in ignorance until now. He
took his father-in-law's arm to lead him into the study.

"Chris will be glad of you. You know about Jemima?"

"They've just told me, at the office," said Old Harry, stiffly.

"I suppose you think we ought to have let you know
before." Simon decided to take the bull by the horns. " It
was really my fault; I didn't see the point of upsetting you
and mother—you know what children's illnesses are: they
are getting over them before your heart's gone out of your
mouth! But I wrote to you this morning—the letter's in the
post now. Chris has had hell." He went on to tell Old Harry
about Jemima; there was a tremendous relief in having someone to talk to, someone with whom it was not necessary to
conceal, or to minimize, his own fears.

Old Harry was in a quandary. He adored his grandchildren
and was very fond of Simon, but he was furiously angry with
him. He had come straight from the office, to confirm his
threat to Daniel, of withdrawing his support from the firm.
He knew in what a predicament it would place them, and all
the way in the car he had chewed the cud of his malice until
his mouth was raw with it.

They would be ruined, eh? Well, people had tried to ruin

him—not once, but many times—and he had found means of circumventing them. If Simon had any guts, he would do the same; meanwhile, let him and his precious partner find someone else's money to back their exploits: someone who had no reputation to lose, who did not mind being made a cockshy in the penny press—it was the latter that sent the blood rushing to Old Harry's head. He had that abnormal sensitiveness to public opinion which is common to those with whom virtue is a matter of expediency.

Not that Old Harry was, as many people regarded him, an out-and-out hypocrite. He had, like the majority of successful business men, two distinct sets of morals, governing respectively his public and his private life. It was not immoral to mislead one's rivals, to bring about an important deal by elaborately dubious means, to sham a bluff honesty while engaged in cutting a rival's throat: this was the meaning of "Big Business"—a highly specialized game, in which Old Harry was a star performer. Jesus was not a business man: that was how Old Harry, and thousands like him, explained the discrepancy between their public and their private Christianity. Sin, in the business world, consisted in double-crossing your partner, in not giving full value for money received; in private life it was almost entirely a matter of sexual relations and conduct, and he counted himself blessed that his circumstances were such as to preserve him from this form of temptation. He was not merely sedulous about his own morals, but concerned himself seriously with other people's—especially with those of whom he spoke, with grandfatherly geniality, as "our young folks," and to whom he preached, with a naïveté no less touching than it was unconscious, his doctrine that Virtue was Pleasant, and Virtue Paid. It paid in acres of bricks and mortar, in glass, chromium and steel; it paid in illuminated addresses, in complimentary speeches, in civic honours; in the deference of important people, in royal favour (he was almost insanely proud of his knighthood) and in personal power.

Small wonder that the association of his name with a shady publication increased Old Harry's blood pressure! He listened, mumbling, to Simon's account of Jemima's illness, admitted grudgingly that Simon and Christian must have been through a bad time—"I'm afraid it's not over yet, father." "That it is not," thought Old Harry, as he curtly demanded to be taken to his grand-daughter's room. Warned by Simon of the creaking board, the pair of them arrived on tiptoe at the door of the night nursery.

Christian was sitting beside the bed; she and the nurse looked up sharply as the two men entered, and Christian gave a little gasp. With a finger laid warningly to her lips, she crossed the room, and silently put her arms about her father. The silence and helplessness of her appeal drove tears of mingled love and sentimentality into Old Harry's eyes; he patted the pretty hair which had lost all its gloss, and looked, in all save its neatness, like the coat of a dog out of condition.

She drew him to the bedside, and they stood looking down upon Jemima—a Jemima shrunk to half her remembered size: whose breath came roughly whistling through dry lips, whose flushed cheek was pressed into a tumbled pillow, against which bristled the short, stubby ends of her hair—she had complained bitterly of the discomfort of plaits, and at last they had cut it off. It made her look very babyish. Her closed eyes were darkly spectacled in black.

"Asleep?" Old Harry's lips shaped the question; the nurse shook her head, and stooped to brush the dry lips with water, an action Jemima gave no signs of perceiving.

Slowly stooping, Old Harry laid the back of his forefinger gently against the hot little cheek.

Jemima's eyes opened: at first slits of vacant brightness, they widened a little, and the struggle to focus made her wrinkle her brows. The nurse frowned sharply, but no one paid attention to her. A very sweet smile came on Old Harry's lips, under the white moustache. Recognition strove with confusion, then gained a feeble victory.

Jemima adored her grandfather. On the distant, blurred periphery of her consciousness, something stirred; her mouth twitched. There was no voice, only a rustle, like a sound of dead leaves, but they all saw her shape the syllables of her name for him—"Granpy"—and Christian held her breath. It was so long since Jemima had said anything sensible, or shown interest in any of the people who looked after her. Her little neck, scraggy as a fowl's, stirred faintly in the opening of the cotton-wool jacket.

Old Harry, snapping his finger and thumb soundlessly, made a peremptory movement to the nurse, to place a chair for him. She did so, with a haughty reluctance that betrayed her desire to protest, but she was not the first to discover that one did not protest with Old Harry. It was useless to appeal to Mrs. Crome, who was just as headstrong, and seemed to think she knew more about nursing than properly trained people.

"Take my coat," said Old Harry.

"He's not turned up, so do you suppose he's gone to Simon's?"

"It looks like it. Damn. I suppose I ought to have let them know——"

"Would you like me to find out?"

"There's no point in it. Well—thanks for trying."

"Daniel! Are we ever going to see one another again?"

"I should hope so. I can't help it, can I—that people are such bloody ferrets?"

"It's foul, isn't it?"

"Everything's foul."

"I wish I could help. I feel it's all my fault, in a way."

"What's your fault?"

"Well, it was I who recommended the thing. You'd never have seen it, if it hadn't been for me."

"Don't be an ass. I'm ready to fight to the last fence for

it. It's a damned fine book. Agatha Mott rang me up about it."

"Has she seen it?"

"No, but Burke's been talking. She says it's the duty of all the intellectual crowd to get together to defend the serious writer from the illiterate majority."

"What does she mean?"

"God knows. She says she'll interest Strachan, K.C., and try and get him to fight the case for us."

"You mean—you're going to law? Goodness, what will father say?"

"It's to his advantage, as well as ours. He's been lampooned as well as us."

"Won't it mean a lot more publicity?"

"Of course it will. You haven't got any rich, potential backers among your friends, have you, who would be likely to interest themselves in a publishing firm that's on the rocks?"

"I can't think—Daniel! Is father going to draw out?"

"That's what he says."

"But won't it ruin——? Oh, he can't!—when he realizes what it will mean to Christian and the children."

"That's the gossamer-thread upon which our hopes, for the present, are strung. It's too melodramatic, even for Old Harry, to go about smashing your son-in-law."

"I suppose Marius Lear is horribly upset?"

"Don't talk to me about Lear," said Daniel peevishly. "Upon my soul, I'm sick of the fellow. If it wasn't a point of principle, I'd throw his book at him and tell him to get to hell. He doesn't back me up; nobody backs me up. Even Rowlandson thinks we ought to withdraw. We're in a devil of a jam—without Simon on the mark. I'll have to get hold of him to-night, whatever happens. He must see, and make Old Harry see, that we've got to fight for the sake of our own prestige. Obviously, we'll be defeated: there's no question of getting justice over a matter like this. But we've got to go down fighting, or sink our pretension to serious publishing for good and all. Good God, if it wasn't the only decent book Crome and Lygon have ever published——!"

"Couldn't we have lunch somewhere and—and talk about it?"

"I've just ordered some food in; I can't leave the office—you should see them! They're like a lot of wet hens. I've sacked Miss Thomas—she's done nothing but pull faces and say, ' But what are we going to *do*? ' since the news came in. I'll have her back, of course—I can't exist without my spot of glamour. But she's got about as much glamour as a scared cat at the moment."

As Lydia clicked the receiver back, Anna, who had come in, and was about to make a tactful retreat, said:

"Why don't you do something about getting a job?"

Lydia was sitting bowed forward, with her head in her hands. Her hair fell forward in a disordered curtain of pale spun silk over the backs of her hands. Every line of her relaxed body showed discouragement and defeat.

"What sort of a job?" she asked dully.

"Oh, I don't know. There are lots of jobs," said Anna vaguely. "You could show dresses beautifully, or help people to give parties. You seem to be getting—I don't know how to put it—disorganized, lately. I suppose it's some chap."

"Anna," said Lydia, "how is a girl to know if a chap really cares, or not?"

"Don't be a goof, darling. Chaps don't care—not what we mean by ' caring.' Do you want to get married—or something?" asked Anna, elaborately casual.

"' Something,' I'm afraid. The trouble is, he doesn't want to—at least, not as much as I do. No, that's not the trouble either. Oh, Anna, it's the most sickening mix-up of family affairs and business! I could make him want it, if it wasn't for the family. Isn't it devilish to wish one was an orphan? I really thought I'd fixed it when I persuaded them to let me live away from home. It never struck me they'd still have the stranglehold on me—and, through me, on other people as well."

"Here, hold on!" said Anna. "What's all the fuss about, anyhow? I suppose he's tied up, as marriage doesn't seem to enter into the picture. But lots of chaps are tied up, and it doesn't seem to stop the girls having a good time."

"It's just that I don't happen to want it that way," said Lydia wistfully. "I know dozens of nice girls who don't seem to mind carrying on with chaps, and sneaking off for a couple of days here and there—but it isn't like that, Anna. I want to make a real thing of it, as real as though we were married.

"You don't mean that you want to go and live openly with some chap?" Anna appeared incredulous. "It's your own affair, of course, but I think you're an awful goof if you do that. Red-hot romance is all very well, but it never works in this country, and it's always the girl who has a filthy time of it and gets edged out of things as time goes on. For my part, I think it's even a bit vulgar. I don't mean that living with somebody you've got a yen for is vulgar, but you must admit, looking round the circle of our own acquaintance, that the women who are involved in some *au pair* outfit aren't the ones for whom one has any particular sort of liking. I don't know quite what it is: perhaps they do it a bit too blatantly, or something. Anyhow, it's a matter of taste," concluded Anna.

"Still, what's a girl to do?" pleaded Lydia.

"Have as much fun as she can get, I suppose, without making an exhibition of herself."

"You can't have fun by yourself," whispered Lydia, "and if the other person won't play——"

That was just it; Daniel, for some reason, wasn't playing. She was ready to do anything: to buy a house anywhere—perhaps in some get-at-able place in France: to cut herself off completely from her English circle—if he would only show some enthusiasm for the idea. The present state of affairs stabbed her continually, she was always being made to feel humiliated—either by Daniel's refusal to accept the suggestions she made for their being together for an hour, or by his nervous abstraction, when they met, for fear of their being observed. She realized fully the disastrous effect the discovery of their liaison would have upon Daniel's connection with the firm, perhaps on the firm itself: but with feminine unreason, she was convinced that if the affair was put upon a proper basis—that is to say, a house, at a safe distance, and perhaps a *nom de guerre* for Daniel and herself—it could be conducted with perfect safety and profit to them both.

Whenever she suggested, as, occasionally, she steeled herself to do, that Daniel was getting tired of their relationship, he always declared, with emphasis bordering, sometimes, perilously upon irritation, that it was not true: that he loved her, if anything, more than ever, but that he simply could not see the point of bringing everything crashing about their ears for the sake of an affair which, as she should realize, could not possibly be kept secret if they did as she suggested.

She was forced to the bitter reflection that she had played her cards badly; had given him too easily the thing he wanted, and now, if not actually tired of it, he had become casual about it. Perhaps he was even interested in some other girl! People were always saying that kind of thing about Daniel, and she had always defended him to herself by saying that he had to have some form of reprisal against Eliza. Since their return from the country he had made no attempt to communicate with her, until this morning, when he wanted to make use of her. It was not a long time, of course: and, with Simon out of the office, he must be kept "at it" all the time: but forty-eight hours (and it was more than that) is eternity to a woman who has reached the emotional pitch that Lydia had reached in her relationship with Daniel.

What she most hated was that Eliza was probably hugging herself over having settled the Matlock girl! That she should be forced into the position of appearing to be frightened of

Eliza Lygon made Lydia's gorge rise; and the worst part of it was that it was the exact truth! Eliza held all of their destinies in the palms of her thin, vicious hands. The tangle of herself and Daniel and the firm and Old Harry was too complicated ever to be solved in the latter's lifetime, and for all Daniel's professions of affection, Lydia's innate honesty would not allow her to delude herself that their relationship contained any of those elements which might have reconciled her to waiting patiently for Old Harry's death. It was a matter, she told herself ruthlessly, of having Daniel while she could get him, and every week that passed rendered more difficult her pitiful object.

It was, she came to the bitter conclusion, a terribly ordinary, passionate affair, filled to the brim with all those agonies and heart-burnings that seem to accompany the most ephemeral of romances. She was more in love with Daniel than he with her: that was the long and short of it, and she had to pay the price of her folly until time liberated her, as she supposed it would, from the worst of her sufferings.

Old Harry had that power with children and sick people which many men of his kind possess, and it was as though confidence sat down with him at Jemima's bedside—a confidence which penetrated even into that dark prison in which the little girl's consciousness was enclosed. Too weak to smile, her eyes in their leaden pits remained fixed upon her grandfather, who, remembering the many times he had jigged Jemima on his knee, started to hum "Banbury Cross" under his breath. It made a noise rather like a large bumblebee, and the nurse frowned disapprovingly. Jemima was to be kept "very quiet." A glance from Christian, however, again checked her protest; she tightened her lips and went into the next room. It was really very exasperating, to take a case where one was not in absolute control. Not, of course, that Mrs. Crome wasn't a wonderful nurse; but, after all, there was a difference, which should be acknowledged, between the professional and the amateur, and if this went on one would really have to complain to the doctor.

The bumblebee, however, did so little harm to Jemima that, by teatime, when she again dropped into one of her fitful patches of sleep, her temperature had dropped a whole point, and Christian, superstitiously eager to catch at the least sign of improvement, declared that it was her father's doing. "Please, please stay with us!" she begged, when Old Harry, not having changed his position for three hours, came stiffly out on the landing. "Simon, make him stay. Please, father—to look after Simon." She gave him the pale flash of her usual smile, and Simon felt an irrational stab of gratitude for the first sign she had given, since the beginning of Jemima's illness, of solicitude for his welfare.

Whether it was the stimulus of a fresh interest, or the actual fact of her grandfather's presence, Jemima had rallied faintly; whether the improvement would continue, it was impossible to say; Christian dreaded the night, the before-dawn hour when human resistance sinks to its lowest ebb, and it was on this account that she implored her father to send to the Savoy for his valise, and to add the strength of his will to hers and Simon's, to draw Jemima through the tunnel of those ominous small hours.

Old Harry was in a very awkward position. He could hardly refuse his daughter's plea, but he felt more than ever angry with Simon, the innocent cause of his being placed in the false position of assuming a benevolence which, as soon as he got out of Jemima's presence, was far from his mind.

Simon, leading the way eagerly into the study, was brought up short by the sight of the tray which reminded him of his neglected meal.

"Good God, father! You've had no food."

"Never mind about that," said Old Harry, deliberately closing the door. He stood silent for a while, biting his thumb-nail, obviously so perturbed and irritable that Simon said:

"Is anything the matter?"

"Anything the matter!" burst forth Old Harry. "It's an unpleasant thing to be obliged to criticize at a time like this, but I think you should keep in closer touch with the business."

"Has something happened?" Simon spoke quickly, instantly scenting trouble. With Daniel, probably! It was just the way luck went—that Old Harry's affairs should bring him to town on a day when Daniel was lording it in the office. "I'm afraid I have let things slide to-day," he began, hoping the soft answer would turn away wrath.

Without deigning to reply, Old Harry tugged out of his pocket a folded copy of *The Cable*, which he slapped down, turned back at the offending page, under Simon's nose.

"Read that, and tell me what you've got to say to it."

Simon felt a sensation in the roots of his hair as he read Eric Neil's article.

"It's an utter piece of infamy!" he said, when he could speak.

"It's all very well for you to say that; you're responsible for it. I think you've treated me—and Christian—abominably." Old Harry's voice trembled with suppressed emotion.

"Hold on one moment, father. I don't quite see what you mean by that. It seems to me that *The Cable's* treated all of us abominably—you, me and the author; but I don't see how Christian comes into it."

"What do you think Christian's feelings are likely to be, when she hears her husband's been publishing smut?"

"Please——" said Simon, suddenly deadly calm, as he realized the dangerous implications of the situation. "Up to the present, father, you've professed perfect satisfaction with my decisions about the books we've published. In fact, you've been more satisfied than I was myself—but that's neither here nor there. Won't you accept my assurance that this was a book of no less moral worth, and much greater merit, than any of our former publications?"

"In the face of this?" sneered Old Harry, pointing to "The Moron."

"Oh, come, father. You know as well as I do what *The Cable's* like: what you probably don't realize is that this is simply a journalistic stunt, that Fleet Street produces every now and again when there's a dearth of bona fide news—did I say Fleet Street?" Former pride of his calling brought the blood into Simon's ears. "It's flattering *The Cable* to say it's produced in Fleet Street. I don't know what particular dung-heap this maggot breeds on, but I know there isn't a single self-respecting journalist who'd work for Ricketts if he was at the point of starvation. Ricketts is an Irishman who earned his living in New York until it got too hot for him, and then managed to oil himself in with the Marshall-Hickmott combine and in six months turned *The Cable* from a comparatively innocuous rag into an imitation of the tabloid——"

"I don't give a damn for Ricketts or the tabloid. I suppose you'll say next that Ricketts wrote the book, stole your imprint and got this fellow to slate it?" said Old Harry, with the bitter and childish sarcasm that invariably accompanied his loss of temper.

"Neil's a lousy little tick who'll do anything he's paid for," said Simon wearily. "I happen to know he's got the third largest collection of pornographical literature in London. The other two," he could not forgo the malice of adding, "are owned respectively by a Cabinet minister and a famous Methodist preacher."

"Will you hold your tongue?" roared Old Harry.

"I wish to God I'd sent you a copy of the book, so that you could judge for yourself——"

"Do you suggest I'd approve of it?" Moral indignation vibrated in the speaker's accents.

"You mightn't have thought it was a suitable book to put into the public libraries, but I don't think that even you could have failed to respect the honesty of the author, and the originality of his point of view."

"Respect smut! As for your wishing you'd sent me a copy, you know as well as I do that's a piece of humbug! You've brought this book out in secrecy; its name isn't even in your current list——"

"For the simple reason that we accepted it after the lists were in print. Our travellers had orders to bear this in mind, when approaching the booksellers; we had, in fact, to arrange a special little plan of campaign, to put it across with the trade," said Simon patiently.

"Do you suppose any decent bookseller 'll touch it, after reading this?"

"Oh, no," said Simon, smiling rather palely. "This certainly disposes of it, so far as the booksellers are concerned."

"And a good job too!"

Simon's patience cracked suddenly.

"You don't know what you're talking about," he said curtly. "However, there's no need for us to start an argument on that side of the question; what argument can there be, when you haven't even seen the book? I fully sympathize with your feelings in the matter, and it's scandalous that your name has been brought into it—although, if you don't mind my saying so, you're partly to blame for that. If you hadn't let your enthusiasm carry you away, no one need have known you had any connection with the firm."

"Nor, I suppose, with you personally—merely being your father-in-law!" sneered Old Harry.

"That's absurd, father. Of course all our personal friends would know about it, but neither Chris nor I get ourselves into the news paragraphs, in fact, I can't think of an occasion since the year we got married that your name and mine have been bracketed together in the Press. I'm afraid I'm a wholly obscure person," Simon was driven to add bitterly, "and even my own profession doesn't think it worth while to make news out of me! It's obvious that we've got to withdraw; it will cost us a lot of money, and it is a frightful blow for Lear, but there's no question of proceeding against a thing like that." He flung the paper disgustedly from him. "The most I can say is that if I ever get a chance to kick Eric Neil's bottom

I'll do it and risk an assault charge! Why on earth do you suppose Daniel didn't let me know?"

"If you take a 'Varsity-bred dolt as a partner——!" snorted Old Harry.

"You overlook the fact that Daniel's my half-brother," murmured Simon. "Hallo—what's this?" He had been staring for several seconds at the pad beside the telephone, and now saw that a fresh message had been added to those already scribbled on the top leaf. "2.45. Mr. Lygon wishes you to ring him up. This came while we were upstairs. Look here, I'm going down to the office. You'll stay here, won't you, sir—to look after Chris? And—I hope you will see the point of this—I hope you'll leave me to tell her about it when I come back."

"One moment. The last time we dined with you, Simon, my daughter"—the ludicrous formality puckered Simon's mouth into an almost irrepressible smile—"told me that she was acting as reader to your firm. May I inquire whether it was she who recommended this—this outrageous publication?"

"Chris didn't read the typescript, and she hasn't seen the book since it was in print." Simon decided to suppress Lydia's share in the matter.

"Does she know about it?" persisted Old Harry. "I mean, know of its existence, and the type of work it is?"

"Christian's knowledge is entirely limited to what I have told her—which isn't much."

"I'm glad to hear you have so much decency," muttered Old Harry.

"I think that's an uncalled-for observation, and I may as well tell you that it was my intention to give her a copy as soon as she had time to read it," said Simon.

"I forbid you to poison my daughter's mind——!"

"Oh, don't be childish!" snapped Simon. "Chris isn't a schoolgirl, and she's got a perfect right to choose her own reading. I don't imagine for a moment she'll like *Cypriana*—

not for the reasons you suggest, but because most of it's rather
above her standard of intelligence——"

"I don't see the need to insult your wife's intelligence,
because she doesn't appreciate a filthy book."

Simon was walking towards the door.

"Wait a minute. I'd better tell you, Simon, that I've
decided to sever my connection with the firm."

Simon whitened. It was what he had been expecting, and
he stiffened to resist the blow.

"You mean, take your money out?" he said bluntly. "Of
course, you must do as you please. It only strikes me it's a
pity you should let yourself be influenced by a—poison-rag
like that."

"It doesn't strike you that my reputation is at stake,"
retorted Old Harry viciously. "Apart from the matter of
principle, my name's been blazoned all over England as the
backer of a firm that publishes dirty literature. How soon
do you suppose that's going to be forgotten? Mud sticks—as
you're likely to find out, in the course of the next year or two.
How many thousands of people, do you suppose, are sniggering
over the fact that my money's been used to float a—a licentious
publication on the market? What do you think the Sellicks,
the Sparkbridges and the Whipples are saying? What do you
suppose they're thinking down at Granedge?"

"My God, you must have done some talking," muttered
Simon.

"What will my future constituents think of a man who
pledges himself to the suppression of vice, and then lets himself be hoodwinked into a thing like this? It couldn't have
come at a worse time," he complained fretfully. "What's more,
you've betrayed my confidence. You've gone behind my back
with a thing of which you knew I couldn't possibly approve,
and, if it hadn't been for this rag, I suppose you'd have got
away with it. This disgusting production would have been
on all the bookstalls—copies would have been supplied to my
own library! You know we have a standing order for Crome

and Lygon fiction." Simon had forgotten it. "Members of our own congregation would have taken it home—into the bosom of their families——!" Old Harry appeared to sicken at the vision.

"So far as your reputation is concerned," said Simon, who had had time, during this outburst, to collect his thoughts, "that can be put right in to-morrow's edition. You have only to make a statement that you knew nothing about the book, and that it's being withdrawn by your orders——"

"You don't suppose they'll swallow that? The general public's so ignorant about publishing, they'll assume, from the connection of my name with the firm, that I see every manuscript that comes in——!"

"*The Cable* public will believe anything their favourite paper tells them. Ninety-nine and two-thirds per cent have never heard of manuscript; they think a book's born in cloth boards with a three-colour jacket; and, what's more, they don't give a damn. The sooner I get this in hand the better. When I come back, we'll go into the other, more serious, matter you've just raised, father. Please be nice to Chris."

CHAPTER THIRTEEN

Simon took a taxi down to the office. He was livid with rage over having been kept in the dark; his anger embraced Nancy and Marius, but was mainly reserved for Daniel.

Daniel's reception of his partner was not soothing. While Simon was absent, and all the responsibility had devolved upon his shoulders, he had taken it soberly, although in a Danielish manner; with Simon's return he chose to revert to the lightheaded junior partner, inclined to suggest that every one, Simon included, was making a most unnecessary fuss.

"I've simply turned the whole thing over to Combridge," he informed Simon airily. "Of course, he started off in his usual stick-in-the-mud style, but I've managed to put gunpowder under him at last, and he's gone off to take counsel's opinion. He rang me up a few minutes ago, to say that the opinion is that we've got some sort of a case—based on the assumed illegal means by which a copy of the book got into Neil's hands——"

"What are you talking about?" was Simon's angry rejoinder. "There's not going to be any case, while I've got anything to do with it. If it hadn't been for your confounded interference——"

"Hardly the word for it, is it?" Daniel raised his eyebrows coldly. "I don't doubt for a moment you would have handled things differently; but you weren't available, so I did what I considered the best thing for all concerned. It didn't—naturally—occur to me that you'd want us to climb down."

"Climb down be damned! If you had a ha'porth of common sense, or had absorbed one-tenth of the ideas I've tried to put into your head since we went into publishing, you'd know the book's already stone dead; and what's the good of fighting for a dead thing? All you've done is to make our position with *The Cable* impossible: I suppose you realize they'll make your precious letter front-page news to-morrow morning, and we'll be the laugh of Fleet Street."

Before either of them knew it, the scene had blazed into a quarrel. Simon's resentment of Daniel's attempt to handle a major situation alone, his discontent with Daniel's dilettante methods, his annoyance with the Lydia-Daniel situation all entered into it: while, on his side, Daniel vented his opinion of what he was pleased to call Simon's weak-kneed policy in the conduct of the firm, accused him of being under the thumb of his father-in-law, of knuckling under to middle-class prudishness and of wanting to run with the hare and the hounds. His thin, cultured accents, the contemptuous half-smile were gadflies to Simon's wrath. The outrageousness of Daniel's presuming to criticize methods to which he was still an inexperienced new-comer almost choked him: Daniel, who had been given a junior partnership only on condition that he accepted Simon's decisions upon all questions as final: who had mastered the superficialities of the business with as much facility as he ignored its deeper implications: whose playboy value barely balanced his essential ignorance—Daniel, daring to set himself up against the weight of his senior's experience!

Daniel let fly another taunt, and somehow—neither of them could ever afterwards recollect how it happened—Simon's clenched right fist connected with the point of Daniel's jaw.

Simon shook his head, as though it had been he, and not Daniel, who had received the blow. Daniel, who had saved himself from falling by catching hold of the corner of the desk, straightened himself, picked up a piece of blotting-paper and wiped his right hand, which had gone into a pool of ink. On the floor, by his feet, was a mess of writing materials and a litter of cigarettes.

"I'm sorry," said Simon dully.

"It's all right," said Daniel, after a pause. "It only confirms an impression which has been growing on me for quite a while; that you and I aren't intended by Nature to get on in double harness."

"Do you want to dissolve the partnership?" snapped Simon. Daniel nodded.

"Ratting—eh?"

"Which means exactly—what?" inquired Daniel flippantly.

"It means that we've got to look round for another backer, haven't we—if Old Harry gets out?"

"You'd better look round for a new partner at the same time. I'm through," said Daniel, and walked out.

There are moments in a person's life when everything seems to have gone so far wrong that there is positive pleasure in contemplating the fact that it cannot possibly be worse. It was in something of this frame of mind that Simon rang for Nancy and asked her to make him a cup of tea.

"How's Jemima?" was her first question, when she brought it in. It gave him another shock to remember that he had not thought about Jemima for nearly an hour.

"About the same—a little better, if anything. Nancy, why the devil didn't you let me know about this business?"

"How could I? Mr. Lygon said you weren't to be troubled. Oh, it is a shame. I'm so terribly sorry for you about it."

"Where's Marius?"

"Gone home; he and Mr. Lygon were on each other's nerves. Marius took our point of view, which I think was pretty good of him, considering everything. He told Sir Harry himself that he wanted the book withdrawn——"

"The devil he did! On what grounds?"

"On the only good and sensible ones: that if the book appears after this, it will be discredited with all the serious reading public. It will go into second-hand catalogues under the heading ' Facetiæ ' and be bought up by all the collectors of that kind of stuff in London. I think he's quite right, don't you?"

"I'm afraid he is; it's a most infernal shame."

"It's been pretty tough here!" Nancy gave a grim little

laugh as she added, "My word, if we want publicity, we've got it. It seems a pity it should be the wrong sort." She indicated a pile of letters, many of them delivered by hand, on the corner of the mantelpiece. "Those are for Sir Harry. I rang through to the Savoy a few minutes ago, but apparently he's not there; shall I have them sent on to Granedge?"

"Give them to me," said Simon, and stuffed them in his pocket. "Oh—and would you mind clearing up that mess on the desk? I pushed something over." While she was quietly and methodically doing things with a duster and a bowl of water, he was making decisions. "Well, Nancy, we're up against it. You may as well know—speaking between ourselves—that my father-in-law's thrown in the towel and we've either got to find some more money somewhere or smash." After a pause, during which she stood silently looking at him, "As a secondary item of news, the firm's no longer Crome and Lygon. Daniel's just informed me he's getting out."

"Well?" she said calmly.

"It's partly my fault. I ought to have known he hadn't the temperament for a business like this; but he seemed keen enough, and he had the money." Simon laughed. "It means a fresh start. Back to the beginning—just when we had begun to gain a bit of ground. What about it?"

"Good. I like fighting," said Nancy.

"You're a grand person. I wish I could make you a partner; you know nearly as much as I do about the business. Crome and Rowlandson; rather long—awkward for the binding. Well, I suppose I'd better be getting back to Old Harry."

"Does Mrs. Crome know? What a shame at a time like this. I suppose she'll be terribly upset."

"I haven't started to think about that yet," said Simon shortly. "You might get me a copy of *Cypriana*: I'm going to try and make Old Harry read it. He owes us that much!"

On the way home he racked his brains to discover some possible backer in Old Harry's place. Apart from the family discord it would occasion, it was not a bad thing to have the old man out of the way. Simon had never concealed from himself his own resentment of the restrictions imposed on the firm by Old Harry's financial interest; but he had always hoped to build up a position that would make them independent of his father-in-law's idiosyncrasies.

But it was a bad time for raising money. The country was on edge with war scares; people were piling their money into armaments, or using it to back pacifist schemes. Books were a secondary consideration—if they were considered at all!

He found Christian giving her father tea in the study; it was the first time since the beginning of Jemima's illness that she had taken a meal downstairs. He looked quickly to see if Old Harry had told her, but she turned towards him a face of guileless welcome and patted the chair beside her with her hand. The two men avoided each other's eyes as Simon sat down.

"Jemima's temperature is still coming down," she told him eagerly. "Isn't it marvellous? I tell Daddy that he's the real wizard with illnesses, although Mummy's so splendid about knowing exactly what to do. Nurse is awfully annoyed, but Jem's sleeping like an angel. Darling, Daddy's promised to go down and see Henry; isn't it sweet of him? I hated the idea of just writing to tell him how ill Jem has been."

Down to see Henry. What about Henry's school fees, if the business crashed? The idiotic tangle of the position nearly made Simon give a hysterical laugh. Old Harry would never stand for his grandson's education suffering: surely he would see the inconsequence of ruining Henry's father and carrying the ruins on his own back?

When they were alone, Simon walked to the fireplace and filled his pipe. When it was drawing, he faced Old Harry squarely.

"Thanks for not telling Chris. She's not to blame for any of this, and it's hard she should suffer for it."

"Who says she's going to suffer?"

Simon suppressed a smile.

"Well, oddly enough, women do suffer—when their men-folk get into messes."

"It's a pity you didn't think of that before."

"One has to obey one's own judgment," said Simon wearily. "In this particular case the judgment wasn't only mine; the book came to us highly recommended, through a usually reliable source"—he wondered what would be Old Harry's reaction, if he discovered the "source"—"and was strongly approved by two of our best readers, as well as by ourselves. It was just the hundredth chance that it came to the notice of a dirty little rootling hog, with his living to earn by the purveyance of offal. If Alec Ray or Agatha Mott had had it, it would have been acclaimed a literary masterpiece—which it remains, in spite of our lick-spittling friend, Mr. Eric Neil."

Old Harry was slightly mellowed by whisky, which Christian had thoughtfully put on the table before going upstairs.

"That's all very well, Simon," he said more mildly. "We know that to the pure all things are pure; but one has to consider one's duty. I mean, one's duty to the young and ignorant, who may pick up a book like that——"

"Father, will you do me a favour? I want you to read *Cypriana* and give me your honest opinion of its literary merit—apart from any moral question that may be involved. You admire the classics, don't you? Well, Marius Lear has a pure, classical style which is almost without equal among writers of to-day; he's got an extraordinary rhythmic sense, that makes whole pages read like blank verse."

"Very dangerous, very dangerous," grunted Old Harry. "Poetry—there's something in it that's like a drug; one gets carried away—one loses one's power of moral judgment—take Byron, for instance!"

"There's nothing Byronic in Lear, I'm afraid!" smiled Simon. Strange, how one could smile, and feel friendly towards this old man who had just dealt one the most shattering blow it was in the power of any human being to deal. It was as though numbness had entered into him, rendering him, for the time being, insensitive to any emotional reactions. "I think when you've read it you'll agree with me that of the one in five hundred young and ignorant people who might start to read it (I'm probably exaggerating the percentage; you've got to have a sound classic scholarship to get through the first chapter), perhaps one in six or seven hundred would have the patience to go on with it, or get more than a vague notion of what it is about! It's essentially a book for thoughtful and experienced people, and not the sort you dip into for the sake of pulling out pornographic plums."

Old Harry looked disappointed, and drew back the hand he had stretched towards the book.

"Well, well, you can put it in my room—where the maids won't see it, I hope; and I may dip into it before I go to sleep."

"Talking about sleep—do you mind if I have a nap, Father? I'm feeling ' all in.' By the way, here are some letters for you; I expect they're all about the book. If you'd like to look over them, I'll turn on the reading-lamp for you——"

"I'll leave them for the present," said Old Harry frowning. He also had had enough of an unpleasant subject. Five minutes later the two men slept opposite to each other, in Simon's easy-chairs.

Christian heard all about it from the nurse, who, as ill-fortune had it, brought in a copy of "The Moron" from her evening stroll.

"Have you seen this, Mrs. Crome? Dear me, how shocking!" She blinked her eyelashes rapidly, to hide the libidinous delight of her kind in an improper situation. "My word, I'd like to have a peep at that book! I suppose Mr. Crome couldn't lend me a copy?"

"I don't suppose he would, if he could," said Christian shortly. She was painfully shocked by the affair; her ears burned with mortification at "The Moron" article, and when she came to her father's name, she bit back an exclamation of disgust.

For her sake, both Old Harry and Simon, when tackled, made as much light as possible of the matter.

"Well, it's taught them a lesson," said Old Harry shortly, referring to the partners. "It's very unpleasant for everybody and for myself in particular, but I don't suppose it will occur again."

"I begged you not to have anything to do with that book!" Her angry eyes reproached Simon, who found that the numbness had gone, and that he was most unhappily sensitive to Christian's desertion to her father's side. For the book's sake, however, he looked her straight in the face as he answered, "I still maintain I was in the right to publish it, Chris."

"How can you say such a thing?" she cried, while Old Harry made noises of impatience. "Supposing some of Henry's school-fellows see it? Supposing the child reads it himself?"

"I don't think we need consider that possibility; 'The Moron' isn't regarded with favour in scholastic circles."

"It makes it perfectly horrible for all of us," she continued. "Of course the servants will have seen it—I thought Hilda looked at me very strangely this morning, when she brought me my tea."

Simon wished they were alone, that he might have talked quietly and gently to her, and tried to make her understand the motives that had influenced his acceptance of the book. But in Old Harry's presence he could do nothing but shrug his shoulders and remain silent.

"And it's beastly for Father!" She broke off, biting her lip. "Do you think Mummy knows?"

"I sincerely trust not," said Old Harry. "Well, never mind: we shall live it down, sooner or later."

This assumption of Christian fortitude drove Simon to say savagely:

"One form the living-down appears to take is that your father is withdrawing his capital from the firm." He was not going to stand for Old Harry's posing as the injured but all-forgiving party to gain his daughter's approbation.

Christian gasped; she grew a little white about the mouth.

"Well, of course, Daddy; I quite understand. You must do as you think best," she said. Although her words were almost exactly the same as his, Simon was irrationally aware of a sense of injury; perhaps it was her manner of speaking them, of going entirely over to Old Harry's side. It made it seem as if nothing could ever be quite the same again. Her eyes avoided his; they were lowered to her hands, clasped stiffly on her knee.

"Of course there's nothing personal in it," Old Harry began to splutter. "But you can see for yourselves the position I'm in. I don't want to make things uncomfortable for anybody—but I've got to defend my own interests—that's to say, my standing with the general public."

"Of course," said Christian, tight-lipped.

"So that's how we stand at present," Simon heard himself say, in a voice almost as flippant as Daniel's. "I'd better mention, as we're on the subject, that Daniel will be wanting to draw out his capital as well."

"Eh?" said Old Harry.

"We quarrelled this afternoon. It's not the first time. We've both come to the conclusion we're better apart."

"I could have told you that twelve months ago," grunted Old Harry.

Christian rose.

"I must go back to Jemima. Are you coming too, Father?" She seemed deliberately to exclude Simon by her manner of giving the invitation; she did not even look at him as he went to open the door for her. Old Harry heaved himself out of the chair, made as though to follow her, and halted. It was evident that he had other things on his mind than Christian and Jemima. To Simon's surprise, his father-in-law laid his hand clumsily on his shoulder.

"It doesn't do to leap before you look," he mumbled.

"We've got to talk things over—I haven't had time—with all this going on—to get things straight. I'm pleased—very pleased—to hear about your half-brother. Never liked the fellow. Never liked what I heard about him. Couldn't bear his wife. Evil communications, my boy, evil communications! When I come down we'll go thoroughly into the matter. Naturally, I don't want to put Chris and the children in a hole. Especially at a time like this. Got to protect myself, though —for my wife's sake. We'll talk it over—talk it over."

"Normal? Are you sure, Nurse?" Christian took the thermometer from the nurse's hand and peered incredulously at the thread of mercury. It was surely at this hour of the night that the fatal little stream started to mount, and she had so schooled herself to discouragement that she hardly dared to surrender to the hope that lightened suddenly in her soul.

"That long sleep did her all the good in the world. You've only to feel her skin," said the nurse, picking up Jemima's little, limp hand. Christian felt the other quickly: no longer that febrile burning! Damp as a little sponge, and nearly as soft, it sent its message of reassurance to her heart. She covered it over tenderly and pressed the bedclothes more closely about the sweating child.

"Too hot," whispered Jemima, too weak to struggle. And, "I want Grampy."

Sir Harry carefully performed the duties which he usually left to his valet, and, far from finding them tiresome, found that they were rather soothing, when one performed them for oneself. Clean handkerchief under pillow; spectacles in case on top of the evening paper; dental plate in neat, covered travelling cup containing disinfectant, on the bed-table at his elbow. He examined the switch of the bed-light, to see that it was in order, and a warm glow enveloped his pillows. Windows open and curtains thrown back; it was one of the pleasures of sleeping alone, of which Sir Harry was always poignantly conscious, that one could enjoy the morning light on one's face. Lady Matlock did not like light in the early morning.

Old Harry knelt down in his dressing-gown, and earnestly prayed to be forgiven his trespasses; he then read his evening chapter—a nightly ritual which Lady Matlock was probably performing at the same moment in her bedroom at Granedge. He switched off the room lights, took off his dressing-gown, and had one knee up on the mattress, when he remembered.

He had not chosen immediately to accept Simon's challenge to read *Cypriana*: it would look as though he wanted to read it, to read a dirty book whose name was already a byword in every honest English home. In his capacity as self-appointed censor to the works library, he had read a good deal of dubious literature: would pause at a suggestive paragraph to mutter with indignation—before reading it again. It was important fully to grasp the salacious meaning of any passage one condemned.

Simon had forgotten to put *Cypriana* in the room; it must therefore still be downstairs in the study. An upward rush of curiosity drove Old Harry back into his dressing-gown. He opened the door cautiously; paused at the top of the stairs to make sure no one was about, and hurried tiptoe down to the study.

So definite was the improvement in Jemima's condition, that Nana, who shared the night nursing with Christian, had prevailed upon her mistress to "take a good night's rest," which Christian agreed to do on condition Nana called her at four, and before that, if there was the least change for the worse.

She came to tell Simon that she would sleep in Nana's room, so as not to disturb him.

"You won't disturb me," he said eagerly, "and you know you never sleep very well out of your own bed. Please, darling, don't make any changes on my account." He was conscious of not being wholly honest in his pleading: the fact of Christian's choosing to sleep apart from him, coming on top of their recent antagonism, seemed to him a symbol of permanent estrangement, that he could not endure.

She shrugged her shoulders, as though the matter were not worth an argument, and started silently to undress. Simon, who was already in his pyjamas, sat with folded arms on the edge of his bed, wondering what to say; whether she was waiting for him to make an apology. This he was fully determined not to do, whatever it might cost him with Chris. Nothing that had occurred was his own fault, nor was any one in connection with the firm to blame.

Christian went into the bathroom to clean her teeth; when she returned, he said in a constrained voice:

"Your Father is reconsidering his decision to remove his backing from us."

"Well, I call that pretty generous," she said coolly.

He did not say to her that he was uncertain whether to be glad or not. Under all the shock and anxiety of that moment when Old Harry announced his intention, he had felt a breathless sense of leaping towards freedom. Now, with the old man's partial recantation, shades of the prison-house again closed about the future. But if the prison-house meant security for Chris and the children——? Simon supposed grimly he would have to accept it, though his pride shrank from the further humiliations which he saw ahead.

"I suppose he's pleased about Daniel?" she added. "So am I! Oh, yes, I liked Daniel in a way, and I loved the way he was with the children—but I can't ever think of him again without thinking about Lydia."

"I suppose it hasn't occurred to you," said Simon, "that the effect of this may be to bring the Daniel-Lydia thing to a head?"

"How?" For the first time, startled, her eyes met his.

"Well, the only thing that has kept them quiet up to now

has been consideration for us. I don't suppose either of them will care what ructions they raise when Daniel's connection with the firm is over."

To his surprise, Christian took this calmly.

"Well, I suppose that's their own affair. Perhaps Daniel will get his divorce and they'll be married. Father's sure to cut Lydia off, but I don't suppose that will upset her much. She doesn't seem to care for any of us these days—she's completely infatuated with Daniel."

"Don't you mind?"

"Of course I mind," flared Christian. "I mind anything that crashes into the family life and makes Father and Mother miserable. I don't see why you should ask if I mind!" she threw at him. "You've just done all you could to make my position with Daddy impossible."

"What on earth do you mean?"

To his astonishment, a gush of tears came to her eyes, so hard and bright a moment before: she swung away to conceal them.

"Putting me in the hateful position of having to choose between the pair of you!"

"Well," said Simon, stiffening. "You did it, pretty plainly, didn't you?" He paused. "It doesn't seem to me that it's your relationship with your Father that's suffered; but our own."

"What do you expect? You knew I loathed the book——"

"Which you never troubled to read."

"Why should I? You'd told me all about it, and I don't enjoy that kind of reading."

"I didn't expect you to do so; but I thought you might have taken the trouble to read it on my account. It's the only one of our books I've been keen about—and I had a kind of notion"—Simon laughed shortly—"that you respected my judgment."

"I'm awfully tired," said Christian suddenly. "Do you mind if we stop this argument and go to bed?"

For answer he switched off his own bed-light, and lay in the dark—she had put out her own—wondering whether to go boldly and take her in his arms, and force her, by loving, to give up this attitude of wounding antagonism that so falsified their relationship to one another: or whether to stand upon what he felt to be a puerile dignity and leave her to come to her senses—as it was impossible to imagine her not doing, when the first edge of the shock had worn itself away. Poor darling—she was worn out, and this was the last straw; no wonder she felt bitter and resentful about it. It was probably better to let her get over it in her own way.

He felt, with a profound sense of gratitude, that he had been right when, towards morning, he felt Christian's arm stealing around his neck, her wet face and soft, scattered hair against his shoulder. . . .

The Daily Cable had, inevitably, the last word.

"A KNIGHT TO THE RESCUE!" it thrillingly announced across its "feature" page.

"The parents of every boy and girl in the United Kingdom have cause to thank Sir Harry Matlock for his timely intervention which has resulted in the withdrawal of the book *Cypriana*, by Marius Lear (publishers, Crome and Lygon), of which Eric Neil, appealing for the defence of national purity, wrote yesterday in these columns:

"'*It is a menace to the whole of our idealism: no young man reading it can retain his reverence for womanhood, upon which all the highest standards of British morality are based.*'

"'I had no conception of the book's existence,' Sir Harry informed our representative, 'and was thunderstruck when my attention was drawn to Mr. Neil's article. Although not directly connected with the firm of Crome and Lygon, I have an interest which enabled me to lose no time in making representations which, I am glad to say, have resulted in the withdrawal of the book. I should like to express my gratitude to *The Daily Cable* for its prompt action in a matter which involves the deepest and most sacred sentiments of the average decent Englishman.'

"BRAVO, SIR HARRY! THE DAYS OF CHIVALRY ARE STILL WITH US!

"The partners of the firm, Mr. Simon Crome and Mr. Daniel Lygon, when interviewed last night, said that they had nothing to add to Sir Harry's statement."

Old Harry, reading his press-cuttings, lifted a hand almost unconsciously to his white moustache. A gratifying conclusion to an unpleasant affair. All the same, he was mystified to know what all the fuss had been about. An odd book. A very—disappointing book.

CHAPTER FOURTEEN

The relief which Simon experienced in the readjustment of the relationship, domestic and professional, with Old Harry, and his thankfulness for Jemima's recovery were mere interludes of comfort in the volume of anxiety which descended upon him with the complete reorganization of the firm which Daniel's retirement made necessary.

Daniel had professed willingness to leave, for the present, his capital in the business; Simon was now faced with the problem of finding another partner, or of making himself into a limited company, with a board of directors. The second course he was reluctant to pursue: first, because he had experience of directoral boards, and second, because his father-in-law would inevitably become a director, with an active and possibly overwhelming interest in the policy of the firm.

This Simon knew he could not endure. The fate of *Cypriana* had made him more sharply aware than ever of the importance of achieving a working independence. He knew that, for the first time since the firm's inception, he had behind him a valuable body of sympathizers, whose goodwill he was not minded to sacrifice to Old Harry's prejudice: and although he was still held down by his obligations to his father-in-law, he felt the time had come to cease playing for safety.

The means of discharging these obligations was his first consideration—of discharging them without delivering himself into further bondage. So completely was his mind taken up with this problem, that he accepted without protest the assumption by his mother-in-law of the disposal of Christian's immediate future.

Lady Matlock arrived with a complete plan of campaign, which she proceeded, with velvety determination, to lay before him.

"I don't suppose you realize for a moment what darling Chris has been through!"

He stared, stunned by her naïve impudence.

"Such a terrible year!" purred Lady Matlock. "Her miscarriage, and all the anxiety about Jemima!"

"I know. Chris is a heroine—the way she stands up to things."

"But, my dear boy, it can't go on for ever! Men never notice, of course: but I'm quite shocked by the change in her appearance."

Change? Of course she was pale and thin; she had called his attention, laughingly, to the grey in her hair, and he had said the usual, the masculine thing: "It's pretty; I like it." She confessed, rather disappointedly, that she thought of having it "touched up." "Do you mean dyed? Do as you like, of course; but I wouldn't, if I were you." "It makes me look so dowdy." "What rot! It doesn't do anything of the kind." "I don't want to be dowdy, when the children are growing up. They'll both expect me to be a credit to them at school functions." He had not paid much attention; it was just the way women went on about themselves at times. One did not seem to expect it of Christian; she was so balanced, so unself-conscious. If it had been Lydia, one would have taken it for granted.

"Such a *shocking* difference," Lady Matlock was insisting. "And really Chris was always so much the best-looking of the two girls! What she needs is a complete change—taking away somewhere and fussing up a little——"

"I think she'd love to go down to Granedge," said Simon, imagining this was what his mother-in-law was driving at, and wondering why she went about it in so circuitous a fashion. Lady Matlock looked at him pityingly.

"Granedge? Oh, no. The children can go to Granedge, as soon as Jemima is fit to be moved, and Henry's term ends. I shall take Christian to the South of France."

"Well, of course, if that's what she'd like——"

"It's not what she'd like, but what's good for her, my dear Simon," said Lady Matlock crisply. "I don't suppose you realize—being a man—that darling Chris has been much too close to 'things' lately. I mean, she's not only had the responsibility of the house and the children, but she's practically had the office on top of her as well. I know you don't mean to be selfish, but I think you might have realized that a girl like Christian—I mean, with Christian's upbringing—needs relaxation sometimes. Husbands are apt to forget that, I know—and of course, like Harry, you are quite wrapped up in your business. But all that trouble," said Lady Matlock vaguely, "and then the shock of that terrible book——! Please"—as Simon opened his mouth—"don't let's discuss it. Harry and I have agreed never to mention it again, but I at least shall never forget to mention in my prayers——"

"We were talking about Christian's holiday," interrupted Simon.

"You must make her sensible about it, Simon! She's got a ridiculous idea about leaving you—as though you couldn't manage by yourself for a few weeks! If you don't like house-keeping, why don't you go to one of your clubs?"

"I'll make my own arrangements, thanks." There was no need for her to take up this aggressive attitude. Actually, it was a relief to know that for a little while Christian would be with someone who could devote her time wholly to her. It was desperately difficult, at present, to give her all that he felt he owed, and it would be a load off his mind to know that she was properly looked after while he concentrated upon the necessary reorganization of the firm.

Yet, when they spoke of it later, it was difficult to crush back the reluctance he felt to allowing her to go so far from him, even for so short a time.

"Darling, I don't *want* to go. Can't we wait until you take your holiday? It's no fun unless you come too."

"If I could be quite certain of getting away——! But it's all too doubtful. I've got to settle something in the next three or four weeks, and when it's settled I've got to see the machinery works properly. It's not fair to keep you hanging about, waiting for the wind to change."

"And you need it so much more than I do!" She passed her hand tenderly over Simon's brow. "Poor old boy—he's beginning to look so careworn! Damn publishing. I thought it was going to be such fun to have a publisher for a husband, instead of a newspaper man, and it's nothing but a beastly worry."

"You'll forget about that when you get to the South of France. Send me some postcards, will you? Frightfully bright-coloured ones, with Prussian blue seas and rainbow-coloured hotels—like we got at Toulon——"

"And a cross to show which is my window," concluded Christian. He felt her gaiety was forced. "I adore Mummy, but she's a frightful tyrant, and somehow, just at present, I don't feel equal to coping with her. I mean, it puts a girl at a disadvantage when every time there's a bit of an argument she dissolves into floods of tears."

"Do you do that?" He caught her against his heart; it was intolerable to think of Christian's bright courage reduced to tears by her mother's well-intentioned bullying.

Christian nodded, swallowing; her eyelids flickered.

"Such an idiotic way of going on!—and so bad for everybody, not only me. I think perhaps I ought to go away for a while, but we seem to have seen so little of each other lately. It's pure selfishness, to want to inflict my nerves on you, instead of on Mother, but I just can't help it."

As he comforted her, he was guiltily conscious that his own nerves would not stand up to much of this kind of thing. A flash of envy for her escape from responsibility crossed his mind; he was tempted to let go, to leave them to muddle on, while he took the holiday which he certainly badly needed. As though she felt the weakening of his will, her arms tightened about his body.

"Simon, couldn't you——? We needn't go so far—just down

to Cornwall, or somewhere. The Draycotts' place at Fowey! I'm sure Pauline would rent it to us—she's sure to be in town for the season."

"Shut up; I won't be tempted. You know we're in a hole——"

She gave a sharp sigh of defeat, as her arms dropped to her sides.

"You mean, about Daniel. We'd have been worse off, wouldn't we, if he hadn't——?" She picked up a box of cigarettes, chose and lit one deliberately. "It was only Daniel's resignation that saved us—with Father." She puffed out a stream of smoke on a nervous little laugh. "Darling, you've lost your scapegoat. You'll have to be awfully discreet, now Daniel's not there to take the blame."

Simon stiffened.

"Blame for what?"

"You must realize Father blames him, and not you, for *Cypriana*," said Christian, arching her brows.

"If he does it's utterly unjust, as you know, and you ought to have told him. I was quite as keen as Daniel about the book."

"There's no need to say so. Father's decided to blame Daniel, so it's all right." He wondered if she would have followed this typically feminine line of reasoning if Daniel had suffered damage from Old Harry's injustice. "Only now he's gone, you'll have to be a bit more careful. Darling, do try not to choose any more horrid books while I'm away!"

"Chris." He put his hands on her shoulders; he was consciously controlling himself, consciously reminding himself how much he loved her, how well she had behaved—after the first shock—over the *Cypriana* affair, as he told her—"There mustn't be misunderstandings between you and me. I like *Cypriana* and I still believe in it; I'd give all I've got for the chance of publishing another such book. I'm not alone, my dear, in my opinion; people you admire have written and spoken wonderfully about it, and I'd be nothing but a traitor

if I were to deny my admiration, even to you. It's the one
book I'm proud to have done, and but for a wretched accident,
Marius would be in a distinguished position as its author
to-day. It was literature, Chris, and I'm afraid my ambition
is to produce literature, rather than best-sellers—though I'm
willing to buy the privilege by giving the general public the
rubbish it wants."

"I wish," she sighed, "I could see why a nasty book is
always called ' literature.'"

This was too much for Simon.

"Of all the fool things to say! I wish to God you wouldn't
say that kind of thing. It's bad enough when you say it to
me, but when I know you're quite capable of saying it in
public——"

"Of course I am. You don't suppose you're the only one
with opinions, do you?"

Had Simon been in a state of mind for clear thinking, he
would have realized that it was Christian's nervous irrita-
bility, after weeks of mental and physical strain, that spoke;
as it was, he was enraged by her foolish reply.

"If that's your point of view it's no use discussing the
matter any further. Well, I suppose you'll let me know your
plans, when you've arranged them with your mother."

"Simon!" She sounded aghast. At the next moment, she
was sobbing in his arms.

"Oh, Chris, don't—don't. Oh, my God, I can't stand any
more of this sort of thing," he was saying despairingly.

"Mummy's right—we ought to get away from each
other." Fighting for self-control, she groped for his handkerchief, which he gave her out of his breast-pocket. "Sorry
I'm so shot-away. Simon." She hesitated, standing with her
back to him. "Simon, it's not so much fun, is it—being so
dependent on Daddy?"

Thinking what an unaccountable creature she was, he
answered gently:

"No. But I didn't know you felt it."

"I don't—except for you. I'm beginning to see the way you're working—with a chain round your neck. I feel it's my fault: I mean, that you wouldn't do it, if it wasn't for me—and the children, of course. Simon, where, exactly, should we be, without Father's capital?"

"It's rather hard to say. Especially at present, when capital's so confoundedly hard to come by."

"But you've got your own money in the business."

"It seems like a drop in the bucket. I have to own I underestimated our running costs, when we started."

"Yet you wouldn't let me put any of my money in."

"Not on your life. I don't gamble with my wife's income."

"Yet you borrowed from Father."

"An entirely different matter. It was a business agreement and I'm paying interest on the loan."

"Why don't you do the same with me?"

"Leaving you broke, if we happen to crash?"

"Is it likely to?"

"I don't think so. But I wish I'd been a bit more cautious."

"In accepting Father's backing," said Christian, with disconcerting astuteness. "Hush—don't say anything: I'm beginning to understand. I'm an awful fool in lots of ways, but in the things that concern us and our feelings I'm not quite so silly. Darling—this is what I'm trying to say: if I go away for a month"—Simon started—"lots of things may happen. I mean, you may have to make decisions. I'm too stupid even to imagine what they're likely to be things to do with the business. I want you to remember that, whatever it's about, I'm on your side. I mean, I want you to do the thing you feel is right, without bothering about me or the children. I mean—we're all right; I've got my allowance—there's no need to think about money—or anything."

"But—Chris!" Simon did not know what to say.

"Oh, gosh—I'm not used to talking—or even thinking—like this. But I'm trying to make up for—for *Cypriana*. I can't help feeling the way I do about that—and I did so hate the upset for Father. We've always backed each other up, and that time I let you down—badly. I think it's perhaps a mistake when private affairs get mixed up with business and—I want you to promise me something: that if you find some way of being quite free, don't consider anything but just *that*—will you?"

"I don't know what's made you say this," answered Simon slowly. "I've never said anything to you—but it's been in the back of my mind for a long time. I'm very fond of your father, Chris: you know it. But it doesn't make things very easy—considering the difference of our views on so many matters—to be in his debt, as we are, all the time."

"I see that."

"Sit down." She did so obediently, clasping her hands round her knees and looking up at him with an expression so like Jemima's that he felt melted with tenderness. "Since you've brought this up, we'd better have it all out. Especially as you're going away, and, as you say, a lot of things may happen.

"Suppose I were to take you at your word—wait a moment. It might come to choosing between—well, between sharing a very much less comfortable existence than you're accustomed to, or going back to your parents, until I'm in a position to give you your luxuries again."

"I see," said Christian calmly. He was grateful for the coolness with which she accepted the ultimatum, the lack of sentimentality or protestation, that proved the sincerity of her offer.

"If I can't find another backer, or a new partner with money to put into the business, I'll have to get out myself," he went on smoothly. "The one thing I've come to the conclusion I cannot do is to accept your father's dictation of the firm's policy."

"But you accepted it to begin with."

"Yes, I am to blame for that—for accepting his help on terms I hadn't fully grasped when I accepted them. To be quite candid, Chris, if I'd known I was becoming Old Harry's literary henchman, I'd have looked elsewhere for my backing, or stuck to editing. Now, if I try to get out of my bargain, it may mean a big loss, and starting over again with an ugly debt on my shoulders. I've done all I can to avoid unpleasantness—as much for your sake as for my own: but, frankly, it's involved too big a sacrifice, both of personal dignity and principle, to be allowed to continue. I've got to get out, as graciously as possible—for the last thing I want is to hurt Old Harry's feelings."

"If we have to retrench and live in—in a small way"—her choice of words made Simon smile, realizing how little she knew of their meaning—"it will just be another adventure. And I feel just as strongly as you do, that we've had too much help from Father and Mother; it's smothering us—and, if we don't take care, it will spoil the children."

"I'll take dam' good care it doesn't do that," said Simon cheerfully. She got up and came to stand close to him.

"Tell me what you really want, Simon. Would you like us to cut and run—now?"

"Heaven forbid." He laughed aloud, as he leaned over to kiss her lightly. "Rather not! I'm not going to sink the ship for want of a good shot at keeping her afloat. As a matter of fact, I'm seeing the bank to-day, and I've got an appointment with Camden. I think he may be able to help—with advice, if nothing else. It's not as if I was trying to get support for a dud concern. I do know my job, and I'm convinced I can make it go if I can get a decent backing. The trouble is, I've got to repay your father's loans, and I've got to find enough to carry on."

"You haven't mentioned it to him yet?"

"What's the good, before knowing whether I'll be able to put it through or not? We may have to go on like this for a couple of years—by which time we'll either be washed up, or I'll be in a position to pay at least half of the loan back out of the firm's financial assets! Besides, I don't flatter myself that Old Harry'll be pleased, because—I don't say this disagreeably—I think he rather enjoys the feeling that we're dependent on him."

"He's rather like that," sighed Christian. "You know he only let Lydia go and live by herself on condition she didn't take a job!"

"And speaking of Lydia—you'll keep this all under your hat, won't you, darling? I should hate the old man to get wind of my intentions before I tell him myself."

"Of course. Anyhow, Lydia hardly comes near me. I don't even know if she knows Daniel's out of the firm—I suppose she does, though I didn't mention it, when I saw her for a minute the other day. Somehow I just can't say ' Daniel ' to Lydia now."

"I'm afraid I've got no time for those two; I've got enough on my mind, without bothering about them," said Simon, more sharply than he intended.

"Well, after all, Lydia happens to be my sister——!" Her flame darted to meet his.

"And Daniel's my brother; and they're a pair of pig-headed fools——"

"I don't see that Lydia's so much to blame—after all, she isn't tied up to somebody else."

Simon opened his lips to give a tart reply, and thought suddenly, "*Christ!* The old woman's right. We *must* get apart." It was too nerve-racking—this pendulum-ing of Christian and himself between tenderness and irritation.

"You're wanted on the phone," said Nancy Rowlandson, pushing the receiver across to Marius, who took it reluctantly. The *Cypriana* debacle had made him phone-shy; although every one in the office had done their best to spare him, he had had several disagreeable experiences. He barked an unreceptive "Well?" into the mouth of the receiver.

"Is that Marius Lear? Miss Audley speaking."

"Well?" said Marius.

"I'm frightfully cross with you."

"What about?"

"Naughty creature! Haven't you ignored my existence for weeks? What is it? A rush of celebrity to the head?"

"I don't know what you're talking about," snarled Marius.

"And considering it was all my doing in the first place! Who gave your manuscript to Lydia Matlock? *Me!*" declared Miss Audley, with more emphasis than grammar. "And I suppose the little beast's reaped all the credit for discovering you!"

"She's not shown any particular keenness about claiming it. Did you want to speak to me about something?"

"I'm speaking; I think you're a thankless brute!"

"Anything else?"

"Not even an advance copy of the famous work! I'm *furious!*"

"I haven't anything to do with advance copies; that's the firm's business."

"At least you can send me one now, can't you?" As the lady's voice rang out into the room, Nancy's eye met Marius's across the table. How was it that so few people understood that when a book was withdrawn it was withdrawn, and that free copies were not available to scatter among one's friends. As Marius was about to reply, the imperious accents of Miss Audley, sharpened by the instrument, trumpeted in his ear. "Is it true—that people are saying—that *Cypriana's* split the firm in half? That Crome's had a row with Lygon and dissolved the partnership?"

There had been no public announcement, as yet, of the change in the firm, but Marius, catching the wink in Nancy's eye, said:

"I'm not a partner, and I don't know what goes on inside the partners' room. If there's been any difference of opinion, it isn't over my book."

"Oh, really? Well, you must come along and tell me all about it. And bring a copy or two of *Cypriana* with you! You needn't bother about the censorship—or whatever it is; I

know dozens of people who'll give five pounds for a copy—
you know, collectors of special books." She broke off to giggle,
but continued before Marius could get his reply in. "And
listen: I've promised Lydia Matlock I'd take you along to her
cocktail this evening, so don't be late. About five at Curzon
Street, and we'll have a cosy chat and go on to Lydia's afterwards. Good-bye!" The gay echoes of farewell were clipped
by the click of Miss Audley's receiver.

There was a moment's silence. Nancy said ironically:

"I can't think of anything I'd enjoy less than a ' cosy chat '
with that young woman."

Marius hunched his shoulders and bent again over the desk.

"So you're going social!" jibed Nancy.

"Who says I am?"

"Gwen Audley."

As he made no reply, a fury seized her.

"You're going to let yourself be shown off by a hare-
brained society woman who thinks she's got a sure-fire sensation for the drawing-rooms! You refuse people like Agatha
Mott and Bertie Manders, who ask you to dine decently in
their homes, and you accept the invitations of a little Mayfair
twirp who wants to put your novel into her smutty library!"

"For Jesus' sake!" said Marius, looking astonished.

Something clicked in Nancy's brain; she gasped, putting
her hands to her head, as she recognized the absurdity of her
outburst. Forcing a smile:

"I'm sorry," she said. "I can't think what it was—I was
in a muddle over these accounts, and that woman's voice
cracked up all my addition. God—isn't this room hot? Open
a window, will you?"

She, too, bent over her desk, her cheeks and ears burning.
She prayed—and knowing Marius, was almost sure—that he
would not connect her outburst with her own suggestion,
earlier in the day, that they should go to a flick after the
office closed—a suggestion which he turned down, because,
he said, he wanted to work. He had said nothing about work

to Gwen Audley—well, she had hardly given him time: but if he did not intend to go, he would surely ring back and say so?

Lydia and Anna were combining for a party. Lydia had just come back from Le Touquet, where she had gone on the spur of the moment—partly because she felt the need to go somewhere, to escape from the emotional strain of her unsettled relations with Daniel, and partly because she thought that a few rounds of golf might hope to tone her up. She stayed three days, had miserable weather, lost more than she enjoyed at the tables and came wandering back, in so obviously shattered a frame of mind that Anna decided there was nothing for it but a party, and spent the evening and most of the following morning in ringing up every one she could lay hands on and inviting them to cocktails at the flat.

So the long, double room was crowded, although its component parts kept changing, as most people had other engagements, and could only manage, at such short notice, to "look in" on their way elsewhere.

"Gwen rang up to say she's bringing Marius Lear," Anna found time to tell Lydia, between directions to a new parlourmaid and greetings to fresh arrivals.

"Marius Lear—what for?" asked Lydia: but she thought, "Now—if I'm cute—I can get some news of Daniel."

He had not telephoned or sent her a line of farewell, although she had been careful to send him word of her plans to the office—cherishing to the last moment the faint hope that he might contrive to join her for the week-end. She had been keeping away from Simon and Christian, more because she sensed their strong disapproval of the Daniel situation than because she minded their knowing about it. Besides, it was too absurd, seeing Christian and not being able to "talk" to her! Christian had evidently taken up a thoroughly "family" attitude to the affair, and was so anxious that Lydia should not attempt to take her, as formerly, into her confidence that

their few conversations were filled with jerkiness and restraint
—which Lydia, up to the last few weeks, would have been quite
willing to break down by a frank discussion of her position.

But since she became uncertain of Daniel she had developed
a painful self-consciousness, which completely put a stop to
her visits to the Cromes; beyond books and fruit and table
games for the now convalescent Jemima, which she directed
the shops to send, she had had no communication with their
household for more than a fortnight. The security of Daniel's
love for her would have buoyed her up in any atmosphere of
disapproval; but her miserable doubts left her stripped and
defenceless. She could no more risk a casual meeting with
Daniel under her sister's eye than she could have asked Christian
point-blank for news of her faithless lover.

She barely knew Marius Lear, whom, in common with
most people, she regarded as a difficult young man; but she
made up her mind to find some opportunity of making herself
very pleasant to him—it should not be difficult, in her capacity
as hostess—just for the sake of coaxing the name of Daniel to
his lips. Daniel, Daniel, Daniel. It was agonizing, never to be
able to name him: to go through life with one's ears for ever
pricked, on the chance of hearing his name spoken. It did not
often happen; Daniel's set did not "play" much with hers.
A casual reference—usually to "the Lygons" (as though they
were one!)—was all that rewarded, in most cases, her strained
attention of an evening. Beyond this, she had to depend upon
a chance telephone call, or one of Daniel's scrappy little notes
—so often to break off an appointment that she had grown to
dread the sight of his handwriting; and just when she had
almost arrived at the point of forcing herself to accept the
fact that it was all over, "something" would happen, or Daniel
for his own mysterious reasons would be prompted to write
her a love-letter of such unmistakable longing and devotion
that it would all start over again—worse than ever!

Here, at last, was someone who knew all that she longed
to know about Daniel; who came, perhaps, straight from the

sound of his voice into her presence. Perhaps Marius Lear
would even have mentioned to Daniel where he was going,
and Daniel, although discretion would prevent his sending a
message, would be thinking of her. Thus desire played havoc
with common sense, and the pulse-beat quickened in Lydia's
—by now—far too slender wrists.

"Lydia, darling, you look positively ravishing! I'd no
idea Le Touquet was so bracing."

"It's not; it was foul," she told the speaker—one of Anna's
tall and drooping young men, who went in for "interiors"
and had helped them to arrange the flat. Anna rather favoured
drooping young men, because, as she said, they folded into
so little space and when bored one could forget they were
about.

"Oh, dear, how sad. Then I suppose it's the party—marvellous party, darling! I'm simply devastated because I've got
to leave before Marius Lear arrives. Bertie says his book was
absolutely stupendous. I'm dying to see it. Do tell me: is it
very naughty?" He batted a coy eyelash and giggled into his
sherry. "Gwen promised to get me a copy, but she's *such* a
naughty girl about keeping her word, so whisper a reminder,
won't you, if you get a chance. Good-bye, darling—lovely,
lovely sherry!" He willowed away, leaving Lydia wondering
a little whether every cocktail party was really so stale, so
foolish, so crowded with unamusing people as her own.

"Hallo, Lydia!"

Gwen Audley was at her elbow, looking, as she always
managed to look, ten years older than her age, by reason of
her swarthy skin and the matronliness of her over-dressed
figure. She was wearing bright purple, with a golden torque
that lay on the upper part of her chest like a forgotten unit of
armour. A faint smell of perspiration, and the perfume she
used to subdue it, made Lydia's fastidious nostrils contract.
Really, Gwen was too much sometimes. She forced a smile,
looking beyond her guest for Marius Lear.

"Am I furious! That nasty little usher's let me down,"

panted Gwen, looking for support, and dragging Lydia with her to a sofa. "Just another dam' swelled head, I suppose."

"Marius Lear hasn't come?" said Lydia faintly.

"I rang up the little beast at his office," went on Gwen, regardless of the fact that the "little beast" was rather more than six feet in height. "You know—your brother-in-law's place—and told him I was going to fetch him here and introduce him to people and arrange for his book to be sold——"

"But that's been withdrawn."

"Don't be silly. It's worth five pounds a copy now, at least, and I know two or three people who ought to be here" —she cast a scavenging glance round the room—"who'd pay twice that for it. I hope you don't mind my saying so, Lydia, but I don't think that firm's got much brains behind it. They're chucking away a grand piece of publicity——"

"Can't you understand, Gwen? You can't sell a book after it's been withdrawn in circumstances like those. You're only asking for a prosecution."

"Nonsense; I don't mean like *that*." Gwen waved a plump, gloved hand. "Every one knows there are ways and means —I got a copy of *The Mangrove Swamp* as soon as the row was over—and I know at least half a dozen people who did the same."

"I don't see Simon agreeing to that sort of back-stair marketing, all the same," Lydia was contrained to retort. "I don't know what happens to a book like that—I suppose it's pulped, or whatever they call it."

"H'm! Very high-minded, I suppose," commented Gwen, looking down her short hooked nose as though she pitied Lydia's lack of intelligence. "All the same, I bet if Lygon had had anything to do with it, he'd have found a way of saving something from the ruins."

"I don't see why you should suggest that D-Daniel's less principled than Simon," stammered Lydia, hating herself for stumbling over Daniel's name.

"Principled my foot!" retorted Gwen. "Lygon was always the live wire of that outfit, and it's a pity he's thrown his hand in."

"What?" said Lydia.

Gwen stared at her, her lips opened, she gave a shriek of triumph.

"You don't mean to say you haven't heard?"

"Heard what?"

"My dear, don't your relations tell you *anything*? The partnership's blown up—dissolved—whatever you call it! Oh, I can tell you there are all sorts of tales about it: that Lygon wanted to fight the case and Crome wouldn't let him, and they had a real, first-class row in the office! Another version is that Eliza had something to do with it—she heard that Daniel was having an affair with a typist or something, and hoicked him out by the collar—I wouldn't put it past Eliza. Anyhow, Lygon's gone—whether he walked out or was kicked, which nobody seems to know. You *don't* mean you hadn't heard? Well, of all the extraordinary things—and your brother-in-law the senior partner—well, of course, he's the whole firm now, and it'll be fun to see what he makes of it." Gwen looked as satisfied as though she had arranged the whole matter herself; it was always the height of bliss, from her point of view, to inform her friends upon matters upon which they might have been expected to have better information than herself—especially when such information chanced to be disconcerting. Her sharp eyes searched Lydia's for signs of embarrassment, but were defeated, for Lydia had learned, through experience, to conceal all signs of facial emotion when Daniel was mentioned. Her hands and her tongue she could not quite control: the only thing was to keep the one silent and the others concealed, until she had regained her equanimity.

"I suppose you've got it right, Gwen."

"Ask your sister, if you don't want to take my word for it. I should have thought you'd have been one of the first to hear," stabbed Gwen. Lydia wondered, with a pang, if she guessed something, but her voice was almost too calm as she replied:

"I don't see why. I don't see Christian often—and I've just been away. We don't go in for correspondence—my sister and I!"

"Oh, don't get annoyed about it. I only think it's most extraordinary," was Gwen's parting shot, as she scrambled to her feet and waddled—she was getting enormous!—away.

In Lydia's heart pounded a painful rhythm. He never told me, he never told me!

Why had he not told her a thing so intimately bound up in their relationship? If he had nothing further to do with the firm there was no longer reason to fear Old Harry's reprisals. Why had he not told her?

Wincing with pain, Lydia forced herself to answer truthfully the poignant question. There could only be one answer: that Daniel no longer included her in his calculations.

CHAPTER FIFTEEN

In removing himself from the firm of Crome and Lygon, Daniel experienced a certain amount of regret, mingled with relief. Although glad to escape from the irksome routine of the office, he was bored with a prospect alternatively blank or complicated by the necessity of finding another outlet for his energies; for, though not economically obliged to earn his living, Daniel had had enough of idleness to have lost his taste for it.

It is tremendously easy to fill one's nights, when one is young, and rich, and indifferent enough to the quality of one's company; it is not so easy to fill the days, when most people have jobs, or pretend to have them. At polo, at the races, one could pick up a few friends; one lunched, too briefly, with people who, at five minutes to three, started looking at their watches and talking about other appointments. Daniel had not, oddly enough, the temperament of the *flâneur*: at least, not while the sun was up. He could act it beautifully—irritatingly so—but it was not until cocktail time that he got into the skin of the part. When the rôle was forced upon him, he found it boring. There was only one thing to do; to clear out—to go away.

And here the thought of Lydia came in to disturb him. If it had been any other girl than Lydia Matlock, it might not have worked out so badly; but even Daniel, with all his selfish inconsideration for other people, knew that Lydia, gentle, loving and hypersensitive under her shining veneer, was not the sort of person to sacrifice to an egoistic determination to have a good time and let the rest burn. The Lydia affair—he faced it coldly—was a failure, as everything cautious and clandestine was bound to be, in these days when people are ostentatiously indifferent to reputations.

It made it no better that Lydia herself was prepared to come out into the open, to risk Eliza's reprisals and family ostracism; for, like the majority of men whose passions are not deeply involved, Daniel did not want to be bothered, either with ostracism or reprisals. What he wanted was a light-hearted and sophisticated mistress, with sufficient independence and sense of humour to be unperturbed by Eliza's behaviour, and sufficient social poise to hold her own against gossip.

Lydia cared too much. Unconsciously she oppressed him with the weight of her loving. Seeking in her only oblivion from his own emotional disturbances, he had met in her a disconcerting will to love, and, as time went on, a perverse possessiveness little less galling than Eliza's. Daniel hated being possessed; but, sweet and true and loyal as Lydia had shown herself, it seemed unfortunate that he could not transfer to her those relics of love which Eliza had left him!

A longing to escape from both women filled Daniel, when he found Lydia's note, telling him that she was going to Le Touquet. He had not seen her since the scene with Simon, and knew he was a brute for treating her in such a fashion. She was bound to hear of the change in the firm's personnel from the Cromes, and he guessed that she was now expecting him to say that, as their actions could no longer affect the fortunes of Simon and Christian, they could freely discuss their future.

In fact, he had half expected Lydia to take some action on her own account. She was careless enough and wild enough to burn her own boats, so long as she was assured that the conflagration would not spread to other people's. It angered him that she could not see for herself—as any woman of sensibility might have been expected to see—that the emotional thing between them had, at least so far as he was concerned, worn itself out.

Or, more truly, it had perished of inanition. Those snatched, difficult meetings had become too tiresome, as well as too dangerous, to pursue in the casual fashion that Daniel desired.

Above all he wanted freedom, ease and absence of responsibility. He could have amusing times with so many people—why strain after something which, sweet as it was, carried so many disadvantages and threatened complications with which a man of Daniel's type could hardly be expected to trouble himself?

The week before Christian went away was the worst since the Cromes were married. As though a spring had snapped, Christian became captious, moody and so unlike her normal self that it was impossible to find precedent for her words or actions. Every one felt the effects of it—from Simon and Jemima to the servants.

"Grumbles at me for the bills and sez we've to economize, and buys 'erself a trooso for the Riviera on the next breath!" was the cook's acid comment, after one of Christian's brief, stormy visits to the kitchen. Her behaviour was that of one who did not know what to be at next; she spent the mornings with her mother, shopping for the trip abroad, Lady Matlock laughingly brushing aside her efforts to keep their purchases within the bounds of moderation.

"No, really, Mummy dear, that's not a bit necessary!"

"Oh, darling, don't let's talk about things being necessary. We're going to have a lovely holiday, and be just as extravagant as we like," crooned Lady Matlock, whose one form of intoxication was to abandon herself to an orgy of buying.

Christian, despairing, and on the verge of tears, found herself in possession of play-suits, beach outfits, sun garments she could not imagine herself wearing; if she rejected anything, the assistant, at a nod from Lady Matlock, added it to the already existing pile. She came back from such expeditions almost hysterical. It was no use insisting upon economy, when she could not explain to her mother for what the economy was needed; Simon was not yet in a position to beard Old Harry and lay his plans before him.

"It's ghastly—Mummy's making me spend hundreds of

pounds; I mean, out of my own pocket, apart from what she gives me!"

"Well, that's all right. I'm glad you're laying in a good stock before the lean time starts!" Simon tried to hearten her.

"But it's such nonsensical stuff—nothing that's of the least use, except on the Riviera. I can't go to the theatre in *plage* clothes!" lamented Christian.

"Oh, for God's sake, can't you enjoy yourself while you've got the chance?" muttered Simon.

The rupture in her usually calm tenor of existence could not have occurred at a worse time for either of them. Simon, distracted as the days went by, presenting no solution to his problems, had nothing left with which to meet the demands her condition made upon his solicitude. She was by turns irritating and irritable; repented in tears for some unwarranted unreasonableness, only to blunder again in a few moments' time. Simon found himself thinking, "Thank God for next week!" It was the first time in his life that he had longed for her to be out of the way—that he might be free to concentrate upon his own affairs.

Jemima, in the fretful stages of her second convalescence, contributed nothing helpful to the situation. She whined because her mother went out and left her, because she was not yet allowed to go down to Granedge, because Christian would not let her play with and try on the result of her shoppings, because Henry was still at school and because nobody came to see her.

"Why doesn't Daniel come? I'm sick of Nana, she's an old bore." Daniel came once, and outraged Nana by teaching Jemima to play poker dice for acid-drops. "It's all that old beast Nana's fault Daniel doesn't come any more!"

"Be quiet, Jemima!" snapped Christian. "I forbid you to speak like that about Nana." She herself had had a tremendous row with Nana that morning, over some underclothes of Henry's which Nana said were only fit to throw away, and Christian said had got to be mended. "They're quite good enough for him to wear at Granedge to play about in."

Nana retorted spiritedly that if Christian wanted her child to go about like a street urchin it was her own affair, and Christian told her not to be impudent, and that if Nana was too lazy to do the darning she supposed she would have to find someone who could; whereupon Nana very nearly gave notice, but, after a look at Christian's flushed cheeks and shadowed eyes, closed her lips tightly and went away.

The climax of misery arrived when Simon came in very late after dining with Roger Burke. It had been rather a portentous dinner, a "stag" affair to which Burke had invited Bertie Manders, Ray and an American whom he introduced as Peter Horne. It took place in Burke's flat overlooking St. James's Palace, and its purpose—transparent, as were most of Burke's efforts on behalf of his friends—was to bring Simon and Horne together, with a view to the latter's interesting himself in Simon's firm.

Simon had been surprised—pleasantly so, by Burke's activities on his behalf. He had known for a long time that Burke's pontifical manner and rather serious attitude to his own achievements in literature covered a heart of gold, and that between him and Manders existed a friendly rivalry in the protection and encouragement of young writers, the kudos of whose discovery they frequently and with acrimony disputed. They had both been loud in their professions of sympathy and support for Marius Lear, although a little taken aback by his indifference to their partisanship. Burke was dryly humorous, Manders inclined to be petulant about it. Patronage is not so common a commodity in these days that one looks for its rejection, when offered! Manders was a born patron; Burke had reached that eminence when he could afford to toy with the pleasures of patronage. Neither was accustomed to being snubbed by young men who might be geniuses but were most certainly paupers, so far as their writing went.

Simon had gone out of his way to try to make Marius

gracious to them both, but had given it up in despair. All he got out of Marius was the terse rejoinder that the small amount of time at his disposal after doing his duty to Simon was dedicated to his work, and not to making himself pleasant to the fatted writers of best-sellers. "Manders isn't a writer, you fool—and he's got enough influence to float a Spring list, if he chooses." "All right, let him get on with his floating," was the good-tempered retort.

Simon desisted; his sympathy was with Marius. He himself was not good at "making himself pleasant" with an ulterior motive; he had left that side of the business to Daniel. But he liked Manders, and he liked Burke, and encouraged by their eager interest in the *Cypriana* affair, had taken each into his confidence about the future of the firm.

Burke's prompt action took him by surprise. "My dear fellow, of course you mustn't throw your hand in," was his reception of Simon's statement of his difficulties. He listened with close attention to all Simon had to say; his high, polished head gleamed with intelligence, with sympathy, with gratification. His enemies said that to get anything out of Burke you had only to flatter him; and, after all, what form of flattery is so subtle as that of giving confidences and asking for advice?

Having made a fantastic fortune out of the old-fashioned, romantic novel, Burke had now gracefully (and some said prudently) retired from the arena, preferring to consolidate his position by the encouragement of moderns rather than imperil it in competing with them. It was freely said that he aspired to publishing, but Simon discounted the rumour, as he did the possibility of Burke's being willing to lend his name and financial support to an obscure firm. Yet what a sporting venture it would be—to a man who wanted to go into publishing less for pecuniary gain than for amusement —to take up a little firm and build it into a great one!

Lest Burke should think this idea was in his mind, Simon became frigid in his detachment from the subject they were discussing: over-did, if anything, his disparagement of the

firm's resources and its achievements up to the present. Burke
listened, nodding gravely. No, no; of course, in his position
one did not go about salvaging derelict publishers; one
became—with suitable drum-banging and fanfare of trumpets
—a member of the direction board of some famous combination, like Gosschalk or Bannister Mills.

"Well, I promise you I'll do whatever I can, my boy,"
said Burke, ending the conversation on a phrase which Simon
thought he had estimated at its true—that is to say, almost
non-existent—value, until he had the telephone summons to
dine with Burke and meet Peter Horne.

"So sorry to give you such short notice, but it's the merest
fluke that I happened to get hold of Horne; he's going back
to the States next week," blared Burke into the receiver. "I
don't know if it will lead to anything—I heard a rumour—
I'll tell you later."

Simon smiled, recalling Burke's old-maidish nervousness
of committing himself on the telephone.

"And I say—I didn't want it to appear too obvious—so
I'm asking Manders and Ray. You'll be surrounded with
admirers—if that's any help to you!"

Peter Horne was small, fair, and, somewhat to Simon's
surprise, young: at a guess, in the early thirties. His skin had
the dry, yellowish tinge of the town-bred American's, and his
hair had receded to the crown of his head, leaving exposed the
full height of a broad, corrugated brow across which ran the
straight bar of his straw-coloured eyebrows, jutting like thatch
over the deep-set, intent eyes of the business man. There was
about him a faintly disturbing tension, which the dragged-out
leisureliness of his speech helped to emphasize. Apart from
the tempo, and an occasional misplaced stress upon a syllable,
he had little accent; he told them he had been at school in
England, but did not specify the school. Simon formed the
impression that it would be very difficult to get any information out of Mr. Horne which he chose to withhold.

The conversation was all of books. Bertie Manders, from

the point of view of the intelligent reader, Ray from the critic's, and Simon, with some diffidence, from the publisher's, kept the ball rolling in a fashion which clearly interested the American. There was a good Château neuf du Pape, to which the Englishmen did full justice; Horne drank ice-water until dessert appeared, when he surrendered to the cognac which Ray, as a connoisseur, recommended. Simon took his first sip, and felt, suddenly, very hopeless. Where was all this leading —this agreeable, literary chit-chat, upon which, so far, no shadow of business had intruded? It was certainly not his place to introduce it. Had he, from Burke's point of view, made the desired impression? He had perhaps been over-cautious; conscious of being "on view," although for what purpose he had not yet discovered, he had done something less than justice to his own conversational powers. He was feeling dispirited, and even meditated excusing himself and returning to Christian, of whom he had seen almost nothing in the last forty-eight hours, when Horne turned to him.

"I hear you've just published a very interesting work, Mr. Crome," he said, with his slow, pleasant smile.

"Do you mean *Cypriana*? I'm afraid it hardly got as far as publication. You know what happened, of course."

"That certainly was too bad. You've got a queer way with books here. That couldn't happen in the States." Horne shook his head. "Not that publishing's in any too prosperous way with us either," he added.

"No. I gather your writers are having a difficult time."

Burke laughed and said that his last novel had been a complete flop across the Atlantic.

"Only eleven thousand; isn't it absurd?" he cooed, with the amused toleration of the author whose successes leave him indifferent to the fluctuations of the market. "I really can't make out what they *want*," he continued plaintively. "*The Green Blade* did very well over here, didn't it, Bertie? And you gave me a lovely notice, Alec; I'd forgotten—I meant to write and thank you."

"I guess we don't know what we want ourselves," Horne interpolated, ignoring the latter part of Burke's remark. "The truth is, we've got the jitters; it's a natural result, isn't it, of over-production? Unless a thing's likely to go over big, it's wiser to scrap it; that knocks out a lot of promising work, and, incidentally—knocks the bottom out of publishing for pleasure. I should know!"

"Are you in publishing?" Simon spoke too quickly to keep the surprise out of his voice. He heard Burke chuckle, as though pleased to have kept his own counsel so successfully.

"My uncle's the big end of Schwartz and Tallant, and I was to have had a partnership this year," said Horne simply. "Now it seems as if the business won't carry another partner, so I just go on doing the chores! I guess I'm pretty sore about it." Again he gave his pleasant smile. "On the other hand, I don't see much chance, at present, for a person with my ideas."

"What are your ideas?" Simon was grateful to Manders for putting the question.

Horne made a cautious, sideways movement of the head.

"Oh, I don't know. Just to produce books! That's all, when it's said and done, isn't it?"

Burke, Ray and Manders laughed. Simon scowled, looking at his plate, with the husks of walnuts upon it. So far as he was concerned, it was a wasted evening. He saw no point in Burke's getting him here to discuss the state of the American book market. Horne looked at his watch.

"I'm sorry, but I must be going. My wife's got a party at the Dorchester and I said I'd join them at eleven. Glad to know you, Mr. Crome." He held out his hand to Simon. "We're going to Paris to-morrow, but I'd like a few words with you before I leave. Would nine be too early?"

"Not at all," said Simon in surprise. "Will you come to the office, or would you like me to come round to your hotel?"

"That surely would be nice of you. My wife breakfasts in her room; perhaps you'll share mine, in the grill-room?"

"Nine sharp," said Simon, smiling, so as not to appear too eager.

"Don't go," Burke was saying to him, while Manders and Ray argued about giving each other a lift. When they were gone, Burke took Simon to his study, saying beamingly, as he closed the door, "Well, how do you like him?"

"Horne? A nice chap; less wearying than a lot of Americans."

"My dear boy, he may be incredibly useful! He's old Carvel's nephew: you know who I mean—Carvel who made a fortune out of canning and put most of it into the book trade. Horne's his heir, and he should have had a partnership —as you heard. Well, even Schwartz and Tallant are feeling the wind, though a firm like that's only got to sit tight and wait for the slump to be over. Still, Horne's not the sort of person who takes kindly to waiting." Burke paused, his myopic blue eyes twinkling at Simon. He produced his conclusion with the satisfaction of a conjurer producing a rabbit out of a hat. "You see what I'm driving at, don't you? He's considering the possibility of acquiring an interest in an English publishing house—with a view, of course, to later affiliation with his uncle's."

Simon drew in his breath. It did not seem possible that the solution could be as simple as that; yet optimism grew as he listened to Burke's account of the American's resources, his reiterated opinion that Simon had (by what means he could not imagine) produced a very favourable impression on Horne.

"*Montage*, my boy! You know what it is—*montage* means almost everything to these people." (Burke was dabbling in the film industry, and *montage*, at the moment, was one of his favourite words.) "I can't help flattering myself I presented you rather well—against a background of Ray, Manders and my relatively obscure self!" He ended with his chesty chuckle, which people who disliked him found unbearably pompous, but which Simon knew as the clumsy veil he drew between his audiences and his genuine simplicity and warmth of intention.

"It's extraordinarily kind of you, Burke," he said. "I really don't see why you should take so much trouble on my behalf——"

"My dear! We're all agreed—Bertie and Agatha and Margaret and I—that you're *definitely* one of the people to be pulled out of a tight corner," boomed Burke. Simon suppressed a smile at this vision of the literary pontificate conspiring to his advantage, but the knowledge of their support lightened his homeward journey, and he was eager to give the news of the evening to Christian, who, when he got in, had, judging by the darkness of the lower part of the house, gone to bed.

He bounded up the stairs and opened the bedroom door very quietly, in case she should be asleep; but the lamp over her head was still alight, and Christian was lying very straight and still, holding a book, which she did not lower at his entrance, up to her face.

"Hallo."

"Hallo, darling. Why aren't you asleep?" He bent over to kiss her; she took the caress upon her cheek, making no response.

"You're pretty late, aren't you?" she remarked coolly.

"I'm afraid I am. Damn—and I have to be up early." He was sufficiently engrossed in his own thoughts not to notice her manner. It did not even perturb him when she dropped her book, switched off her light and turned over, pulling the clothes up to her ears, with her back towards him.

"Chris," he burst out. "I oughtn't to tell you—because it is still all in the air—but I think we've got a chance of coming through."

"Roger Burke?" she mumbled.

"Partly, yes." As he undressed, he told her about the conversation, about Horne and his future plans.

"Very nice—if it comes off," said Christian shortly.

"Very! And if it doesn't, I'll sell him *Cypriana*, and that'll please Marius."

Her silence at last attracted his attention. He went up to her bed.

"Chris, is anything the matter?"

As she did not reply, he looked down at the book, which was lying where she had dropped it, on the floor. To his surprise, he saw it was *Cypriana*. Blast! thought Simon. He really began to feel he had had enough of the book, which had done nothing but make discord between them since he accepted it.

"So you've been reading Marius's book," he said quietly, stooping to pick it up.

"It's exactly what I thought—a filthy book!" exclaimed Christian.

"Oh, well, for God's sake, let it alone. You needn't have read it, if you didn't want to."

"And I simply detest that young man Lear! I suppose you know he's been on the telephone while you were out?"

"How should I know?" said Simon coolly.

"I left you a note on your desk."

"I came straight upstairs. What did the note say?"

"Merely that he'd rung up. Apparently I wasn't to be trusted with a message!" sneered Christian.

"Don't be silly. It probably wasn't important enough to make a fuss about."

"Then why should he ring up your private number?"

"How the devil do I know? It's not unnatural he should do so; Marius and I are very friendly——"

"So I gathered—when he asked for you as Simon."

"Why shouldn't he? I call him Marius. I suppose he knew he was speaking to my wife."

"Well, I hate people who presume on an office friendship." Simon forced a laugh.

"I don't suppose Marius knows the difference between an office and an outside friendship. Anyhow, I'd have had him here if I hadn't thought that you and he wouldn't get on."

"Many thanks for being so considerate! I certainly shouldn't have stayed in the house with a person like that."

"You're just behaving like a little fool," snapped Simon, losing his patience. "I suppose you're one of the people who confuse what a person writes with his private personality? It is really time you'd got over that kind of thing, Chris."

"I suppose you mean I'm a complete failure as a publisher's wife?"

Simon was really too tired to think of what he was saying. He answered, as he flung his trousers across a chair:

"I think a good many women would have tried harder to identify themselves with their husbands' interests."

There was a terrible, cold pause before she replied:

"Perhaps you'd rather look for—another woman."

Simon stood up, facing her in his vest and underpants, feeling helpless with anger and disappointment.

"That's just being idiotic. You know"—he blundered—"I've never looked at another woman since I knew you."

"I know——? How should I know? I only see you for a few hours each day; what do I know about the time you're away from me?"

"You can check up on that any time you choose, at the office," muttered Simon, feeling that the whole thing was a bad dream, from which he would waken at any moment. To hasten the process, he found himself pinching his thigh; the bruised flesh winced, but nothing further happened.

"You don't expect me to believe you spend every minute of the day in your office?"

"Chris—this is vulgar!" he heard himself saying weakly.

"Any more vulgar," she retorted, "than picking up a girl in a teashop?"

"I've never in my life——" he was beginning.

"Please don't lie to me, Simon." Her face was crimson with anger; she was sitting up straight, with her hands pressed down on the bed at her sides. "You told me yourself——"

"I remember now. If there'd been any harm in it, do you suppose I'd have told you?"

"It's an easy thing to say, isn't it?"

"Chris," he said despairingly, "you simply must not say things like that. What's come over you? Don't you realize you're spoiling every lovely thing there's ever been between us?"

"It's you who've spoiled them," she said brokenly, "with the horrid company you keep and the—the things you bring into our lives." She pointed at *Cypriana*. "Things like that. Suppose Jem and Henry had been grown up: suppose they'd had to see that horrible paper——"

"Oh, God," said Simon, "if you say another word about the book I'll go crazy. Can't you leave it alone? The whole thing's over and forgotten except by ourselves; you're just using it as a pretext for picking a quarrel. Why? For God's sake, why? Can't we have a few days of peace and quiet together before you go away——?"

"I suppose you're glad I'm going away," sniffed Christian.

"With this kind of thing going on most of the time—do you blame me?" he flung at her. He made a last effort to control himself, to speak gently and with understanding, as he added, "I don't mean to be rotten to you, Chris: but the truth is we're two worn-out people who've got right on each other's nerves in the last few weeks. It doesn't make a spot of difference to the way I love you or, I hope, you love me. But can't you manage, in our last few days together, not to say foolish and hurtful things that you don't mean—any more than I mean the answers I give you?"

"I suppose it's always I who say them first," she muttered.

Simon thought carefully.

"You know, darling, I honestly think it is. I know how rotten you feel, with all that long time of nursing Jemima, and your illness before that, and all this fuss about getting away; but can't you see you're making it much harder for yourself——?"

"Oh—don't *preach*."

"I'm not preaching. But you know when you say a silly thing—like that thing about the girl in the teashop—you're hurting yourself, while it only makes me mad. Now, Chris!" He sat down on the bed and tried to take her hand, which remained pressed tightly on the mattress. "You know that was just a piece of nonsense, that you laughed and teased me about at the time."

"I laughed because I didn't want you to know how much you'd hurt me," said Christian—as Simon knew, untruthfully. Could she have forgotten all of those days—all of her very self, the self he had loved and trusted all the years he had known her? He knew he could never have loved or trusted a foolish sobbing woman, who indulged petty and vulgar jealousies, and objected to the friends he made in the course of his work. The thought flashed across his mind that Christian might have begun the change of life, and, as many a man does in his place, winced at the prospect of the years ahead; then he dismissed the idea as absurd. She was far too young —not yet forty. "How am I to know you won't do things like that when I'm away?" she was sobbing.

"Things like what? I tell you, I've never 'done' anything," cried Simon. "I've been perfectly faithful to you in word and deed, and if I can't speak four words to a miserable little chit in a Lyons' restaurant——! Oh, don't be so absurd."

She was looking at him, with her lips trembling and the tears now coursing unhindered down her flushed cheeks.

"Will you tell me something? Have you ever been to one —to one of those—women?"

Simon's jaw stiffened. There is always something vaguely distasteful to a man, in being forced, by a woman to whom he has given every proof of devotion, to recall a past which he is satisfied to forget. The necroscopic feminine instinct is one to which it is given to few men to understand, and the nearest Simon came to understanding it in Christian was his assumption that it was another symptom of her nervously over-wrought condition.

"No. At least—I once went to a place in Paris, with some other fellows; but I was bored and a little scared. I had some drinks—and came away."

"Was that before we were married?"

"Of course."

The tension of her lips relaxed.

"Then I was—the first?"

He was deadly tired; his instinct was to say "Yes," and to escape her further questionings in sleep. But the thought of their relationship, hitherto based upon complete truthfulness, warned him of the ignobility of such an evasion. In a glass on the opposite side of the room he saw his long, bony, stooping figure, in the absurdity of underclothing, and wondered if the Victorians looked any more ridiculous in their nightshirts. He straightened his shoulders and answered her calmly.

"We've been married thirteen years, Chris. Is there any point in raking up these things now?"

He saw her shrink, saw the blank, stricken expression that came into her eyes, caught her shoulder and shook it angrily.

"You little idiot, have you ever thought how much of your own happiness you owe to not being 'the first'? Haven't you the sense to be glad you escaped the shock of experiment with a groping ignoramus?"

When she had finished crying in his arms, she began to tease him for particulars. What sort of a girl was she? Was she of his own class, or a common creature? Simon was completely nonplussed; it was a Christian of whom he had no previous knowledge—a foolish, irrational creature making a grievance out of events fifteen years old—that had happened before they had even met each other. It was a state of affairs he might have understood—even expected, in a nervous young bride, but in a wife of thirteen years' standing it was preciously near to ludicrous! He silenced her at last by kissing her mouth.

"I refuse to pander to your morbid curiosity," he told her. "If I swear that if I were to meet either of them—yes, there were two—in the street to-morrow, I wouldn't know her from Eve, you ought to be satisfied. You weren't the first, but I promise you, my darling, you're the last."

"Sure?" She was clinging to him. "You know it would kill me, if—if—I mean, I could be anything, except——"

"I can't imagine what put such thoughts into your head. Aren't we everything to each other?"

"It's—it's that poisonous book. Somehow—it destroys all one's securities." She put him gently aside, found a glass and powder in the drawer of her cabinet, and began to repair the ravages of her tears. "I am a sight, aren't I! Please forgive me—and forget this, Simon. I don't know what's happening to me—I've been an utter fool lately. I suppose this is what they call a nervous breakdown. I don't envy Mummy, when she gets me to the South of France."

"You'll be all right in a week," said Simon, with a sigh of relief at the re-establishment of normal conditions. "You've had too much on your mind, and if I'd been worth my salt I'd have seen it before, and packed you off as soon as Jemima was through her trouble."

"Do you think I'd have gone?"

"You would if I'd made you—my rebellious wife!"

After he was in bed, she said:

"I suppose you wouldn't do something for me."

"Most things—if they weren't too silly."

"Simon . . . couldn't you get rid of Marius Lear?"

He paused before replying.

"I think that's an unreasonable suggestion—and most unfair to Marius."

"I don't care a damn for Marius—as you call him. There must be dozens of young men who could do the work he does for you in the office."

"Not exactly dozens. We've taken a lot of trouble—Nancy particularly—in training him, and a change of personnel is

always to be avoided, unless there's an uncontrovertible reason
for it. Marius is shaping very well—and, incidentally, there's
a reason why I couldn't possibly sack him at present."

"What reason?" He could hear her trying not to allow
her voice to sharpen.

"About ten days ago Bridgeman of *The Athenian* rang up
and—prompted, I imagine, by Agatha Mott—offered him the
job of second reviewer on the paper."

"Well?"

"Marius turned him down."

"Why?"

"For a variety of foolish reasons, which he gave me—and for
the real reason, which he gave Nancy, and she, with the typical
treachery of her sex, passed on to me. It was that, if he took
on the *Athenian* job, he would not be able to fulfil his proper
duties to me."

"Doesn't he rather exaggerate his own importance?" said
Christian coolly.

"As a matter of fact, he doesn't. I've put him practically
in full charge of the foreign department—which is growing
enormously—and if he were to leave us just now, it would
plunge the department into chaos for the time. You don't
find someone who can do French and German and Spanish
correspondence—and translations—for Marius's money, under
every mulberry bush."

"Still, you could give him notice, and look round in the
meanwhile," she persisted.

"No, Chris, I couldn't. *The Athenian* offered a fiver a week
and Marius chose to stay with me at two pounds ten; one
doesn't play ducks and drakes with that sort of loyalty."

"Oh, well, I suppose you know your own business best."

"Why, apart from the book, do you dislike him so much?"
asked Simon.

"I can't think of him apart from the book," she answered,
with surprising frankness. "And, to be quite honest, I'm afraid
of your friendship growing——"

"I'm afraid you must be prepared for that, my dear; but I promise it shan't be allowed to cause you any annoyance—or inconvenience."

"Do you think I'm horribly mean, Simon?"

"No, darling; only—prejudiced."

"We've always shared our friends, haven't we?"

"I'm sure Marius would be quite willing to be shared," Simon could not refrain from saying.

"Oh, I don't think so." Her voice was delicate with disdain. "I shouldn't imagine that Marius Lear has much use for virtuous women."

Simon opened his mouth to answer sharply: it was ridiculous that Christian should have an *idée fixe* like this about Marius, whom she had only met two or three times. Then the solution of her extraordinary obstination came to him, and, in any other circumstances, would have made him roar with laughter. Christian, like the majority of maternal women, had the persistent habit of regarding her husband as a small boy, liable to be led aside into mischief by other small boys, unless she kept a watchful eye upon him! What she actually feared was the influence Marius Lear might gain over him.

It was too late and too risky to start a discussion on those lines; he permitted himself a chuckle and edged his shoulder more comfortably into the angle between mattress and pillow.

"Good-night, my darling; sleep well."

"Good-night," said Christian, and he heard her give a little sigh, as she settled down as well. Poor Chris! It would be all right, when she got away from all the responsibilities which had taxed her strength for so long.

CHAPTER SIXTEEN

In the long summer evenings Simon had no objection to staying in his room at the office; it overlooked a yard in which stood three plane trees. Pigeons strutted hopefully on the paving, seeking the remainder of the crumbs which the typists scattered during their lunch hour. It was very quiet, and the business-like atmosphere was better for concentration than his own study.

When the telephone rang a little after seven, it surprised him. Who should know he was still in the office? Expecting to hear the voice either of Nancy or Marius, he lifted the receiver.

"Hallo—is that you, Simon? Lydia speaking."

"Good lord, what are you doing? I thought you'd dropped off the edge of our planet."

"Can we have dinner together somewhere? I'd like to talk to you."

"Well, I'm devilishly busy——" He liked Lydia, but felt it was too much to expect of him, to sacrifice the rest of the evening in trifling with his sister-in-law. He was also a little cross with Lydia, who had not even taken the trouble to ring Christian up to say good-bye.

"You've got to eat some time, haven't you? I'll come down there, if you like—I suppose there's some low chop-house in your quarter!"

"Meet you at the Ivy, if you like, at eight sharp," he cut in. Lydia—and "low chop-houses"!

"Oh—not the Ivy, please. Every one you know's there—and I don't want to change."

"All right. I'll pick you up in twenty minutes' time—and mind you're ready! I'll have to make it short and sharp, so make up your mind where you want to go while you're waiting."

She sounded as though she were in some sort of trouble. Daniel, of course. An angry resentment at being dragged again into Daniel's affairs almost inclined him to ring back and say that, after all, he was afraid he could not spare the time to dine with her.

He had not seen Daniel since their quarrel, although the latter, with his masterly capacity for ignoring an awkward situation, had rung up in the friendliest fashion, to say that he was quite prepared to carry on until Simon had made other arrangements, and that he hoped their disagreement would not affect the publication of his Roumanian book, which was now ready and contained some really good stuff that should certainly sell.

Simon rejoined that he was naturally expecting to handle the book he had commissioned, but that the greater distance Daniel kept from the office the better he (Simon) would be pleased.

"Right!" said Daniel, with provoking good humour. "Dine with me one night, won't you?" and rang off. There was no way of embarrassing him. He had made a graceful gesture, too, in leaving his capital in the firm; it would have taxed Simon's means to the breaking-point—this was before his conversation with Horne—to buy out Old Harry and Daniel.

Horne's suggestion (which was precisely that outlined by Burke) was still in abeyance; it was impossible to sign any agreements until he had talked the matter over with his firm, but he had given Simon to understand that he did not anticipate much opposition, and he took back as a *douceur* Marius's novel, for which he signed outright a cheque for a much larger advance than Simon had felt justified in offering.

Lydia was waiting, in a black hat rather excessively draped with veil; her little face was just visible, like a pale silver moon seen through a thicket. She named a not very modish restaurant, notable for the indifference of its illumination. He ordered Amer Picon, at her request, and noticed that she drank hers straight.

"Have you heard from Christian?"

"She rang me up on Sunday."

"Lovely, expensive call! How mother will enjoy paying for it," she murmured smiling. "I always feel I'd get on better with Mummy if I let her drench me with erratic luxuries, instead of standing out for a perfectly sound and regular allowance on the first of each month. Chris manages the family so much better than I do—no wonder she's their little favourite."

"It's a blessing she is. She badly needed a change, and I couldn't have managed it just yet," said Simon dryly.

"I thought Daniel's withdrawal from the firm meant you'd suddenly become fabulously rich," she said, with a pretence of flippancy which did not deceive Simon. "You know—the fortune made and Daniel retiring to sit on his nest-egg. Doesn't sound a bit like Daniel, does it? He'd make omelettes with, not sit on, any nest-eggs if he had them."

"I suppose so."

"What happened?" asked Lydia.

He looked at her in astonishment; she avoided his eyes, playing with the stem of her glass with thin, restless fingers on which glittered too many rings.

"Don't you know?"

"Should I ask you, if I did?"

Swallowing his surprise at this evidence she was not in touch with Daniel, Simon gave her a toned-down version of the quarrel; he omitted the blow he had aimed at Daniel; in decency, one did not repeat things like that.

"It's a pity in a lot of ways. Daniel was certainly a big social asset, but he hasn't got the staying power to make success of a job like ours."

"Did you think he would? You ought to have known him."

"I agree; but, in spite of our being half-brothers, we hadn't seen so very much of each other since he grew up. He seemed to be keen, and he'd got the money, which he was determined to put into publishing. Candidly, I didn't see why Daniel's money should profit some other firm when it could give us a start on our own. There seemed no reason, either, why it shouldn't work; we'd always got on well together, in spite of the differences in our temperaments. But—well, you can imagine for yourself: we'd arrived at the point of rubbing each other up the wrong way. Daniel wasn't willing to accept my ·judgment—a hopeless state of affairs, in a partnership— and it was he who chose, I think sensibly, to resign."

"I thought you'd chucked him out," said Lydia wearily.

"Good lord, no. You can't chuck a partner out. It has to be a matter of mutual agreement."

"I suppose Father's satisfied."

"Yes, I think he is."

"He always loathed Daniel."

"I'm afraid he did."

"Perhaps he's going to loathe him some more." She caught the waiter's eye and touched her glass. "Another, please."

"Look here, aren't you going to eat something?"

"Oh—order some fish. I don't care what it is."

Simon ordered *truite au vin blanc*, and wondered what to say to Lydia. Should he tell her not to be a fool—to put Daniel out of her mind? Something warned him that matters had gone too far for that.

"How much do you suppose Daniel cares for Eliza?" she disconcerted him by asking.

"I haven't the faintest idea. There's only one thing on which I'd stake my soul: Daniel cares more for himself than he cares for man, woman or devil."

"That's just masculine, isn't it?" sighed Lydia. "I think Daniel cares—cared—a bit for me, for instance. Though I suppose you don't believe it."

"Yes, I do. I thought it was a pity."

"For conventional or other reasons?" she mocked him.

"Oh, damn it, Lydia. I suppose it's reasonable to mind if you're unhappy?"

"Yes; I suppose even Christian feels the difference between me and herself," she said, so softly bitter that he hardly caught the words.

"Why 'even' Christian? You know how fond she is of you."

"There's nothing like happiness for making people self-centred. Dear Christian; she's always been so well regulated! Everything happened for her along the lines she wanted—the safe, comfortable lines of our provincial convention. One can't expect her to sympathize with any one so wild and foolish as myself."

"That's not true," said Simon. "I don't know much, because Chris is very loyal about her family relationships—but she's been terribly cut-up about you and Daniel."

"Cut-up? Yes, I suppose so: for fear there'd be a scandal, for fear Father would hear about it and make trouble for everybody. Well, she's not got that to worry about now. Whatever happens is between me and Father: it won't affect any one else."

"Are you going to do some dam' fool thing with Daniel?" frowned Simon.

Lydia laughed.

"My dear Simon, I don't know. That's the ridiculous part of it. Daniel hasn't been near me for weeks. I've yet to find out if he's been near Eliza. I suppose he's thinking what he means to do. It's awkward for him, I know, being forced to a decision. You see, the only thing that kept us apart, up to now, was our fear of complicating the business: now that fear's removed, I suppose Daniel's trying to make up his mind if he's really done with Eliza. He never was quite sure." Again she gave her hard little laugh. "This sitting about and waiting—it's not very good for the *amour propre*! But what's a girl to do? I may as well face the fact that life without Daniel is just no value, so far as I'm concerned."

"It's a devilish shame," said Simon, deeply touched.

"Daniel's a charming cad, isn't he? Of course I know he is; but I ran him in for it, in the beginning. I've been crazy

about him for ages, and I used his wretchedness about
Eliza——" She broke off, catching her lip in her teeth.

"Lydia, darling, you oughtn't to tell me these things," he
said miserably.

"Why not? It wouldn't hurt so much," she went on, "if
Eliza wasn't utterly worthless. It's such a waste of all Daniel's
emotion. . . . What is it? Can't you tell me? Why do men
go on caring about women who treat them that way? Is it
just sex?"

"I suppose so," said Simon.

"God! Why haven't I got more of it? I've given Daniel
everything I knew how—I'd give him all the rest—even my
life—even my life."

"My dear, sweet Lydia, you don't know what you're saying.
Don't you know Daniel isn't a normal person, in some ways?
It was something perverse that turned him to Eliza in the
beginning, and it's the same thing that won't let him break
away from her now."

"Do you think she's awfully beautiful, Daniel?" Ignoring
her slip of the tongue, that made her call him by his brother's
name, Simon replied:

"It's a type that doesn't happen to appeal to me. I can't
stand decadence." He leaned back, for the waiter to put the
plate in front of him. When the man had gone, "Lydia, can't
you chuck it?" he asked. "Even if Daniel leaves Eliza, what's
the good? She'll never divorce him, and I'm afraid you've
scotched your chances, between you, of divorcing Eliza.
There's no future for either of you, that I can see."

"Except living in sin! I know. It's not what I'd have
chosen. I've got just as much preference as Christian for
safety, for the wedding-ring and the happy family circle—
even for children. But it seems I'm not to have those. Sensible
people make the best of what they've got, don't they?"

"But you haven't 'got' anything," pointed out Simon.
"Can't you see what you're doing? It's impossible for people
like you and Daniel to live like that—in England."

"Yes," she sighed. "England's a hell of a country for lovers—I should know! But perhaps we needn't stay in England; perhaps we could both get jobs abroad. In Paris, even. I'd have to try and earn something, or of course Father 'll 'cut me off,' and we're both so extravagant; it couldn't be done on Daniel's money—as I suppose he'll have to keep Eliza as well."

"Well . . . if you want to kill Old Harry, you're going the right way about it. If that's any consideration."

She looked at him stonily.

"Do you know, I don't think it is. Father and I were never in sympathy; he's never stopped trying to kill everything in me that didn't conform to his own pattern. I've been made to suffer hell through his miserable religion—most of which meant 'minding what people would say' and going to chapel for the sake of making a good impression upon business acquaintances—all as muffled up in Methodism as we were ourselves!" She drew a gasping breath. "Do you blame me for having to get away from all that? Do you know I've been fighting all my life, just to be honest? I couldn't help falling in love with Daniel, Simon. I'd waited such a hell of a long time for love, I thought it was never coming, and when it came—I just couldn't believe it was no good."

"But Daniel wasn't the first——"

"The first to make love to me? Oh, dear no. Only the others didn't count, I just wasn't interested, so I didn't want to give them anything. It didn't seem as if I could be interested —until Daniel came along; and then—I hadn't time to think."

"Bad luck it should be Daniel."

"Wasn't it?" She spoke almost brightly. "Is your fish good, Simon? No—I don't want mine. I don't seem to want any food these days. I'm getting a divine figure—even my dressmaker admits it!"

"You're much too thin. Christian will be furious when she comes back."

"Furious with envy, darling! Let's stop being serious,

shall we? Perhaps it's all about nothing. Perhaps Daniel will decide he doesn't want me—and it'll all turn out a storm in a tea-cup. But I wanted to prepare you; I want you to take my side, if anything happens—try to make Chris see, will you, that it's my way of trying to be happy? She can't blame me for wanting a little of what she's got in such full measure!"

Simon realized the futility of trying to make Lydia sensible, but her unhappiness was an added load on his mind, and, for a time, he played with the idea of speaking to Daniel about it. What, however, could he say? Apart from the unwarrantable impertinence of meddling in another person's affairs, he could not advise Daniel to leave Eliza and live with Lydia, nor could he play the heavy brother-in-law and warn Daniel off.

Life was complicated and exhausting. He had to keep in touch with the children, to write every day to Christian, and to carry on the work of the firm with its still unsettled future upon his mind.

One afternoon he had an attack of nose-bleeding in the office. His nose bled and bled, in spite of all his efforts with cold keys and compresses to stop it. Extended on the floor, he had practically fainted when Marius found him, and called Nancy, who instantly rang up Simon's doctor. The doctor dictated a treatment, and said he would come round as soon as he had gone through his afternoon surgery. When he arrived Simon was again at work, and submitted grudgingly to examination.

"I suppose you know you're played out."

"Well, what about it?"

"This about it. You must slack up, or run the risk of a crashing breakdown."

Simon began to laugh.

"Don't be an ass. I've known that for the last five years."

"Then you're five years nearer your breaking-point. I'm not fooling you, Crome; if you don't obey orders, I can't be responsible for results."

"Who's asking you to be? My dear chap, I'm perfectly

willing to obey orders, but circumstances won't let me. I frankly admit, I feel like a yard of chewed string, my energy's gone and nothing about me's functioning up to standard. What I want from you is some dope to help me carry on until this job's finished——"

"What job?"

"The comparatively childish one, from your point of view, of reorganizing a publishing house."

"Where's your wife?" asked the doctor abruptly.

"Gone abroad for her health; you, if any one, ought to admit she needed it. And you needn't suggest dragging her back into this mess. I hope to have everything squared up by the time she returns, and then—oh lord!" said Simon weakly. "Don't you see that all I need is to be tinkered up to finish my job, and then I'll go into a nursing home or take a rest cure or any dam' thing you like to order?"

"You'll do that before you've finished your job, unless you do as you're told, my lad," said the doctor. "How much time have you had off in—say—the last fortnight?"

Simon laughed again.

"Don't be silly. This isn't a station bookstall. I'm all right, I tell you. I stop work when I can't concentrate any longer—and that's been pretty early the last few days," he was driven to admit.

"You're telling me. Got a car?"

"Courtesy title—yes," grinned Simon.

"Chauffeur?"

"I'm not a millionaire."

"How are you about driving?" Simon stared. "I mean, do you find driving an effort? Does it get on your nerves?"

"Not a bit. It's a relief, if anything. Even the traffic helps —makes one focus away from the work. I'll soon get out into the country—drift along—taking my time——" Simon's voice trailed away; how long, now, was it, since he had had that pleasant experience?

"All right. Do it now—take yourself out for the evening.

Get some fresh air—that's the best prescription I can give you; it'll do you more good than this," said the doctor, as he finished scribbling on a pad, and handed the leaflet to Simon. "I'll drop in to-morrow, and see what you look like after a good sleep."

"Is this to make me sleep?" Against his will, Simon could not keep the eagerness out of his voice. He had hardly slept since Christian went away.

"Yes; take it last thing—but remember, it's the fresh air that counts."

It was impossible not to be tempted by the prospect. Simon gave grudging assent, got rid of the doctor, and worked on until six, when Marius came in with the letters to be signed. He stood scowling over Simon.

"Well, what did the leech say?"

"What bloody business is it of yours?" asked Simon, good-humouredly.

"You needn't tell me. I've had a nervous breakdown myself."

"Oh, you have, have you. Then you don't need telling anything—except, Mr. Know-All Lear, that I haven't the slightest intention of having a nervous breakdown—either to please you or that damned apothecary!" said Simon, rapidly signing letters.

Marius glanced at the clock and lit a cigarette. He was scrupulous about not smoking in office hours.

"Going home now?"

"What's that got to do with you?"

"Nothing whatever. It's just as easy to get on with my work here as in my digs."

Simon leaned back in his chair.

"I've got a good mind to give you the sack," he said, in a tone of mild exasperation. "Upon my soul, you and Nancy between you seem to have a conspiracy to treat me as if I was a child of five sickening for whooping-cough. If you can't behave normally you can, both of you, get out."

"Your loss if we do," said Marius calmly, as he proceeded to close the letters. Simon looked at him affectionately. As usual, Marius had the towsled, greasy look of one too engrossed in important affairs to pay attention to his appearance.

"You may be right, you conceited fellow, but you might leave that to be said by other people. What a sight you are, Marius! Why on earth don't you get your hair cut and make some small effort to conform to decency in your turn-out?"

"Why should I? Will it make me do better work? If it did, I'd alter to-morrow."

"Nothing really matters to you, does it, except your work," Simon commented idly.

"Not a dam' thing," said Marius cheerfully. "Unless—in a less degree, of course—it's yours."

"What a fool you were not to take that *Athenian* job. You'll be sorry, you know, if we crash."

"We won't crash," said Marius, with calm certainty.

"Suppose we did. . . . What will you do? There's one good thing, anyhow: you won't find it difficult to find work—after *Cypriana*. And I dare say Agatha would see you got a chance with *The Athenian* again."

"To hell with *The Athenian*. I don't want to do reviewing; I'd rather preserve my self-respect."

"Shut up, Marius; all reviewing isn't corrupt."

"You're telling me. Anyhow, this suits me better."

"You mean, you'd rather work for me."

"You've been very good to me," stammered Marius, seriously taken aback by Simon's frankness. "If it wasn't for you I'd still be holding on to that lousy job in 'college.' I'd like to find some way of repaying you for that—I can't see how I'm to do it."

"Rot. What are you doing to-night?" it came into Simon's mind to ask.

"Getting on with my book, I suppose."

"You wouldn't take a run into the country, with me?"

Marius considered the suggestion, with his head on one side.

"No," he decided.

"As usual, the *ne plus ultra* of old-world courtesy," murmured Simon.

"There's no point in my coming with you. All we'd do would be to talk shop. Find somebody else."

"One of my thousands of friends," grimaced Simon, remembering how he had neglected them.

"Or pick up a tramp," offered Marius. "You don't want an intelligent person, with a vocabulary and literary ideas. Find somebody to whom books are punk and the *Daily Cable's* literature; that's the type of mind in which you'll find relaxation. I know what I'm talking about. Good-night."

Nancy, to whom Simon repeated the conversation, approved of Marius's advice.

"Your mind's worn out—it needs rest more than your body. I'd love to come with you, but Marius is right—except that I'm not sure if you wouldn't be better by yourself. Why don't you find a country pub and spend a night in fresh air and surroundings? There are some delightful little places around and near Cookham. There's no need to chase back in the morning—you've got no appointments until twelve, and I could shift that to the day after, if you like: it's not vital."

"Don't bother—I'll be along in time. That's not a bad idea of yours, Nancy. I'll probably take it."

"I'll ring for the car."

While he waited, Simon remembered that he was hungry. He had not eaten since lunch-time, when he had snatched a sandwich and a glass of beer between two appointments. At this time of day the car could stand outside the office for half an hour without police interference. He went to wash his hands. He felt very light, exhausted, and yet serene. Work had withdrawn to a great distance.

At the nearest bunshop he had just ordered a pot of tea and some toast when he remembered he had not written his daily letter to Christian. Fortunately he had a loose-leaf notebook in his pocket; he had the table to himself, and he started to scribble his usual account of the day's occurrences.

There seemed little to write; the usual routine happenings —and an invitation from Henry's headmaster for Speech Day. "I accepted for both of us, as you'll probably be back by then; if you aren't I'll try and get Lydia." His pen hung idle; he could think of nothing more to say.

They had written so few letters to each other since their marriage that Simon was out of practice. During their few separations they rang each other up night and morning, a course which Christian had cheerfully proposed to pursue from the South of France. "Mummy won't mind paying for the calls; she never thinks she's getting her money's worth unless there's an enormous telephone bill." "Not on your life," returned Simon, capitulating, however, to the extent of a weekly call, for which he and his mother-in-law could pay alternately. "It means so little to Mother," Christian had protested, but Simon stood firm.

It should have been so easy to write; it was so difficult. It was that scene, so shortly before their parting, that, try as he might to ignore it, had set a rift into their perfect-seeming relationship which it would take time to heal. It was as though their previous unity had been an illusion. He felt that, at a time when he most needed reassurance, Christian had failed him—a thing he had never believed her capable of doing.

His love for Christian was unalterable and eternal, but something of its magic, its rainbow quality had departed. Instead of lovers, they seemed to have become a married couple, held together by custom, rather than by the electrical quality of a mutual passion which, he could have sworn, would never fail. That cheap doubt of his fidelity had done it; he wondered if things could ever be the same again.

Her letters to him showed an equal feeling of constraint, although they were warm and loving and full of amusing comments upon her surroundings. His heart ached for her return, knowing that the only hope for the re-establishment of their happiness was to hold her in his arms again.

"Excuse me—would you pass the sugar?"

Muttering an excuse, Simon pushed the electro-plated horror across the table without looking up. Some woman had come to sit there—he hastened to finish his letter and get away.

"No news yet from Horne, but I don't expect anything until he gets back. I believe we'll flourish, if we can only get the right kind of support—Nancy's reports on the last batch of MSS. are almost too good to be true; I'd accuse her of losing her critical faculty, if I didn't know about that armour-plated brain of hers! But one can't overlook the fact that, for their own mysterious reasons, the agents are sending us quite a different class of stuff from——" He was going to put "from what they were sending us before *Cypriana*," and altered it, crossing out the "from" and substituting a full stop. "I've got at least two good novels, one of which I am sure you'll like, and a lot of good non-fiction about which I find it a bit difficult to make up my mind. I do want to get together a strong fiction list." After hesitation, he added:

"I had dinner with Lydia the other night—I forgot to tell you in my letter." (It was not quite the truth; he had not intended to mention it, as he did not want to disturb Christian with an account of their conversation. Then it occurred to him that Lydia might refer to it, in one of her erratic letters to her sister, and Christian would think it odd that he had said nothing about it.) "She doesn't look very fit. I tried to persuade her to join you both for a week or ten days, but I don't think she took to the idea. She's still obsessed with Daniel; I wish to heaven she'd get over it."

He ended with one of what Christian called their "pet-phrases"—scribbling it hurriedly, half ashamedly; it seemed like the empty shell of a once lovely thought, and he would have omitted it, save for knowing that its omission was bound to raise questions in Christian's mind. Perhaps her next letter

would contain something that would breathe life into it
again. He folded the detached leaves and put them in his
pocket, thinking that he would address an envelope in the
post office on the next block.

For the first time he took a glance at his vis-à-vis to find
her staring at him with lively attention. On catching Simon's
eye, her own flickered, and drooped with conscious demureness
to a half-eaten ice. She held the spoon genteelly with a quirk
of the manicured little finger.

Were all girls of that class exactly alike? wondered Simon,
his mind going back to the previous occasion, whose untimely
resurrection in Christian's memory was the main cause of his
present unhappiness. What on earth interest could a man of
his type be expected to take in these pathetic little standardized
models—each one so like another that they might be graded
test-tube products, of the Huxleyan imagination?

Their very clothes amounted to a uniform: there was the
neat, dark suit, the crisp white collar, the little round hat,
perched as far back as it could balance on a sleeked blonde
crest. Oxford Street versions of the Bond Street original—
Simon assumed that it took a feminine eye to detect its subtle
"wrongness"—reproducing themselves a hundred times in the
course of a walk down any of the city streets. To the average
man these little typists or shopgirls were as well dressed as
their own wives and daughters; it was only when they opened
their mouths to emit the egregious cockney vowels that they
gave themselves away, placing themselves in the social scale
as accurately as though crochet gloves, toeless walking shoes
and "halo" headdresses did not exist, for the pleasure of all
classes.

How could Christian imagine that he could be attracted
by one of these little bazaar puppets? Finishing his toast,
with an occasional eye of analytical curiosity upon his neigh-
bour, since he had no other subject to occupy him, Simon
guessed her age to be between sixteen and twenty-two. She
had a clear, rosy complexion etherealized by powder and the

usual bright smear of lipstick on her full, greedy little mouth. Jemima, made up, might look very much the same. Powder and paint had made it impossible, in these days, to be sure of girls' ages.

Having finished her ice, she opened a handbag of red patent-leather, and, with the help of a square of looking-glass, conscientiously repaired the scarlet outlines blurred by her feast. The concentration she brought to this task drew an involuntary smile from Simon, which was intercepted by a quick, upward glance from the girl. To his surprise, she snapped her bag hurriedly, and remarked with a giggle, " Pardon!"

"Why?" asked Simon—naturally. After all, she was only doing what every young woman does nowadays—making her toilette in public with a frankness which would have outraged her grandmothers and which the younger generation takes for granted.

"Well——!" There was a coy satisfaction in her tone, in spite of the flickering of her eyelids. "Some gentlemen aren't supposed to like it when a girl does that, are they?"

"It seems entirely a matter for your own choice," said Simon, signalling to the waitress for the bill. She acknowledged the summons with a nod, which Simon interpreted as "Coming presently," and immediately disappeared through the serving door at the end of the room. He felt irritated at having to wait, and sat frowning, and rapping softly on the table with the shilling he had taken out of his pocket.

"Have you got a date?" asked his companion sympathetically. She was not a bad little thing—less unattractive than she would have been had she not been obviously young and a little in awe of her company.

"No," said Simon shortly. He was not going to be inveigled into another verbal flirtation with teashop hussies—even if he had learned his lesson about repeating such to Christian. Harmless as they were, he saw there was something cheap, or, at least, lacking in taste, about them. Daniel could do that

sort of thing without losing caste; he was not so sure that
he himself, in his anxiety to put people at their ease, and not
appear superior to his companions, did not overdo the "all
friends together" business.

"Close, isn't it?" she observed presently, as though embar-
rassed by his silence.

"It's about time we had some summer, I suppose," Simon
felt bound to agree.

"Hasn't it been a *n'awful* year?" she came back eagerly.
"Except that fortnight in March—and what good's March?
That's what I'd like to know. Nobody has their holidays in
March."

"No, I suppose not."

"I mean, the seaside's no good in March, is it? Unless
you're on the Riveera, or something. Coo—I wouldn't half
like to go to the Riveera."

Simon, still looking for his waitress, could not forbear a
smile of sympathy. Why not? he was thinking. Fundamentally, what was the difference between this child and the
ten-cent store heiresses and cinema stars and Mayfair chits
who lolled about the *plages*? Put her in a beach suit, give her
a coiffeur and a couple of diamond bracelets, and there would
not be a pin to choose between her and them—physically or
mentally. All a matter of money and a cockney accent. As
for morals, she was probably infinitely their superior.

Cursing the waitress, who continued in retirement, he
remarked that he supposed his companion would be going
for her holiday soon.

"Don't know. It depends." The full lips pouted, but she
did not say what it depended upon. "But you do get sick and
tired of London, don't you?"

"Some people do. I'm one of them."

"You don't say!" she returned, in her own idiom of genteel
incredulity.

"Why not?"

"Aren't you one of them West End toffs, that goes places

every night?" she flattered him by replying. Simon laughed.

"Bad guess. I'm a working man with a family to support."

For a moment she looked as though she did not believe him, then some of the interest faded from the rather prominent, china-blue eyes which, for the last few minutes, had been fixed upon his in unwinking attention.

"Well—it *is* close," she repeated. Her voice had lost its note of genteel affectation, and held a note of tired petulance. She turned back the high neck of her little jacket from the base of a throat milkily white and curved like a vase. It had that slight over-fullness which, lovely in its beginnings, threatens later disease.

"Why don't you go in the park and get some fresh air?" he advised her.

"What, by myself? That's fun—I don't think. My boy friend's in hospital, and he doesn't like me to go out with other fellows when he's not there." It obviously did not occur to her to seek the society of her own sex. "Is that where you're going?" she insinuated.

Simon, intent upon catching the eye of the waitress, who had at last emerged from the service, and was bustling about two distant tables, muttered something about taking a run into the country; his mind was not on what he was saying —he was telling himself not to forget to post Christian's letter, and wondering if there was enough petrol in the car to take him out on the Great West Road before getting a fill-up.

"Got a car? Aren't you lucky?"

Her tone warned him sharply to take care. He found her looking at him with moist lips parted—obviously prepared to accept an invitation. Evidently the boy friend's wishes did not carry as much weight as her previous words suggested. Silly little ass! This, supposed Simon, was how trouble started— ending in a "Daily Moron" splash heading: "Blonde in Car Assault . . . Miss Patsy Prim, a petite blue-eyed typist of Finsbury Park, described how she was flung from the car. . . ."

"What's your favourite newspaper?" he asked, with apparent inconsequence.

She stared at him, disappointed and taken aback.

"I'm not much of a one for reading," she pouted. "What I mean—you don't want to read, do you, after you've been working all day? All the girls in our place take *The Cable*— that's a nice paper, isn't it? Lovely snaps of girls and fellows in swim-suits—and Vivienne Wood's page: I like that, though I think she's a bit soppy sometimes—still I'd like to meet her and see if she's like her photos——"

"Not much world news, is there?" said Simon ironically.

"World news? Ow, what's the good of world news?" was the scornful reply. "Chinese and Japs and Spaniards and Italians all cutting each other's throats—nobody knows what for—and that big fat pig Mussolini, and Hitler and Swastikas —ow, you get sick of it!"

"You aren't interested in politics?"

"Who? Me? What's the good of politics to a girl? I know a chap that's a Nazi and another that's a Red, and they're both on the dole—so what about it?" she concluded.

"Somebody to whom books are punk and the 'Daily Moron's' literature!" Marius's recommendation flashed into Simon's mind. This, surely, must be the perfect specimen. Supposing he took her—damnation, it would not be playing fair by Christian. Yet what earthly harm could there be in it? No one in his right mind would accuse Simon Crome of "intentions" towards a girl of this class—no one, that is to say, but his own wife: the one person of whom he would have said, a few months ago, that she understood everything and to whom he could tell everything, secure of her under-standing. Taking this girl for a drive would now mean not telling Christian; that in itself was enough to prevent his doing it. Besides, the girl would be no less bored than he; her idea of a joy-ride would run to cuddling on the back seat, a blaring gramophone and ginger-beer at a cheap roadhouse. Nothing in that to tempt one to deceive one's wife.

He morosely contemplated the alternative: a lonely drive —buzzing engine—buzzing thoughts. Thoughts of Christian, of the business, of Lydia and Daniel, of the deferred interview with Old Harry, of Horne's scheme—the sort of thing that kept him awake at night. There was some sense in Marius's prescription. If he adopted it, it would mean, of course, cutting out the night in the country, but this he hardly regretted. What was the use of one night—probably a sleepless one (he had temporarily forgotten the doctor's prescription which lay inside his pocket-book), to be followed by the effort of getting back to town in time for his noon appointment? Much better to get a little fresh air and return to his own bed.

"I once had a lovely drive," she was saying. "A—Pa had a friend" (he wondered why she had faltered) "that owned a taxicab, and he won one of them football competitions, so he thought he'd take a day off and we—I mean, Ma and Pa and me and him—drove all the way down to Ramsgate! Coo—it was lovely! I do think motoring's lovely. I often envy them girls that win beauty competitions and get all sorts of things given them. I heard of a girl that got a car given her by a fellow—not that Pa'd ever let me!" she corrected herself hurriedly. "I mean, when, when a girl takes presents like that from a fellow—well, people talk, don't they? Even when it's quite innocent——"

"Tea, toast and an ice," said the waitress crisply, as she put the slip down in front of him.

"I didn't have——" Simon was beginning, when he remembered Christian's chaffing remark about paying for a girl's tea. The laugh he gave was not very pleasant, as he felt in his pockets for the extra coppers to add to the shilling he already had in his hand.

"Well, did you ever? What a mistake!" Plump, manicured fingers were fumbling in the cheap handbag. "The ice was sixpence, wasn't it? Have you got change for a shilling?"

"You can stand it me another time," said Simon, rising. She looked up at him, eager, prepared to giggle, yet on the verge of disappointment. The flaxen hair, dragged back from the brow she had forgotten to powder, had a childish fluff at the roots. "Silly little pigeon!" Simon was thinking. "Poor, silly little London pigeon—looking for any old crumbs!"

"Oh, well, thanks very much, I'm sure! Have a nice drive."

"Care to come?"

The words were out before he had time to consider them, and regretted as soon as spoken.

"Mean it?" There was a sudden, shining dilation of the china-blue eyes.

"If you like. I'm tired—I shan't be a very lively companion. But if you'd like a breath of fresh air, there are worse ways of getting it."

She could not possibly interpret that, he was thinking, as an expression of enthusiasm for her society. Unless she really wanted the drive, she would not come. She was a harmless kid, he decided, as she jumped up, picked up her gloves—one of which had fallen under the table—and followed him to the cash-desk.

"I've got to post a letter."

"I know, I saw you writing it. Was it to your girl friend?" she coyly inquired. "What'll *she* say when you tell her you took me joy-riding?"

"Very much the same sort of thing your boy friend will say when he hears you've been," retorted Simon, feeling that settled it. She giggled, but the glance she shot at him was surprisingly sly. "All right, madam," thought Simon. "You may think you're for it, but at the first signs of funny business out you get, with your fare home in your hot little hand!"

CHAPTER SEVENTEEN

"You're a lovely driver, aren't you?" she sighed. The little round hat was on her lap, and the wind blew a frail flaxen halo round her head. She looked like a child—not much older than Jemima—except for the flaring lipstick and the crude, coral-pink nails. "It's a lovely car, isn't it?" she offered, a little farther on.

"I'd begun to think of entering it for the Old Crocks; but it's running nicely to-night."

"What's the 'Old Crocks'?"

He told her, and she was plainly uninterested. Anything outside the radius of her own small experience, he had discovered, interested her not at all. Mindful of Marius, he was amusing himself secretly in trying to make an analysis of this small and shallow being, so innocently unaware of her own flimsiness. Had she any emotions that were not hysterical? Was she capable of strong grief, or passion? This was the type of girl, he found himself marvelling, for whom a certain type of fellow gets himself into hideous predicaments: into gaol, into debt—and worse. Men shot themselves—and sometimes other people—for the sake of these pink and white bits of flesh. Even the girl herself was sometimes the victim of her own sheer insipidity; unable to deal with the passions she apparently had power to rouse, she was found behind bushes on commons, under the seats of railway coaches, with marks on her throat . . .

"Coo—did you see that girl? In *shorts*. Some people don't seem to care what sights they make of themselves."

"I rather like shorts—on the right person."

"Oh, well—I've got a pair myself. I look nice in them too—though I say it that shouldn't—but I've got that kind of figure! But Pa says he'll take the skin off my back if he ever catches me outside the front door in them."

"Then they're not much use to you, are they?"

She bridled, again giving him the sly look which he had noticed before.

"Oh, I manage—now and again. I'd like to have had them on to-night."

"What's the good of them in a car?"

"They're cool—and comfy," she said evasively.

"And you'd get your legs bitten to pieces when we get down by the river," said Simon, as he swung the car off the main road into one of the many by-ways that lead straight to the "pastoral heart of England" from the great traffic routes running east and west. The tall, neglected hedgerows imprisoned a green tranquillity, between dusk and dark, which, here and there, the overshadowing trees permitted to be patched with the bright saffron after-glow of sunset. He hoped she would not chatter too much, as he allowed his body to sag and his wrists to go slack on the wheel. A lovely relaxation of mind and body was at last succeeding the tension of the day.

"The country's lovely, isn't it?" she reminded him anxiously.

"I didn't think London girls liked it, as a rule."

"Oh, p'raps not to live in. But in an evening, like this——! P'raps I'm romantic!" She giggled at the suggestion. "D'you know what I like on the pictures? I like it when the girl comes through a wood, with her arms full of flowers. You know —in a thin white dress, with the light behind her; ow, I think that's beautiful. And then the man falls for her! And there they are, all alone, with the song of the birds and the apple-blossom all falling down, like confetti at a wedding—and she sort of melts into his arms! I expect it sounds soppy, but it always makes me cry, that bit!"

Simon had the sense to realize that she was perfectly sincere. It was an amazing experience, to come face to face with the reader who patronizes the twopenny libraries; for whom Crome and Lygon had published *Heart of the Sunset* and *Blue*

Roses! He suddenly recognized Christian's mentality, translated into a lower sphere of life—the mentality that feeds on
illusion, and shrinks from harsh, undecorative reality. In the
case of a girl like this, it seemed to him far more reasonable,
that she should seek escape from her probably sordid surroundings to the honeyed falsehoods of Hollywood.

What would Christian think if she could see him now?
She had once had the sense and good taste to think just nothing.
She would have been the first to encourage his wish to give
a town-tired little typist an hour or two of country air. For a
conventional woman, Christian had always been extraordinarily generous and open-minded; jealousy and suspicion
were alike vulgarisms to her fastidious nature. On the one or
two occasions when Simon had done things which were
admittedly eccentric, her heart-warming laughter had eased
the explanations he felt bound, in love, to offer her. Her
teasing, when she teased, was without bitterness, her mockery
so tender that it was almost a caress. This was the Christian
he had known, loved and depended upon for thirteen years.
In what relationship did she stand to the whining, petulant
Christian who had reproached him with forgotten incidents
of his pre-marital days?

He could so easily picture himself saying to that former
Christian:

"I was so damned dull without you, and so tired, that I
picked up a little misery I found in a teashop and took her
for a drive in the country."

And Christian, tenderly mocking, making a joke of that
which was only jokeable because it was unthinkable as well:

"So long as you didn't seduce her, darling, I'm sure it was
very nice for both of you. Poor kid, I hope she thanked you
nicely, when you took her home."

It was so easy to imagine, so simple, under the terms of
their old relationship; but brought into contact with the
poison which seemed latterly to have entered into her veins,
who could foresee its outcome, if Christian were to find out

what it was now obviously impossible for him to tell her? Simon felt suddenly miserable, and cursed himself for a fool.

"You aren't very talkative, are you?" his companion was complaining.

"I'm sorry—I told you I was tired. I think perhaps we won't go as far as Windsor. I'll do a few more miles, then we'll probably find a decent pub, and have a drink, and go home."

"That's a nice way to behave! Asking a girl out for the night, and taking her home after a drink."

"Now, none of that," said Simon, viciously accelerating. "For one thing, I didn't ask you out for the night, and, as you dam' well know, I took this trip on my own account. You happened to come in on it because you were snivelling about town being stuffy and I offered you a ride."

"Sorry—I'm sure!" In spite of an absurd assumption of hauteur, she wilted so promptly that Simon relented.

"I don't mean to be beastly; but the truth is, I'm rather a sick man, and my nerves won't stand argument. If you'll be so kind as to remember that, we'll have quite a pleasant drive."

"I'm sure I never wanted to argue——" she started to whimper.

"Then that's all right—but don't be silly. Look here, why don't you tell me about yourself? I don't even know your name."

"You never asked, did you?"—with an abrupt revival of sauciness. "I suppose that's the sort of chap you are—just pick a girl up and pop her down without so much as a ' When do we meet again '?"

"Picking up and popping down aren't habits of mine—and if it comes to that, you didn't make any fuss about credentials, did you?" She batted her eyelashes; he could see her pondering on the word "credentials." "Pretty risky game, isn't it, for a girl like you? Do you do it often?"

"What are you getting at? Do you think I'm a tart?" she inquired indignantly.

"If I did, you wouldn't be sitting where you are," said Simon patiently.

"Oh, well—I could see you were diff'rent."

"I suppose they're all 'diff'rent'?" said Simon dryly.

"You're proper sarcastic, aren't you?"—but she was dimpling. "I never go out with chaps I don't know—or'narily."

"Really?" He did not try to keep scepticism out of his voice.

"Reelly! It's a soft thing to do, isn't it? I mean, look what you read in *The Daily Cable*! Every day—girls getting murdered and being assaulted, and what-all!" she said, with virtuous horror.

"Then I take it you fancy you're a reader of character?"

"A how-much?"

"For God's sake, child, don't you know any English?" Simon was at last exasperated The last hour or two had driven forcibly home to him the shortcomings of the English council school as a medium of education. "I suppose you thought, having had a look at me, that I wasn't the sort of person to abuse your—kindness?"

"Abuse?" She fastened with relief on the word she understood. "Oh, no. I could see you were a gentleman; and gentlemen don't use bad language to girls, do they?"

"Well, what's your name?" asked Simon, giving it up.

"Mildred Harris. What's yours?"

"Simon——" he was beginning; then it occurred to him that it was foolish to give his name away to a girl of this sort. "Well, Simon will do, won't it?" he ended lamely.

"I bet it's not your real name!"

"Why not?"

"Who ever heard of a chap called Simon?" It seemed to tickle her.

"What do you do for a job, Mildred?" It seemed better to create a diversion.

She wriggled her shoulders, as though the question irked her.

"Ow—not much. What do you do?"

"I'm a publisher." He wondered what it would convey to her.

"What—do you make books? Coo!" It seemed to have impressed her. Shy, like the rest of her kind, of "impression," she jibbed away from it, to ask, "Are you fond of dancing?"

"Very; but I haven't time for much."

"I'm crazy about it!" Her face lost its inanity, was almost beautiful, lit by her enthusiasm. "I should think you'd be a lovely partner. It's a pity we can't dance together. You're just the right height for me—not too tall. There's two sorts I can't stand: the very tall ones, that drag you up by the shoulders, and the fat ones, that make you bend over!" She tittered. "I think *you'd* be lovely."

Yes, you're blowing up for trouble, thought Simon. He had begun to realize that her seeming naïveté was only the cover for a considerable degree of cunning. He did not for a moment believe that he was the first to win her companionship for a casual outing.

She had twisted sideways in her seat, so that her knee touched his—a small, plump knee, straining at the web of shiny near-silk that covered it; her costume skirt, caught by the wind, lay carelessly, midway across her thighs. Simon recognized a technique which no doubt, in its day, had proved irresistible to those favoured by Miss Harris's company. Yet how it would enrage her to be called a little harlot! These wanton gestures were only part of what she and her kind regarded as legitimate fun. The best sort of fun, from their point of view, was exciting the animal instinct of the male, and squealing denial when it sought fulfilment. For of course, Miss Harris's virginity (such as it was) was reserved for the boy friend, when he had saved enough to establish them in some one-room apartment south-east of the river. Simon, a connoisseur in London accents, had already decided that, whatever might be her present domicile, Miss Harris's birthplace, and the scene of her rearing, was within bowshot of the Elephant and Castle.

Whatever might be her designs on him, he found her harmless and pitiable. He had always had sympathy for these children of squalor, whose horizon is the chimney-pots, their paradise the picture theatre. He sympathized with their crude attempts to realize their ideals in their own persons, with their sporadic efforts to snatch at something thrilling and dangerous, because it came from beyond their own sphere.

The old engine had started to miss—which did not perturb Simon because he knew that, in this part of the country, there is, on the average, a garage to every square mile. As they stuttered into Datchett, he saw a likely one, and drew in.

"Just go over the plugs and fill her up; I'll be back in about half an hour," he left instructions.

"Now, Mildred," he said, as they leaned on the counter of the pub. "What's yours?"

Mildred had a gin and ginger-ale, Simon two beers, and it was dark when they picked up the car and made for the Great West Road again. He thought it better not to risk any more by-lanes, as the lights were poor, and Simon, who knew the batteries had been recently charged, feared the bulbs might be failing. The garage was unable to supply these, so he made for safety and a route of which he was sure.

Mildred, for some reason, had turned sulky. With her elbow on the window-ledge and her chin in her hand, she returned only monosyllables to Simon's attempts at conversation. She had made one or two more attempts to flirt with him—on one occasion had plainly offered her mouth for a kiss—which Simon turned jokingly aside.

He felt some compunction. Poor little devil, it must have been a dull trip for her. She was probably regretting that she had not stayed in town, with a chance of picking up one of her own kind and getting taken to a cinema. She did not look as if she had much fun, and had probably thought she was in for a parcel when she accepted his invitation of a drive into the country.

It is, difficult to entertain a person who speaks another

language, and has a different vocabulary of thought. Ignorant
of the idiom, Simon had not even the current "wisecracks"
of her kind, with which to maintain the conversation at
giggling level. Convicted of social failure, he sat and grimaced
in the dark. One more kind action gone bad on its performer!
If he had been what she had hoped and expected, this, of course,
was the moment to start the cuddling: draw in under a hedge
and make up with kisses and fumblings for his other shortcomings. Unfortunately, she did not inspire him with the
least desire to do so.

Simon was one of those lucky people to whom the idea of
sexual philandering unaccompanied by love is so unimaginable
that they are able to contemplate it in cold blood, without
even being revolted. It was a curious phase of human conduct,
that he could examine as impersonally as something on a
scientist's slide. He could not in any circumstances imagine
himself kissing the forlorn child who sat by his side, but he
could perfectly imagine her own sentiments, and blamed
himself for her bitterness and disappointment.

"Now we shan't be long," he told her—as though, by
shortening, he could lessen her ordeal.

"That'll suit you, won't it?" she snapped back at him.

Ahead of them the sky blazed orange with the signs of one
of the big roadhouses, patronized mainly by rich young Jews
and their West End mistresses. In a flash, Simon took a
decision.

"Look—that's the Knave of Diamonds; have you ever
been there? We could have a dance, if you liked."

Instantly she was sparkling.

"D'you mean it? Coo, the Knave of Diamonds! I've heard
of that. But it's posh, isn't it? Oughtn't we to have on evening
dress?"

"Nonsense."

Simon swung the car in between the packed Bentleys and
Hispano-Suizas of younger Jewry.

"People come in just as they are, off the roads. You can

go and make yourself tidy before you dance, if you want to. I'm going to have a wash myself."

It struck Simon that it was a long time before she returned to him, but he had secured a table, and been obliged, to his annoyance, to order a bottle of champagne. "It's a gala night," the waiter informed him, with an air of take-it-or-leave-it. No wonder, thought Simon, as he watched the crowds pouring into the room, that they did not worry about a standard of courtesy in places like these.

Brushed, re-powdered and flaming with lipstick, there was a glitter of excitement over her that touched Simon's heart. She seemed positively sequined with delight! She had carefully removed all traces of dust from her little office suit, which had, nevertheless, a touching, naïve shabbiness under the garish lights.

"What do you think?" she informed him. "The girl in charge of the ladies' cloakroom used to be a friend of mine! I mean, she went to the same school as me—only that was before I went——" She was babbling with excitement, as though the unexpected encounter had put the coping-stone on her evening's pleasure. "She fairly couldn't believe it, when I told her I was here with a toff. Aren't those girls lovely?" she broke off to exclaim, as a group of luxurious prostitutes, naked to the base of their spines, passed on their way to join their Semitic lovers.

"Frightful, since you ask me," said Simon. "There's a tough crowd here to-night—come on, let's dance and get it over." He wondered if he should have brought her; it seemed a surprisingly vicious place—much more so than any he had been in of recent years.

"I think it's lovely," she assured him.

"You've been darkening your eyelashes!"

"Yes—Doris—that's my friend—lent me some stuff. Do you think it's elegant?" It obviously satisfied her. "Coo, what a lovely band! I'd like to come here every night."

"Come on," said Simon, slipping his arm round her waist.

The floor was crowded, and a considerable percentage of the dancers were, if not drunk, elevated. There were several men, in varying stages of over-amiability or truculence. There were a number of suburban girls, behaving like tarts, and an equal number of tarts, behaving with the supposed demureness of suburban girls. There were short red-faced men dressed like golfers, who danced with tightly corseted elderly women in Oxford Street "semi-evenings," and several professional couples who, at intervals, performed surprising ballroom acrobatics under spotlights. It was, in every particular, the type of amusement place that Simon abhorred.

"Isn't it heavenly?" Mildred was pressing herself to him. He laughed and gave her a light squeeze. "I knew you'd be lovely to dance with," she was assuring him.

She, he discovered, danced beautifully, with a kind of breathless lightness that glorified a commonplace rhythm. A wave of the sea was no more perfect in its rhythmic reaction than her small, boneless and sexless body, soft as a child's. Her eyes were bisected by their drooping lids, the smile on her lips was tranced—she delivered herself body and soul to an art in which she excelled. Simon caught a few curious glances, which irritated him, as they went round; he realized that they were a conspicuous couple in that gathering.

"Well—had enough?" he asked presently.

"Oh, no—please let's have another!" she begged, as the second band launched itself with saxophonic fervour into the next number.

"We'd better have a drink first. I had to order something —it seems to be part of the racket," grumbled Simon. He did not care for champagne at any time, and doubted its quality at a place of this sort.

"Champagne! Crikey—I didn't know you were a millionaire."

"I'm not—and I advise you to go slow on this stuff." He lifted the bottle out of the ice-pail and half-filled her glass. Tasting it before he gave it to her, Simon pulled a face. "I

thought so—sweet! I'd rather drink prussic acid." He called
the waiter and curtly ordered beer. Mildred dipped her little
muzzle into the glass.

"Ooh—fizzy! Of course, champagne ought to be, oughtn't
it? I once had some at a wedding—I thought it was lovely."

"Well, don't drink too much, or you'll be sorry in the
morning," he advised her.

"Me—sorry, after a night like this? Not much! It's worth
getting squiffy, to have all this fun."

"You try getting squiffy, and I'll put you in the car."

At the end of an hour, Simon insisted upon leaving: the
heat, noise and tobacco smoke having undone all the good,
so far as he was concerned, of the outing, he was suddenly
overwhelmingly tired. Mildred pouted at being taken away.

"I could go on dancing all night."

"Next time you must find a younger partner."

"Pooh—you're not old!" She flicked his face playfully with
her hand—dancing and champagne having given her a good
deal more confidence than she had shown in the earlier part
of the evening: although Simon had taken care that she had
not overshot discretion, by pouring most of the contents of
the bottle into the ice-pail. She hung closely on his arm.

"I must say, though you weren't in dress clothes, you made
some of the chaps that were look downright common. I always
say—don't you?—you ought to be able to tell a gent from a
waiter."

"Look out—the fresh air's gone to your head."

"Do you mean I'm tipsy?" she giggled.

"God forbid. But you've forgotten your hat." As she ran,
laughing and stumbling a little, towards the cloakroom, he
called after her, "You know where the car is: I'll be waiting
for you there."

The car, as it happened, had got wedged in among those
of later arrivals, two of whom had been so considerate as to
lock their doors. Annoyed by the delay, Simon went to find
the parking attendant, a showy individual in uniform, more

intent upon his tips from the Bentley owners than upon his general duties to the rest.

"Why can't you look after your job properly? It's your place to see that locked cars aren't parked in front of others already standing there."

The man muttered something about having more on his hands than he could manage, and went surlily to find the owners of the locked cars. It was twenty minutes before an irate person with a crimson carnation in his lapel came to remove the Lancia which was the main block on Simon's retreat. With his unwilling assistance and that of the attendant, they managed to push the second locked car, a small Hillman, whose owner was not to be discovered, sufficiently aside for Simon to get out. When he had done so, his humour was not improved by the discovery that Mildred had meanwhile struck up a lively flirtation with the attendant, which she terminated with barely concealed reluctance at Simon's peremptory summons.

By way, probably, of amends for this hardly graceful behaviour, she became, as soon as they had set out, rather embarrassingly affectionate, insisting upon encircling Simon's neck with her arm, and singing, in the peculiar, drawling tone of her kind, "Alone—with love—on the top of the world," which she interrupted to press a fervid kiss on his cheek, just as the traffic lights turned from yellow to red.

"For goodness' sake behave yourself!" snapped Simon, as he brought the car up, with a shriek of brakes, in a little more than its own length. He had to back to the line. "Do you want to get me had up for dangerous driving?"

A factory clock proclaimed the hour of midnight; they were still well on the wrong side of Hammersmith.

"Where do you want me to drop you?"

"Oh—I don't mind; where are you going?" She had sobered herself to search for her hat, which had slipped on to the floor of the car.

Simon had remembered some papers left in the office, which

he might need, early in the morning. Driving in London after midnight was so effortless a proceeding that he thought he might as well go down and fetch them.

"Down to my office—near where I met you this afternoon."

"That'll suit me."

"Can I send you home in a taxi?"

"Coo—I can see Pa, if I was to come home in a taxi, at this time of night!" she jeered at his simplicity.

He wondered what, in her world, was the subtle difference between arriving home on foot or in a taxi, at this hour. A taxi might have been assumed to be more discreet.

"Pa's awfully particular," she announced—a trifle defiantly.

"What will he say to your turning up after midnight?"

"Oh, I can look after myself."

He took this to mean that she had some way of getting in unobserved, and left the matter alone.

"Well, here we are. Good-night—and thanks for a pleasant evening," said Simon, as, half an hour later, he helped her out of the car.

She looked up at the façade of the building.

"Is this where you work?"

"Yes—it's my office."

"Crome and Lygon"—she pronounced it "Lie-gon"— "Which are you?"

"I'm Crome," said Simon, thinking it was perhaps unfortunate that the council schools were not so ineffectual after all. "There isn't any Lygon now," he added superfluously.

"Fancy that now!" she said pertly. "Well, good-night— *Mister* Crome—and thanks ever so much. P'raps we'll meet again some time."

Not if I know it, thought Simon. It would be tiresome to have to forgo his occasional lunches or cups of tea at the corner restaurant, which was cheap and handy, but he had seen enough of Miss Harris by now to realize the risk of continuing an association of this sort.

Instead of being refreshed, he felt irritable and uneasy, as he let himself into the office. He could not think why—until he suddenly remembered that he had not dined!

"Nor that miserable child either! She must have been starving—and I thought she was sulking because I didn't make love to her!"

The absurdity of his misconception made Simon fling himself back in the chair and laugh himself hoarse.

"Good lord, I wonder what she thought of me! And I wonder if dancing at the Knave of Diamonds made up to her for her poor little empty stomach!" He reflected that it was a miracle that the champagne she had drunk, and his beer, had not laid them both flat on the floor.

He telephoned the garage, which was an all-night one, and told them to fetch the car; then took a taxi, ordering the man to drive round by Rule's on the chance of still finding it open, and the possibility of a meal. But Rule's was closed, so he had to stop at the Coventry Street Lyons, where he ate some food, went on to the druggist in Leicester Square and got his prescription made up, and then drove home—to sleep until after ten in the morning.

Having played poker as long as his eyes could see the cards, Daniel left his friends and let himself in with his latch-key. He could hear the telephone ringing and wondered whether to answer it. Twenty-past one; a fool hour to ring up. The thought crossed his mind that it might be Lydia; but Lydia, these days, was preserving a dignified silence, behind which he guessed at her pain and anxiety. Oh, God, if he could only make up his mind about Lydia!

The telephone stopped ringing. He gave a sigh of relief, mixed himself a drink and took it to his room. An unpleasant, dissipated reflection met him from his mirror. He must get more exercise, play squash, ride, or do something to get back his condition. If there were only some work to be done. He was not a "hearty," finding the be-all and end-all of existence in physical exercise; sports and games he indulged in more

as social gestures than for the stimulus he drew out of them.
If only Simon hadn't been such a fool about the firm.

The telephone started ringing again. He let it ring until
it got on his nerves, then snatched off the receiver.

"Well!"

"I wondered how long it would take you to answer."

"I've only just come in."

"Well, for God's sake come up and have a drink or something. I've got a hump the size of Gibraltar!"

"I don't want a drink and I'm just going to bed."

"If you don't come up I shall come down."

"Challenge to the old-fashioned chivalry, what?"

He heard the receiver clip back.

Well, he supposed there was nothing against going up for
an hour. He and Eliza practically never saw each other these
days. He wondered, as he touched up his face with powder,
and added a silk scarf to his dressing-gowned effect, if she
wanted money. He had settled a generous allowance on her
and she had money of her own, but was always overdrawn and
in trouble with her creditors. She had once, when Daniel was
hard up, offered to do without the allowance, but he refused the
suggestion. "The money's there for your use as long as I've
got it—on condition you never let any other chap pay a penny
towards your bills." "I'm not that sort of tart!" she flung at
him. And he believed her.

Eliza was in her yellow drawing-room, with the magenta
bookshelves and a Modigliani someone had given her in
payment for a debt and which she was always trying to give
away because she had got tired of it. All the lights were on,
and Eliza was in a high-necked, steel-coloured gown which
reflected in its satin shoulders the burning flag of her hair.
Her face was the face of a woman of forty, set on the body
of a girl of sixteen; actually, she had only just had her
thirtieth birthday. She looked as if she did not care if it was
her sixtieth.

"Been out?" She made a vague gesture towards the drinks.

"Playing poker at Lupton's." He pressed down the latch of the syphon—not really wanting any more to drink, but conversation was easier when one held a glass in the hand.

"Lose much?"

"Only a bit over a fiver."

Eliza walked once or twice up and down the drawing-room; her hands were on her narrow hips, with the elbows pressed back. Between her lifted shoulders the white stem of her neck and her narrow, pointed chin were thrust forward as though in quest of something her blank eyes denied.

"I thought you'd like to know . . . Gavin's chucked me."

"I'm sorry," said Daniel gravely. He supposed it was the correct answer.

"It's new stuff for me, isn't it—being chucked? It wasn't quite like that either. They offered him a post in Greece, so, naturally, he took it."

"Need it make any difference?"

"His wife's going out with him, and all's to be domestic bliss and unity!" she gave a croaking laugh. "It's comic, isn't it?—when you think of all the trouble I took for Gavin. All that smoke-screen stuff, so that no one would notice what we were up to. And then he goes off to Greece with his wife."

"He couldn't do anything else, could he?"

"Other people have," said Eliza darkly. "Well, anyhow, that's all—except I'm pretty sick—with everything. If it comes to that, I'm sick of living here: mewed up like a cat in half a dozen rooms, with a key I'm always losing!"

"It was your suggestion," pointed out Daniel. "And so far as that goes, there's nothing to stop your having the run of the house; I'm not in all that amount."

"It's so stupid!" stormed Eliza. She looked so like a sick child who does not know what to be at, that Daniel's heart—an organ of which he disliked to be reminded—ached for her.

"Well, make a suggestion."

"What suggestion is there to make? Should we do a cruise or something?"

"With me?" Daniel's voice betrayed his astonishment.

She gave her low, throaty laugh, came to him, and linked her hands behind his neck.

"We seem to go on being married, don't we, in spite of—things? The truth is, we're a curse to each other—the sort that descends from generation to generation: only, luckily, it will die out with us, as we haven't been careless enough to produce any progeny!" she said lightly. He could feel the thin circle of her arms burning through his dressing-gown and her eyes made green light under her down-drawn brows. She had something better—or worse—than beauty, now; something that compelled him. . . . He tried gently to unclasp her arms.

"I don't play understudy to other people," he reminded her. She flicked aside the suggestion with a restless movement of her neck.

"You can't escape a curse, Daniel!"

"Let's not talk drama, shall we?" he lightly suggested.

She looked at him, smiled, and unlinked her hands. Sauntering across the room to light a cigarette, she said casually:

"Have you still got a thing for that Matlock girl?"

"Does it matter?"

"No; except that—of course—she can't have you." She blew out the match she held between her pointed fingers. "You see, I happen to want you. It's an odd thing—but I always do."

"Perhaps you'll allow that you've got an odd way of showing it."

"Not really," said Eliza, on a note of sweet reasonableness as she sank into her billows of steel-coloured silk on the sofa. "Because a child in the nursery has got dozens of dolls, it doesn't follow she's willing to give away one of them."

"With all respect to you, my dear Eliza, I refuse a, to be classed as a doll, and b, to accept your analogy between your attitude to me and that of a child with its toys."

"It wasn't so good, was it? It was just what came into my

head." The head dropped back on the cushions. "Oh, God—
I'm so tired—and I'm so fond of you, Daniel."

"Now don't start that."

"Why shouldn't I? You know it's true—and you know you
might have affairs with a dozen Matlocks but you'd always
come back to me. That's what I mean by our curse. It's mine,
really. I've always done it to people—often without meaning.
I meant to in your case, that's why it's so strong. So strong
that even I'm a little afraid of it. It's like a projection of
myself, and I'm not answerable for what it may do.

"Can you deny that, in all the times you've held Lydia
Matlock in your arms, you've thought of *me*?"

"For God's sake! We needn't be indecent."

"If you'll answer that," she persisted, "I'll tell you something that might interest you too."

"I suppose," he retorted bitterly, "that you've never thought
of any one but me?"

"Well, it happens to be the truth. What do you make of
that?"

"Since you ask me, I think it's pretty revolting. If you
betray one person with another, the least you can do is to make
it a complete betrayal—not that sort of double-crossing stuff."

"What about your double-crossing, with Lydia Matlock?"

"It wasn't. At least," said Daniel, "I never attempted to
hide from her that I cared—for you."

"And I suppose she believed it! Really, Daniel, you are a
frightful idiot sometimes!" She was actually laughing.

"Well, don't let's talk about it. I don't discuss you with
Lydia; it doesn't seem in the best of taste to discuss Lydia
with you."

"I'm afraid I don't fall for the old school tie thing," she
mocked him, shaking her head. "It doesn't suit you particularly well—or me, either, if it comes to that. Let's face
it, shall we? It's always fun facing things. We're a couple of
cads, Daniel: the real, deep, dyed-in-the-wool sort, and that's
why we suit each other; why we can never get away from

each other for any length of time. You're happiest with me
and I'm happiest with you, because we don't need to keep up
any pretences and we can laugh till we're sick at other people's
illusions. I'd hate you not to be a cad, my dear!—it puts edge
on you. It gives you a kick, as they say—and that's what I want,
more than anything else in the world. That's what you want too.
You can't look me straight in the face and tell me you've met
your 'soul-mate' in that little Matlock girl—with globules
and globules of nonconformity running all through her system!
A globule popping up whenever you least expect it——"

"You don't know what you're talking about. Her sister
—Crome's wife—is like that; but there's no more nonconformity in Lydia than there is in you. She loathes everything
to do with her upbringing."

"Revolt, darling; that's all. The wheel always turns full
cycle. When Lydia Matlock is fifty she'll be playing the organ
in chapel and running rummage sales!"

"Don't be absurd." Nothing more unlike Lydia, her gaiety,
her elegance and light-hearted frivolity, could be imagined;
yet the shaft told. In Daniel's circles there was always something slightly ludicrous in nonconformity, and he was snob
enough to realize that—apart from Lydia—the Matlocks were
of no value: successful *arrivistes*, who were received for their
money—although he had heard that Lady Matlock came of
a good family.

"She's not really smart, you know, either," Eliza was murmuring. "She'd probably look best in arty things—those
Schiaparelli styles don't suit her at all."

Subtle, Eliza, and cunning; Daniel recognized both the
subtlety and the cunning, and, to do him justice, every drop
of his feeling for Lydia rose in defence of Eliza's clever
depreciation of her qualities. At the same time, it was as
though an ugly crease had been laid into a delicate fabric; it
could not alter the weave, but it could never be pressed out
without ruining the material. Eliza had shown him, deliberately, that people—her sort of people, who were also his—

might laugh at him for his affair with Lydia, and laughter against himself was a thing Daniel could not tolerate.

"You're a hundred per cent feline, aren't you?" he muttered.

Eliza smiled and stretched herself. She really looked, for a moment, like a lovely grey cat, as she twisted her body on the cushions. Then she sat up, with an assumption of energy, patting the palms of her hands together.

"Well, listen. I've had my game with Gavin, and you've had yours with Lydia. We can't throw stones at each other, so let's call it a day. I'm getting old, or something. I want some sun—the real sort, not this watered-down, English variety!—and I think—I'm not sure—but I think I want to settle down a bit."

"I've heard that before."

"I know you have. It's a nice sentence for tiding over awkward moments. But this time it's true—truer than usual, I mean. Oh, Daniel, what's the use of talking in terms of the future? There's only the present for people like us. We're here, and we're still fond enough of each other to have a good time. Let's take it while it affords! I won't make silly promises, but I can tell you one thing, my dear: this Gavin affair is going to last me for a long time. It's hit me somewhere where it hurts. I can't explain. Please help me to get over it!"

"What about helping me to get over Lydia?" he said—not meaning it: for, alas, what was there to get over? It was already a sweet, half-forgotten dream, fading in the revival of old fires.

Eliza smiled her fine, incredulous smile.

"You can just go and have a little talk with her, and say thank you for the party, like a good little boy. I don't see why I should be so generous—but I've gone a bit soft, over Gavin. It's luck, isn't it, you're out of that ridiculous publishing business?"

She stretched up her arms, and with a little, despairing sound, Daniel dropped down into them—accepting his curse.

CHAPTER EIGHTEEN

"Anna," said Lydia, "shall you be in this afternoon?" Her hand was clasped over the mouthpiece of the receiver, as she stood at the door of her bedroom. Anna, fixing her hair in the hall looking-glass, shook her head, smiling. Lydia said into the telephone, "Yes, three o'clock will do very well," and dropped the receiver into its place. Then she appeared to forget that she was holding the apparatus, for she stood, leaning against the door, with it in her hand, until Anna came and relieved her of the burden.

"I wasn't going to be in, in any case," she said, "but if I'd thought of it, you needn't have avoided telling me I wasn't wanted."

"Can you," said Lydia, and paused. "Can you," she resumed, "suggest a suitable toilette for a lady, on receiving her *congé*?"

"Is that the way of things?" muttered Anna.

"By the pricking of my thumbs," said Lydia, attempting —not very successfully—bravado.

"Oh, to hell with men," said Anna softly.

"Not *black*," said Lydia, contemplating her wardrobe. "Too suggestive: though that new one I brought back from Paris is far and away the smartest I've got. Still, he's seen it—once." She drove back the memory of the occasion on which he had seen it—the dinner at La Crémaillere, when all heaven seemed patined with the fine gold of happiness . . . women, she supposed, had got to get used to these things.

Humming beneath her breath, Anna reached across her shoulder to tweak out a fold of silk, grimaced and rejected it.

"No—perhaps not that, either; I have a sort of feeling those stripes and splashes are for one's brighter moments—"

"I think you'd better have it; yellow's more your colour than mine," said Lydia; it occurred to her that there might not be, for a long time, any "brighter moments," and that the

L

frock, which was very up to date, would then be démodée.

"Thanks, I don't go in for grave-robbing," said Anna. "Some moment, when you're feeling your bright, bonny self, you can offer it me, and see what I say." She surveyed Lydia, frowning. "Go and have a coiffure and a face massage; you've got heaps of time for both, and they're so bolstering. And then you can put on that demure little pink affair you got for Celia's luncheon."

"Will you be in for lunch?"

"Yes, but it's my apple-and-Ryvita day. Don't order anything for me."

"Cook's getting horribly out of practice; either we're out or we don't eat anything."

"Then you can tell her to fix a soufflé for you. I'm going to the Book and Wine shop, by the way; there's hardly a drink in the house, and I shall bring back a half-bottle of Roederer for your lunch."

Anna was certainly a treasure as a house companion. She never fussed, never questioned, but was always practical and stimulating.

As Lydia sat with her head under the drier she had almost persuaded herself that Daniel's message meant, not that he was coming to tell her that everything was finished, but that he had made up his mind to leave Eliza and to take her away to bliss in some other part of the globe. If it had been the other thing, would he not have written? Men were supposed always to avoid scenes. Whatever came, there should not be a scene!

The face massage freshened her, and her skin felt as soft as petals; the little pads of lotion they laid on her eyes took away the ache and the slight puffiness under them. No wonder women went in for beauty treatments; they were so soothing. She did not quite dare to dwell upon that possible future with Daniel, but her mind kept filling itself with little dancing half-shaped images, and her heart, which had ached with an actual, physical pain for many days, contented itself with beating a little faster than usual.

In spite of this, and the Roederer at lunch, and Anna's cheerful conversation, she was almost overwhelmed with nausea when the hands of the clock pointed to five minutes to three. "Suppose when he comes I'm being sick?" In despair, she took a large spoonful of brandy, which she had heard was supposed to steady the stomach, but nearly had the opposite effect. Her knees shook so much when she heard the bell that she had to sit down suddenly, and doubted whether she would be able to rise to welcome him.

When he came in, she could not help remembering the first time he had entered the flat—when he stood in the doorway, looking like a dandified scarecrow—a Brummel among scarecrows—with his silk hat on the back of his head and the scarf half slipping off his neck. He looked very much the same to-day—allowing for the difference in garments: thin, fine-drawn and hag-ridden, with a nerve jumping between his cheekbone and his temple. Her dreams died; she knew before he spoke the business on which he had come; she wanted to forestall him—she rose, and felt her lips shaping themselves into their accustomed smile.

"Hallo, Daniel."

"Pretty frock," said Daniel. He did not move towards her —thank God!

"It's rather early for tea; would you like some coffee?"

"No, thanks; I've just come from lunch."

"I think we'll have some coffee." Ignoring his protest, she laid her hand on the bell; it was something to do—to say. "Bring some coffee, please," she told the maid who had replaced the pert Agnes. There was a new cook, too; Anna had got rid of the old one while Lydia was in France.

There was a long silence. Daniel, who had rehearsed every word of this conversation—at least, of his own end of it—was, for once, tongue-tied. He had done what seemed to him the least caddish thing. It would have been so much easier to write to Lydia, but he felt that the least he owed her was this call. And now that he had come, all his prepared sentences—

sentences framed so as to hurt her as little as possible—had gone from his mind.

"Well, Daniel?"

"You've guessed," he muttered.

"Yes."

"It's an abominable *cliché*, but it happens to be the truth; I'm not good enough for you, Lydia."

Her lips smiled; she was surprised, and glad to find that they were not trembling.

"The trouble is, people don't always care for what is good for them; they generally prefer—the other."

"I shouldn't—I've been a monster of selfishness, from the beginning." Words came more easily now.

"You needn't worry about that. It was good, wasn't it—while it lasted?"

"It was my salvation," said Daniel, with complete sincerity. "But you—my poor sweet—what was it for you?"

"Good." She flashed a smile at him. It is wonderful how one can smile, with all of one's inside twisting in agony! "Are you sure it's got to—finish?"

"Sure."

"On your account—or mine?"

"On both."

"Don't count me," said Lydia quickly.

"Why not? You're the only person who counts, in this. I deserve all that's coming to me, you've been nothing but an angel, and I suppose I'll burn in hell for what I've done to you."

"What happened? Please tell me. I don't mind what it is, so long as I know. Did you get bored. Did I do something?"

"Nothing—nothing that wasn't perfect. You know yourself what it was."

"Eliza all the time."

He nodded.

"But now, Daniel, darling, you've got nobody! How can you go on—with nobody?"

He had not meant to tell her the cold-blooded truth; she would hear it soon enough. But her tragic tenderness defeated him; he could not take from her, on top of all the rest, the gift of her compassion.

"Eliza—wants me to go away with her."

In the silence which followed the beauty stripped itself from her face like bark from a young tree. The maid returned, put down the coffee between them and made her rustling withdrawal.

"Eliza wants *you* to go away with *her*?"

He sat miserably silent.

"And you're going?"

He wondered if this in any way resembled the scene between Eliza and her lover, when she was told of his appointment to Greece. She was quite devil enough to have foreseen it: deliberately to have insisted upon his seeing Lydia, as though, in passing on her pain to another woman, she could rid herself of some part of it. He execrated himself for causing Lydia unnecessary suffering, through playing into Eliza's hand.

"Yes."

"Well, then . . . there's nothing more to say, is there?"

"I suppose you think it's weak-minded of me—allowing myself to be whistled up like a dog, when it suits Eliza? There's no excuse for it: except that, for good and evil, I seem to be bound to her as long as we're alive."

"It's all right," said Lydia, "so long as you're happy."

He laughed.

"If you think I'm expecting happiness in connection with Eliza——! On the contrary. I'm going to get paid out for the way I've treated you."

"Daniel." She was on her feet, swaying before him. "You mustn't! I can't stand it—I can't have you punished because you gave me a wonderful thing——"

He took her in his arms.

"You can't prevent it, my sweet."

"But—we *love* each other!" It was the lost and puzzled whisper of a child, seeking reassurance.

He shook his head, unable to believe that the prickling sensation in his eyes was caused by tears, until a great, humiliating drop rolled down his cheek.

"I'm not built for love—what you mean by love. It scares me—like having to go to Communion used to scare me when I was a kid at school. It fascinated me, and I hated it. My hate was part of my fear—do you understand? Eliza and I have a thing in common: our dread of permanency, our desire to live wholly in the moment, to take what we want when we want it and then to throw it away—for Christ's sake, Lydia, what's the good of that to you? What's the good of it to you?"

She looked at him for a moment almost with horror, and then withdrew herself from his arms and went back to sit in her chair.

"What's the good of it to me?" she murmured.

Daniel had gone, and the untouched coffee stood on the table. Lydia got up and wandered about the room, touching things without seeing them. Everything must be different, everything must take another pattern, now Daniel had gone out of her life. Nothing could ever look, or sound, or taste, or smell the same again, because a change like that struck right down into the roots of one's organism, and altered the very cells of one's body. Now the ripening time was past, the time of harvest, of all bright colours. . . .

Her hands lingered upon a book which Anna had left on a table; as they idly lifted it, it fell open at the last pages. She glanced at the meaningless print; a line detached itself, and sped like an arrow through the vapours of her tired mind:

"*In the Spring my life began; in the Summer, happiness; in the Autumn, let me die . . .*"

She put the book down, with a shiver. No, it was not as simple as that. Nothing ever was as simple as that.

In spite of his exhausting evening, Simon came down to the office very much on the top of the wave, to deal with his noon appointment. Among the pleasanter ingredients of the morning mail was a very friendly letter from Horne, saying that although no settlement had yet been reached, he had every hope of an amicable agreement, and expected to bring good news on his return at the end of the month. This encouraged Simon to open the next envelope, addressed in Old Harry's neat and crabbed style—a rather ominous departure from his usual typed epistles. Old Harry had, however, written in person, to say how sorry he was not to have looked them up lately; that he hoped shortly to be through with his present rush of affairs—and would Simon dine with him at the end of the week? "Ever affectionately his, H. M." It cost Simon a pang to recognize the old man's genuine warmth towards him, for he knew that Old Harry would be, not merely offended, but deeply hurt, when he learned of Simon's intention of dispensing in future with his financial and advisory help.

Still, it was something of a relief to know that the interview was postponed; there was a fair chance that the business with Horne would be settled by the end of the month, and Simon would have solid ground upon which to take his stand against Old Harry's displeasure. He felt so satisfied with the way things were shaping that he invited Marius and Nancy to lunch with him at a nearby chophouse: a friendly rather than a business occasion—although, of course, little but office matters were discussed—for he felt he had of late paid little personal attention to these two devoted followers of his fortunes.

"Honestly, Nancy, don't you feel the worst is over? We've got all the ingredients of success in our hands now."

She looked at him, surprised at this rather childish optimism. She knew too well these signs of disequilibriated nerves—the insane despair, alternating with a crazy confidence. Not that Simon's confidence in the present instance was altogether crazy; Nancy herself felt that success was within their reach, but, being by nature cautious and unwilling to commit herself to premature rejoicing, she felt it would be wise to

get the Horne contract signed before "sending up the balloon."
She smiled slowly.

"Things are certainly looking brighter, and it looks as if
our autumn list will be a whacker," she admitted.

"Schwartz is crowing like a game cock over *Cypriana*," he
told Marius, seeking from him some of the enthusiasm which,
for her own mysterious reasons, Nancy appeared to grudge.

"Is he?" mumbled Marius, in the tone that lent his most
agreeable pronouncements an air of disgruntlement.

Simon leaned back and laughed.

"I must say you're an encouraging couple! I know what
it is, of course. You both need a holiday. I'll try and fix it
as soon as we've got through the accounts."

"I haven't the least wish to take a holiday," grumbled
Marius. "I'm on my new book, and when I change environ-
ments in the middle I find it breaks the thread. Having just
succeeded in adapting myself to the present routine, I don't
see why it should be disturbed."

"It's no use my taking time off until Dennis gets his
holidays," put in Nancy, "and I've fixed up for him to spend
the first fortnight with his grandmother; so the end of August
will suit me better than going away now."

"Oh, all right," snapped Simon; their lack of graciousness
had exploded his bright mood. He thrust his chair back. "I'm
going back to do some letters; I don't need either of you, so
you needn't hurry over your coffee."

They looked at each other after he was gone.

"He's awfully near the edge," said Nancy.

Marius grunted, tapping ash into the saucer of his cup.

"I don't know why it is . . . I hate to hear him talking as
if we were out of the wood. Supposing Horne decides against
this partnership? American firms have all they can do, from
all accounts, to meet their own commitments at present; it's
hardly likely a firm like Schwartz would choose to recoup
by putting money into a business like ours."

"Well, in that case, I suppose we'll put up the shutters."

"Good God, don't you realize what that means to Crome?"

"The same as it means to all of us, I suppose—except on a larger scale. One takes things as they come."

"Marius, are you *really* indifferent to success or failure?"

"Is any one—except a fool? Perhaps I'm a fool. I think I am indifferent—to the sort of thing you mean. Our ultimate success is within us; all the drum-banging in the world can't count, if you've failed to satisfy your own innermost judge."

"But failure? When one's given all that's in one to something—and it crashes——"

"How do you mean—'all'? The thing that inspired you to your first effort will inspire you to your next, so long as you don't prostitute it."

"One needs a lot of faith, to believe that." She looked doubtfully at his heavy face, his long, lugubriously-sprouting hair. "Have you got faith—like that?"

"Of course I have—faith in myself. That's why I didn't care so much about *Cypriana*. You all went on as if the book had been murdered; it was only the pruning back of a tree that grows too fast. The good of it will come out in my next book. *Reculer pour mieux sauter*: isn't that one of the principles of progression?"

"Then you're not sorry for the failures?"

His violent eyebrows drew together in a scowl.

"Sorry? Do you mean pity? I don't believe in pity; it's vitiating. If a man's got anything in him, he derives impetus from scorn—never from pity. Scorn's a high and holy thing; especially scorn for oneself, for one's mistakes and follies."

"You're pretty inhuman at times, aren't you?"

He surprised her by laughing.

"That, if I may say so, is a typically feminine remark."

"Well, do you despise women?"

"Don't be a fool; you've read *Cypriana*."

"I never asked you before," said Nancy slowly, "because it's such a fool question. But I suppose that's all autobiographical."

"Most of it—I'm afraid."

"Why ' afraid '?"

"Because all fiction ought to be creative. Any fool can put down bits of autobiography, and one in twenty can make it readable. *Cypriana*'s a useful record—that's all. And, of course, a statement of creed. It's not a bad idea, if you're a writer, to start by stating your creed. It helps to equilibrize your future work."

"Is that where you got your views on scorn and pity?"

"Yes."

"They seem pretty hard."

"Hard?" He rose, jerking the belt about his hips. "Life's hard—if you live it for what it's worth; that's how it's good. The harder you live the more virtue you get out of it."

"A man's theory, Marius."

"And a woman's—if she's the right sort."

She rose as well, picking up her gloves with a little laugh.

"I'm sorry for the women you have to do with, if those are your views."

"Sorry?" He narrowed his eyes at her. "You asked me a minute ago if I despised women. At least I've never insulted them by pitying them."

It was a few minutes before six, and Marius was finishing some letters which he had taken to Simon's dictation. His shorthand speed was considerably less than Nancy's, but his typing was exquisite; he had a way of spacing which, as Nancy herself admitted, made a sheet of typescript look like Early English lettering.

The telephone purred and he lifted it mechanically.

"Yes?" He covered the mouthpiece before turning to Simon. "There's a person asking for you downstairs. He seems to refuse his name."

"Oh, go down and see what it is, will you? Say I'm engaged, and—anyhow—I never see people without appointments.

Marius replaced the receiver and slouched out of the room.

Simon was going through the Aldebaran returns, and had practically forgotten the incident, when Marius returned.

"Well?"

"Not so well."

"Eh? Oh, I'd forgotten about the chap; what's he want?"

"He won't say; atmosphere of veiled threats and general unpleasantness."

"Well, have you got rid of him?"

"I'm afraid not." From his jutting lower lip, Marius regarded this as an aspersion on his own powers of compulsion.

"What's he look like—a dun?" Simon tried to remember where he owed money; he could think of none of his usual creditors who were likely to dun him.

"Might be. Some sort of out-of-work clerk with a grievance. I wondered if he was somebody you'd sacked."

"Good heavens, I don't know. Tell him to clear out and not make a nuisance of himself."

"Shall I kick him out?" asked Marius helpfully, turning at the door.

"If you aspire to a summons for assault. Try peaceful measures, and then mention the police."

Ten minutes later, Marius was back.

"I say," said Simon, "do you mind taking another couple of letters? I know it's after six."

"Look here. That bastard's camped in the waiting-room, and short of running him out by the seat of his pants there doesn't seem to be any way of getting rid of him. The people downstairs want to go home."

"Did you mention the police?"

"I did; and he gave me to understand I was at liberty to call the whole of the force if I felt like it."

"Bluff!" said Simon scornfully.

"I just wanted to make sure it was," said Marius slowly, "before taking him at his word."

"Here—what do you imagine I've been doing?" Simon was astonished.

"I haven't the least idea."

"Well, seeing my conscience is clear, perhaps you'll be so kind as to take this letter for me—and meanwhile you can ring down and say that Mr. Whoever-it-is can send up his name or go to hell."

Having translated this into suitable terms for the switch-board attendant, Marius took Simon's letters and retired to the typewriter. Simon settled down to write to Christian. Presently Marius brought the letters for signature.

"Anything else?"

"Nothing to-night, Marius. I suppose Nancy's gone?"

"She went out about four to see the *Comet* people, and those new agents in St. James's who sent us the Rankin manuscript. She rang back at five to see if she was wanted, and said she'd be at Blessington House until six; if no message came through she'd go straight home from there."

"The efficiency of that woman is paralysing. You and she get on pretty well together, don't you?"

"Yes?" said Marius, on a note of inquiry.

"Have you ever thought of getting married?"

"To Nancy Rowlandson?" Marius was startled, and showed it.

"Of getting married in the abstract, you ass. To Nancy—if you happened to feel that way. She'd make a damned good wife."

"I think marriage would interfere with my work. That's the vital thing, for the present. Besides which, women expect to be kept. I can't keep a wife."

"I don't see why you shouldn't manage—if you were both earning."

Marius shook his head.

"I've no use for that sort of independence. It's all right in a mistress, because it absolves one of responsibilities. But it's the devil in a wife. I want to get on with my work. I don't want—emotionalism in my environment."

"I suppose it's never occurred to you," said Simon, "that

your work might profit by a little emotionalism? Don't be too sure of those cold, Parnassian heights; they'll let you down, sooner or later."

"That's for time to prove," returned Marius, unimpressed.

Simon wondered if he was right; whether he himself might have gained if he had foresworn for a while the soft and sweet delights of marriage to Christian. He would at least have been spared some mental agonies. . . . Then he thought of Henry and Jemima. That was the real meaning of human fulfilment!—not the cold, egoistical cleaving through space of a path to glory, but the propagation, through love, of a fresh line of endeavour.

"Well," said Marius, "I'll be off."

"Leave the door open," said Simon. "This place is like an oven."

It was owing to Marius's leaving the outer, as well as the inner, door open that Simon overheard the encounter upon the stairs.

"What are you doing here?"

"Now then, none of your lip! I've come to see Crome, and I'm seeing him."

"You're trespassing on private premises, and we can have you summonsed for it. You were told to get out, weren't you?"

"By who? You think I was goin' to do as I was told by some piddlin' little orfice boy?"

"What's all this about?" Simon went to the door at the head of the stairs, on which Marius and his companion were having their altercation. It was too dark to identify the latter, whose truculence instantly vanished, to be replaced by a kind of whining pleasantry, even more disagreeable than the previous aggressiveness. As Marius, obeying a nod, ceased to bar the way, the man came a few steps up, removing a seedy bowler to display a shining bald head, thinly streaked with dark hair.

"What do you want?" asked Simon sharply. "My secretary's right—you're trespassing; I suppose you know what that means."

"Now, mister, I won't keep you a minute," said the fellow plausibly.

"Why couldn't you send up your name?"

A cunning upward glance, which was in some way familiar to Simon, caused him a faint uneasiness.

"No good filling folks' mouths with a pack o' gossip, is there?"

"I don't know what you're talking about. Say what you've got to say and clear out."

"What—in front of 'im?" He contemptuously indicated Marius, now behind him, barring his flight. "Come on now, Mr. Simon Crome: have sense! You know folks don't come in like this—riskin' the coppers—for nothink! I only want five minutes' chat with you, and I'm sure the 'ole business 'll settle itself to everybody's satisfaction."

It struck Simon that, in spite of the man's glib use of his name, he was being mistaken for someone else. Feeling sure of his ability to prove an alibi in the case of any inconvenient misunderstanding, he stepped back, jerking his head towards his room.

"I can give you five minutes; that's all."

"You can say a lot in five minutes. Hey!" said the visitor to Marius, who was showing signs of following. Marius and Simon exchanged glances, and a flicker of the latter's eyebrow sent Marius into his own little office, which had been Nancy's until she took over Daniel's quarters on the second floor. Simon closed the door upon himself and the man, who turned out to be a short, pot-bellied person with a clean-shaven face of the type which an older generation christened "knowing cove." A strong stench of beer and onions immediately pervaded the already close air of the room; its originator spat carefully into the fireplace, gave a quick look round and marked the three doors, one of which he had just entered, one communicating with the secretary's room and one wth Simon's lavatory.

"No funny business? No eavesdropping?"

"There's no one here but ourselves and the person you've just seen. Get on with it; I'm a busy man," snapped Simon.

"So 'm I, if it comes to that; but not too busy to look after the int'rests of them belonging to me. I dare say, Mr. Crome, the name 'Arris conveys somethink to you?"

"Not a dam' thing," said Simon irritably. He detested circumlocutory talkers. "Come to the point."

"I'm coming, I'm coming. So that's your story, is it? You don't know the name 'Arris, and I suppose you didn't keep my girl out till one o'clock this mornin', neether?"

"So that's it," said Simon. "I see. Well, what about it?"

"This about it." The man's air became threatening. "We all know what chaps like you is up to, when they take a girl like my Mildred riding in the country. She says you took advantage of 'er."

"I *what*?"

"Got 'er drunk on champagne and took advantage of 'er." The father's tone held something of unction which, in different circumstances, Simon might have put down to the mollifying influence of the word "champagne." There was a difference, after all, in getting a girl ginned up with shandygaff and raping her on champagne! "That's a nice thing for a father to 'ear, ain't it?"

"She's a dirty little liar—or else you are. You'd better go before I have you kicked out."

"Now then! Not so fast, will yer? There's a law of assault, you know, that goes for the poor as well as the rich!" Mildred Harris's father had nimbly nipped round to the farther side of the desk from Simon. "Callin' my girl names now, are you? You got to prove what you say, you know."

"What do you mean? Your girl says I seduced her; I say I didn't. It's her word against mine, and I don't see how you're going to prove who's in the right," said Simon slowly. This couldn't be serious! It simply did not happen to people like him.

"I'm likely to believe my daughter, aren't I? She's always been a good girl to 'er parents, and she'd rather cut off 'er right 'and than 'urt 'er daddy's feelings. Cried bitter, when she told me about it. ' I wouldn't 'ave said a word, daddy, but I'm that frightened.' And there was 'er mother an' me, worryin' our 'eads off when she didn't come 'ome early, the way she always does——"

"Never been out at night in her life, I suppose?" sneered Simon.

"What 'ya gettin' at? I tell you, my girl's decent."

"So far as I'm concerned, she's as decent as she was the night before last."

"Seduction apart, it's not going to sound so good in the courts, when it comes out that Mr. Simon Crome of the publishing 'ouse of Crome and Lie-gon took a girl out in the country an' filled 'er up with champagne: a girl of fourteen!"

"Fourteen my foot!" exploded Simon.

"I got 'er birth certificate!" said the other quickly

"I don't believe it."

"Well, that's up to you." Mildred Harris's father replaced the greasy bowler on his head. "I don't arsk nobody to believe nothink I'm not prepared to prove before a judge an' jury. So as my lawyer's kindly promised to wait till I step round, I'll wish you good-day."

"Wait a minute.... I suppose this is blackmail," said Simon. Harris grinned.

"First time you've met it? Some folks is lucky."

"It's more than you'll be, when the case is through."

"Oh—fightin' it, are you? Go on, Mr. Bloody Crome: fight it. An' fight the case I'm bringin' against you for seducin' my daughter. I suppose you're countin' on the Mr. A. business if you sue me for blackmail? Well, there won't be no Mr. A.'s in my case; there'll be full names an' addresses *and* a reminder to the jury that you're the chap that got 'is name in the papers for publishin' dirty lit'rature!"

Simon had a sensation as though his diaphragm muscle had descended into his pelvis, followed, for a shocking instant, by the desire for the first time in his life to commit murder. This creature held in his dirty hands the power to ruin him in every possible way: domestically, financially and socially. If this matter were to come into the courts, he could see no possible way of proving his innocence to a jury already prejudiced by the *Cypriana* affair.

He wondered how much of the conversation Marius had overheard; little, if any. In winter, with the windows closed, it was possible to hear conversations in the adjoining rooms; in summer, with the hum of the traffic pouring in through the open windows, Simon found it necessary to bawl half a dozen times before the camel-like head and shoulders of Marius came through the intervening door, vaguely inquiring, "Were you saying anything?"

Which of his friends would stand by him, if he were convicted of this hideous business? Burke, Ray, Agatha Mott, the immaculate Manders—all who had eagerly championed him through the *Cypriana* disaster, would recoil from one accused of a dirty little sexual crime. He tried to remember the sentences people got for seducing girls under age. "The age of consent." What was it? Sixteen? Eighteen? Whatever it might be, and whatever age Harris's daughter might be, she knew all about consenting. The very stuff she rubbed on her mouth, the sly droop of her lashes, the way her shiny, fat little knee sought his, were all gestures of consent.

Simon was just about to say, "What's your price?" when Marius walked into the room.

"Here—what's this?" asked Harris, startled.

Simon pulled himself together.

"My secretary has come to remind me that there are letters to be got off on the night mail. I can't spare you any more time now."

"That's as you please, mister. I'll be moving on to that appointment I mentioned."

Making a pretence of consulting the pages of his engagement pad, Simon said:

"I can give you a few minutes at the same time, to-morrow.
Here, between six and seven."

A glint of cunning came into the other's eyes.

"Oh, you can—can you?"

"Provided, of course, you cut the appointment you spoke
of."

Harris chuckled.

"Well, I'm in your 'ands, aren't I?" he said ingratiatingly.
"And I guess, in the circs, I can trust you not to let me down."

"See him out," muttered Simon.

"Who's your seedy pal?" inquired Marius, when he returned.
Simon was standing with his back to the door, looking out of
the window. When he turned, the flippancy was smitten from
Marius's lips. He stifled an exclamation, his oddly-shaped
eyes narrowed, he took a step towards Simon, who made a
gesture of defeat as he dropped into his chair. He sat there
for a few minutes, covering his face with his hands. He heard
Marius go to the cabinet, and heard him mixing a drink with
the doubtful movements of one unaccustomed to the task.
Marius was standing by his shoulder.

"Here's some whisky. I don't know if I've put in the right
proportion of soda."

Seeing Simon incapable of action, Marius held the glass to
his lips. Simon was dimly aware of the almost womanish
tenderness he had surprised in Marius on other occasions.

"Blackmail," he managed to say, at last.

"I guessed as much. It's amazing how the game goes on,
considering what they get for it. Well, that's soon fixed."

"Not so soon. In fact—I've got to—pay up."

"Don't be a fool!"

Simon told him the history of the previous night. Marius
sat looking between his knees; his hairy forearms hung over
the arms of the chair. He did not move or make any comment
until Simon had finished. Then he drawled:

"It's a frame-up."

"Of course it's a frame-up; the oldest trick in the world. The only variation on the classic theme happens to be the age of the girl."

"Didn't you guess?"

"Guess what? That she was fourteen? How should I? She might have been anything, from a schoolgirl to twenty. That's the way they all are, these days."

"But when you got her in the car?" persisted Marius.

A note in his voice told Simon the horrific truth: that even Marius, who knew and was fond of him, did not believe in his complete innocence. The discovery paralysed for a moment his powers of speech; when he recovered them, he said:

"Will you believe I didn't touch the girl?"

"I'll believe anything you tell me; it doesn't seem to matter."

"God in heaven, of course it matters. I love Christian, and I'd as soon take a servant in my own house as that little cockney bitch!"

"What's kissing a cockney got to do with loving your wife?"

"Everything. Anyhow, I didn't kiss her. I didn't want to kiss her. She bored me to tears—and I imagined I was doing the same to her. That's why I took her to the roadhouse—I was sorry for the little wretch, and felt she was disappointed with her outing."

"Did she say so?"

"More or less."

"And tried to get you to make love to her."

"In a clumsy sort of way. In fact, so badly, I didn't catch on to it for quite a while. She's not an old hand, that I'll swear; but she's made—a promising beginning!" grinned Simon bitterly.

"What attracted you to her?" asked Marius curiously.

"For God's sake! Haven't I told you i wasn't attracted?

In fact, if you like to put it that way, I was only following your prescription. You told me to get out in the country with someone to whom books were punk—it didn't seem a bad idea. I was too tired to scare up any one I knew, and there was this kid, at a loose end, and looking a bit forlorn—of course, telling it like this makes it sound as if I thought the whole thing out. I can only say I was too fagged to do any thinking. It was practically a reflex action."

"Dangerous things, reflex actions. I've performed quite a number of them."

"Keep your wisecracks," snapped Simon. "If the girl had been Aphrodite and made me advances, I'd have regarded them with as much emotion as something on the fishmonger's slab. She happened to be a peaky little East Ender with a yen for fresh air." Marius gave a yap of laughter. "It's no good talking to you. Clear off, if you don't mind. I've got to think this out."

"I didn't mean to laugh, and I beg your pardon." Marius chewed a corner of the protuberant lower lip before he announced, "You'll fight it, of course."

"How the dickens can I fight it? You can't get these cases tried in camera, and the very fact of being mixed up in a thing like that will do me in."

"I should fight it on point of principle: for your wife's sake—for everybody's sake," said Marius stubbornly.

"Thanks. I don't feel like being a martyr for the cause of humanity."

"People who pay blackmail ought to be forced to do time for it themselves; it's conniving at crime," scowled Marius.

"I know all those smart generalizations. What about the children—Henry at school? What about Old Harry and Peter Horne? I see Horne going into business with a fellow who's been had up for a shady affair with a kid of fourteen!"

"At least," said Marius, after a pause, "you'll see Combridge and get his slant on it."

"He won't believe what I say," said Simon bitterly.

"He probably won't; but it won't prevent his putting his finger on the weak spot in their case—if they've got one."

Simon threw up his hands with a beaten gesture.

"So it's no use living a perfectly straight and decent life of complete content and understanding with one's wife? I suppose not—if every one's going to take it for granted one goes off the rails at the first opportunity? You! Combridge! That means every one else—all the people that one might have expected to count upon——"

"Steady on." Marius laid his hand on Simon's knee. "It's no use bringing sentimentality into this. It's not unheard-of for a man, however ideal his relationship with his wife may be, to go off the rails under certain conditions: say shock, or overwork——"

"So that's what you think."

"What the devil does it matter what I think? It's what the jury 'll think. I fancy that's the line you will get off on, if the case ever comes into court."

"I'd rather do time," said Simon simply, "than that Christian, or any one I care for, should think that. It's infamous! Do you mean I should plead guilty to a thing I've never done?"

"Of course," said Marius, transferring his attention from the corner of his lip to his thumbnail, "there might be such a thing as a forged birth certificate."

"There's also such a thing as finding out if the girl's *virgo intacta*. She probably isn't, but if so, it's none of my doing."

"Anyhow, nobody pays any attention to that in these days; intact virgins went out with the vaulting horse and women's sports! Let's ring up Combridge and get him round for a talk."

Combridge's wife answered the call.

"Who? Mr. Simon Crome? Oh, well—I'm sorry; but my husband's gone to see a client in the country; he isn't expected back until to-morrow."

"What time to-morrow?" asked Marius, cursing the delay.

"I'm not sure—before lunch, I should think. Is it an urgent matter?"

"Like hell it's urgent," Marius prevented himself with difficulty from replying; he knew the etiolated accents of suburban refinement. He managed to imply that the matter was pressing.

"I'll try to get a call to him after dinner," said Mrs. Combridge, obligingly. "But of course he mayn't be at the hotel. I don't even know if the house is on the phone."

"Find out," said Marius curtly, "and ask him to ring us back if he can."

"Oh, yes—well, where?"

Marius looked at the clock, and looked at Simon, who did not seem to be aware of what he was saying. He gave Nancy Rowlandson's number, added curt, conventional thanks, and rang off. On pretext of collecting his papers, he went into the secretaries' room, shut the door and dialled Nancy. To his relief she was at home.

"Are you by yourself?"

"Yes; do you want some food?" She was about to enumerate the not very lavish contents of her larder when Marius cut in:

"I want to bring Simon. He's in trouble. Yes, it's serious. We might want to stay the night."

"Come along," said Nancy.

"Well," said Simon heavily, "I suppose I might as well be going home." He spoke like a man who has been hit on the head.

When Marius said quietly that they were going along to Nancy's, he made no demur. The power of ordering his own actions had left him.

Just after he and Marius left the office the telephone bell started ringing. It rang at intervals for more than an hour.

CHAPTER NINETEEN

"Have you heard from Lydia?" asked Lady Matlock, drawing her needle through the heart of an improbable magenta blossom.

"Only the post-card I showed you; Lydia doesn't write letters much, you know."

"I do wish she'd get married," frowned Lydia's mother. "It seems so very unnatural for a girl in her position, and with her opportunities, not to have found herself a husband before now."

"There's plenty of time, isn't there?" said Christian, a trifle nervously. "Lydia's so sweet—and she's probably having a good look round. It doesn't suit everybody to marry young."

"Nonsense, darling; it's the natural aim of every woman to settle down in a home of her own. I can't help worrying about Lydia rather a lot," said Lady Matlock plaintively. "I do so detest this bachelor girl nonsense, and I'm sure I don't know what to think of this Miss Pryde she lives with. I suppose Lydia pays for them both."

"Oh, no. Anna's an awfully nice girl, and I know she pays her share whenever she can afford it."

"No doubt it's a great advantage for her to live with Lydia," said Lady Matlock fretfully. "But I must say I think it's a most irregular existence, for two girls like that, living by themselves and going everywhere unchaperoned. Of course, I know the chaperon is out of date——"

"Mummy darling! They're neither of them children. Lydia's nearly thirty and Anna can't be much younger."

"I can't help that; a girl who goes about in society unchaperoned, as Lydia has done—heaven knows it was against my wishes!—ever since she was twenty-one, loses value in the eyes of the kind of man she ought to marry." Lady Matlock's eyes filled with easy tears, and she turned appealingly to her daughter. "I know it's stupid, Chris—but I'm always dreading to hear that Lydia's got herself into some horrible tangle. It seems to happen so often to girls who lead that sort of life."

"Mummy, dear." Christian took her mother's soft, un-useful little hand. "You don't know how capable Lydia is of looking after herself——" She broke off; was it true? For weeks now Lydia had not mentioned Daniel's name; did it mean the unhappy affair was over, or that Lydia had decided to follow her own inclinations and keep her own counsel over it?

Lady Matlock quickly dried her eyes.

"So selfish of me, darling, worrying you with my stupid fears—when you've been through so much yourself."

"Oh, that's all over. I feel like a war-horse—ready to tackle anything. My only worry is poor old Simon, sweltering in town, while I lounge about here."

The delicate acrimony of the mother-in-law was in Lady Matlock's tone, as she replied:

"Oh, I'm sure Simon will take the first opportunity he can find of a rest. I expect he has a great deal to do, to set the business in order again after that *dreadful* affair."

Christian's lips tightened. She might herself recriminate Simon, but she would brook no such criticisms from other people—not even from her own family. Poor darling Simon; so harassed, so desperately anxious to secure the future for them both. How, knowing the extent of his love and devotion, had she ever come, during their last fortnight together, to behave to him in such a fashion—a fashion wholly alien to the character of their relationship, as well as to her own very definite ideals which, up to latterly, had governed their married life? She wished passionately that she had an abler pen, to convey to him her contrition: but she was as shy and clumsy as a schoolgirl in conveying her emotions to paper, and she knew there could be no hope of a restored understanding until they were together again.

Already she was chafing under the terms of an exile she

could find no colourable excuse for breaking. Leading the life of a super-invalid, in a suite of rooms for which they were paying about twice the usual rates, to ensure for "dear Christian" perfect quiet and at the same time guard her from boredom (their long balcony extended almost the whole way along the first floor, and commanded the gardens reserved for the hotel residents), she found herself smothered with attentions for which, very often, she had no taste.

It bored her when Lady Matlock insisted upon having the chef up in person, to discuss what special dish might be most tempting to an invalid palate. The elderly holidaymakers, among whom, to Lady Matlock's satisfaction, were a famous Wesleyan divine and an English (Evangelical) bishop, who made sedulous daily inquiry after her progress, irritated her almost to screaming point.

She was not even allowed to go down to the *plage* unless her mother's maid was in attendance, with a whole para-phernalia of restoratives, in case Christian should feel faint, or be overcome by the sun; and her bathing was restricted to ten minutes in and out of a sea whose blue warmth tempted her to let herself be swept out—out to oblivion of all this unnecessary fuss and agitation about her welfare.

She was crazy to get back to Simon, and her impatience was increased by an odd sort of jealousy of the people with whom he was now spending his time: Nancy Rowlandson, and that unpleasant young man, Marius Lear, whom, sub-consciously, she blamed for all the differences which lately had arisen between herself and Simon. Like many simple and forthright people, Christian had strong prejudices, which, roused on the first occasion of her meeting with Marius by his unprepossessing and uncouth appearance, had been rein-forced by the *Cypriana* incident. She felt him in her life and Simon's, not precisely as an evil element, but rather as some-thing which might possibly menace their relationship, by providing a cause of friction between them. It irked her that Simon should continue to hold in his good graces a person whose attitude to herself was no less antagonistic than hers to him. Whenever they met, Marius accorded to her the barest minimum of courtesy and immediately found an excuse for withdrawing from the company. She suspected him, for some inscrutable, impertinent reason of his own, of despising her: not, as he might reasonably have done, for her lack of literary parts, but for something—something in connection with Simon. How dared he criticize their relationship—a thing of which he knew nothing?

"Darling, do put on your glasses," Lady Matlock was murmuring. "You've been frowning for the last ten minutes; it's so bad for the skin."

Christian stabbed on the coloured glasses which had been lying in her lap with a movement of uncontrollable impatience which brought her mother's eyes to rest in mild surprise upon her.

"Are you feeling nervy? I wish you'd try my bromide that Dr. Vaizey gave me just before I came away—so risky to trust these foreign doctors; they think nothing at all of prescribing the most shocking drugs and things—you know, habit-forming," concluded Lady Matlock vaguely.

"No—no; I'm all right. I just wonder a bit—naturally— about Simon."

Lady Matlock's small, crumpled lips drew together.

"You know, darling—I don't want to hurt your feelings; but I can never *quite* regard Simon in the same way, after that horrid *Daily Cable* affair. I simply don't understand how he could do it. One would think his respect for you——"

"Do you mind if we don't discuss it?" Christian felt the tips of her nails pressed into the soft flesh of her palms.

"My dear child, the very last thing I wish is to discuss it —with you or any one else. One can only pray it will soon be forgotten; but when I think of your poor Father—and how we were all made to suffer——! There are times when I positively wince, wondering whether the person I'm talking to knows all about it and connects us with it."

"I shouldn't trouble, if I were you; memories are short, and it's not as if your name was Crome!" said Christian. There was a faint bitterness in her voice which reached her mother's heart. Lady Matlock was not really badly disposed towards Simon; such faint jealousy as she felt towards the man who had usurped her favourite daughter's affections was based upon the illusion that he was responsible for the differences of opinion which, as Christian grew older, asserted themselves—not to the point of open rupture, but sufficiently to show Lady Matlock she had not, as formerly, complete control of her daughter's mind. It was on this account that she took every opportunity that offered to invent some little disparagement of Simon—usually so playfully worded that the only possible rejoinder was a laugh that concealed Christian's vexation.

She was more vexed than usual, this time, because, fundamentally, she was in agreement with her mother. Having forgiven Simon for his share in the *Cypriana* affair, she still harboured a faint resentment for the way in which the family name had been dragged into it: far more on her parents' and on the children's account than on her own. And this resentment kept flashing to the surface in stupid and indiscreet little remarks like this one to her mother, which she regretted as soon as spoken, because it implied disloyalty to Simon and instantly drew upon her her mother's gratified sympathy—far more distasteful in her present mood than maternal disagreement.

"My poor darling, how thoughtless of me! Well, never mind; I'm quite sure this has been a great lesson to Simon, and that he'll work hard to redeem the past. Of course, we both—your Father and I—blame him less than that unpleasant young half-brother of his. By the way, has he got his divorce?"

"I thought you knew it was off," said Christian indifferently.

"What a mercy! I do so hate these scandals; they get so much more publicity than they ought, and it's so difficult," said Lady Matlock plaintively, "to keep the minds of our young people clean and pure nowadays, with all the things they read in the papers."

"Do you think that page is looking for us?" asked Christian, snatching at a chance of diverting her mother's conversation from personalities. The white-clad page was threading his way between the chairs, his gloved thumb clutching a salver with a message on it. Neither of them was expecting a note at this hour of the day, and a little premonitory pang, which almost always accompanies the reception of a telegram in a foreign country, ran through both, as Lady Matlock took up the envelope.

"*England.* Your Father!"

Christian took the message from her mother's hand. As she read it, she had the oddest sensation that she had known about it in advance. She read it aloud, very calmly and clearly.

"'*Lydia ill. Return at once. Reservations booked on Paris plane this afternoon five. Harry.*'"

"Plane!" Lady Matlock blanched. Her needlework had slipped to the ground; she looked suddenly very crumpled and old. "Your Father knows I never travel by air! Oh, Chris—Chris—it must mean——"

Christian laid a calming hand on her mother's arm.

"It doesn't necessarily mean anything," she said firmly, "except that Lydia's ill, and there's no one to be with her. Don't cry, Mummy; I'll see to everything. Just go and get ready quietly; we haven't much more than an hour."

Refusing to listen to Lady Matlock's agitated conjectures, Christian shut herself into her own room to do her packing. There was no time, she kept reminding herself, to think. Yet, through all the confused dread and apprehension of the moment, one thought insistently repeated itself: "I'm getting away from here—getting back to Simon!"

There was no doubt that Lydia was seriously ill; otherwise her father would never have submitted them to the ordeal of air travel, which Christian disliked as much as her mother

dreaded the idea of it. What had happened? Not daring to
follow the thread of conjecture which, despite self-control,
had begun to shape itself in her mind, Christian continued
steadily to fit the few necessaries of the journey into her
dressing-bag. The maid, a middle-aged, experienced woman,
was to be left to make her way back by rail, with the rest of
the luggage; meanwhile, she had her hands full, in attempting
to calm her mistress and to get Lady Matlock into travelling
clothes.

Their arrival in Paris was delayed by weather conditions,
and the courier whom Old Harry had arranged to meet them
told them that the London plane had left. Leaving her mother
in his care, Christian put through a call to the Savoy, London,
where she had learned Old Harry was staying.

"It's all right," Old Harry told her, after inquiring how
the two women had stood the journey. "You'd better spend
the night in Paris and come on the morning plane. She's not
in danger, but there's no one in particular to look after her.
I can't stay in town——"

"What happened, Father?"

"Tell you when you get here." The connection was
deplorable, the line crackled with electricity, and Christian
could barely recognize her father's voice. "I've had her moved
to a nursing home, but she ought to have someone with her
—I mean, someone belonging to her."

"Anna Pryde——" began Christian, but Old Harry did not
appear to hear.

"I'll send the car to Croydon and come down myself, if it
can be managed."

"Daddy, let Simon know I'll be back, will you? Or ring
the house; they'll tell him if he doesn't happen to be in."

"All right. Try not to let your mother worry . . ."

Nancy, Simon and Marius talked through the night.
Combridge rang through about eleven, and said he would do

his best to be in town by three next day. Nancy cooked a meal
which no one ate, and thereafter made relays of coffee; for
Simon's sake, both she and Marius maintained a curt, commonplace attitude to the whole affair, but inwardly they were
appalled. At two in the morning they managed to induce
Simon, stupid with exhaustion, to lie down on Nancy's bed.
He fell instantly asleep. She and Marius sat in the sitting-
room, until the sky grew pale with incipient dawn.

"You'd better go home and get some sleep. Somebody's
got to be clear-headed in the morning."

He went without argument; she ran a warm bath, then,
moving softly, so as not to disturb Simon, wrapped herself
in a dressing-gown and lay down on the sitting-room couch
to snatch an hour or two of rest. At eight she rang up Marius.

"He's still fast asleep. I don't like to wake him."

"No, let him alone. I'll come round after I've had my
breakfast. By the way, oughtn't we to send some message to
the house?"

"I'll see to that."

When Marius arrived, Simon was still sleeping. Sprawled
across the broad, low bed, he looked cadaverous; the sunken
flesh of his cheeks revealed all the fine, bony structure of the
face, its pitiable, premature lining. His unconscious face had
a kind of defeated nobility. Marius and Nancy looked pitifully
down on him.

"If you go down to the office, I'll stay here."

"What about his wife?" said Nancy suddenly.

Marius scowled.

"What's the good of dragging her into it?"

"I don't know. I was only putting myself in her place.
I'd want to be with him at a time like this."

Marius shrugged his shoulders.

"How's she likely to take it?"

"God knows. I like her—but she's very young in some ways.
Very inexperienced. I believe she's devoted to him."

"Let it alone—at least till we've seen Combridge."

Nancy got to the office a few minutes before nine; except for the charwoman, on her knees scouring the outer office, she was the first arrival. She collected the mail and went upstairs. She had hardly taken off her hat and straightened her hair when the telephone bell started to ring.

"Can I speak to Mr. Crome?"

"He hasn't come in yet." It was a woman's voice, unknown to Nancy.

"Can you tell me where I'll get at him? I was ringing up the house and office all yesterday evening. It's very urgent."

"I'm afraid he's not available just at present. Is there anything we can do for you? I'm his secretary."

"Well—look: I'm Miss Pryde. I'm a friend of Lydia Matlock's, I live with her—and I want to get at some member of the family."

"I see. Is anything the matter?" asked Nancy quickly.

"Yes."

"Have you rung up Sir Harry? I'm afraid he's the only member of the family I know of."

"I happen to know she'd rather I didn't ring Sir Harry."

"Well . . . I don't know what to suggest. I can't get Mr. Crome for you; Mrs. Crome and Lady Matlock are abroad—as I expect you know."

"Then"—there was evident reluctance in the voice—"I suppose there's nothing else for it. Is Sir Harry in town or at Granedge?"

"Granedge, I think—but I should try the Savoy first; he's always there when he's in town."

"Thanks. The point is," said the hesitating voice, "I've got a job—rather a valuable one, to me: but I can't leave her to the servants, and I didn't exactly care to pop her into a nursing home without communicating with the family."

"Is Miss Matlock ill?" asked Nancy, wondering how many more complications she would be required to shoulder. "Perhaps you'd like Lady Matlock's address, to cable to her?"

"I don't want to raise the roof," said Anna Pryde. "It's

not necessary, and it won't do Lydia any good. I wanted to
get hold of Mr. Crome if I could because I know Lydia likes
him, and I'm sure he isn't the kind of person to make a fuss.
Look here: I'll tell you what it is, if you like. Lydia took an
overdose of sleeping draught. There's not the least question
of attempted suicide, or anything of that sort; she's not that
kind of person. But she's been upset about a few things lately,
and I think she got rather desperate about not having any
sleep. I found out in time and got the doctor, and we did the
right things; but she's really not in any sort of state to be
left by herself."

"I should imagine not."

"On the other hand, you can understand I don't want to
raise a hullabaloo and upset the whole family, and Lydia herself is all against the nursing home notion—which makes it
pretty difficult for me. You see, don't you, it isn't exactly a
job for Sir Harry—who's a nice old thing, but isn't likely to
take our view of a matter like this."

"No; but I don't see who else you can get hold of. He'll
probably send for her mother, but that's his affair. I'm so
sorry not to be more helpful, but it's absolutely all I can
suggest. Let me know if you find him, won't you?"

Anna thanked her and rang off. Nancy had hardly replaced
the receiver when Marius was on the line from the flat.

"Look here; I'm going to get the doctor to Simon, Yes,
he's come to, but he's in a complete state of jitters. I'm trying
to prevent his coming down to the office. He isn't wanted,
is he?"

"No—except someone's just rung through to say Lydia
Matlock's ill. They wanted me to get Simon, but I refused."

"Well, can you give me the doctor's number? If he gives
Simon a shot of dope he'll at least be fit to talk to Combridge.
I was right, by the way, about his wife; the only coherent
thing I've got out of him up to the present is for God's sake
not to let Christian know."

"What are you doing with him?"

"Taking him home, if he'll go; it will be much better for him to see Combridge down there than at the office."

"Isn't that Harris creature coming here again at six?"

"Combridge will tell us what to do about that," said Marius, as he jotted down on the blotting-pad the doctor's number, which Nancy had found, and given him.

"The trouble, so far as I can make out," said Combridge, when he sat opposite Simon in the latter's study, "is that your case for blackmail isn't complete. Apparently this man made no explicit threats, beyond the one that he intended to bring a case against you for seduction of his daughter."

"Good God, isn't the inference obvious?"

"Obviously enough, but, unfortunately, in the absence of mentioning money, insufficient."

"We were interrupted," muttered Simon. "Someone came in."

"A pity. However, we'll probably get all the evidence we need this evening. I'll ring up Carleton, and get him to send in a couple of men. I don't think there's any doubt we'll get your friend cold."

"Whereon I proceed for blackmail?"

"As Mr. A., of course. They're very careful about these cases, nowadays."

"And supposing I succeed? Is there anything on earth to stop him, or some person acting on his behalf, from starting the prosecution on the seduction charge? It simply means I'll have the thing hanging over my head."

"Crome, exactly how much is there in what Harris says?"

A profound despair settled in Simon's heart. It was Marius over again. Even the people who knew him best could not accept without reservations the fact of his innocence. He replied with a gentleness of resignation:

"I've told you. Nothing at all. Why can't you believe me?"

"My dear chap, I'm not doubting you. It only occurred to me that, if his motive is blackmail—a point we have yet to

M

establish—our friend must feel very sure of his ground to risk
a return to the scene of his first effort. He must know you'll
have prepared yourself. That's the part I don't like. It suggests
that he's prepared, as you say, to proceed in any case; it looks,
in fact, as little like blackmail as anything that has come
my way."

"Then why should he come?" persisted Simon. Combridge
hunched his shoulders.

"Search me. If it was blackmail, the logical procedure
would be to ring you up from a call-box. I can't imagine any
blackmailer—even the most bungling amateur—giving notice
of his arrival and then dropping in for a friendly discussion
of terms!" He opened his case, took out and absently tapped
a cigarette. "In fact, it looks as if he knows he's got all the
cards in his hand."

"But what cards can he hold? Where's the evidence, except
the word of a lying little bitch?"

"There isn't any, of the assault; but I presume they can
muster the usual proofs that you were drinking with her at
Datchett, and you bought her champagne at the Knave of
Diamonds—a name which carries a certain significance with
most people. The rest, to the vulgar mind, follows in sequence.
I don't want to scare you unduly, Simon, but those two facts,
taken in conjunction with the birth certificate, are going to
prejudice your case badly with the jury."

"God!" groaned Simon. Combridge gave him a kindly
look.

"Of course, a lot will depend on the impression the girl
herself makes when they put her in the box. No doubt she'll
have had a good coaching, but the judge is used to that kind
of thing. The trouble is, as it is in nine cases out of ten in the
English law courts, the jury. If you were being tried by a
jury of your peers, I should say almost certainly you'd get
off; but if it should happen to be twelve good men and true
of the same class as the plaintiff, primed to the ears with class
antagonism, not to mention the indignation which most right-

minded people feel over the seduction of a minor by a middle-aged person, it's not going to be easy."

"You take it for granted I'm going to plead."

"What else do you propose to do?" said Combridge sharply.

"Say I'm guilty and get it over quickly. It means ruin for me, whichever way the verdict goes."

"Nonsense."

"Of course it does—and you know it. That kind of mud sticks."

"What about your wife and children? Not so good for them."

". . . I forgot," groaned Simon. During the last few hours he had sedulously thrust the thought of Christian and the children into the back of his mind. Whether or not Christian believed in his innocence, she could never recover from this.

"They're abroad, aren't they?"

"Christian's away—thank God. She must be told to stay, until this is over."

Combridge looked doubtful.

"Well, I'll get those men of Carleton's on the job. I suppose you've got some place to secrete them, for your interview with Harris?"

"Plenty of places," said Simon wearily.

"Always assuming," said Combridge, "that he turns up."

"And if he doesn't?"

"If he doesn't, and if you hear nothing further—it looks as if you'll have to go through the hoops."

At seven o'clock Simon was sitting in his room at the office; the three doors were wide open; the door of a small coat-cupboard was also open, to form a bolt-hole for the two plain-clothes men who sat conveniently placed to take up their observation posts at the sound of the arrival of the expected visitor. Simon was pretending to read; the men were silent —one immobile, the other doing a crossword in *John o' London's Weekly*. The clock on the mantelpiece chimed the quarter after seven. The men looked at each other; the elder cleared his throat.

"Looks as if he's funked it," he observed.

Simon looked up.

"You mean, he's not coming?"

"Looks that way. If I was you, sir"—he stood up and stretched himself—"I'd stand by for a telephone call."

"You mean—wait here?"

"Unless they've got your private number."

"I'm not in the book," said Simon. It was one of the means he had taken, on Old Harry's advice, to secure his domestic privacy.

A ring came through about eight, but it was Combridge. He advised Simon to wait a little longer, and then to give it up.

"If you hear nothing by nine, we can take it for granted he's thought better of his blackmailing effort."

"So what?"

"So you can wait for the next move."

"Which is?"

"The police court, probably. Of course, you'll be allowed bail. It might save some delay if you'd think which of your friends would be likely to furnish it. I'm afraid they're liable to fix it rather high."

His friends! A stream of bitterness gushed to Simon's lips, and was held back.

"All right. What I can't understand is, that if the swine doesn't mean blackmail—and it looks that way—what does he stand to gain by a prosecution?"

"He probably thinks that, if you're convicted, he will follow it up later by a civil action for damages."

"And could he succeed?" Simon was startled.

"He might; but you couldn't afford to fight it."

"Well, if I'm convicted," said Simon bitterly, "he'll be welcome to all he can find afterwards. I shall be sorry for any solicitor who acts for him, hoping to get costs out of me!"

"You realize I'm deliberately taking the blackest view of the affair? It's quite probable it'll all fizzle out. It depends on who Harris has got to advise him."

"Yes, yes, I know all that." Simon hung up. To hell with Combridge's sops—he was not a child.

At nine he was alone. It was dark; he had drawn the curtains and switched on the lights. The room had a kind of stark grace; on Daniel's advice, he had spent money on his private quarters. The furniture was modern, the carpet and curtains suggested a dignified luxury, in keeping with success. Simon himself had never believed in this shop-window stuff; his editorial training had accustomed him to workmanlike squalor, and he had always felt a little conscious of this impressive apartment, more like a library in a private house, than the headquarters of its owner's business activity.

All façade!—veneer over worm-eaten structure. Finished. The end of the biggest gamble he had ever undertaken.

A flash of imagination gave him the future: porters carrying out the upholstered chairs, rolling up the carpets, tearing down the hangings. Notice in the papers—"Disposal of office furniture"; scene in an auction-room. A few weeks'—or perhaps only days'—abandonment to dust, grime gathering on the windows of empty rooms. Then a new tenant. . . . In the book market, a flux of "remainders"; pulping machines working overtime; transfer of contracts to unimpressed rivals. . . .

He went to the fireplace, and came face to face with the photographs of Christian and the children; against the frame of Henry's rested a card, inviting them to his Speech Day. Suddenly, disconcertingly, a sob tore itself up through Simon's body. He was crying, noisily, painfully, like a little boy.

"It's ridiculous—even to imagine a thing like that in connection with Simon!" Nancy was saying indignantly. "I've worked with him long enough to know. He doesn't notice girls; I'll bet you what you like he wouldn't recognize any of the typists if he met them in the street!"

"That doesn't prove anything. He's been overdoing it now, for months. He was due for a breakdown, and that's a common enough form for it to take."

"Picking up a girl in a teashop? Don't talk rot."

"Teashop nothing. It's a woman, isn't it?—the natural form of relief to which a man turns when he's down and out."

"You—do you mean to say you think Simon *did* it?"

"Why not? It seems reasonable, in the circumstances."

"That's infamous!" she blazed at him. "You know he isn't capable of a thing like that. It's a betrayal of all his ideals—of Christian—of the children."

"Oh, don't take such a high-hat view of it," drawled Marius. "In Simon's state of health a man doesn't act according to his normal nature."

"Then you think he's lying, when he tells you he didn't?"

"Quite possibly. It's equally possible he doesn't remember a thing about it. He admits he'd been drinking at Datchett; he admits the champagne—and he hadn't had a bite of food since morning. Those lunch sandwiches don't count. The combination of an empty stomach and an exhausted mental and nervous system would account for a lot—with any reasonable individual. Anyhow, where was the harm—except for the little bitch's being under age?"

"Do you suppose his wife will see it like that?"

"To hell with his wife. If she was worth anything, she wouldn't have gone gadding off to the South of France at a time like this."

"That's absolutely unfair," Nancy was driven to retort. "She's had a rotten time, and it was as bad for Simon as it was for her to have her around when he'd got so much on his mind."

"I've got no damned use for that woman," muttered Marius, as he lounged across the room, to pick up the receiver and dial the office with a pugnacious and not over-clean finger.

"He's not there," he said presently. "I suppose he's gone home."

"He must have done. I hope he's all right. I hated the look of him this morning. Why don't you like Christian?"

Marius pulled a face.

"It's a type I loathe; it makes me sick," he said shortly.

"I suppose she's too decent for you," Nancy found herself stung to reply. He looked down at her contemptuously.

"Meaning exactly—what?"

"You don't like women who live virtuously—who aren't promiscuous," she stammered, taken aback with the sound of her own words after they were spoken. Her cheeks flamed beneath the look of mockery and understanding that he gave her from the corner of his heavy-lidded eyes.

"Nonsense. Don't be hysterical."

"Well, why don't you like Christian Crome? What has she done to you?" she persisted, feeling furious with him for that humiliating look.

"Done to me? Nothing. I don't give women of her sort the chance of doing things to me," he answered. "It's only fools like Simon who fall into that trap," he added viciously.

"You have no right to say things like that!"

"Why not?"

"What's the use of blaggarding him when he's—when he's——" To her horror, Nancy's voice broke. Now, she thought, he'll have a right to call me hysterical.

Oddly enough, Marius appeared not to notice. His lips were pursed to whistle, but no sound came. They parted, to inquire:

"What will you do, when the balloon goes up?"

"Do?" With a great effort, she pulled herself together. "Oh—find another job, I suppose."

"I'll very likely go to Paris," he disconcerted her by announcing. "I suppose I'll get my American money, and that'll keep me for a bit. There's no sort of environment for work over here—my kind of work, I mean."

The floor rocked—steadied itself. Well . . . there was Dennis. Nancy clutched at the philosophy which had supported her through worse things than losing Marius Lear. A folly—for which she deserved to suffer. Her voice was purposely tart as she replied:

"You're certainly able to look after yourself—now."

"What do you mean by 'now'?" he shot at her.

"You weren't so good at it a few months ago—when Simon met you."

A slow, triumphant grin broke out on his face.

"Well—for crying out loud! I suppose that's meant as a slap in the face."

"Interpret it which way you like." For some reason, her mind had flown off at a tangent to Lydia Matlock. She felt a little guilty at having kept Anna's message from Simon. She ruffled the pages of the telephone directory, and presently dialled Lydia's number. A servant answered.

"Is Miss—Pryde"—for a moment she hesitated for the name—"in?"

"I'll find out, madam. What name shall I say?"

"Say Mrs. Rowlandson—from Crome and Lygon." Inevitably the old style slipped off the tongue.

Anna came quickly.

"Oh—hallo. I'm so sorry; I promised to ring you up, didn't I?"

"It doesn't matter. Did you find Sir Harry?"

"Yes—and Lydia's in a nursing home. Lady Matlock and Christian are expected to-morrow——"

"Marius!" Nancy hardly waited to put back the receiver. "They're coming back."

"Who?"

"Christian and her mother."

"Like hell they are!" It gratified her to see him shot out of his complacency. "Does Simon know?"

"I don't know."

"Who sent for them?"

"Sir Harry—on account of Lydia's illness."

"Damn the woman. Ring up the house and find out if he's heard."

Nancy glanced at the clock, whose hands pointed to nearly eleven, and hesitated.

"I'd hate to disturb him if he's asleep; I expect the servants have gone to bed.

"You must risk it. Go on."

It struck her afterwards that there had seemed nothing odd at the time, in taking orders from Marius. It was some moments before the housemaid's voice, familiar to Nancy, replied.

"No, ma'am; Mr. Crome isn't in yet."

"Would you leave him a note to ring me up when he comes in?"

"Yes, ma'am; I'll leave it by his bed."

"You haven't——" said Nancy hesitatingly. "You haven't had any word from Mrs. Crome, have you?"

"No." The woman sounded surprised. "She's still on the Continent, you know."

"All right," said Nancy. "Don't forget the note."

Marius, hunched in a chair, was chewing his thumb.

"If that isn't the devil!" he was saying.

CHAPTER TWENTY

"Don't fuss, don't fuss," Old Harry kept on saying; but Christian, less sunk in her own private emotions than her mother, could not avoid the hurt, puzzled and half-angry look in his eyes. It was the look of a man who does not fully understand, and does not wish to understand, what he is up against. They had neither of them—he nor her mother—ever understood Lydia. "It's all turned out well, except that the silly child's in a nursing home." He was speaking unnecessarily loudly, as though he wanted to drown another voice than his own—a voice which bade him wonder if it had turned out so well, after all. Two young women, politely and silently denying his authority over their actions, mutely resisting his right to question his own daughter!—behaving, in fact, very much as though it were all no affair of his, though one at least of them had been scared enough to call him in. It was all confusing, irritating, contrary to his notions of fatherly and daughterly relationship. "I'm sorry to break up your holiday, but I think it's quite time Lydia came under some other influence than that fly-away young woman she lives with."

"It seems to have been just as well she was living with her," Christian murmured, *sotto voce*.

"*Sleeping* draughts, Harry! It sounds so ridiculous—at Lydia's age."

"Ridiculous? So I should say. It's all part and parcel of the racket of modern life," snorted Old Harry. "I don't know what the medical profession's up to—prescribing them for girls in their twenties."

"Oh—it was a prescription," said Lady Matlock faintly.

"Of course it was a prescription; how else do you think she'd get the stuff? Apparently they're both—both those girls —in the habit of taking doses; that Pryde young woman stood and argued me out that they were harmless—harmless!"

"These dreadful cocktail parties and late nights! If only she listened to my advice—a good rest and change in the country—no need for those wretched drugs." Lady Matlock was catching her breath between the little disjointed sentences.

"It was an overdose, wasn't it, Father?" Christian heard herself saying.

"Downright slapdash carelessness!" trumpeted Old Harry. "If this Pryde woman hadn't happened to go into her room——"

"My poor little girl!"

"Now, please, don't let's have too much of that." It was so rarely that her husband spoke to her in that tone that Lady Matlock gasped, and involuntarily straightened her shoulders. "What Lydia needs is a good straight talking to. You've got to get it into her head that we're not having any more of that Park Lane establishment. She can either come and live decently at home, or she can find a suitable companion and lead a respectable life in a proper environment."

It was useless, as Christian knew, to attempt to persuade Old Harry that a young woman of twenty-nine cannot be ordered about as though she were a child in the schoolroom. She made an effort to change the subject by asking after Jemima.

"Very well—very well indeed; Nana's keeping her at Granedge. No sense in bringing a child up to town in the summer."

"Did you let Simon know I was coming?"

"I rang up the house after speaking to you, but he wasn't in, and the maid seemed half asleep. I suppose they'll have the place ready for you."

They drove straight to the nursing home; Lady Matlock cried and crooned over her daughter, but Christian was speechless before the white resignation of Lydia, prone in her narrow bed, with the shoulder knots of her nightgown dragged taut across her thin shoulder-blades. It was as though all the living part of her had been drained away; that which remained was only a limp and punctured web, incapable of inflation by their breaths.

Lydia agreed with her mother that she had been careless over her sleeping draught, murmured something about a stupid nursing home, but seemed to care so little for their company that Christian, saying she would come in again in the afternoon, went away. She had tried to find out where to get Anna, but no one at the nursing home seemed to know. She rang the office, to find out if Simon was there, but was told he was not, and that Nancy had gone out to lunch. Convinced she would find him waiting for her at home, she took a taxi, and rang her own bell (she had left her key with the rest of the luggage) with a feeling of excitement only partly tinged with apprehension. There seemed to be something momentous in this reunion with Simon; her arms and her bosom tingled, her heart quickened at the prospect of clasping him again. Once it was accomplished—that physical rejoining—all the sad remnants of their disagreements would melt away.

When the door was opened, she stepped lightly into her hall, her housewifely eye marking the fact that it had been well cared for during her absence. "Well, Stephens!" She put out a hand mechanically to spread the sheaf of gladioli that stood upon the hall table—why could servants never arrange flowers? She found herself deliberately protracting the seconds of anticipation, before the opening of the study door. . . . "Everything all right?" she asked brightly.

"Very glad you're back, madam."

She had barely time to notice that the woman looked at her rather oddly, when Marius Lear came out of the study. Christian stiffened involuntarily; it was a set-back she had not been expecting. Had Marius Lear, during her absence, formed the habit of coming to the house? Had Simon invited him to lunch? He might surely have put off the invitation—if it had already been given—on receiving her message!

"Good-morning, Mr. Lear," she said, coolly. She walked

past him quickly, to meet Simon—and Simon was not there.

"Where's my husband?"

"I—don't—know," said Marius, bluntly.

"You——?" She faced him, noticing, with distaste, that he had not shaved; in fact, it was doubtful if he had used soap and water that morning. Her nostrils contracted delicately; like many hyper-fastidious people, she was apt to construe disorderliness in others as a form of personal insult: especially in the case of people she disliked.

Wholly indifferent to her scrutiny, Marius slouched over and closed the door.

"We don't know where he is, Mrs. Crome. He didn't come home last night."

She felt the blood draining away from her heart; then, pride coming to her aid, pulled herself together. She stood by the desk, stripping off her gloves, altering the position of a pad, of a photograph frame, with the unconsciously possessive movements of a person accustomed to ordering every detail of her environment. She forced herself to say lightly,

"What a pity. He can't have had my message. I suppose he went away for the night." It was not an unheard-of thing for Simon to take a night away on business; she reproached herself for the folly of allowing Marius's hangdog air to disturb her. Turning, she spoke as pleasantly as possible, though on a note of dismissal. "Thanks very much for coming to let me know; I'm afraid this is your lunch-time—don't let me detain you any longer."

Her eyes met his, and she suddenly caught her breath. It was startling to be hated like that! Startling? It was absurd! Simon must be made to see the absurdity of it. There had never, until Marius's arrival, been anything but goodwill between her and the office personnel.

"You've got it wrong, Mrs. Crome. Simon is—lost."

"*Lost?*"

It became more and more absurd—until a possible explanation came to her: Simon—overworked—losing his memory!

She moistened her lips before continuing:

"How long has he been lost? Have you made inquiries? Have you told the police?"

"We've made all the inquiries possible. We haven't told the police—yet. I've come to tell you why."

It was a moment of vengeance for Marius—vengeance not only upon Christian, but upon the whole type she stood for in his eyes; the antipathetic type of the soft, spoilt, luxury-bred woman whose untested virtue increased her egoism. God help Simon—that he should have such a one in his life! Marius's heart contracted at the thought of Simon, lying asleep on Nancy's bed—worn out with his bitter experience, his suffering increased by his feeling of responsibility to this pampered being, this silk-sheathed vision of self-indulgence, brown from the Riviera sun—now biting her lips with impatience at Marius's silence. Let her be impatient.

Knowing nothing of the side of Christian that Nancy knew, knowing only Simon's love for her, and unable, by reason of his prejudice, to picture her noble qualities, he hated her. Sensitive to the opinions of others, for all his assumption of contempt, he had always felt her antagonism. It did not need Simon's casual admission that she "did not care much" for *Cypriana* to tell Marius that she was one of its bitterest opponents. She was in the enemy's camp: it was this, and not her disparagement of his work (regarding which he cared for no one's opinion) that Marius resented, because it proved her disloyalty to Simon, whose championship had gained his devotion.

His inarticulate gratitude for all the help Simon had given him, and for the confidence it proved, burned in Marius like a red-hot coal, stinging him to reprisals. He had, without telling Nancy, who would surely have vetoed the suggestion, taken it upon himself to meet Christian on her return, after a morning spent in searching for Simon in all possible and impossible places—a search hampered by the need of not publicizing his disappearance: Nancy, meanwhile, holding the

fort at the office, a task for which she was better equipped
than Marius.

"Well, I suppose you are going to tell me about my
husband?" said Christian crisply. She was formidable; she
was Old Harry's daughter, as she faced him with authority—
the authority of being Simon's wife—in her eyes.

Marius told her—he took pleasure in telling her—without
mincing matters.

All the structure of her life was crumbling about her.
There was no aspect of the situation her electrified brain did
not grasp, from the disgrace to them all to their financial ruin.
Vague as she was about finance, Christian did not pay much
attention to that. The fact which hammered at her brain was
the possibility, which Marius, by his manner of telling, had
clearly revealed to her, of Simon's guilt; or rather, of the
virtual impossibility of proving his innocence.

"Of course he's innocent!" one part of her mind was crying,
while the other whispered, "Suppose he isn't?" Like a spear
darted into her memory that light and chaffing conversation
about the girl who had "picked him up" in the tea-house.
"The age when an old man's fancy lightly turns to thoughts
of the *détournement des mineurs*." Could he possibly have jested
upon such a subject if there had been a shadow, a grain of
truth in it? Common sense rejected the possibility; instinct
—the instinct of fear—pawed at it.

Another thing returned to Christian's mind: that he had
actually let her go away without making love to her—a thing
which had never occurred before. She had not made much of
it, because, since her miscarriage, they had been "careful";
another reasonable explanation was their mutual over-tiredness,
coupled with the slight friction which, owing to all their
worries, had recently underlain their relationship.

Was it some upward-flaring of animal desire that had
driven him to betraying her in this cheap and hideous fashion?
An overwhelming sense of nausea wrenched at the pit of her

stomach; instinctively she doubled over, pressing her hands against her diaphragm. His failure to meet her on her return —what was that, if not a sign of guilt?

"I can't believe it," she was groaning.

"Believe what? That Simon seduced the girl? What the hell does it matter, whether you believe it or not?"

She stared at him, stupefied.

"Your belief makes no difference to the fact that Simon's got to pay for a thing any man might have done, and got away with, except for the girl's age," he added brutally.

"Doesn't he deserve to pay?"

"Deserve! That's just the way you would look at it. I suppose no woman like you would admit it's the natural way for a man to seek relief when his nervous system goes back on him?"

"To betray his wife? His home?"

"There you go!" cried Marius, with a kind of savage triumph. "Betrayal—family affections! You've got them so twisted up with sexual relations you can't see straight. You wrinkle up your nose at sex, and it forms the boundary of your whole horizon. Like the majority of virtuous women, you'd burn up hell with your sexual jealousy."

"How dare you accuse me—the mother of Simon's children —accuse me of jealousy in connection with such—such a creature?"

"'Such a creature!' Your very scorn shows you're jealous. Your jealousy comes before all your feeling for Simon, for the way he's cared for you, slaved to provide you with all your comforts, worn himself out for the sake of you and the children. Women have no generosity! I mean virtuous women," he flung at her, "if they allow a man the priceless gift of their bodies, it's not out of tenderness; lord, no! It's just a way of binding him to them, of forcing an obligation on him. They don't give a damn for his happiness; that's what makes them resent his accepting kindness from another woman."

"A prostitute's kindness!" she sneered bitterly.

"At any rate, a prostitute's honest; she gives value for money."

"Exactly—for money."

"Why not? What's a pound or two compared with the blood money a married woman forces from her husband as the price of her virtue? 'You've had me, so I can claim support from you for the rest of my life. I've given you children, you must be for ever grateful.' An eternal levy upon the sentiments, the emotions, the intellect. Spiritual blackmail. God, give me the gay, realistic coming-together of people who love each other without these dirty ties; give me the honest, animal instinct that takes a man to a prostitute—at any rate, he won't be made to pay for it to the end of his life."

Christian rose coldly; under the downpour of Marius's rage her brain had recovered its equilibrium.

"That's quite enough. If there was a word of truth in the poisonous suggestions you've made about Simon and me, I might not be able to forgive you; as it is, I think you're out of your mind. What should you know of what Simon and I are to one another? You call yourself his friend, yet you obviously think he's guilty of a sordid crime."

"It isn't criminal to sleep with a girl; he knew nothing about her age."

"Will you please be quiet?" She drew in a deep breath, her nostrils quivered. "You can say what you like—I believe, absolutely, in Simon's innocence." She was surprised to find it was true.

"I said before, what does your belief matter? I believe nothing, I disbelieve nothing; I want to find him, to find some way of bringing him comfort."

"Don't I want that as well?"

"Only on condition he's innocent! Otherwise your pride would suffer—your miserable little matrimonial pride!" He laughed. "And your social pride as well. What will your family say, when Simon's charged with seducing a schoolgirl?

Who are you going to side with this time—them, or your husband?"

A slow enlightenment dawned upon her strained face.

"I understand—now. That's why you dislike me: because I didn't take your part about your book. This is your way of getting back at me—how petty, how mean!"

"Listen," said Marius. "I don't expect you to believe this, any more than the other truths I've told you. But I do not care a hoot for your opinion—either of me or of my work. What do you know—about either? All I care about is Simon, and the fact that he's charged with something that might never have happened if you hadn't gone off to enjoy yourself on the Riviera, when he was on the edge of a nervous breakdown."

He saw her wince.

"Do you really think that?" she whispered.

He shrugged his shoulders.

"It's what most people would think, if they knew the facts. Unfortunately, facts—of that kind—don't come out, in a case like this. Well, what are you going to do? I suppose you'll have to start by telling your father."

"He'll want to separate me and the children from Simon!" The unspoken thought shot into her mind.

"Why should any one be told—until we've found Simon? Oh!" she cried, walking across the room, "what's the good of talking, when we ought to be looking for him?"

"What's the good of looking, when we don't know where to look? I only came to ask you if you're prepared to tell the police. It's the kind of thing I didn't care to do on my own authority."

"You surprise me," she lashed him. "I should have thought your own authority was sufficient in itself, since it permits you to come and accuse me of disloyalty to Simon."

"Well, what sort of loyalty is it"—Marius stuck to his guns—"that depends on a person's innocence? Loyalty doesn't take that into account."

"Are you blaming me?" she demanded. "Are you blaming me for believing Simon innocent?"

"No. I only think you're trying to make it easy for yourself."

"And for him. You fool!" She turned upon him, her eyes blazing with sudden access of anger. "It's you and Combridge —with your cynical indifference to right and wrong—that have driven Simon away! I can see the whole thing. Simon —sick of your jesuitry—seeking the truth——"

A tap at the door heralded the parlourmaid, who entered with that lively consciousness of something amiss that characterizes servants on such occasions. She was not in the habit of knocking; the fact that she had done so showed Christian that the staff had started to gossip.

"If you please, madam, lunch is ready, and are you expecting the master?"

"You can serve it for Mr. Lear and myself; if the master comes in, cook must make something fresh for him," said Christian. When the woman had gone, she looked at Marius. "We shall have to eat, to stop them talking."

"Conventionalist!" he mocked her.

"It happens to be a form of loyalty, which I don't expect you to appreciate," she retorted, as she led the way to the dining-room.

Their own servants; yes, there would be all that to face. As she crumbled her bread and gulped the food—keeping up all the while a pretence at conversation, for the benefit of the maid who lurked, all agog, in the background—she wondered if she had really the strength to face it; then knew she had to, for Simon's sake.

Marius did little to help her; despising the falsity of the situation, he answered her remarks with monosyllables; he did not even pretend to eat.

"I'll get Mr. Combridge—and you needn't wait here," she told him, at the end of the seemingly interminable meal. Her mind agonized, wondering who she could get to help her.

Her family she rejected. Roger Burke she thought of dimly as an influential friend, for whom Simon had always professed affection; but Burke was bedded in social success and discretion. There were many influential people with whom, through Old Harry, as well as through Simon, she had some acquaintance: but she could think of nothing that entitled her to call upon their help in such a crisis as this.

She was waiting for Combridge, who had said he would be round within an hour, when she heard Simon's footstep in the hall. With a cry of thankfulness, she flung open the door. He stood staring at her, his chin dropping, aghast. It pierced her to see him looking almost as unkempt as Marius, with a day's growth of beard, his collar smutty and his suit bearing traces of contact with some grimy resting-place.

"Simon—my darling!"

"What are you doing here?" He was trying to hold off her attempt to take him in her arms. "Don't—keep away— I'm filthy."

"Where have you been?" she asked tenderly, drawing him into the room.

"I don't know. Walking." He looked down at his shoes, as if they surprised him. The ragged edge of a sock hung over his heel. "Walking. Since last night—some time. I don't know." He passed his hand over his harassed face. "They had no business to send for you," he frowned.

"They didn't; Mummy and I came back to look after Lydia."

"Lydia?"

"It's nothing. Tell me about yourself—tell me everything. I don't care what anybody says," she declared, clinging to his hands.

He looked at her for a moment, as though he had gone beyond words, and then he began to weep. The tears coursed helplessly down the soiled channels of his face; Christian felt her own in her heart.

CHAPTER TWENTY-ONE

The case came on, with a thunder of publicity, just before the long vacation. The children had gone to the seaside, with Nancy and Dennis; Christian had stood like a rock against her parents' efforts to claim them. She would have no dealings with Simon's enemies—as from the first moment of the news breaking, Old Harry had declared himself to be. Whether or not he was guilty, Simon had, in Old Harry's judgment, put himself outside the consideration of decent people; Lady Matlock inevitably sided with her husband.

There was hardly time for Christian to dwell upon the fact that she had parted, irrevocably, from her parents; if there had been time, the knowledge would have brought her something like a feeling of relief—so difficult and so irksome, of recent times, had the connection become.

Daniel, abroad with Eliza, wired his sympathy, and wrote his intention of being at hand to support Simon through the trial. Lydia, recovered, but for ever dimmed, was passionately sympathetic; also in revolt against her family, she offered all she had, from her flat to her private means to the Cromes. The means were much diminished and the flat was doomed; Old Harry, in an attempt to undermine his daughter's independence, had halved Lydia's allowance, a measure which she countered in part by taking a very small, ill-paid job in an employment agency, which, under the title of Ladies' Helps, Limited, professed to cater for the domestic embarrassments of working gentlefolk. One day cooking the dinner, another taking an obstreperous Pekinese to exercise in the Park, Lydia was doing her best to re-equilibrize her existence in a world that had stripped itself, so far as she was concerned, of all reality. People sometimes looked round at the beautiful girl, who had the air of a somnambulist, as she wandered past the Achilles statue, or stared vaguely into the windows of shops that no longer commanded her custom.

Marius, finding himself useless, had gone off self-containedly to Paris, from which he sent long, admirably impersonal letters to Simon, and the best encouragement the Cromes received was that of the many friends who wrote in terms of warm sympathy, and helped Christian to keep up her pretence that it was all rather a ridiculous fuss about nothing, during the agonizing weeks of waiting. Among these letters was one from Peter Horne, expressing his sympathy in carefully composed phrases, and saying nothing whatever about the proposed amalgamation. Naturally! Not deluded into optimism for the future by these expressions of personal goodwill, Simon found plenty to occupy himself with in winding up the firm's affairs. With no money to carry on, it was foolish to fight a losing battle. The case—they had briefed a famous K.C.—was going to exhaust his few remaining resources.

Christian's first glimpse of the Old Bailey took her breath away. She had not realized the enormous amount of interest that the case had aroused; Combridge procured her a passage with difficulty through the crowd that surged about the doors. When she had got through, she discovered that Simon was no longer with her, and the discovery gave her a sickening shock, which was repeated when she saw the long line of people who had been marshalled behind the wooden barriers leading to the court where the trial was to take place. She had expected—foolishly, no doubt—that Combridge's presence and her own connection with the case would procure for her some preferential treatment; yet she was curtly told to get behind the barrier with the rest—most of whom, she found, carried some sort of card or letter which seemed to insure their admission to the court.

She saw Combridge talking to one of the barristers, and they both approached the policeman in charge of the queue —apparently without effect. Combridge's small, sallow face was flushed with mortification; she clutched him as he returned.

"Can't I go in now? Do I have to wait? What happens if the court's full?" There seemed to be at least a hundred people ahead of her.

"You'll certainly get in; this place is full of red tape," muttered Combridge, evidently mortified by his failure to obtain preference. A sudden wild dread that he might be wrong made her clutch the policeman's arm as he passed her.

"Can't you let me through now?"

"'Ave you got a letter?"

"No—no; I'm Mrs. Crome—my husband's being tried."

"Can't find your name on the list." A blunt pencil travelled down the sheet he held in his hand.

"Don't be ridiculous; why should my name be down?" Nervousness splintered into anger. "I'm Mrs. Crome, I tell you—I've come to hear my husband being tried——"

"Get in the line, please." She found herself thrust back among the others, several of whom—within earshot—now regarded her with stares of curiosity.

"I'm sorry," Combridge was mumbling. "It's my fault—I should have got you a card from the Under-Sheriff. I didn't expect there would be such a crowd."

"Why is it?" whispered Christian. Her eyes wandered, seeking Lydia, who had promised to be there. At this rate, she would never get in. Roger Burke walked past, booming genially with a couple of barristers; no one stopped them. Christian felt her cheeks flaming; the palms of her hands were wet.

"Why do they let him past?" she asked indignantly.

"Well-known patron of the Old Bailey. Shall you be all right? They'll be letting them in in a moment," said Combridge, anxious to take his departure.

"What shall I do when I'm in?"

"There will be plenty of seats—but I'll try and get you a place at the table," whispered Combridge, as, sighting Simon's counsel, he ducked under the barrier and went to join him. Christian lost sight of them; a few minutes later, the queue started to move up. She found herself again opposite the policeman.

"'Ave you got a card?"

"No; I told you, I'm Mrs.——"

"'Ave we got your name on the list?"

Speechless with indignation, she found herself told to stand aside, while thirty or forty people passed ahead of her. Her eyes were glassy with tears; she bit her lips to force them back. The insolent indifference of the man in charge made her want to scream, to swear, to perform a dozen actions foreign to Christian Crome. "If they don't let me through I'll slap his face—I'll spit on his beastly list!"

Combridge was again at her elbow.

"Come along; I've got things fixed."

Her knees seemed turned to jelly as she followed him into the court, to the place at the solicitors' table which he had managed to procure for her.

There seemed to her first confused glance hardly an inch of space in the court. The benches at either side of and behind the dock were packed with a conglomeration of pressmen and public, and the gallery was crowded with the type of spectator invariably attracted by this type of trial. On the lower gallery on the left of the judge, reserved for the elite, Daniel's white, cynical harlequin-face stood out like a carving in ivory against the dark background. He had succeeded, after a tussle, in excluding Eliza from this expedition; she had been anxious not to "miss the fun," but, fortunately, the opening of the case coincided with another social event she was equally anxious not to miss. She departed for the country, leaving Daniel free to carry out his promise of contributing, by his presence, moral support to Simon during his ordeal.

Roger Burke, bland and pink-faced, by his manner very much above and outside the whole thing, was there, sub-pœnaed as a witness to Simon's character; Bertie Manders, very much hoping he would not be called, as appearances of this kind were an offence to his conception of good taste, was there for the same purpose. Just on the right of the dock Lydia had belatedly found a place, supported by a barrister friend of Anna's; she was very much be-veiled, and her eyes were anywhere save upon Daniel, who, after one quick look in her direction, turned slightly away and sat with arms folded and one leg slung over the other, in an attitude of exaggerated nonchalance.

There was a flashy little group of witnesses for the other side, among whom, when he entered the dock, Simon thought he recognized the waiter from the Knave of Diamonds and the landlord from the inn at Datchet.

The jury was the usual assortment of mixed types, reluctantly diverted from their private interests to the business in hand; their attitude to this kind of charge could be determined from a glance at the tightly controlled, conscious faces. There were two women, one stout, motherly and possibly belligerent, the other elderly and virginal. The men were without interest, except a sharp-featured, youngish man in eyeglasses, who was the foreman, and looked as if he might himself be a solicitor's clerk.

"There isn't a single gentleman among them," whispered Christian despairingly, after a glance at this assembly. Combridge compressed his lips. Exactly; there never was, in this type of case.

She sat, clutching her hands tightly, while the members of the jury were sworn. At any rate, things were moving at last. Having fretted through the slow processes of police courts, depositions and adjournment, it was almost a relief to find oneself at last in the Central Criminal Court, with the end of the ordeal in sight.

The only sensation provided for the public was the appearance of the plaintiff herself, and even Simon gasped when he saw Mildred Harris, in socks and gymnastic tunic, with cotton gloves pulled over her prim hands and a schoolgirl's cap and badge on the back of her head. With her appearance the prosecution scored heavily with the galleries; the absence of lipstick and mascara, the drooping eyelashes and convincing assumption of childish embarrassment impressed all but the legal faction, used to such metamorphoses. Simon saw Harris nudge his solicitor with a grin; at the same moment Simon's eyes met Christian's. In them he saw troubled astonishment and consternation. He shook his head at her gently, and she flashed into a smile. "I believe *you*," her eyes said; and Simon hurriedly looked away. He looked very pale and lonely, standing there in the big dock, whose size seemed to reduce his own.

She tried to be very calm: looking at the dais, at the great sword of justice, half tilted above the row of chairs. When the judge entered her heart leapt, strained towards him, cried out with a passion that her bitten lips held back. Under all that pomp of wig and robe and bouquet, surely there was something that would help Simon? He looked very small and old, and for a moment she wondered wildly whether age was to be trusted; surely the administration of the law required the knife-edge of a brain unblunted by custom and precedent? In the little, lined face under the heavy wig she found something terrifyingly impersonal; something almost old-maidish in the perch of the shell-rimmed glasses upon the small, fine nose. Was this the kind of man to understand Simon's predicament?

Mildred herself coyly testified to the alleged assault, in childish language that drew a murmur of sympathy from all the women in the gallery. There were calls of "Silence" from the ushers, and the judge mildly threatened to clear the court. Mildred tripped down, blushing with conscious heroism, to bury her head in the shoulder of a typical East End virago who retained through the encroachment of years and adipose sufficient likeness to be identified by the onlookers as Mildred's mother. As the procession of witnesses started, Combridge bent over to encourage Christian. "Did you ever see such a set of toughs?" he whispered. She nodded, and tried to smile;

the most formidable of the "toughs" was the woman from the toilette-room at the Knave of Diamonds, to whom, apparently, Mildred had boasted she was out for the night with a "real piece of hot stuff," with the obvious implication that intimacy had already taken place.

Steered by a wily judge, the case for the prosecution reached its conclusion sooner than Simon had expected. By the time the court adjourned for lunch, the Harris side had said all it had to say, and had had the mortification of witnessing the destruction of Mildred's virginal assumptions by a number of her acquaintances, who, skilfully cross-examined by Simon's Advocate, ended in testifying to some of her livelier moments: in particular to the use of cosmetics, which Mildred had demurely denied.

Finally her boy friend, convalescent from hospital, well-meaning but witless, gave the reluctant lie to her claim of "never having anything to do with boys." Apparently taking this as an aspersion on his virility, he declared plumply that he and Mildred had been "carrying on" for six months; nothing serious—kissing, yes, and perhaps a bit of fun now and again; but Mildred was "just a kid," and he didn't want to get into trouble.

"You carry her photograph about with you, don't you?" smoothly insinuated Simon's counsel. "Would you mind letting the jury have a look at it?"

The newspapers had it next day: the portrait of Mildred Harris, a credible imitation of the blonde film stars she admired, halo-hatted, bare-shouldered, with lashes that swept the powdery surfaced cheeks in a fashion hardly compatible with the stubby fringe that outlined the now pink-rimmed edges of their owner's eyes. The jury frowned over it; there was not one among them who had not been prepared to award the verdict to the innocent little schoolgirl of fourteen who had taken the oath, admitted she was a Girl Guide, said she was in her first job and gave all her wages to her mother.

Combridge was enchanted, when, during the luncheon

interval, he took Christian out and insisted upon her drinking brandy and soda with the sandwiches she was unable to swallow at a neighbouring tavern.

"By George, I wasn't expecting that! Jacquard's a clever devil, I wonder who put him up to it? It's given our innings a tremendous start, and I rather fancy we'll knock them after all."

"Shall we get through to-day?—Simon looks terribly ill ; I don't believe he'll stand another day of it."

"I don't think there's the smallest doubt of it. It'll depend largely on how long the judge wants to sum up. So far, it's a perfectly straightforward case, and as we've thoroughly discredited the plaintiff's statements (what an ass that boy friend of hers is!) there seems no reason for carrying it over."

It was hateful, she was thinking, not to be able to get at Simon, who had vanished down the stairs from the dock without even looking at her, though her eyes had been fixed upon him to give him encouragement. She was grateful to Combridge for bringing her out of the court; she had not wanted to stand about, being brave and bright for the benefit of Simon's friends. It flashed across her mind to wonder what Daniel and Lydia were doing: whether they were together. It was most unlikely.

Simon took his cross-examination easily; Combridge had signalled to him that there was nothing to fear. He could feel the judge's eye upon him, with an ironic kind of sympathy. He was aware that he was being made to look a fool, but this was better than appearing a knave. He took without the flicker of an eyelash the prosecution's suggestion that he was responsible for the publication of *Cypriana*, which caused another stir in the court. Simon's K.C. was on his feet immediately, objecting; the judge, with a nod, upheld the objection; the implication failed.

The summing-up was a masterpiece of judicial direction. Near as she was to the dais, Christian had to lean a little

forward, to catch the soft, muffled syllables, the mild, almost
diffident-sounding phrases in which, like a bee in amber, the
verdict lay. True, it was to come from that sharp-eyed young
man, with the authority of eleven other worried, well-
intentioned minds behind it: but its true origin lay in that
brain which functioned under that heavy wig, expressing
itself in the courteous and measured terms of a gentlemanly
argument, with which the listeners might or might not agree.
In the midst of her suspense, Christian found herself being
fascinated and charmed by the personality which, by some
virtue of its own, lifted the subject under discussion on to a
plane of pure reason, and in so doing, dismissed all the rancour
and acrimony of the combatants.

"I must remind you," said the tender and indistinct old
voice, "to weigh the evidence particularly carefully, since, in
this class of case, where corroboration is invariably absent, it
is the word of one person against that of another, and I will
repeat what learned counsel said when he addressed you—
that the accused is always entitled to the benefit of the doubt,
if doubt there is.

"While, on his own admission, the defendant has acted
somewhat foolishly, although, according to the evidence, not
out of accordance with his character—which some of you will
no doubt regard as lacking in the quality known variously as
worldliness and sophistication—you may arrive at the conclusion that the girl Mildred Harris is not quite the simple
young woman the prosecution has invited us to think she is.
Although her consent, being of the age suggested by the
prosecution, would not, if it were established, clear the
defendant of the charge, the evidence given by her own friends
in cross-examination might well weigh with you in estimating
the value to be attached to that given by the girl herself, and
prompt you to ask yourselves whether there was anything
more in the outing which occasioned these proceedings than
there is in what, I understand, is generally referred to as a
'joy-ride.'

"If, on the other hand, you are quite satisfied that the evidence of the girl is a true statement of what actually occurred on the night in question, you will not allow considerations as to the standing and character of the defendant to weigh with you in arriving at your verdict."

The jury, which was absent for less than twenty minutes, returned the verdict: "Not guilty."

Clinging together, they found themselves at last outside the whirlpool of congratulations. "God, Christian, let's get away from this nightmare," Simon had whispered, when, his arm shaking with handshakes, the sweat of exhaustion beading his brow at the roots of his greying hair, he felt he could endure no more of it. Christian, who had driven herself down to the court, had left the car across the road.

"Shall I drive?"

Simon nodded, climbing into the other seat. She saw his head drop forward, his eyes close; when she had taken off the brake and put in the gear, her hand pressed hard down upon his.

"That's right; relax. It's all over. Oh, Simon, thank God —it's all over!"

"All over—and nothing left," he answered her bitterly.

"How can you say that?" she reproached him passionately. "Haven't we got each other? Henry? Jemima?"

His hand twisted under hers, pressed it silently.

"You've got to face it, darling. I'm done for—for a while. Of course I'll get back—some day; but what's going to happen immediately? Now?"

His dependence upon her touched her to the heart.

"Never mind about now; it's the future that matters. We've got my money, and we've got freedom. Yes, Simon; I know how you've longed for freedom. I know what you've given up—just on my account—because of me, and my silly way of clinging to the family—because I just couldn't imagine life without them."

"Why should you? They're your people—and they've been

damned good to us. Chris, you mustn't let this separate you from them. Don't feel that you've got to take sides, will you? I mean, I know this has finished me with Old Harry, but he's devoted to you. It will break his heart if you stop seeing them, if you act differently towards them. After all, it's so natural they should hate me; I've done nothing but bring you a packet of trouble, and they must be sick of my name after this. Don't get any silly ideas of loyalty into your head."

"My darling idiot." She was silent. "I'm glad this has happened for one thing. It's shown me the stupidity of running with the hare and the hounds. No—don't interrupt. When a person marries," she said slowly, her attention divided between dealing with the traffic lights and what she was trying to say to him, "she's got to accept a new life. The less of the old one she brings into it the better. I've done nothing but trail the old life after me, ever since we were married. It was my way of being comfortable. It was just sheer selfishness—wanting to eat my cake and have it. I do love you—I have always loved you; and I thought the ideal thing was to combine my love for Mummy and Daddy with my love for you."

"Well, that sounds reasonable enough."

"But it doesn't work out that way. It's unfair all round. Marriage means—should mean—a clean break with the old; a complete acceptance of the new—all its different conditions, its different points of view. I've let you down badly over that, Simon; I can see it now. It's been bad for you and me, and very bad for the children. I've allowed Mummy and Daddy to interfere in matters that were no concern of theirs, and I've allowed their ideas to influence me, even when they were against your interests. I want you to know that that's all over. Our lives are our own and our children are our own (I must remember to send a wire to Nancy!) and all that we make of the future will be our own making."

"Why the devil do you choose to tell me all this now?" Simon's voice was unsteady.

"Pardon?" said Christian, shooting the lights with a dexterous bit of acceleration. She was inclined usually to be a timorous driver in London, but somehow, to-day, a new courage had flowed into her. She wanted to laugh, to take risks. "I'd like," she announced inconsequently, "to kiss that judge!"

"You may have an opportunity, if I kiss you now, and you knock down that old woman and get run in for manslaughter."

"No, don't—get back, you little beast!" A small boy had just stepped perilously off the edge of the pavement. Christian trod hard on the brake and there was a squeal of brakes behind them. "Sorry—but did you notice him? He was the image of Henry——"

"Oh, lord, what about Henry? We can't send him back next term. Do you think they'll let us off the fees?"

"I should think so. I had an awfully nice letter from the Head's wife."

"It's ruining the kid's education."

"Nonsense; it's just what he needed. We'll send him to a good Grammar school, and he'll get a scholarship; what's the use of those brains if he doesn't?" said Christian firmly. "Jemima can go to the High School and find out if she's got any—I'm afraid the poor sweet hasn't, not really, but she might struggle through School Certificate and get some sort of a job, if she needs to, by that time."

"You mean—you believe in me? You're willing to start again, Chris?—much lower down than last time. I expect I shall have to take any old thing, until I've found my feet."

"And we'll live in the suburbs and you'll come home at two in the morning and sleep all day, and I'll be a real newspaperman's wife! Oh, darling," said Christian, quietly, as, with the red lights against them, she took out the clutch and turned towards him, "what do any of those things matter, so long as we're together?"

THE END